LIBERTY

Other Books by Kris Ralston

Sending in the Clowns
Raising Angels
Project Hope Event
Precious Cargo

LIBERTY

Kris Ralston

Copyright © 2014 by Kris Ralston.

ISBN: Softcover   978-1-4990-7758-2
         eBook   978-1-4990-7757-5

All rights reserved. No part of this book may be reproduced or transmitted in any form or by any means, electronic or mechanical, including photocopying, recording, or by any information storage and retrieval system, without permission in writing from the copyright owner.

This is a work of fiction. Names, characters, places and incidents either are the product of the author's imagination or are used fictitiously, and any resemblance to any actual persons, living or dead, events, or locales is entirely coincidental.

Any people depicted in stock imagery provided by Thinkstock are models, and such images are being used for illustrative purposes only.
Certain stock imagery © Thinkstock.

This book was printed in the United States of America.

Rev. date: 11/10/2014

To order additional copies of this book, contact:
Xlibris
1-888-795-4274
www.Xlibris.com
Orders@Xlibris.com
686596

CONTENTS

Foreword 13
Introduction 15

Rolling in Diamonds 17
Darkling 24
Acceptance 29
Shards of Truth 34
Treading Upon Solid Ground 43
Catch the Dog 49
Call Me In the Darkness 53
The Spattered Crystal 64
Synthesis 70
Whispers of Faith 96
The Lone Cold 116
Identity 129
The Warmth of a Stranger 151
Climax 185
Gardens of Hell 213
Barking Up the Wrong Tree 264
The Fullness 285

Epilogue 313

This book is dedicated to the following:

Ryan Dupuis
Tieta Ralston
Jerry Ralston
Bill and Teri Tilden
The Dupuis Clan
All my sisters and brothers

"Now the Lord is the Spirit; and where the Spirit of the Lord is, there is liberty."

II Corinthians 3:17 (NKJV)

Everybody has a choice in life, to make decisions or ignore them. With bright decision-making you are living your life. With negative decisions, you are condemning yourself. You have a choice, and at any time you can change your mind. That is liberty.

FOREWORD

Liberty is a multi-level success, joining sweetness and suspense, the high road and the low. Ralston finds the thread of truth in the reality of her story; she finds liberty, sometimes in unexpected places.

Liberty contains a mystical wisdom, an outcome borne of the author's own steady walk on a path no one can master in their imaginations. Her work is one of patience, grace and goodwill, even though she is pushing through great mental challenge as she creates. The true sense of Liberty enters the reader even beyond the print on the page. Ralston's latest book is sweet and beautiful, even as it entertains dark and shocking events. Courageous self-acceptance is clearly her own gift and the gift of her character heroes. She writes with original brilliance.

One of the many accomplishments of Ms. Ralston's work is the triumph she has earned regarding reality. Although she has suffered from a disease in which reality is constantly transformed, often into terror, she has created a reality of hope, character and liberty. Overlaying the level of art is the level of unique worldview. Ms. Ralston takes her liberty to double back between realities, the way the metal in a samurai sword is folded and re-folded until it no longer matters what the separate bands of metals once were.

This book was written in love, passion, courage and detachment – another samurai creation of triumph.

-Julie Jirus, MSW MHP

INTRODUCTION

You have come here with a purpose. A purpose of finding out what a book called "Liberty" is all about. This is not a book about governmental and legal rights. It is about finding your own way and realizing you have the right to choose your way in every situation. You can guide the way of your life and learn to choose good decisions as you find out that you can learn to love yourself in every situation.

No one will come knocking on your door telling you what you must do. You have the chance to make a choice, your right in every circumstance. You never need to stay stuck in a rut when you have the liberty to rise out of it if you claim that right. You can design your own future, and understand that what you do affects other people. All circumstances are filled with possibilities. It is your right to choose your own will, and make judgment with policies of living for the good and freeing yourself from damnation.

God's will is the ultimate will, but He did give us freedom to use our own will. This is the liberty to do what is right fundamentally, and provocative in every situation.

The essence of provocation is growth, and denial is religion thwarted. Living for what is right seems bright, and executes judgment on infernal policies that don't appear righteous.

Making up for instances in subjunctive situations, rely on your own authority to make an impact. Take your liberties, it's your justification, your personal boundary of life and growth and achievement.

ROLLING IN DIAMONDS

There are three worlds in which reside a schism pertaining to what is natural, what foretells the future, and how we learn from our pasts. It is a wind around the truth that takes great stake in learning of the inert, where wind gives no liberty but for you to stand there exuding opinions from onlookers letting leaves blow in your face. Art thou a statue not at liberty to move? Then crumble. You must do something, or at least be admired for the perfection of a corrupt life, broken and useless. Do your part, and God will do His part. Only reach out with what you have learned and pertain to the past as the history of life, a troublesome life indeed, as have we all. Yet the fortuitous bounty of the future calls for a trust in the present, that we may use it.

Farley Cadwell, a man in his early forties has had more than his share of troubles. He isn't very active. He listens to the radio, and puts a restriction on the amount of TV he watches. Farley is a simple man with a convoluted past and an enjoyment of going on walks. He also works.

He likes to watch the crows, and throws bread to them on the park lawn. He reads avidly. He likes to go fishing from a pier not far from his home. But after three years of fishing, he has only caught three fish; all of which were too small to keep. This frustration he endures, as he likes to experience the fresh, windy air and lapping of waters below. He enjoys gazing out across the bay to the mountains, where there usually hangs a fluffy fog. To his embitterment, he one day lost his gold watch in the waves beneath the pier.

He remembers watching the prized jewel sink out of sight, feeling utterly hopeless as he felt its loss, watching the timepiece disappear underwater. The catastrophe was three years ago, and yet it did not deter his fishing habit, which allowed for peaceful meditation, if no rewarding fish.

He liked to sit and read with his lure in the water. The first fish he ever caught jolted him like a shock of electricity. As he panicked before realizing what he should do, his heart flipped until he put down his book to reel in the fish. The small, sleek, slippery catch sent chills of accomplishment throughout him. Inadvertently, the ferocious reeling and reaching for the fish net some how loosed his watch from his arm and he saw exactly where it fell, between the fifth and sixth posts of the pier.

Farley was devastated and elated, mostly devastated because the fish was too small to keep and he had lost his watch.

The two other fish he had caught one day after another in his second year of the habit. He felt like a rich man that second day, and reveled in the tugging on his line. As was his first, the second two trophies were too small to keep so he threw them back, with a sense of wellness.

With his fiancé, Sally Comber, he likes to cook. They have been together for ten years. At meal times they talk and share and argue. She hates his gambling addiction and has come close to getting him to promise he would stop. Farley, however, enjoys the thrill of winning too much. On days when he loses, he immediately goes fishing, or for a leisurely walk.

The tension of loss can be depressing, but Farley deals with it well. He doesn't go as often anymore, because the sting of losing has burnt him one too many times. He would like to stop, but can he?

Farley's fiancé, Sally Comber, wants to become Sally Cadwell, but their combined incomes causes them to refrain from getting married. They are both on disability income and SSI, and would lose a significant amount of money when they took the loving step of marriage.

So they stayed together and loved each other, sleeping in separate rooms, abstaining from intercourse, which they believe ought not happen outside of marriage. It wasn't always that way. In the beginning they made love quite often, but Sally was adamant about sexual immorality and the necessary practice of abstinence. It was odd she thought, that their inability to get married lay in the rules of government income, but she knew that God had that day coming ahead of them. She prayed for it. Daily. - And nightly.

Self-control, she deemed, was necessary. But she was caught in a trap. If one burned with passion for another, the Bible says that they should marry. But Sally and Farley could not marry. They couldn't afford to.

Sally believed it was in the works, however, for she kept praying for their marriage. They had even selected a date, believing that God would somehow provide for them financially. Maybe Farley could find a decent job, and Sally, too. But neither one had landed a job in over the ten years since they met. Their disabilities made it difficult to work. Sally got tired easily, and Farley got overwhelmed too easily.

Spiritually they were rolling in diamonds, with faith, courage, hope, and blessings. Maybe they should just do it, they thought. But how tight could they pull their purse strings?

One fine day in the middle of summer, July 31st the two joined in the holy institution of marriage, Sally taking Cadwell for her name. Gilmore, Farley's only brother, and Sally's friend, Mae, stood up with them at the wedding. It was a small Church ceremony, which meant they must manage their money like hawks. Sally forbade Farley to gamble any more, and reluctantly he agreed. Now they were really rolling in diamonds as foreplay and making love gradually seeped into their marriage union and bonded them with physical liberties together.

They were a quiet couple, and didn't impact their society in any large way. They embraced and tears came down. Sally did find a job filing papers for their mental health institution, and Farley also found part-time work doing a little landscaping for the City Parks. God had blessed them mightily. It was a great liberty for them to have part-time jobs on top of their disability income. They were able to survive.

Farley fished twice a week, and still ached over the lost golden watch. The watch had a diamond at the tip of the minute hand. Gilmore gave it to him for his twenty-ninth birthday. Right after two months in the psychiatric ward where he first got acquainted with his mental illness. He was diagnosed with undifferentiated schizophrenia combined with major depression. Sally had been with him through this, for she had become ill at the age of twenty-one with schizoaffective disorder.

Neither one knew how their illnesses appeared, they just one day took over after an onslaught of confusion and bitter nuances as they compared themselves with others around them. They both seemed very shy, but were known to be disruptive, especially if they tried going off of their medications. They tried this many times together and ended up in pathos every time, signifying hatred, common feelings, and elation.

Sally was extremely soft spoken and dealt well with the ravages of her illness. She cried a lot, softly at night, and now had Farley to hold her during these bouts of emotional expression. Together they shared their bodies tenderly, exploring every part so gently.

The two are dependent on their disability income, and need the little extra that comes with their working. Sally is a house mouse, and dreaded going to work. She did it though, for Farley and their marriage.

Carefully they eased into a work and rest routine. There was plenty of time for enjoyment, and they took their liberties, going out to eat, taking walks, and sometimes Sally would go along when Farley went fishing, so that they could spend time together.

Sally liked to exercise and tries to workout daily. This included walking with Farley, or using a fitness DVD when the weather was bad and she wanted to stay indoors. This was hard and she really needs discipline to perform that nearly insurmountable feat to make it to the end, breathing laboriously and letting the sweat run off of her forehead.

As for walking, they sometimes went around the high school track, mixed in with neighborhood walks, and they liked to hold hands while walking. Sally also swam at the high school pool, and took part in a "water walking" class, which exercised her entire body and felt good.

Sally kept a journal and wrote down the "downers" of her days plus the good parts too. She learned from this, and reread her journals to focus on patterns of illness, and when she was feeling good and what set her off to feeling nasty. The voices in her head tormented her throughout the days, causing her to get reticently violent, keeping her anger to herself.

Her faith in Jesus was central to her life. She commonly rebuked the devil and reminded him of his future, to burn forever in a lake of fire. Just recently she had learned to roar out loud in her hideous depressive anger, to chase away fear and the devil who constantly tugged at her making her feel miserable.

But Sally had Farley too, and she shared her voices with him, believing in him, and knowing that he always helped her with uplifting words and care.

Farley was quiet about his illness until it became overwhelming and depression fed upon his being. His shyness and his voices caused a place of worry and mistrust. He could not always count on himself to come through, thus his life was broken and he lived in dismay were it not for Sally, his most precious diamond whom he would never want to lose.

After the loss of his golden watch with the diamond minute hand and rotating sun and moon, Farley ceased looking forward to events and just lived for the mightiness of his days. Lost, confused, dependent on Sally to keep him going straight, he mourned the loss somewhat obsessively.

Next they took part in Church. They were avid Apostolic Christians and attended as many Church meetings as possible. They had Church every Sunday morning and Wednesday evening. Then on Tuesday nights, they sometimes showed up for an hour of prayer. Both Sally and Farley believed in the power of prayer. God had found them jobs so that they could marry. Now their lives were full, and rewarding, as well as could be under the schisms partaking of a gloomy past, natural element, and stones cast to the future, elements of forgetful anger.

Their negative thoughts were held at bay, turning them around the world in enigma of what makes them happy, and what brings them sadness. Separation hurts, and Farley and Sally knew themselves blessed to be eternally together. Forever and ever they would master the art of life, the will of the Lord, and living to the fullness of the days.

They knew not to take life for granted. Farley had lost a close cousin, two aunts and uncles, and all of his grandparents. And it hurt. He had always had a close-knit family, and as a blessing, he still had his his dear brother, Gilmore. But his parents had "disowned" him and moved to the Philippines. The thought of having lost them made him treasure life that much more.

The cost of a jewel for living, as a diamond of hope and necessity, living alone can cause the most pain, when there is no one to turn to except yourself other than God, Jesus. Farley knew aloneness. When the feeling of loneliness reigns, especially when you have only God, and others have moved away from life there is a feeling, and Farley knew it. It is like being caught in a rattrap with rats bearing down, and settling within inches of the body.

When he became mentally ill, he became socially withdrawn and afflicted with loneliness. No one could understand him anymore. His social withdrawal stopped his social growth. There goes one point for the rats as they bite.

This made life even more difficult. So when Farley met Sally, who could understand him, he rolled in diamonds, growing together with her, learning from her, and loving her. They needed each other, and loved one another, cherishing each moment.

Working as they did, they came to depend on a rigorous schedule, which meant they had to show up for work, for case manager meetings at the local Mental Health and Wellness Center, and to keep psychiatrist appointments as well. Life had meaning. Earning money brought a sense of responsibility and accomplishment. Working wasn't so bad, once they got used to the idea. It gave them a feeling of contributing to society, no matter how small the contribution.

Farley and Sally Cadwell had carved out a life for themselves, both having "failed" at college due to their mental illnesses. This didn't keep them from reading and learning and taking educational therapy groups at the Wellness Center. Looking to the future, a rolling diamond in their path, they walked each day, something constantly to look forward to. They walked towards God. Each day, throughout each day, if only to keep walking toward God, it would keep them on the right path. This was their liberty.

It was midsummer, but in the wintertime, their fireplace danced with red coals and flame, and cookies baked in the oven. Snow kept them inside and unable to drive. Luckily there was a corner grocery store at the end of their street. Farley liked to smoke his pipe inside on cold days, and this did not bother Sally, for she rather enjoyed the smell of his tobacco. She liked to read by the fire, her feet up and her back reclined on a cow skin with a pillow for her head.

Her senses translate the world she lives in as not a favorite world of all worlds. What is a world? She covers it up nice and neat and fixes tea every morning while also enjoying coffee drinks throughout her day. In her younger years, Sally used to hang out in coffee shops with her latte and a good book. It is here she began to take notes on her life.

She began keeping a valuable journal, which eventually led to her first book, "The Big Enigma". It is a book about schizophrenia and other severe mental illnesses, and what causes them. Sally has published another book, entitled "You Stepped On My Grapes!" A hilarious story of the misfit encounters of the mentally ill and illuminating them in a happy, recovered state. The mind is a weird place to go. Sally knows that, and having first hand experience she writes delicately about her mental illness, and Farley's, too.

"*The World According to Garp*" is a favorite of hers, and is actually the book that first inspired her to write. Reading and writing are her favorite things, and walking and swimming too. It is today that she decides to go fishing with Farley, to experience his big attraction. He welcomes her company, and tells her how to hold the pole and jig it gently.

Farley screams suddenly and points down. Sally nearly drops the pole in the water and at the same time hooks a fish. "What is it? Farley, what's wrong? I've got one! Help me Farley, Farley!"

Farley comes out of his reverie and grabs the pole from poor, helpless Sally, reeling in the fish and whistling. "That's a keeper, Sally," he drawls. He nets the fish and puts it in the small cooler that he brings every time he comes here, for chances like this one. "How'd you do it, Sally?" He was in awe, perplexed, and jealous at the same time.

Next he shows Sally the golden shiny object about nine feet down off to the right side of the dock.

"I have to get it, Sally, that's my watch from Gilmore. It's gold and has a diamond in the minute hand. Here, watch our stuff. I'm going in for it."

Sally was reluctant. She knew how important that watch was to Farley. But she didn't even know that Farley could swim. "Don't stay down too long," she said worriedly.

"It won't be that long. Look it's right there. I have to get it before the algae covers it up. See? *See?* Look! It's right there!"

Farley was wearing shorts which he kept on, and stripped himself of everything else. Then, not wanting to stir the waters, he gently lets himself down over the side on the little wooden ladder connected to the pier.

He comes up spurting water, takes a deep breath and goes down once more, praying that the shiny object wouldn't be covered. The clock ticked and Sally panicked. That was her Farley down there, risking his life for a silly old watch!

DARKLING

Underwater the swimming is good, until you run out of oxygen intake and choke on sputtering gulps of muddy liquid. His head in darkling thought patterns clears a liquid way for Farley to die in his incessant search for that watch. Just as he turns to go up, up, up, he sights the shiny golden object once more and snatches it away. "More time!" he thinks cloudily, his lungs bursting in pain as he gasps and coughs fiercely, swimming blindly to shore under the pier where he lands upon the dry beach, rolling and holding himself.

"I've got it! I've got it!" Farley was beside himself, and looked lovingly at the watch, which he noticed was still working. Sally sat in amazement as she watched her husband clip the timepiece around his wrist.

"Look, Sally, it's the watch from my brother Gil, that I lost more than two years ago. Every day I come here I look for it, and now, look, here it is, right here on my arm."

Sally looked at the watch with appreciation. She was proud of her husband, the feat he had just performed. "I guess it's not just a silly old watch," she thought, as she perceived her husband's emotional response to the finding of his lost gold watch. Gilmore was his only brother, the only one who cared about and understood his mental illness. His parents had disowned him long ago.

Sally turned her attention to the fish in the cooler. It was a perch at least eight inches long. Sally gutted it right there, dropping the wasted portions into the waters, and scaling it before cutting off its head and throwing that over the side as well.

Here was dinner, for the meat part. Sally decided on a spinach salad, and hoped that Farley would do all the cooking, knowing she wasn't a queen of the kitchen.

They decided to wait there for a while and to fish some more. Ten minutes later Sally had hooked another fish, this one even bigger.

"How on Earth did you catch that?" Demanded Farley. It was her second fish of the day, all within two hours of fishing.

Farley was amazed, and keeping his jealousy to himself, he glanced down at his watch and realized how lucky he was to have it back whole, and not in wreckage, or full of maggots.

Generally, Farley was not a violent guy. He knew better than to hurt people on purpose. He was nice, not naughty, and perplexed at the finding of his watch today. It was a pure miracle. And now Sally had caught two fish using the little shrimp for bait.

The grass was green on the bank up from the water's edge, and many trees were reflected in the shallows of the water. The sun reflected brilliantly on the small ripples in the waters of Turnip Bay, an inlet from the great Ocean itself.

It was blinding if one stared for too long, and both of them were noticing a slight sunburn on their exposed skin. Sally had on a halter-top, and Farley was stripped down to his shorts.

It was so nice that Sally didn't feel like going home, she wanted to lay her towel down on the bank and lie there soaking up sunshine, and water, too, if she decided to go for a swim. She was relaxed and happy about her two fish.

Farley, on the other hand, wanted some of Sally's luck and decided to continue fishing. He casted and let the lure sink down as he slowly reeled it in to the dock. There he let it bob up and down slowly as he maneuvered the pole slightly, skillfully in an up and down motion, praying for fish.

The time went by and after an hour, Sally turned over and let the sun hit her front side. She was lazy, sleepy, and thinking over the reality of her life.

She was married to Farley, her long time lover and now husband. For years they had abstained, and now she was free to be with Farley in her mind and in their bed.

It was freezing in the winter here, and Sally loved the warmer months, liking to play tennis with Mae when she had free time on the weekends. The two also engaged in intense Bible study together with Farley and James, Mae's significant other. They currently were reading the book of Proverbs in the Bible, and discussing the positive influence that following its guidance would provide for them. There was nothing else as important as the Bible, in Sally's mind, except for God, Jesus, Himself.

They followed each other throughout the passages and learned gently, slowly, as they applied themselves to the knowledge before them. There was nothing so great as God.

Now both were getting hungry and it was time to get heading on home. Farley felt suicidal about not catching anything when his wife had caught two perch without any strange or weird technique. Well, at least he had his watch back. That made up for all other disappointments.

Sally was covered with grass, as the two had rolled around a little "in the hay" on the bank, celebrating their coed union. Sally knew she would never have a child, since Farley had long ago had a vasectomy. Also, she would have no one other than her beloved Farley. Together they hugged and kissed more before getting up to walk home.

Above them the clouds had begun to whorl about, in darkness, threatening rain and thunder, perhaps lightning too. In fact, they were caught in the rain two blocks from their home. Together they ran the rest of the way, Sally squealing as she got wet. She hadn't gone swimming so the water on her skin was jolting as the raindrops peppered her and rolled down off her arms, soaking her shirt and shorts. Farley was attuned to the water, having been already in the water by their favorite fishing pier.

The water began to flow down on them in a violent torrent, making them eager to get inside the door.

They slammed it shut behind them, and dashed to the bedroom where they could dry off and get into dry, clean clothes. Farley chose to shower first, and Sally went into the kitchen to make coffee for their appetite, as well as two tuna fish sandwiches for lunch. She put the two fish, scaled and cleaned into the refrigerator so they could have them later for dinner. Sally felt secretly proud of herself, having caught two fish on her first try, and attained to the beauty of success, now having provided for their dinner.

Thinking ahead, Sally had decided that spinach salad would go best with the catch. The wild catch that she had caught herself. She glowed inwardly and outwardly, feeling like a hunter-gatherer, for the spinach would come from her own garden. Beets, carrots and peas would go well too.

Farley liked to make salad dressing with balsamic vinegar, olive oil, and left over mustard. Then he would add spices like pepper, garlic, and thyme.

At the moment Farley was singing in the shower, "Amazing Grace", at the top of his lungs. The soap was flowing down his body and cleansing off the bay water. He was wearing his golden watch, since it was waterproof, he need never take it off again.

By now, Sally was in the bedroom changing into her bathrobe and curling her grassy clothes up into a ball in the hamper. She didn't need to shower, and rather liked the slight sting of her sunburn.

Never again would Sally stray away. Before their marriage, there had been an interloper trying to come between the beautiful relationship of Sally and Farley. That was in the past.

To Sally this break would be enough. Farley disagreed. He planned to surprise her with a Rottweiler puppy for her birthday. It would grow up and learn to guard the house, front and back, night and day. It would need a kennel in the back yard, daily care, walking, feeding and love, as well as vet bills. Marriage was holy, but a thwarted perpetrator could be mean as a one-eyed raven.

Sally was going on forty-two and her birthday was only two months away in October. She loved dogs, Farley knew, and it would be an added responsibility, but with no kids, it might be nice to have another buddy around the house.

Farley breathed his secret to Sally as he lay down with her on their bed. "You could call him anything you want. But I need this for you and me, for the both of us, for that villain Oscar who is a maniac and may be dangerous when having been thwarted this last time."

Guns and knives were in Farley's mind, and the fear of losing his precious Sally. Tomorrow. Tomorrow he would go buy a Rottweiler puppy. He asked of Sally, and she said she wanted a boy dog. Neutered, of course, as she thought Oscar should be.

She hadn't actually seen Oscar for a few months since her wedding and felt like she was free of his snares. But a monster can have many mouths, and claws beyond numeration. She felt safe with her God. Surely He would protect her from harm. If Oscar were to strike out at her now, he must really be a maniac, a psychopath and a villain beyond description.

Farley and Sally rolled around on their bed for a while and snuggled and made love. What a release from all the aggravation of the day. Each dressed in jeans and T-shirts walked out of the bedroom into the kitchen.

"I'm going to go out to the garden and get some spinach and other stuff. The mustard is almost gone; do you want to make some salad dressing with it? Remember, a mustard seed of faith can grow to move a mountain, and I have faith that eating mustard can kind of get us into consuming faith religiously. I have faith that everything will work out for the better. But a dog is a dog, you know. I mean it would change our lives a lot, wouldn't it?" She paused at the door.

Farley was silent. He needed to get a guard dog for them. For their small house with a big back and front yard. They would need to build a high fence to keep the dog inside, and a kennel for it in the back yard.

ACCEPTANCE

Once you recognize that fear is a nervous reaction, you can overcome it. Farley didn't need to worry, his life was in God's hands, and God loved them. Sally's birthday was coming, and he searched the newspaper for Rottweiler puppies. He found some that were three months old for $350.00. He was sure she would be happy about it. He picked out a lively male, and decided to let Sally name him. It would be best to neuter him at five or six months so he could develop fully and properly.

What a cute little critter it was. When Farley brought it home it peed on the kitchen floor in the corner. Farley and Sally were aggravated and put the poor little puppy outside. They would need to get an indoor kennel for the dog. Sally had yet to name it. "Thomas", she said adamantly, wanting the dog to have proper respect for his masters, it was a name of dignity.

Days went by, and Farley and Sally grew to love little Thomas who was not so small anymore. He was a playful dog and barked at strangers. He welcomed Mae and James, and had yet to meet Gilmore. His attitude was tender and his long tongue hung out of the side of his mouth after a playful run around the yard retrieving toys.

Farley and Sally gave the dog rawhide bones to chew and gnaw on. He was a joy to their little "family". His black and brown hide shone glossily, and his brown eyebrows added character to his lively face. Thomas loved to be petted, and made himself at home on the living room couch. He was not, however, allowed in the bedroom, except to wake up his masters in the morning when he needed to go out.

Gilmore had yet to meet Thomas, and Farley called him daily to come visit. When he did, he was overwhelmed by the bouncy, playful dog, which jumped up to hug him. Gilmore was set back at first, but the puppy calmed down and sat when Farley told him to. He was pleased to see the golden watch on his brother's arm, and Farley told the story of how he had seen the timepiece glimmering in the water below the pier, and how he had gone after it.

"I nearly didn't get it, except at the last moment. I had no more air and kicking upwards violently was my only salvation. Thanks again, Brother," he said, "my life revolves around this watch."

The two brothers embraced, and then got back down to business.

"Well, if you need the added protection, a Rottweiler is sure a good way to go. Who are you afraid of, or do you just feel safer this way?" He questioned them mildly.

"Well," spoke Farley, "we've had some problems in the past with perpetrators, villains who want to make mash of our relationship. It seems that Sally has an admirer who can't accept the fact that we're married, and he just isn't the one for her."

"What's his name? Do I know him?"

"No, his name is Oscar and he's very intelligent, that's why I fear for Sally and me, mostly for Sally. I mean homicide is not far off of his list of things to do if we ever got in a tussle. I've already warned him to stay away, not wanting to need my gun after all.

"I'm not a killer by instinct, but if it came to the safety of Sally, there's no telling what I might do. And I don't want to do the worst of all options, which would be eliminating him from the picture. If it gets any worse, I'll have to get a restraining order against the guy. He's not very big, but he's quick and liable to act hastily. I know that he hates me already, so I'm glad we have Thomas now for added protection." Farley spoke slowly and seriously, giving thought to the dangerous matter at hand. If Oscar ever showed up at his doorstep, he would be gracious and civil, but would not let him in.

Oscar was a thorn in their sides. He was a blister on their toes, a headache during the night. Constantly pursuing them, especially Sally, and she swore that she sometimes heard his voice in her head. It scared her and tripped her up, as she often had trouble deciphering between her thoughts, and Oscar's obsessive ones. He wanted her. He wanted to make her his own.

Not in the throes of her illness, but when Sally began to blossom in her relationship with the Lord, and her love for Farley grew, it was then that Oscar came sniffing around her door. Quite obsessively, Oscar could not bear the thought of not having Sally for his own.

There was nothing they could do, for Oscar was sly and would not let himself be caught in sin against them. His hideous presence subdued Sally and kept her slightly fearful almost all the time. His voice, how did his voice get into her head?

Embarrassed by herself, Sally blossomed into a creature of beauty, recovering and learning to live with her illness. Farley was relieved when they finally were able to get married. Thomas fit in perfectly, and now allowed Sally to go on walks again on her own with him as her loyal companion who loved her dearly.

They trained him basically, and he became a very well mannered dog, who hated the mailman and anyone walking by the fence in the front yard, or down the alley in the backyard.

Sometimes Farley and Sally saw Oscar in Church and they avoided him there as well as they could. Sally felt wretched about their relationship to him, and feared the surprise attack that might some day come along their road.

Farley instructed Sally on how to use his pistol, if ever Oscar got in the house or threatened her up close. He also bought her pepper spray to put on her key chain. This mischievous devil was hard to predict, so it was best to be prepared to handle him at any time. If only Oscar would go his own way, realizing that he couldn't have Sally for his own, that he was unwanted company for them, and a pain they wished they could be without.

After Sally had arrived home from college, she was a very sick individual who saw her psychiatrist once a week for an hour, and hated every minute of it. As years went by, she grew to value her relationship with Dr. Nett. He made her understand her devastating illness, the constant voices being a part of that, and that recovery could be obtained if she was careful and kept trying to accept her illness rather than fight it.

By the time she married Farley, Sally had learned to accept her illness, and was well on her way to learning how to love herself. She was also able to have a stable, loving, and caring relationship with him.

Guidance was the answer to their stumbling block- what to do with their lives? The threat of Oscar was lucid enough, but obtained no further vision. The belief in his evil intent was enough to provide a backdrop for their cherished home life, including Thomas.

Sally had many voices, and they popped up at the most unexpected moments, just when things were going well. She believed there was a devil, and that some of her voices came from it. It was bewitching and seductive, a matrimony of love and hate, neither side winning, and owning up to a certain ambivalence about creativity and spontaneity. Curdling worms in the grass, slugs on the cement, sea urchins pulsing at high tide, and masses of floating algae with dead bodies floating past. Thoughts could flow.

Indeed, Farley, on one of his fishing excursions had seen a dead man without clothes float by him as he stood on the pier. He had hastily pulled out his lure and called 9-1-1 on his cell phone to report this disturbing entity. A fire truck came with three squad cars, and Farley went home, not wanting to see the body again out of the water. He became miserable, grossed-out, and sick with vomit at this strange apparition. This happened two years ago, and remained in his memory.

He had confided in Sally, who sympathized with him as his symptoms escalated, and he began seeing things.

Up the hill from their home stood a large cross with a bench by it and a huge pile of rocks. Sally had walked Farley up to the wooden monument, giving him the liberty to pray at the feet of Jesus who had died on a cross. Together they prayed for the dead man's soul, and then added a rock to the large pile to the left of the tall wooden cross, which stood nearly nine feet high.

They sat on the bench together that day as Farley wept having witnessed death in an ugly manner. Sally remained quiet and let him talk out the unnatural scene slowly, and stuttering, as Farley was not good with words and tripped over them a lot.

The day passed, and time went on, the memory buried. Acceptance of fate and the way of the world blessed their kitchen, blessed their home, work, and outside activities. Mostly at liberty, was the walking together that sewed their relationship tighter and tighter.

They had good neighbors, and Gilmore visited regularly. Gilmore offered his assistance in any way possible to get that Oscar off of their tails, who was constantly chasing them around in circles.

Their Fiat was running well, and they carpooled to work. Farley dropped Sally off at the mental health center, and then drove to the current site of landscaping where his team was working. Their work schedules were therapeutic, and Farley didn't have to worry about his stuttering, he just basically took orders and left it at that.

Their lives were fit, if not slightly confused during miscommunications and small arguments over minor matters, like what to have for dinner.

SHARDS OF TRUTH

When there are equal divisions between opposing forces, there are visions equal to the innate or the untouchable cataclysm that betrays all in all. Indecision. It is thus lived out by the odd equation of building truth on pleasure, in conditions under forces of evil, and condemnation of pieces that have tremulous tendrils reaching goodness in reaction to aloneness. Cleaving to little pieces of nervousness keeps the devil at bay as it cannot grab a solid hold on jumpy creatures who are nervous in denial of the truth. Ejection of the truth is denial of the belligerent.

Emptiness in control of carnal knowledge, causes one to carefully consider that there are attitudes to the rest of life where belief falls here and resides in the minds of Farley and Sally like a diamond rolling on truth. Piercing goodness is easy here and there, to the left and to the right. Mistaken ignorance is like a plastered piece of porch left unturned in the earthquake of social awakening, in the guilt of frozen abstinence, and the common law of invitation that is left to the commotion of the thick relays of lives built on journeys.

Hideous anger is a rage where social catastrophe gives pieces of goodness to fall all over the land that gives water to wanderers with the habit to go pick up and glue what had fallen to pieces. Farley and Sally live lives of honor and just want to be left alone to their own simple, quiet way. Together they are like a quilt designed by puzzle pieces, complete and shimmering with truthful patterns.

The puzzle is concluded as the last piece is put into place, leaving necessity behind with the world of flowing ignorance, a favorite of fools holding back their opinion of the dead floating in the waters of peace and solution. People stand by and hold back tears for the loss of a good soul, one who could have and might have changed the world again if only in some small way.

Blackouts and negative influences fly a high kite in the instance of betrayal where life is understood and misaligned with the aggravation of overturned blackouts. Blanketing an illness, the cursory respect found here, is for the ignorant, who cannot help but claim the end when the truth is found and fully known. Passing along disease, and failing in conduct blows the shards of truth to all creation, where we poison one another in an act of love. Coming together for purposes and destiny, there is the destitute, uncommon of belief in the appalling shards of broken truth and misguided situations. Shards of truth need only to hold onto a common resignation of the end of the reality, of the faith and overcoming of clarity in it, one for all. We are none of us supposed to be completely trusted, for betrayal breaks the back of the innocent, the naïve, and those who can't judge for themselves. It is all partitions of faith, where clarity reigns and the belief in wretched circumstances portrays the guilty of faith where recklessness must abide. The avenue of justice builds trust. Faith clears away cobwebs and fills in nature with voluminous portions of factored agendas growing in filth.

Falsehood and nastiness grow like leaves on trees with poisonous berries. Mountainous shards of truth come in the common knowledge of bites versus burst, where the explosion is one of danger and death, seeping through the body as pepper spray comes rolling off your face and you paw at the nastiness, giving in on sin. Thomas took pepper spray from the mailman once, and Sally never saw him look so helpless and in pain. No wonder he hates the mailman.

Sally is tired and wants to go out in the yard to play with Thomas. Farley is at work, and she is already done with her day of work, coming home earlier than Farley as usual.

Then with a strange suspicion, she calls Thomas to her and he sits by her side. She has the intense feeling of being watched, but she sees nobody. "Come, Thomas," she orders, "let's go to the front yard to see if anyone is there."

As they round the corner of the house, Sally sees Oscar closing the front gate as though leaving. "Go! Thomas," she releases him to go charging at the gate. Oscar is seen running down the street in a panic. He had gotten too close this time, and Sally thanked her lucky stars for Thomas who chased him away.

Believing she had a narrow escape, and so did he, Sally watched the frightened Oscar until she could no longer see him around the following blocks at the dead end where there was a trail leading through the bushes on the other side of the block to the main arterial.

Sally knew not what to do. She was shaken with fright, and held Thomas closely, who was no longer barking at the intruder. Sally decided that she would leave Thomas in the house at night, where he could give greater protection than to run around the yard possibly being nipped by a gun and bleeding to death.

During the daytime he would have to stay out, but his warning bark kept strangers at bay and his senses could sort out the truth of a perpetrator, and insolent intruder, or potential killer.

When Farley came home that day and Sally told him of this close encounter, he was incensed and grateful for Thomas. "Thomas, you're such a good boy," he said and gave the loyal dog a big hug around his middle. Thomas wanted to play. He liked chasing after strangers, and he hated ones who came in the yard without invitation or welcome.

Gilmore came over and they told him about Oscar trying to get in, and the near escape from Thomas's fierce jaws and claws.

"That dog is a blessing," Gilmore told them. He came into the house with Farley and Sally, leaving Thomas outside to play with his chew toys and to chase people along the fence, barking loudly.

All three wondered if Oscar might be making plans for another surprise visit. He was obviously not welcomed, and Thomas now knew his scent, and his scent made a hasty retreat from their yard. For Sally it was a bite of bitterness to have to swallow, not feeling safe in her own home.

Gilmore worked with Farley on the back screen door which Thomas had broken one day, inadvertently, as he charged through what looked like an open door, but turned out to be an obstacle. His head tore through the screen, and there he was, half in and half out, whining pathetically, and Sally had to laugh.

The gift of the qualm was the shard of truth, expressed but retracted before going into reality. Broken and waiting, the mental illness with which she lived allowed her to live a different lifestyle with Farley, and his mental illness. They still had the liberty to live the way they wanted to. For instance, by grace they were able to marry, and now they had Thomas and their friends and relatives who knew about them.

The time came to go grocery shopping, so the two lovers hopped into the old orange Fiat and clattered down the street to the store. Here they must manage their money. As always, they had to put something back at the cash register. They lived on a stern budget, which they needed to stick to. Racing down the aisles, for neither one enjoyed the grocery store, they managed to fill their cart with enough food for two weeks, including food for Thomas.

On the way home, Sally found herself looking out for Oscar, not in hopes of seeing him, but rather in a matter of defense. Distress. Rudimentary oblivion. Needing the passion of fear to die. Quaking beyond the level of servitude. Negligence on her part could cause inadvertent consequence on the other side, of a dastardly nature. Better to be prepared, and then to have faith in God. *"Now the Lord is the Spirit; and where the Spirit of the Lord is, there is liberty."* 2 Corinthians 3:17 (NKJV) "I'm free!" shouted Sally in the car on the way home as she read her Bible in the passenger seat. There was always a Bible in the car, old and beat up, but the Word of God nevertheless.

"And I live on rainbow milk," she sighed, referring to God's promise of the land of milk and honey where the sun would shine on cascading water falls, the fruit of which grew to great proportions, as they were feeding on the wild berries next to streams of milk and sugar cookies beyond rainbows which signified God's promise never to flood the Earth again.

Sally sighed again, thinking of Oscar, and wondering why he just couldn't let her go, let her enjoy her liberties. What if worst came to worst, she thought. Belligerence, it was the feeling she had in this frustration of twisted truths and shards of anger, the real truth beneath her fear. It was her faith. He was a nuisance and a belligerent reality. Her stifled anger sufficed to keep her from panicking, and helped her to be fine-tuned in the way of this seemingly stalking predator.

Both Sally and Farley needed to see their case managers this week on the same day. Sally saw Kirk, and Farley saw Nate. For shards of truth, it would suffice to say that neither one had the answer to the Oscar threat. It made her nervous, and it made him wary. Except for trespassing in the yard, he had never done anything blatantly wrong except act as a curse in Sally's mind, and a worry to Farley. Not to mention the annoyance he was to them in Church. Sally was learning to overcome it, to accept the anger that went with it, and to cling to Farley when Oscar made her feel threatened. It was just a shard of indigenous hope as to who held the territory, and rights to it.

Behold there was a nuisance in their lives of enigmatic learning. Forcing the oblivion away, and covering sin with anger, they claimed to deter any other forces of evil, of which there were none. Just the constant threat of Oscar getting inside Sally's head and inserting thoughts which misguided her until she learned to recognize them and their origin.

A peaceful catastrophe kept Sally looking over her shoulder, and scanning the way before her for any signs of danger. She was always happy to see Thomas after walking home from work and nestling into their loving home where harmony resided except for this one constant danger from a deranged man who had his hooks on their doorstep, leaving Thomas to patrol the yard.

After walking home from work, Sally was pleased to take Thomas out for a neighborhood walk. They crossed paths with many people but had not yet run across Oscar, who appeared insanely jealous at this time.

Thomas was a polite walker and didn't pull on the leash, not even to chase after squirrels, small dogs, and cats. He gave his full attention to the walk itself and to Sally, the one he adored.

Sally would not let herself be resigned to staying home all the time for fear of Oscar. Who knows, he might come knocking on their door sometime.

Courageous as she was, Sally allowed no fear to hinder her in enjoyment of life. She liked to walk to Farley's favorite pier, and Thomas would go swimming with her as she threw tennis balls for him to fetch in the water. Together they swam in circles, and Thomas would swim to shore and pad out on the pier to the end where Sally pulled herself up on the ladder. There she sat, kicking her feet in the water, and putting an arm around Thomas who sat next to her peacefully.

It was getting near time for Farley to come home in the old Fiat, and she wanted to be there for him. So she walked briskly home with Thomas at her side, appreciating the crows and smaller birds in the trees and bushes along the way. A cat crossed their path, and Thomas hardly noticed it.

As they made it to the front gate, the Fiat pulled up in their driveway and Sally rejoiced as she ran to the car and put her arms around her husband as he clambered out of the car.

"Oh Sally, I love you so much," his molten words warmed her very being as she held him close and asked about his day.

"G-give me a moment," he stuttered, "I'm just now getting home. Let me unw-wind a little b-bit. Yet he returned her embraced as Thomas snuggled his way between them.

"We're just coming home from the pier," Sally said brightly with a smile on her face. She kissed him softly before releasing him and leading him and Thomas to the front gate. Into the big yard they went, and Sally and Farley went inside, leaving Thomas to guard and play outside with his many chew toys.

There was a hornet's nest in one of their rhododendrons, and Thomas, curious as he was, stuck his nose into the bush. Inside the house, Farley and Sally heard a yelp, and then another. Fearing the worst, they ran outside to see their dog and found him smothered with hornets, helplessly crying out and pawing at the air. Thomas dashed around the yard until the last of the hornets had left him to be. Farley and Sally shut the door as hornets buzzed around their heads. Thomas was safe under the cherry tree in the back yard. He lay down with his head between his paws, morose.

Inside, Farley called pest control and within the hour the service man showed up and could see immediately where the problem lay. Suited up, the man sprayed and removed the nest from the rhododendron, and put it in a canister.

"You should be free of hornets soon," he said.

"How soon?" Inquired Farley.

"Oh, a couple of hours. Their nest is destroyed so they'll be lost and on their way soon. They might be a little mad and persistent at first, but the problem should disappear. I would stay inside for the next two to three hours." The man looked at Thomas as Farley wrote him a check. "Quite an animal you've got there. Looks like he's in shock. Make sure he has plenty of water, OK?"

"Gotcha'," replied Farley. "I think we'll let him in for awhile for a little well-deserved pampering."

Poor Thomas had suffered the brunt of the attack and raced through the front door, as he was welcomed in. Dog love. Farley and Sally loved Thomas as their own.

The hornets outside darted angrily to and fro, searching for their nest. Now would be a good time for Oscar to visit, thought Sally cynically as she imagined the stalker being surrounded by hornets.

The truth being told, and a shard at that, no one knew when Oscar would make his next move or if he had given up.

Sally imagined a snowball fight, and she and Farley were assaulting him with snowballs as he cowered and ran away. When and if he showed up with knives or a gun, Farley had his own gun just inside the front door on the third shelf to the right.

Sally shuddered, hoping she would never have to use it. Maybe she could get by using her pepper spray and then calling the police. It was an itch that could not get scratched. A darkling image of evil in and on itself, the shard of truth was that Oscar appeared to be on the side of the enemy, making him all the more dangerous and unpredictable.

As Sally woke the next morning, a giant dog's head greeted her on her side of the bed. Thomas needed to go out to pee.

The hornets were all gone and there were no other nests in their yard. Thomas bolted out the back door and ran to the fence with a big "Woof!" He ran to the cedar tree in the corner and peed long and luxuriously. Next he nosed around the yard, wary of the hornet's nest that was no longer there. He pooped. He scampered back and forth and brought Sally a toy for her to throw. She obliged and Thomas surged across the yard to retrieve it. But Sally didn't want to play now, she needed coffee and breakfast tea, and to make breakfast. She would enjoy coffee after her breakfast of eggs and bacon with toast on the side, and tea before that.

It was already seven-thirty and the sun was climbing up. Frost on the grass and birds in the trees welcomed the day. Sally closed the door on Thomas so he could get to his routine of guarding the fences, and chasing and playing with things in the yard.

Thomas knew he was loved, so he didn't mind being left outside where he could express himself more violently, yet without mischief.

Sally made breakfast and went in to rouse her husband from his sweet slumber. "Come on, Sweetheart, time to get up!"

Farley rolled over and groaned, but smelled breakfast and knew he had to make coffee. It was enough to get him out of bed, but first he pulled her down on top of him and squeezed her tight as he kissed her passionately. Breakfast could wait, now it was time to make love, and they did with a shudder and a release. Holding each other gently, Sally asked him if he'd known about the hornet's nest?

Farley admitted that he did, but hadn't thought it a bother, up until yesterday. Poor Thomas sure got his violent surprise. "Thomas will be fine, he'll get over it," Farley reassured her.

"Too bad Oscar didn't choose yesterday to pop by," quipped Sally. "Oh well. To hell with that bastard. We don't want him around here anytime, anyway, anyhow, any whatever."

"Come on now, I've made breakfast and the coffee's waiting for you to turn it on."

"Sally," he admonished her, "we shouldn't use such vulgar language around here. It's fitting, but only makes matters worse. Remember, 'love your enemy, treat him well, and you are pouring hot coals over his head.' That's a paraphrase, my love, from the Bible."

"I'm sorry, Farley," she said, "it just gets my hackles up to always have to worry about the next minute, or hour, or day, or place that he will show up, even though we see him at Church sometimes. If only the Pastor knew about that leprechaun. He's deceiving the Pastor by giving false praise to the Lord, or so it seems, and he's always in my face. I hate it." Sally lay there agitated until Farley pushed her out of the bed into her bathrobe and out to the kitchen where breakfast and tea were ready and waiting for them.

As was habitual, Farley turned on the coffee and drank it with breakfast, as Sallly enjoyed her cup of black tea. Morning was fresh and full of wonder, and they both had to work today. Sally started at 10:00am, and Farley went to his work site at 11:00am. They enjoyed getting up around 7:00am to have breakfast, a little Bible reading, and coffee as they played with Thomas in the yard. He was overjoyed, and chased all the toys that they threw for him, as he brought them back and happily put them at the feet of his masters.

Sally was first to take a shower and get dressed for the day. She came out fresh and clean, allowing Farley to shower and dress also. She tied blue ribbons in her brown hair. She prepared her purse and made sure she had her wallet. She found the car keys and put them by the door with her purse. Farley would drive her to work, leave her there, and go on to his job site. Sally would walk home when she was done.

As for Thomas, he was put in the outdoor kennel run for the time that they weren't home. He barked loudly and jumped up and down violently at his fence when they left.

Farley and Sally listened to classical music as they drove through the streets to the mental health center where Sally had her job. She would work three hours and then walk home.

Farley, on the other hand, worked from five to six hours daily, landscaping. He was happy to come home to Sally, and Thomas too. Sally always tried to be there for him when he got there. She and Mae had begun walking with Thomas, and they would talk about "Oscar the Perpetrator", and how Sally shouldn't have to live in such fear of him. Mostly, Sally didn't want to lose her mind.

TREADING UPON SOLID GROUND

Gruesome figures align the sides of the world. You could reach out to touch them, without hurting yourself completely, or you can put your mind on Christ and know He won't hurt you. Blubbering insinuations keep foreign matters at bay. Always have a word, and if you don't, remember you have the right to remain silent. And silence is a virtue. Sometimes Sally chose to be silent, as was her liberty, yet the lemon moon at night abhorred the possibility that there was an integral force that kept her quiet there, beyond her own will. It was the silence of her mind, the words she heard in her head before she spoke them. She was upon solid ground, always testing her words first when they came into her mind. There were other times when she was candid.

She was an extremely quiet person and talked, really *talked* to just a few people. There was Mae and her fiancé James, there was Farley, of course, and she had come to know Gilmore quite well also. She spoke candidly with people at work, but never about personal matters like her mental illness.

Sally was on friendly terms with the people of their Church, but hadn't met anyone yet that she was close to. Tina Makron spoke to her a lot and they prayed together. Sally was hoping to make a better friend of Tina. She was at peace with the Pastor, and although she didn't always believe with him, it all worked out in the end.

Sally's Church was an active one as Apostolic Churches are. She expressed herself loudly in that place and worshiped, praised, and spoke in tongues. Sally had been baptized at the Church and received the Holy Ghost. From there it was a new world, and as she paid tithes, the Lord took care of their financial situation at home. Plus they were blessed in many ways. For instance, Farley had just been reunited with his long lost watch.

Thomas was also a blessing and a faithful friend. He was so polite and energetic at the same time. Except for that first pee in the corner of the kitchen, Thomas had never made a mess in the house since Farley brought him home that blessed day.

Farley didn't come home on time today; in fact he came home three hours later than his usual five o'clock and Sally grew suspicious. She knew in her heart where he was. Playing slot machines with their well-earned money. Either he would come home beaming, or sour faced.

Bless their stars; Farley had won again. He came in the front door with Thomas and apologized for being so late. But he couldn't contain it.

"I just won $212.00," he said proudly. Sally was happy for him but still she sulked. Here she had waited at home to meet him, all the while reading a book, not knowing where her husband had been. She knew he would never cheat on her, but she had hoped the gambling phase had passed. Now it was back more than ever, as Farley had just made a happy win.

"Let's go out to dinner, Sally," he implored. I'll treat us; we can have whatever we want." Yes this was one positive aspect of his winning, but she was not always sure the Lord approved. She had repented herself, and never went to the Red Tornado Casino anymore. But it was his liberty, if he chose to do it, she could not stop him.

"Yes, let's go out to eat," replied Sally, a bit edgy. "Next time could you call before you're going to be late?"

"I'm s-sorry Sally, Sweetheart. I was j-just having a little bit of fun. I never use more than two twenties, you know-? Where do you want to go? I'll let you choose." He waited expectantly.

"McDonald's!"

"*What*?"

"I'm just kidding. How about 'The Old Barnyard'? They both liked to eat there. It was a nice restaurant built out of an old farmhouse, restored, with many windows and three floors. "The Attic" was the nicest and most expensive part of the restaurant and looked out on an old barnyard with acres of grass stretching out beyond. The land was just waiting to be bought up.

"Let's go!" shouted Farley.

"Yes, let's go," Sally said quietly. Her husband agitated her when his schemes of getting rich got in the way. She knew he wanted her to be proud of him, but she wasn't. She wasn't displeased however; at least he was having harmless fun. And now she didn't have to wait for him to make dinner. She had been about to start cooking sausages and potatoes.

They put Thomas in his kennel outside and Farley drove them to the pricey restaurant where he parked outside and held Sally's hand from the car to the restaurant. The couple asked for a booth - "in the attic"- and waited their turn to be seated. The sumptuous smells from the kitchen caused Sally's stomach to tighten up in anticipation for the good food they were about to have.

Up they went to the attic when it became their turn to go in. They climbed up the stairs and took an Eastern facing window table overlooking the real old barnyard that was there still with old and rusting farming equipment.

They both ordered coffee, Farley ordered the "Widow Maker" hamburger, and Sally had a Cobb Salad Sandwich.

They didn't need to wait long for dinner to come and they luxuriated in the fine food when it did. Farley drawled in his catchy way of speaking about how good his food was, and wasn't she glad they could come here?"

Sally smiled and kept eating.

As they were leaving, Sally clung hard to Farley's arm. There in the parking lot was Simon; a young man from Church, and walking next to him purposefully was Oscar in all his silly get up. Sally felt his eyes on her and ignored him completely. She felt violated being stared at like that. Farley took her arm and steered them around the parked cars to the rear lot where he had parked. He didn't even give Oscar the time to say "Hello".

Now came the voices and she boxed at them in her head. The unclean gossip, the side talk about her soul needing him, and then what a loser Farley was.

Sally was incensed and cried as she looked helplessly at Farley.

"The worm," Farley said. "Don't listen to the voices, Sally, he can't really hurt you, you can stand up for yourself, don't be afraid."

Sally wilted and both of them felt distracted and disturbed. Like Mae had told her, he's just a symptomatic mealworm trying to get inside of her, trying to slide himself in between Farley and Sally. Sally didn't feel confident talking to the Pastor about him. Maybe someday she would, maybe someday.

Sally couldn't wait to get to their warm and cozy house where she would let Thomas inside and give him big doggie hugs. Thomas ran around the inside of the house, his claws scuttling on the floor as he turned corners and ended up on the living room couch.

Sally said she was tired and went into the bedroom to lie down. Thomas went into a noisy slumber, and Farley, left counting his money went to go read the Bible for a bit. Tomorrow was Friday, they had missed the Wednesday night service and Farley felt low on the Holy Ghost. He awakened almost two hours later, his head on the kitchen table, and slobber pooled up under his chin. He had closed the Bible after reading from the book of John, and rested his head momentarily.

Now there were clouds and raining quarters falling all around him. He took shelter in a Church foyer until the raining stopped, and as he stepped back outside, the sky was clear and there were balls of hail all over the Church lawn, which he had volunteered to keep mowed this year, and they were well into fall when he would rake leaves instead.

The Church sported two beautiful maple trees in the front, and several dormant cherry trees all around the back and sides. It had a big cross on the roof of the front entrance, and lots of windows around the sides and a huge tall window in the front that looked out on a little stream of water.

Farley moaned and came back to the waking world. He felt guilty and bad for Sally. She knew she must forgive Oscar, and continue her walk with the Lord, praying for Oscar to keep his funny little distance away from her.

The way he controlled her mind was beyond her, and she had long trained to focus on a certain point, from her years of rowing on the high school crew team. It was here where she found her stamina, and during her first year of college on the Freshman Crew Team. She used this to keep strong, and reminded herself again and again that Oscar was a poor, pathetic person whom she didn't need in her life and was basically harmless, she hoped. What he wanted he couldn't have, and this she surmised might make him either reluctant to let go and be gone, or mad as hell for being thwarted. Other than the voices in her schizoaffective mind, she knew not how to deal with the hold he had on her. His ways were possessive, leery, threatening, and sadistic.

Farley lumbered to the bedroom where Sally lay sprawled out on the entire mattress. How to negotiate this situation, he wondered. Very carefully he lifted her legs and moved her to one side of the bed. Next he changed into a pair of boxers and slid under the covers on his side of the bed. He was fast asleep, dreaming about a Rottweiler chasing dollar bills that were flying in the sky. Each time the dog caught one, it brought the dollar to Farley. Throughout the night, Farley's stack of dollars grew, and when he finally awakened in the morning, Saturday, he had taken a bucket to put all the dollars in, which he fed to the dog in its bowl.

What useless thing is this? He wondered to himself. He heard heavy breathing and a whine. There was Thomas at his bedside needing to be heard, desperate to go out and do his business.

Farley got up and let the huge animal outside into the backyard. Farley thought about the restaurant last night and remembered how good The Old Barnyard food was. He appreciated the thought and thanked God for the experience and delicious food.

Farley left the door open and brought Thomas's food bowl to the closet where they stored his food and filled the red bowl with dog food and brought it back to its place by the kitchen cabinets. Next he scrubbed out Thomas's blue water bowl and put fresh water in it, which he placed on the steps outside. Thomas could make a big watery mess when he drank thirstily. Then, Farley put two big vitamins mixed into the food, which fortified his dog with energy and health.

Thomas was nearing onto seven months old and needed to be neutered soon, very soon; he was a big dog. His big bullish face and fine lines of brown and black with a tongue hanging out of the huge mouth was a fire engine of sorts, he slobbered so much.

Farley was waiting for Thomas to come in but the dog was nowhere to be seen. He must be in the front chasing squirrels, thought Farley and started making breakfast. It was his turn to get it ready for Sally. Eggs, bacon, biscuits and a half slice of grapefruit were ready for her in the next half hour. Still Thomas hadn't returned.

"Sally, Sweetheart, wake up my little queen." She moaned. She still hadn't changed out of yesterday's clothes and had dreamed horribly about Oscar coming at her with a lasso. Just as the noose landed around her neck, she felt Farley's warm, loving hands on her shoulders, pushing her gently and waking her up.

"Farley! It's you! I knew you would come and rescue me. What is this? I didn't change last night? I must have been exhausted. I forgot to take my pills."

Farley was anxious for his coffee in the kitchen and wondered why the dog hadn't come back in for food and water. And attention.

"Breakfast is all ready," he said to her softly. Then he went around to her side of the bed and kissed her gently on the ear. Breathing into it, he spoke, "eggs and bacon and biscuits and tea – and grapefruit Sweetheart, waiting for you." He stroked her hair gently and helped her to sit up. "I love you, Sweetheart!" Farley left her there and went back to the kitchen where he saw the dog's water hadn't been touched.

"Thomas! Thomas!" he called, now wondering what his dog was doing. He quickly donned a pair of blue rubber garden shoes and went out to find the missing dog. To his horror, he saw that the front gate was wide open, and Thomas was nowhere to be seen.

"Thomas? Thomas!" He called but saw no sign of the big dog.

CATCH THE DOG

Religious nuances question whether or not you will see your dog in Heaven. Farley and Sally both believed that they would, and it would be a perfect form of Thomas, what he had always aspired to be. Cats too. But chase your dog through life and you find that its ways are unique to its species. You walk your dog and it goes poop. You are responsible and pick up after it. Remember that your dog should come when called. So it is a game of touch and go. It is tremulous dreaming, and knowing that you can always talk to your dog.

Just don't get bit by the neighbor's dog. But now, call as he might, Thomas was not being an obedient comer to Farley. Farley ran into the street and looked up and down both ways. No Thomas. He stopped to listen. Why didn't Thomas come? He whistled. No Thomas. Then he turned and saw Saucy, the neighbor's grey cat mangled in the roadway. His heart dropped. Had Thomas, . . . did he kill the cat?

Farley decided the best thing to do was to go inside and eat his breakfast, have his coffee, and come up with a plan with Sally who would be horrified at this news.

Sally was already eating when he came into the kitchen. "Oh dear, Sally! Thomas is gone – the front gate is open, Thomas is not in the yard, and Saucy is lying dead, mangled in the street. I think Thomas killed Saucy! What are we going to do? Thomas isn't even neutered yet and he's running wild in the neighborhood. I told you we should have gotten him micro-chipped. Now he's gone, and somehow, you and I have to find him. Where would he go?"

"Well, there's a young female chocolate lab on the walk that I take with Mae now and then, and Thomas always goes berserk when we go by her house. She runs up and down the fence, and Thomas tugs like mad to get to her. I think they're friends. Maybe he went to go visit her. Thomas wouldn't go far, he's always eager to get back home when we go walking. Who knows? Maybe he'll come back on his own. If he doesn't get shot first."

Sally's face went into a pout and she started to cry. "What if he's gone? What if a car hit him? What if he's out murdering innocent cats? What if he goes and mates with another dog? We could be in big trouble, Farley."

"Let's finish eating," prodded Farley, "we have to hit the streets and f-find the silly bugger." Farley was trying to make light of the situation, knowing it wouldn't be proper to panic. "Let's go," he said, "We can finish eating later." The two rose and went outside, after dressing for the outdoors and downing the last of the coffee.

"I'll drive," said Farley. So away they went, slowly through the streets of the neighborhood, and then to the town park in the center. And there he was, sitting at the foot of a George Washington monument, tongue hanging out and panting heavily. Sally saw him first and screamed and pointed. Farley stopped the car and she got out.

"Come here, Thomas!" She called. "Thomas!" The big animal came running toward her. Sally realized she had no leash to put him on, but grabbed his collar when he came near. Thomas lunged at a squirrel, but Sally held him tightly. Farley came running with a leash and hooked him, just as the massive animal lunged again, this time pulling free of Sally but being caught on the leash by Farley. "Stop it, Thomas," ordered Farley. "Sit."

Thomas sat but he had a wild look in his eye. "To the car, Thomas," spoke Farley. Sally was hugging the big dog and talking to him quietly, and he calmed down slowly.

"We need to have him neutered! What if he already. . . -" Farley looked at Sally and the two giggled. "We might have a Ma-Ma dog in the neighborhood soon. Let's take him home," said Sally. Together they put the now quiet dog into the back of the car, and left the leash on him. Farley drove the two miles home and parked in front of their nice little turquoise house.

They put Thomas in his kennel outside and securely locked the gate. Next Farley needed to check on Saucy. He was quite sure that Thomas had done the dirty deed.

When he arrived on the spot the dead animal had been removed. There were just some smudges and tufts of fur. Farley looked around and started whistling a tune; putting his hands in his pockets and walking casually back to his house, closing the front gate behind him.

The couple was relieved to be at home again with their precious animal. Farley brought him his breakfast with vitamins and his big blue bowl of water. Thomas made a big mess of it all, going from bowl to bowl trying to make up his mind if he wanted water or food or both at the same time. He was being very sloppy.

Farley double-checked that the front gate entrance was locked, and walked back to the house, hungry now for his breakfast. The eggs and bacon were cold, but he didn't mind. The coffee, however, needed to be remade. Farley got it ready.

He sat down relaxed and looked over at Sally who was watching him. She smiled, the smile that always won his heart and said, "I love you." She was laughing at him now in a funny way. "I just realized how cute those puppies are going to be, if Thomas really had it with the chocolate lab. They're so cute together and always bark and Thomas tugs like a mad thing. Maybe he's had his way with her. Didn't he look triumphant to you, sitting there like that at the monument of George Washington? I mean, he took pleasure in sin, which is not a sin in the reproductive case of a dog. We can't let him out again. Maybe you and Gil' can put a better latch on the front gate?" Sally was having her turn at the coffee now. Both had finished breakfast, and Thomas was whining outside.

The clouds were mounting in the sky to the East, dark and luminous. There was lightning and thunder across town, and going outside, Sally saw why the dog was so agitated. A huge storm was blowing near them, and it threatened to take over the skies above them. With mercy, Sally opened up Thomas's enclosure and called him with her to the house. Thomas dove into the house, relieved to be out of danger of the storm and with his two beloved masters.

Farley sat down to read a book, while Sally took to sewing a patch on her favorite old jeans. Classical music played in the background, and they drank from the coffee pot until it was gone. The soothing brown liquid opened Sally's eyes and brightened her mind.

She was lost in thought and enjoyed the coffee mindlessly, grateful for the plenty. She fixed the pot again, putting in three scoops of grounds for a twelve cup coffee pot. She was eager and couldn't wait for it to be done. In the meanwhile, she continued to sew the patch on her jeans, humming along with Bach's Third Brandenburg Concerto. "Want to play chess?" She asked her husband, who was innately ingenious when it came to that game. She could hardly challenge him, so he usually played with Gil', who was equally talented.

"Oh, no, Sweetheart, I'm too busy reading John right now. I'm reading about Nicodemus, who didn't understand rebirth. Jesus sure tells him what's up!"

"Oh yes, He really does, doesn't He?

"Farm life must have been disastrous, in the old days, when huge storms came upon the crops like the one that's coming toward us right now. I wouldn't be surprised to see it hailing out there. Our poor Fiat; hopefully we won't have smashed windows. Let's go watch the storm come." Sally was intrigued by nature and Her violent problems. Explosions here and there, lightning striking, broken dams. Fallen trees, crops destroyed, rivers swelling, and avalanches initiating near the tops of the mountains. She loved to go snorkeling during the summer months, and windsurfing, too.

She made love with hurried ecstasy, rushing to her climax and overcoming any insecurity that either one of them might have. They blew up, together, exploding on top of one another, insecure yet forgiving. Open wide and dissolute, prepared for the worst and expecting the greatest dams exploding as their love reached their hearts for a total eclipse of nature.

It was in both of their natures to take care of the other and to give the most where it came to pleasuring the other. It's a side story, too precious for words.

Lightning struck outside and hit the dog enclosure, harmlessly on a sandy portion. Both Farley and Sally thanked God that their dog was inside.

CALL ME IN THE DARKNESS

When the wind is whipping outside, your dreams make sense of darkness. Cleverly made, the mind can do most anything. We need light to survive, so if you get lost on me in the darkness, call and I will come bearing light.

Sally penned the poetic words and planned to work them into her next novel. She reached out to Farley here and raised her mind up against Oscar, who hadn't bothered her for some time. Farley and Sally went to Church faithfully every Sunday and on Wednesday evenings. They had been married for two years now, and fellow saints were wondering if they should expect a child.

Sally and Farley did not discuss it. They had long ago opted not to have children. They had Thomas instead, and with their mental illnesses, they didn't feel competent as parents for children.

It was a sacrifice they made, opting to forego children. They both liked children, but watched them from a distance. Neither one felt secure or authoritative enough to care for them. Children needed to be managed, and Farley and Sally each had their own mental illness to manage first and foremost. Thus, there was Thomas.

Thomas was agreeable. He needed them, and sometimes acted like a big baby. Now as the storm raged outside he lay down next to the coffee table on the living room rug. The rug was decorous with vines and leaves and pretty red flowers.

Breakfast had been satisfying and so had making love. They were agreeable to this nature, and neither one kept the other waiting or neglected.

Sally called Mae to see how things were going with her and if she and James had set a date yet. Nobody answered, so Sally called Tina

Makron from the Church and chatted with her. The two could talk about a lot of things in a short time, and Sally appreciated her friendship that helped balance out her life with Farley. Finally they agreed to meet for coffee that afternoon at the Turnip Bay Coffee Shop.

Sally let Farley hear her plans, and got ready to go meet her friend who also had the Holy Ghost. She had a better time talking with people in the Holy Ghost, and could relate better. She interrelated as well, sharing aspects of their lives together.

Sally took the old orange Fiat and putted into town where she found parking across the street from the café. There was Tina getting out of her car across the street and she waved. The two girls smiled happily and ran to give each other Holy Ghost hugs. The spirit was with them in the Coffee Shop and they sat in a corner near a tall Hawaiian Umbrella Plant. Its lush leaves grew towards the window, and some were flattened up against the windowpane.

They looked outside and watched the cars go by. There wasn't much traffic here on a stormy Saturday afternoon. Both girls ordered coffee and a sweet. Tina had brought her Bible and laid it on the table. She leaned back in her chair and commented on the large hailstones. It hailed around Turnip Bay quite regularly, so people were generally well prepared and also looked for the signs of the oncoming weather.

Next Tina giggled and mentioned that there was a new flame in her life.

"Who?" questioned Sally with great curiosity. On the other side it was easier. Sally didn't like discussing her mental illness and saved that for Kirk and her psychiatrist and of course Farley. Here she dove deep into giving support to her friend and the need to feel needed or appreciated. "Does he go to our Church?"

Tina paused with embarrassment. "It's Leroy, Simon's brother," she said. "He's only two years older than me and we just seemed to click."

"How long has this been going on?" Sally reached out with interest.

"Since last Saturday when I bumped into him at the grocery store. We exchanged phone numbers. He lives about two miles from me, and I visited his house last Tuesday. Leroy sings in the choir, you know."

"I think I've noticed him up there before, doesn't he sometimes sing solo?"

"Yep. He's a really nice guy. We kissed once as I was leaving his house, and I can't wait to see him tomorrow. I'll introduce you if you want."

"Of course! Maybe we could all go out to dinner with Mae and James and me and Farley. Farley and I have been married for about two years now, but we've known each other for over ten years."

"I'm not quite ready to make that step at this preliminary point, but I imagine something exotic coming out of this relationship. He really, really likes me. One problem is that he lives with his brother, Simon, and I don't know how it's going to work out if we decide to move in together. But maybe I shouldn't think about that now. I don't want to rush things."

"Well congratulations," Sally said warmly. "I'm glad you found somebody. It's so much nicer to have someone there all the time. Someone you can count on, and invest in things together, like our new Rottweiler, Thomas. We got him at the perfect time. Since Farley and I can't have kids, we remain totally devoted to each other, and God. I have fun watching the kids in Church, but I could never raise one. Not with my mental illness," she spoke in raw order.

"Well you and Farley make a great couple."

"I love Farley very much."

"I can hardly wait for tomorrow when I see Leroy again. I'll plan to sit by him. We'll see you there and I'll do introductions with you and Farley."

"We sit on the right side middle back."

"I won't know where he'll want to sit, so I'll leave it up to him."

"I'm so happy for you! – What do you think of Simon, his brother? Is he older or younger?"

"I think Simon is three years older. Leroy just turned forty and I'm thirty-seven. I'll be thirty-eight next month. So we're pretty close in age, all of us. What are you?"

"Forty –two."

"I guess I'm the baby," said Tina with a grin. Her coffee was good and she was enjoying her cinnamon roll. "Do you mind if I get a refill?"

"No, go ahead. I don't want any more but I might have some water." Sally had drunk four cups of coffee this morning. Now she had to tell Tina about Thomas's escapade.

Tina came back with her refill and a cup of ice water for Sally. Sally thanked her quietly and accepted the gift. "Thomas got out of our yard this morning, before the storm hit. We think he killed the neighbor's cat and mated with a local chocolate lab. What a mess! We found him at Washington Park, sitting on the monument platform. Luckily he came when I called him and we were able to get him into the car. Then we got home and this storm hit. Guess what!! Lightning struck Thomas's outdoor dog enclosure. Thomas was inside with us when it happened."

"Lucky dog. Are you going to Church tomorrow?"

"I think so. I'm looking forward to meeting Leroy. So, Tina, are you familiar with Oscar at all? I think he's friends with Leroy's brother, Simon. Farley and I saw them together when we were leaving the restaurant last night, The Old Barnyard. Farley won some cash on a slot machine at the Casino, so he took us out to dinner. I don't think I'll ever get him to break that addiction. But so far it's been pretty harmless."

"I, actually, go there myself sometimes," confided Tina "But about Oscar, he's a funny kind of guy. I mean, he goes wild in worship, and people say he's a new convert. He seems OK."

"I was just wondering what you thought. He seems harmless enough, but he has a weird eye out for me. Sometimes I look up and he's right there. Kind of eerie, sort of. I don't trust him."

"Well I guess you just have to keep your guard up, Sally. There's a reason God brought him to our Church. But if he makes you feel unsafe, I would go for avoiding him, if not hiding yourself with your own camouflage. You know, when you feel threatened, it's an unsafe, scary kind of feeling. I would avoid him." Tina was wise in her words.

"Yes, it's a dangerous situation. My schizoaffective side would go to say that he's part of the CIA and trying to undermine my trust in God for political reasons. It's a dirty situation. Tina, sometimes I hear his voice in my head and I'm just learning how to ignore it or let it go. Every time I feel safe, he pops up again and the threat starts all over again. I think he's adamant about Church, but has a certain regard for me as well. I wish he would just go away.

"Farley has a gun by our front door, and has showed me how to use it in case Oscar ever comes calling. He also bought me pepper spray to put on my key chain. Loathe that I were ever to need to use it."

"I think you can handle this problem, Sally. Just trust God and go with God. Do you know what you need to do for your own safety? First trust in God, then make sure you don't fall into temptation. Remember, Jesus is your number one, and He always will be. Farley is also your number one here on earth. You need to stay bound to him and confide in him with everything."

"He always will be. Farley, and the Lord Jesus Christ. – Who comes first before everything."

"Just don't let go of Farley, and you'll be all right. Remember, you're married, bless your lucky stars. No one can come between that. You and Farley are so close, that even if you weren't married, no one could come between the two of you. You and Farley have a rare love Sally. Don't let anyone spook you," Tina spoke reassuringly.

"Oscar has no part in your life, and if he thinks so, he's dead wrong. What is holy is not to be soiled. Also, you are not a toy to be played with, although sometimes people helplessly get into that situation. Then it's time to turn toward Jesus and run to Him. No more of this CIA stuff. How could it be and why?"

"I'm indifferent about most of it, just the invasive threatening feeling gets to me. I'm scared.

"Then there's Simon, his friend and Leroy's brother. I feel like Simon and Oscar are good friends trying to outwit my feelings of security. I'm broken, and every time I go to Church the pain starts again. But I feel like I need to be there for the sake of Jesus Christ in my life. I can't escape it. Pastor says that God says to grow where you're planted. Farley and I aren't going to uproot and move somewhere else. Oscar and Simon would probably follow us anyway." Sally needed mercy.

"Well, for now just let it play out. But remember, Farley comes first. – After Christ."

Outside the hailing had relented, and the streets were wet with chunks of ice.

"We've been here awhile," said Tina. "I'd better get going home. Thanks for confiding your darkness in me. I'm there for you if you ever need me, OK?"

"Yeah, I guess we better go. Thanks for meeting me here and listening to what I have to say. I feel better, now I'm not in this thing all alone."

The two ladies left their seats and went outside, where the sun was now shining, and steam was rising from the street. They said goodbye and waved to each other as they got in different cars and drove their separate ways.

Sally remembered what Tina had said about Leroy, and felt happy for her friend. Tomorrow was Church again. It would be just another day to face off with Oscar and his little friend Simon. It was too much to think about all at once, so Sally ignored the thought and went home to Farley, her one and only true love.

There he was in the living room snoozing on the couch. Her heart leapt for joy. She opened the back door and saw Thomas curled up on one side of his enclosure. Needing the love and company, she walked to his cage and let herself in. Thomas was asleep. "Thomas," she spoke softly and knelt by the dog as he wagged his docked tail. She embraced the beast and tears rolled down her face as a rattle and hum went through her mind, tearing at features and certain anomalies in her life. She gave up on grace and held fast to the faith that God had placed in her heart. There she sat, stroking Thomas gently and burying her tear stained face into his soft fur.

"Please leave me alone," she whispered. "I just want to be. Free. Filled with liberty to live my life the way that I want to."

It was a windfall thought that had come to her. The fact that she had liberty in Christ to live her life as she wanted to, with the liberty to make decisions and choose what she wanted to do. That was smash on Oscar. He dare not interfere with her liberty to live her own personal life without being intruded upon. She had the liberty to shove him away, and avoid him, as Tina had suggested.

As for Simon, who seemed harmless enough, he might be the more dangerous of the two. Scary thought. Imprisonment. "NO!" she cried. Nobody is going to step on my grapes. She had written a book about just that, about people stealing other people's liberties and manufacturing fake lives without hurting themselves. The idea had first come when Sally wanted to write about the four times she had been raped, and the equality that she found in the world after much pain and suffering.

People try to hurt people through injustice, but everything balances out in the end.

So it's important to know where to put your faith, or the act of being cheated can ruin your entire life. Instead, you have the liberty to choose your own way and walk your own healing path, deciding who and who not to let into your life. Some people breed ugliness, and don't care who they hurt.

Sally sobbed into Thomas's big shoulder and laid her head on the dog's belly with her arms around him. People would laugh at her demise, but being a Christian she had hope in Jesus Christ, and that He was healing her. The mention of strange others was repudiating. She needed softness in her rest. For rest she needed Farley.

After half an hour, Sally pulled herself together and went back into the house, leaving Thomas in his kennel. Farley was still asleep on the couch, snoring like he so often did. Careful not to wake him, she put the coffee on and sat down in a chair, staring at a blank wall. "Why should she feel fear?" She asked herself. "It's not like Oscar brought guns into the Church, but she feared him anyway. He was manipulative and point blank. Sally believed he wanted to make her his own, which would NEVER happen. She had Farley and Jesus. The CIA could screw itself and her delusional thinking, due to her mental illness needed to pipe down.

Screw this and screw that. She mumbled to herself that she was important. "I am a brave woman. I can overcome my fears. I am Courageous!" It was Sally's mantra that she must always tell herself when she felt scared or insecure. The more she said it, the more she believed it.

She tried to let go of her fears, to overcome them. She would face up to Oscar in Church tomorrow, unless she felt it better to avoid him. She just didn't want him ruling her life. Why should she feel uncertain fear all the time, never knowing when Oscar would strike next, or how, for certain?

It was an ugly situation. But she couldn't ignore her feelings and the fact that he was a threat to her in her own little world with Farley, which together they had built.

She smelled herself and realized that she hadn't yet showered today. Quietly she left Farley in the living room on the couch and made her way to the closet, chest of drawers, and bathroom.

The steamy air soothed her pungent thoughts and cooled her guardian vigor. No one can get me here, she thought to herself. She lathered her hair with shampoo, rinsed, and applied conditioner to the long tangled strands that stuck to her body.

She took a bar of sweet smelling lavender soap and gently massaged her whole body with it. She rinsed her hair and turned circles, getting the warm water all over her.

Finally it was time to get out. Sally put on her favorite jeans which she had just finished mending, and a flowery shirt that sported mesmerizing patterns of flowery leaves and petals. She brushed through her hair carefully, applied a leave-in conditioner, and scrunched her long hair to encourage the natural curls that she had.

What should I do now? She thought. I guess it's time for Thomas's walk. Sally grabbed a sweatshirt, Thomas's leash, and then bent over her husband to murmur sweet things in his ear till he awoke. "Wha-?" Farley came to through a cloud of consciousness. "I'm taking Thomas for a walk, Sweetheart. Just wanted to let you know where I would be."

"Bring your pepper spray, Sally," he said slowly, a bit concerned and just waking up.

"I have it sweetie. We'll be back soon, OK?" Sally shut the back door behind her and was sure to lock it. She had two legs; she could run if she had to – but not like she was thinking. She was no longer the great athlete she had once been. She realized that her body was weak, due to her medications over time. In fact, she could hardly run at all. At least she would have Thomas by her side.

She opened his enclosure door and leashed him up. He sat obediently as she arranged his collar and got ready to go. Out the door they went, into the yard and around to the front where the gate stood firmly latched.

Sally guided them out through the gate and closed it behind her. She looked left and right and relaxed. It was another fun day with Thomas. They began to walk. Sally chose to go right. She wanted to go to Washington Park where there was a dog park enclosed on the South side. But she thought better of it. Thomas needed to be neutered first. So they walked to the pier instead, and Thomas dove into the water as his master hurled a tennis ball out for him.

He swam easily to shore and ran back out on the pier to Sally. Again she threw the ball, and again Thomas launched himself off the pier to make a big splash as he landed in the water, chasing after the ball. It was enough for Sally. She laughed at the wet animal who came running to her on the pier where she sat.

She thought it wise to move, so she leashed Thomas up again and they wandered on, around the inlet, back into town, and past the Turnip Bay Coffee Shop where she'd met with Tina earlier.

Sally had no qualms walking Thomas through town. He was majestic and very well behaved. She left him at the door of the café, and went in to order a tall lemonade. She took it with her back out the door and sat at a sunny table where Thomas lay obedient at her feet. She didn't feel safe however, and rather exposed. Her mental illness was kicking in and she was having strange thoughts about CIA people all around her, focused on her, and trying to force her to do something. She knew not what, only that her faith in Jesus Christ would save her in the end.

Sally fidgeted in her seat as she slowly downed her lemonade, putting up with the paralyzing fear of a panic attack. She managed her feelings and used her head to self-talk herself into a place of safety. Just as she was growing more confident, she looked across the street and there was Oscar, walking and whistling a song, threatening her with his very presence. She scratched Thomas's head and ignored Oscar. When she looked up again, he was gone.

She couldn't help but feel watched and knew she couldn't escape that. It was her mental illness again. She froze in her seat and knew not what to do, so she finished her lemonade and got up to throw away her cup. Thomas came with her and was happy to be on the way again. He seemed oblivious to danger.

They reached home again after another forty-five minutes, as Sally had slowly built up confidence on the way home. She latched the front gate securely and let Thomas have the run of the yard. He played wildly, chasing shadows, squirrels and birds. Sally went inside the back door.

Farley was watching Animal Planet, one of their favorite TV stations. Tomorrow would be an I Love Lucy marathon on the Hallmark station. There on the living room table was Sally's journal and she poured out her thoughts and feelings into it. Afterwards, she craved a glass of wine, but resisted knowing that it clashed with her medications.

She picked up the novel she was deep into and began to read again, feasting on the words in the book. Sally had a great love for reading and their bookshelf was nearly full. She often checked out books at the local library, but she also collected some as she bought them intermittently.

"How was your walk, Sweetheart?" asked Farley.

"Oh fine," she said. "We need to get Thomas neutered so he can go play at the dog park. Other than that everything went fine." Then she blubbered, saying "I saw Oscar across the street when I was trying to enjoy my lemonade outside a café. I got so scared, I clutched up, and then when I looked again, he was gone. Farley I don't know what to do. You know Simon, right? Well Leroy is his younger brother, and Tina told me today that they have it hot for each other. Simon is Oscar's friend, I can tell, and I think they are both ganging up on me, as if to pull me out of Christ's clutches."

"Sally, no one can do that." Farley was angry.

"Tomorrow Tina wants to introduce us to Leroy. I think they're going to become a couple, like we used to be before we got married. Which is good. I just worry about Simon and Oscar becoming buddy-buddy with Leroy to get to me. Through Tina. I have to talk to Mae and make sure that we sit by her and James tomorrow. I need protection from those lunatics."

Farley closed his eyes and leaned back again. He had been resting for most of the afternoon. He got up and poured a cup of coffee, with which he sat slowly and drank appreciatively. Tomorrow would be Church. The two hooligans would probably be there, so not to be surprised. He knelt by the sofa then and prayed for God's safety and protection on them, that the losers in Church wouldn't hurt them in any way.

Sally prayed and kneeled next to him. They both prayed for their subsistence and relaxed knowing that God loved them, and wanted them in Church. This was just an obstacle in their paths. Maybe they were making matters bigger than they should be, but Farley trusted Sally's feelings, and her gut told her to be wary of the two would-be perpetrators.

Farley and Sally prayed next to each other for the next five minutes, and then Sally felt she needed to go read the Word for awhile and get more of God's truth in her. She found herself lost in the Book of Acts. She read about the Lord coming to Peter and through a vision making it known that he should not judge and call anything unclean which by the Lord was made clean. Maybe Simon and Oscar weren't unclean, just CIA. She let her mind whirr at a high rate, learning from herself that her judgment might be too harsh. She recalled believing that she worked for NASA, and perhaps this CIA thing was just as fictional as

NASA had been. That was in the hospital. She went to the moon, and to Saturn, and to Jupiter, finding that Jupiter was too big, and Saturn was just right in size for Heaven to be.

In carnal knowledge there is therapy in rest with the infinitesimal tatters of worn clothing and ill-fitting shoes. The poor and the restless not deceiving mindless games, but playing for the therapy of uncanny knowledge, reach out and come when one knows Christ. We all have our big, dark secrets and clouds that rain on otherwise sunny days.

Bringing into subsistence the need to mature and to trust, especially if one is found to be trustworthy, and Sally was told by the Lord long ago that she was trustworthy, also that she had time. Sally needed to grasp these two concepts and make pilgrimage through the hot spots where touch and go is the only way to communicate.

Funky knowledge, learned by ill behavior and response patterns, just means that dipping into the truth too much brings sadistic response as people close up and want to stop hurting each other.

Languid and seemingly salty are the portrayals of good habits and polite behavior. Unless there is something unwanted, such as being in a microscopic lens, there is fortitude and anxiety in riches of faith and glory for the Lord.

Behavior sins when one takes liberty and turns it around, saying that all actions are worthy of God. No. There are lessons to be learned, and behavior might still be cross, but giving up and letting go, that is the only way out of indecision and microcosm of fruitless behavior. Beheld that evil is wrong for the wrong doer.

Initially, sin was made for the wrong doer, knowing that in happenstance, it can be wrong. Sally might well be being sinned against by the bastards in her Church. If only she could say so.

THE SPATTERED CRYSTAL

Like the Earth when it collides with a powerful force, all things will go flying into the wind and torrential outpours of violent waves and things floating on the water. Your head like a crystal ball is powerfully shaken and falls like a glass to the floor. So God made medicine that cuts down on the input and confusion. Your mind, broken apart, is disfigured and you are mentally ill, trying to put the pieces of your shattered glass skull back together.

That's my head again, Sally said as she wrote the words into her journal. My crystal head, smashed to pieces where I look, everything is distorted. It's my mental illness, which I treat with a number of different medications. Farley has it too, just a little bit different. He didn't have thoughts of persecution. It's a divine conspiracy, taking place in the Church, of which no one is aware but me and Farley, and those two hooligans.

Reaching the thought of indecision, it is best to act, and act quickly without too much pondering. It is clear in the indicator of our minds, that unfinished behavior comes around again until it is met and resolved. If you forgot something from your childhood, it will be made aware to you at a later date, such as Sally when she first had memories at the age of twenty-eight of being raped as a small child in a foreign, Far East country.

It displayed itself in an ugly matter, and as time went on, Sally began to deal with the rotten truth, in an ugly matter, which would close down on Sally's social life and leave her a helpless chicken in a tornado. Mad and crazy, life for love, there is learning to be guiltless, and that a wrong was done upon her uninvited. She forced herself to forget, and to merge into a world where numbers counted and figures made sense, but not in the rampant equality where good outdoes bad, because behavior is learned on experience.

As she thought back on these truths, she understood that she didn't need to fear Simon and Oscar. She had been through worse than what they were able to throw at her. She might just comply and be their friend. In the instance that she picked truth with scattered, spattered glass, a cage breaking and setting free a small bird, yellow and high in a tree.

Carefully she must make a cave for herself to go to when she needed to escape. Waking up she might find herself in a prison, a prison of her own Hell, which she needed to escape. In finding friendship with Oscar and Simon, she could release her fear of them, looking for the best in them, and realizing that God was bringing them all together for a reason. As long as they didn't mess with Farley, her one and only true love.

Lacquer on a sleek surface only makes it shinier. And then it can reflect the sun. Sally had a wooden bead necklace that shined it was so smooth, and she wore it on days when she felt especially bad, making into something a hopeful piece of strand and beads. She had hooked a small cross at the center length, of silver, and she prayed with this necklace as though it were a Holy Rosary, only she didn't speak the Catholic words or count the beads for Mary, which didn't exist on her necklace.

Everyone needs a prayer piece, or a charm that has special meaning, like Sally's glass necklace made of Murano. It spoke to her and she felt extremely religious when she wore that one.

But not a woman of many jewels, she treasured her wedding band and the ruby/diamond ring, which Farley had given her at the time of their union.

It was a beautiful union, on a sunny day, by which Farley and Sally became engaged, thus, their union. It happened easily. They both asked the other to marry each other. Both agreed with a "Yes!" And happily they went for a while until they were finally able to get married. That day meant so much to them.

They were tired of people in Church thinking they were fornicators. It wasn't true. They never slept together, and their relationship for many years had been built on trust, love, respect, and understanding. They gradually got to know each other, learning about secrets dark in the past. It was as though each word they spoke tied them closer and closer together. Their love grew and grew, and their affection for one another sprang into a desire to please one another.

Farley endearingly called Sally his "Little Clown", based upon his avid collection of Emmett Kelly the Clowns collectible clown figures. He had over forty of these characters, and always had an eye out for clowns at yard sales. Sally became his "Little Clown" when she spoke of her many facets as separate clowns with names. It was how she described herself, to remain silly and not get down about these many sides of her personality, each another clown with a name.

Sally invested a lot of time in defining her personality. The more she knew about herself, the less complicated her life became. She hurt a lot, and not trusting had very few relationships. She believed that God wanted her to start building relationships, to grow confidence, and to keep her job.

The building where she worked was an excellent facility for helping people with mental illnesses. Her job was basic, but important, as she worked with clients' files and progress notes. Each client had an open and running file, which was cycled through the system each month, documenting case management reports, doctor meetings, physician appointment records, and notes on therapeutic groups such as art therapy, writer's group, meditation group, chemical dependency services, a group for domestic violence and one for Voices. These among many others were provided for "consumers" who took advantage of the system.

Farley and Sally had to pay for their own dental care, but medications were blessedly covered through their insurance. They once a month received a disability government deposit to their individual bank accounts, as they managed finances together but from separate sources.

Sally recalls her days as a freshman in college, and having to leave after two years due to her illness. She always felt like a failure, but now was carefully building a new life for herself. This included eating healthy, exercising regularly, and keeping part of Church. Now she had a job, and felt confident about that, because it helped their income and made their marriage possible.

Thomas was howling outside in his enclosure, and Sally went out to bring the poor beast in. He got hungry at night as they fed the dog twice daily. Thomas dashed around the yard, and Sally watched him play as he threw his toys into the air and wrestled with them violently.

"Thomas! Thomas, come here." He came immediately to Sally who let him in the house while she got his food and water bowls ready. Carefully she placed the two items on the back steps and Thomas attacked the food and slurped the water noisily. She smiled; he looked so silly wagging his rump and gobbling food and water.

It was getting dark out, and goblins were coming out of hiding, to linger around the doorstep wanting to come in. Not a chance. Sally could see them and rebuked them away. She was well familiar to the spirit world, and saw ghosts, goblins, ghouls, even occasional demons and also she saw angels and spoke to them. Call it an aspect of her mental illness; she was gifted with the ability not to fear any of these entities.

Her favorites were the ghosts that she saw, every now and then when she had walked with Farley, and they loomed around them laughing and waving their fingers back and forth in admonishment. This didn't scare Farley or Sally, for they knew they were doing nothing wrong. Ghosts liked to tease and often put shiny objects in front of them as they walked; so that they were deceived into thinking they were diamonds. But on closer inspection there was nothing there. A mirage. Ghosts were good at that, making fun of their vision, but never in a harmful way.

One time Sally long ago was driving home and a ghost had a laser gun beaded upon the back of her neck as she drove recklessly trying to avoid it. Careening around corners and running stop lights she finally got home where the laser gun car drove by her and she panted, sweating in terror at this near encounter with terrorist ghosts.

Once she saw Elvis in a tree. She couldn't believe her eyes. This ghoul shimmered and hung there for five minutes then disappeared.

Goblins came out at night and caroused the city streets, both preventing and causing automobile accidents. They looked like shadows out of the corner of the eye, slipping out of sight.

Demons threatened to inhabit her body, and indeed her mental illness could attest to that, but she rather believed that God protected her from the demons entering her body, and she never felt threatened because she could dodge the shackling creatures. They were everywhere, some spreading germs, others spreading rumors, and still others trying to steal souls at death. Farley and Sally were protected against them, for they believed and were baptized in Jesus Christ.

He did everything for them, from bringing Thomas into their home, to dissipating the fear surrounding Oscar and Simon, as avid Christians, finding a place to worship.

Their background was unknown to Sally, and the mystery surrounding their somewhat friendly demeanor exacted Sally into realizing that God was doing something significant with their Church, and these martyrs were reaching out in a ghostly world to make contact with people and citizens of the Church, routing out evil and worshiping wildly.

Politics could be involved, but Sally and Farley knew next to nothing about politics and didn't mind keeping it that way. They learned bits and pieces as time went on, but mostly they gave up to theology and God, knowing their time would soon come to meet their Maker.

Following the demons come the many angels that have touched their lives. An angel had been with Farley the day he recovered his watch and Sally had caught two fish.

They were negligent neither to beginnings or ends, and timelessness did not matter, for they had time and kept in step with the agreement of ability, with source and truth.

Devilish figures didn't scare the couple, for angels, guardian angels kept watch over them.

Evil did not amount to much in the lives of Farley and Sally, because they had Christ, and there was to be no condemnation in Christ. He loved them, blessed them, looked out for them and kept them safe no matter the circumstances. In return, Farley and Sally lived for Jesus, worshiped Him, loved Him, and gave him praises with prayer and thanksgiving.

But back to Sally feeding her dog and rebuking the nosey ghoul at the doorstep, we see that the dog has eaten all his food and drunk most of his water, and now lay curled up on the couch by the TV. Together they watched Animal Cops and mourned for the many abused and abandoned animals. Thomas would forever have a happy home.

Thomas would sleep inside tonight as usual. They let him out to do his business before going to bed, and walking through the intrusive apparitions that garlanded their home on a regular basis. One friend they had was a spider that had a web by the front porch light. Sally called it Carla, and kept track of the web and bugs caught in it. Darkness was the best and most fruitful time for this arachnid as bugs darted around the porch light and got stuck in her web. She was a big, fat spider.

Farley and Sally thought of her as a good luck charm. She had lived there for two or three months now, but as morning came and Sally went out on the front porch to get the paper, she noticed that Carla was missing. There was her web, torn and shredded. Most likely a bat had found her juicy body and made a meal of her.

Sally's heart dropped, as she was made aware of the missing spider. Did this mean their luck would change? So far they had had a happy marriage. There had been no deaths in the family on either side. Gilmore hadn't been by for some time, so she decided to call him after Church today and see how he was faring.

Church was at ten-thirty, and Farley got their breakfasts ready early so they would have plenty of time to take care of Thomas and get dressed and ready to go – after coffee and Sally's morning tea.

They put the big dog outside in his enclosure after his morning bowl of food, and they put his water bowl outside in the enclosure as well. Everything set; they grabbed their Bibles and went out to the car after locking up the house. Together they drove to their Church, Hillside Apostolic Church, and parked and got out.

There was Oscar at the front entrance, greeting people. Sally said, "Thank you" and Farley said, "Good morning, Buddy!" Sally felt a warmth go through her body as they passed him by and headed to the sanctuary. There was Simon chatting with guests and laughing with them. Nothing seemed wrong or out of the ordinary. Perhaps God had moved in their hearts to find this acceptance of one another. Fools would be greedy, but these were no fools. They were wise, brilliant men of God who exuded a powerful spirit in their presence, and Sally was aware of this power. She was clairvoyant to a degree, her mind was a crystal ball that had spattered, and she saw so many things through so many points of view. Her shattered pieces made up her life like a crystal ball being pieced back together.

SYNTHESIS

Comb through your hair as with a salve that puts everything back in order. Sally played with her locks in the bathroom to fix her look in the mirror. She realized in horror that she had dreamed about having lice in her hair last night. If it had been real, and Carla still alive, she could have harvested the lice and sprinkled them in Carla's web. She felt sadness at the loss of her friend, the spider. Not that she liked spiders particularly, but she had become fond of this spider at their doorstep who now was dead in some bat's belly.

She screamed and there were bats all over her. She came back to consciousness and realized she had passed out on the bathroom floor in the Church. No one was there to witness this event as there was Church service going on. She and Farley where sitting next to Mae and James. Tina hadn't yet come over to introduce Leroy to them. There was Leroy singing in choir. The music ended and everyone took seats.

Sally sat next to Farley, and told him nothing of her fainting in the bathroom. What was it? Too much worry? Too much pressure on her? She disguised herself as a pretty little clown, and started counting numbers to occupy her mind and keep voices from intruding. She tried to pay attention to the Pastor, but she could only put her head in her hands and mope on the floor with her eyes. Intermittently she looked up and around her. She felt so lost.

Everyone was singing now, and worshiping, screaming and crying out to and for the Lord Jesus Christ. But Sally felt quiet in her heart and couldn't join in the crescendo. She folded her hands and swore an oath never to misjudge people again. Not to be judgmental, and to be forgiving in all circumstances.

There was steam coming out of her ears as she felt the presence of the Holy Ghost but could not vocally join in the chorus. She did begin to clap her hands together to the music, finally lifting her arms and waving her hands in the air.

Thunk. She sat down hard on her chair as the worshiping overcame her and her back hurt making her need to sit down. She kept her arms up, though, and waved her hands back and forth, finally joining in with the singing and a much lighter heart. She was confused in herself and couldn't synthesize the time with the worship. It was all suspended as the Holy Ghost swept through the Church and combined spirits all together.

Feeling sort of back in sorts, Sally connected with her spirit and allowed herself to praise the Lord with the music and the praising Church of people around her. She was lifted up, and thought of Carla, wondering where the little spider had gone. She thought of Thomas, now safe in his enclosure at home, and then she remembered Tina, who she saw was making her way toward them with Leroy as the congregation made its way to the alter to pray and be prayed for.

Sally smiled at Tina and put her hurried morning behind her. She smiled with her freckled face as here came her friend to talk to her with Leroy in tow.

"Hi!" They greeted each other. Farley said, "Praise the Lord!" and shook Leroy's hand. Tina greeted Farley as well. Then it was Sally's turn to meet him. "Hi, brother Leroy! Sister Tina has told me quite a bit about you."

"This is sister Sally," Tina spoke to Leroy. "She's my newest friend in Church."

"Sally and Farley are married," Tina spoke up. They've been coming to this Church for four or five years now. How long have you and Simon been attending?"

"Oh, me and my brother Simon moved here a few years ago, but just started going to Church here at Hillside about six months ago. I like it here and so does he. We're planning on getting separate apartments soon, but for now living together is quite convenient," said Leroy with a crooked, odd little smile.

"I don't know if you've met brother Oscar? He's my brother's best friend and has just started recently coming here too. You should meet him. It's hard being new and not knowing anybody."

"Oh, would you introduce us?" asked Sally beside herself. Her curiosity was getting the best of her.

"Of course. Maybe we could all sit together next week." Leroy meandered through the crowd in search of Oscar. Farley and Sally eyed each other suspiciously. They were about to officially meet the fiend from Hell whom Sally now wanted to befriend.

Oscar and Leroy walked up to where Tina was standing by Sally and Farley, and Mae and James as well. He made introductions, and Sally introduced Mae and James to Tina, Leroy, Simon, and Oscar.

Everyone stood and sat around each other in wavering curiosity for a few moments as Oscar reached out to shake Sally's hand. She bowed her head curtly but was too shy to say anything. Here was the "big monster" that had been pursuing her for the last six months, frightening her, and haunting where she lived. He was just a nice guy that Sally had obviously misjudged. As she spoke to him now, she realized that he could never come between her and Farley. She had been suspicious for no good reason. Still, she felt a twinge of something out of the ordinary with Simon and Oscar. Like people hiding behind trees on a windy day.

Leaves were falling everywhere, waiting to be filled out by pen as to tell a story in their cycle.

A golden moon hung overhead. It was one of those days when the moon shone during the daylight hours. The sky was partly cloudy. The group of new acquaintances remained talking and chatting in a friendly manner as Church came to an end and the people at the alter slowly made their way back to their seats.

"It was nice meeting you," said Oscar to Sally, and then to Farley, Mae, and James. "See you next time," he said, and turned and walked away. Simon also took his leave and left Tina and Leroy with their new friends Farley, Mae, and James, and he shook Sally's hand as he departed.

Outside the wind was blowing ferociously. Trees were waving and there were gusts of wind on the small pond next to the Church. A flock of crows inhabited the lawn in front of the Church. Two small squirrels raced around to the back and up the cherry trees.

Sally noticed that Oscar was sitting in his car in the parking lot with his engine running. She waved with Farley as the couple walked by on the way to their own car, the old, orange Fiat.

At least it still ran, so they didn't complain.

On the way home, Farley was smiling. "See, he isn't so bad like you thought, Sally."

"You're right, but there's still something odd, and I can't put my finger on it."

"You're right about that," came a hallucinatory voice in her head.

"Farley! I'm hearing voices about Oscar. He says he hasn't been misjudged and that there is something 'odd' about him." Sally praised the Lord and rebuked the devil. "Leave us alone!" She wailed. "With the authority of Jesus Christ, I command you to leave!" Sally admonished the devil and sent it on its way.

"I'm sorry, Sally," said Farley. Do you want to go to Starbucks for a coffee drink? We could just sit there and relax, and make plans for the rest of the day."

"Yes, Farley," Sally said sullenly, "Let's go to Starbucks. I could use an Americano right about now. I need some cheering up. Those men are dangerous. I can feel it in my bones."

They reached Starbucks, parked carefully and went inside. There were Tina and Leroy sitting at a corner table.

"Humph. This must be divine ordination," Sally whispered to Farley. It was too late to back out; they had already been seen.

"Sally! Farley! Won't you join us?"

Sally smiled at her friend and walked over to their table in a dark corner without windows.

"How did you like Church today?" Came an innocent inquiry from Tina.

"Fine, fine. I forgot to mention to you guys that I fainted in the ladies' restroom during service," she looked apologetically to Farley. She hadn't told him about it and he was shocked and surprised.

"What? Why didn't you say anything, Sally? Are you OK?"

"Well, I do have a bump on my head and my left shoulder hurts, but I'm all right in general. I think I'm just under a lot of pressure right now, with Oscar and everything, and Simon, his buddy. I'm scared. Something doesn't seem right. I'm just praying for the best. I'm sorry, I shouldn't have brought that up."

Leroy nodded affirmatively and said that everything was fine.

"Here, let us go get our coffee, and then we'll join you. Are you staying much longer?"

"Actually, we were just leaving, but it was nice to bump into you. See you next time," Tina and Leroy got up to go.

"See you next time. We love you!" The gates broke and Sally hugged Tina and then Leroy, and Farley warmly shook their hands.

Tina and Leroy went on their way; so it left Sally and Farley to order their drinks and sit down to enjoy them. They chose a window table with big, comfortable maroon chairs. They sat for a while to let their drinks cool a little so as not to burn their tongues.

"What do you think of *that*, Farley?" questioned Sally, a little shaken. "I probably shouldn't have mentioned Simon and Oscar, Leroy being Simon's brother and Simon Oscar's best friend. I wonder which way the beans will scatter, now that I've poured them out." Sally was solemn and drank her Americano slowly.

"I wouldn't worry about it. If there is something fishy it's bound to come out anyway."

"I just don't want to get hurt, and I don't want to hurt anybody. Those are my gut feelings."

"Well, Sally, y-you're not a hurtful person by nature. You always want the best for everybody. You always put yourself first in a line of defense. It's probable that you would curse away evil rather than entertain any of it. So maybe th-the truth had to come out. Too much pressure. And you fainting in the bathroom. I'm worried about you Sally. We've got to be careful now. Who knows how this thing might pan out?" Farley was tired and deeply concerned.

"So what do you want to do today?" implored weepy Sally.

"Let's go fishing at the pier! That would get us out and away from the nest, a target zone for unwanted villains. It's not good to be too predictable, and we shouldn't have to worry about that. God is on our side. Who could stand against us?"

"Yaaaay! Fishing sounds fun, Farley," squeamish Sally leapt at the opportune idea.

"Let's go."

"Let's go."

They threw away their empty cups and walked out to the car and got in. Within ten minutes they were home, and there, paws on the gate, was Thomas who had escaped his enclosure. Most likely they forgot to lock it properly.

"Oh Thomas!" Cried Sally. She darted inside the gate and ran to the dog, which ran to her. He jumped up and gave her a big doggy hug. Sally held onto him and cried. Then she let go and they watched as he tore off around the house bringing back a toy for them to throw.

Sally hurled the toy across the yard and the Rottweiler pounced after it. Then he paused and looked up, ears cocked sniffing a familiar scent. There was Oscar, across the street and smoking at a bus stop. Thomas went ballistic and charged at the fence. He knew this intruder and associated him with fear and escape.

Farley waved, and said "Hey!" Sally kept quiet. Oscar waved back and put out his cigarette. "How are you two doing?" He asked curiously.

"Oh fine. Did you like Church today?" Sally became aware that they were shouting across the street at each other. Her stomach felt knotted up.

"I'm tired, Farley, I'll take Thomas back and put him in his run. I'll be inside, OK?"

"I'll go with you," said Farley, and waved goodbye to Oscar.

Oscar waved back and started jumping up and down. "Praise the Lord!" he bellowed. Then the bus came and he waved goodbye.

Farley went inside the front door, and found a weeping Sally on the davenport in the living room. "It's obvious he was following us, Farley. He was in his car when we were leaving Church today. Where is his car now? How did he get to our bus stop? Something mysterious is going on. But I don't feel quite so afraid anymore. He seems of a friendly sort, we just don't know him yet. But isn't it strange? It's like he's following me, and then leaving right when I can't stand it anymore. Boo-hoo. Church time. Church should be a pleasure not a battleground. Well, Farley, we are Christian Warriors, are we not? So it's to be expected that there would be some conflict going on. I'm going to call Tina later and find out if anything sprung from our little talk at Starbucks."

"Are you feeling OK? Do you still want to go fishing?"

"Yes, I do. Let's go."

"Let's go."

Instead of walking with all their gear they drove to Farley's favorite pier and parked next to the gate. Out on the end of the pier they cast their lines out into the water in opposite directions so as not to tangle up their lines.

Sally had a bite immediately, and then she had a fish on. She reeled it in, and Farley gaped at the huge perch that she pulled up and netted. They knocked it out and put it in their bucket. Sally smiled at Farley, who had cast his line again. Three more times he cast his lure and on the third try he got a bite. Then he had a fish on and was so excited he could hardly reel in the fish. It was a medium sized perch just big enough to keep. Farley was elated; for once a success!

Two hours went by and neither one caught another fish, but they were both eager and excited by their angelic luck today. Sally went down to the water and quickly scaled and filleted their fish. Here was dinner. They packed up in the car and went home. It was five o'clock and beginning to get dark outside. Everything at the house seemed normal. They let Thomas out of his enclosure and all three went into the house.

Farley volunteered to fry the fish, and Sally filled Thomas's red bowl with food and scrubbed out his blue bowl and filled it with water, placing the two bowls on the back stairs.

Thomas gobbled up his dinner and then came in to lie on the couch. All was right with the world. Ghosts and goblins surrounded their house, all curious and harmless. They knew better than to try and haunt God's children.

After some time went by, and they had eaten the fish for dinner with salad on the side and two baked potatoes, Sally decided it was time to call Tina and see if anything had come from her admission today at the coffee shop. She wondered what Leroy thought, being Simon's brother who was Oscar's best friend.

Or so it seemed the two communicated often in Church, even from opposite sides of the congregation. Sally saw them grin at each other and nod.

They played out their positioning which always seemed concurrent to where Sally was sitting or standing. Somehow, one or the other were in her way, but she had said little until now, having formally met Oscar and shaken hands with Simon.

They were wildly active in worship, and jumped up and down and yelled and screamed "Hallelujah!" and "Yes, Jesus!" Speaking other words of praise and worship as well. Both had been recently baptized, and had the Holy Ghost within. Most likely they were speaking in tongues also.

How can God love them, and also love me, yet pit us against each other? Maybe I'm misunderstanding the cues, and they just want to get to know me, about life and what is happening these days. Obviously they had a mission to ferret me out of the crowd and make me feel targeted for some big, important reason. I know I'm no more important than the next person, but I feel singled out by reason of which I am not sure. If I stick this thing out, the truth is bound to be revealed.

She picked up the phone to call Tina. It rang, and Tina answered. "Hi Tina!" She greeted. "It's me, Sally. I just wanted to follow up on the conversation that we had today at Starbucks. Thank you for introducing us all to Leroy in Church this morning. And thanks for introducing Simon and Oscar as well. Do you know where they come from?"

"Leroy said they've been living here for about ten years, before which I don't know where they were. They both went to the same college together, I think, and have kept their friendship all this time. Both are very strong, trustworthy Christians, so I don't know what your hang-up is all about."

"Did Leroy say anything to Simon about it?"

"I think he may have mentioned something, but he said not to bother about it; it's all just hogwash. Simon loves this Church and so does Oscar. They've been coming for about seven months now and feel they have found a Church home. I don't see why you're so concerned, Sally."

"Oh, I just have my reasons I guess, but I suspect they're up to no harm, otherwise we wouldn't be in the same Church together, and love the Church as well. Hillside Apostolic Church is the most truth – based Church I've ever attended. I wouldn't want to be forced out, so there must be room for all of us.

"God is just uniting his children, I guess, especially me and Simon and Oscar, who seems so intrusive.

"Well I shouldn't keep travailing on about this whole thing. It's just my suspicions anyhow. So how are you and Leroy faring? Any little rainbow hearts in the future for you two?"

"Oh my God, yes! I have never been so in love with anybody. Leroy is everything I've ever looked for. We're talking about marriage already, and it's only been a couple of months. It's breathtaking. We're not fornicating, don't get the wrong idea, but all the more reason to get married, right?"

"Of course. Farley and I abstained for almost nine or ten years before we got married. I believe it's the right idea - *love,* I mean. Be sure you are in love before you make a mistake for sex.

"God tells us to have self control. But all of us fall short of the glory of God. I admit I sinned not less than once or twice before I found Farley and we subsequently got married."

"Well pipe down little tea pot! I love Leroy, and he's not weird, and neither is his brother, and neither is Oscar. What ever gave you that idea?"

"Oh, I have my reasons. I don't feel at liberty to tell them to you. But I just wanted to hear from you what happened out of our conversation at Starbucks. I love you Tina, and I hope you don't get the wrong idea. Let's keep in touch and have coffee again soon."

"I would love that. Thanks for calling me."

"Thanks for listening! – Bye."

"Bye-bye."

Sally walked out of the kitchen into the living room and found her mate busy reading a novel. It was one that she had already finished. "Hi Sweetheart," she said resignedly. "How's the book coming?"

"Great. I've never read a book where the author has so much control over the plot. Not a boring word in here."

"That's what I thought. It's sort of a spiral plot from beginning to end. It's makeshift, and real. I liked it a lot, too. I called Tina and tried to ferret out whatever came of our talk at Starbucks. She basically told me to get my head on straight and stop worrying. She said that Oscar and Simon and Leroy moved here about ten years ago. She said they love Hillside and want to make it their Church home."

"I don't know what to say. You've always had good radar in understanding relationship and organizations. Remember how you uncovered a cocaine dealership through your last boyfriend, how he used to put cocaine in the coffee grounds and kept you hanging on in lust and misery? Now if there's something fishy going on with Oscar, and I think there could be, seeing how he was at our bus stop today when we got home from Church, you'll see it to the truth. Sometimes the truth is painful. Sometimes you have to hurt other people to keep them from taking advantage of you. But we're not sure that they're out to take advantage of you. Worry less, think more."

"Remember, God is in control, and he will protect us, I believe. What if he sides with both of us and we crash somewhere in the middle?"

"Well, Hillside is a powerful Church if it can house both us and them. We just have to stay alert and on our guard and protect ourselves from invasion and intrusion. Say, wasn't that fish delectable? I must say I had a good day, finally catching another one. Yours was huge!"

"It's a good habit to have. Keeps you out of the Red Tornado where you swindle your money, God's money. Remember, we have to pay tithes on any of your winnings. I can't see God approving it any other way."

"I love the Casino! But I know it worries you, so I'll try to stop going, and maybe just go fishing instead. Or I could go bike riding through the hills. I want to go up to the big cross again sometime. I feel like I could lay some garbage at the Savior's feet so he can get rid of it. First there is my Casino addiction. I'm sorry Sally. I can only try to stop. That's all I can say for now. You know how much fun I have . . . but I shall try to stop. It's borrowed money from God, anyhow. I love Him, and I love you."

Darkness was settling outside, wrapping the little house in all sorts of spirits, goblins, and ghouls. It was a haunted house, but God ruled over all of it. So much spirituality was tied up in this one little place. It was good to have God as King and ruler over all. He kept them safe and protected.

The couple was used to seeing spirits of all sorts in and around the little house with the big yard and cherry and cedar trees. The fence bordering their neighbors cut under an old green apple tree, so they harvested the ones on their side. They were the best apples on Earth, and Sally liked to make them into pies and applesauce.

The salty air surrounding their city off the shores of Turnip Bay was healthy for their lungs, and provided for much therapy in being outside. Sally wanted to call Mae and set up a tennis day.

She called Mae. Mae answered. "Hello?"

"Hi Mae! It's Sally. How are you doing?"

"Oh hi!" she replied.

"We need to play tennis again soon."

"I would but I have 'tennis elbow' from rampant gardening and I have to wear a brace on my wrist. Take it or leave it, but it's my tennis arm that got hurt, so I can't play. I'm sorry."

"I wasn't aware of that. Do you want to walk Thomas with me tomorrow?"

"I would love to. How's Farley?"

"Farley's wonderful. He's really well and always there for me. I love you Mae, let's talk later. How about if I call you after work tomorrow so we can walk Thomas together?"

"Sounds good to me. OK."

"OK, see you then! Bye."

"Bye."

Farley and Sally relaxed in their living room among the ghosts and goblins, the ghouls, spirits and invading demons plus intrusive angels that balanced the whole situation out.

Sally wanted coffee. There was none and she didn't want to make a new pot. It could wait till morning. At nine o'clock she told Farley she was tired and got up to go to bed. She was submissive to God and said prayers after brushing her teeth and changing into her pajamas. She rested easily and never heard Farley come in two hours later.

She dreamed about cremating people and spreading their ashes all over the hills above the bay. She felt threatened by Oscar and this came through in her dreams as a skier skiing faster than her and bearing down on her two little skies until she toppled over and fell out of his way. Only he did not just leave her there. He made sure she was not hurt.

Morning came and the couple arose to make breakfast, shower, and feed, water, and let out the dog.

Sally's head hurt where she had bumped it in the bathroom at Church yesterday. She groaned and got up. Farley had made breakfast already. Soon they were ready and carefully put Thomas in his outdoor enclosure, securing the latch so that he wouldn't escape again. Both agreed that it was time to have him neutered.

Farley drove Sally to work and dropped her off at the mental health center. Then he drove to his current work site and put on his armor to be a man at work without concurrent problems. He focused solely on the task at hand, which was planting little pine trees on a central lane divider. The work hurt his back, but he didn't complain. It kept him strong, and he looked forward to biking in the backcountry.

Sally's job that day consisted of data entry, filing, and ordering supplies while manning the phones as well. She was challenged, but enjoyed the activity.

After work Sally walked home and went to Thomas in the back yard. He whined excitedly and jumped up and down at the fence of his enclosure. Sally opened the latch and swung open the door, letting Thomas out wildly. He stormed around the yard, running to and fro, excited to be moving his big body in big ways. He raced around the whole house several times and came finally to Sally and sat at her feet.

"Good Boy, Thomas," she said rewardingly, "You're such a good dog." Then she went in the back door of the house and he came with her. She put a bowl of water down for him, and he lapped at it energetically.

Next she picked up the phone and called Mae. "Hello, Mae," she said when her friend answered. "Are you still up for walking Thomas with me?"

"Yes," she said excitedly. "I've been waiting for your call, I could really use the exercise."

"Where do you want to meet?"

"What if I meet you at your house in half an hour?

"That's great. Then I can get ready to go."

"OK! See you soon! Bye!"

"Bye."

Sally fixed herself a quick sandwich and had an apple with it. Then she finished what was left of the coffee. After that she went and sat in the front room, waiting for her friend to arrive.

She picked up a Bible and started perusing through it. Then she set it down as she heard a knock on the door. It was Mae.

"Hi Mae!" She squealed as she let her friend in the house and gave her a big hug. Mae returned the hug with equal fervor. "Let's go!" She said.

Together they went around back and let Thomas out of his enclosure. Sally had a long leather leash that she used with Thomas. It was sturdy and she liked it. She hooked it up to Thomas's training collar, a choke chain that she seldom needed but was there in case the dog ever did get a mind to take off. His collar would restrain him with metal prongs.

"Can I take him?" Asked Mae, who loved dogs and had a Chihuahua.

"Of course you can," said Sally. "Let's go around front to the gate out there." Carefully Sally opened the gate and shut it behind them. They decided to go left up into the hills. Sally wanted to stop at the big cross and say a prayer regarding Simon and Oscar, and then put a stone on the huge pile of prayer rocks at the Savior's feet.

Mae prayed along with Sally, adding her own prayers to the session. When they had finished they looked into each other's eyes, a sign of confidentiality. Nobody forced conversation, and together they walked Thomas into the backcountry to a little stream where Thomas drank greedily. He lunged after a rabbit but Mae held him tight and secure on the leash, which was beginning to wear thin.

"Sally," spoke Mae in consequence, "don't you think you should get a nylon leash? This one doesn't look like it has much life left in it."

"I agree, Mae, this leash won't last very much longer. I want to get a red leash for Thomas. That would look cool."

"Yeah," said Mae. "A big dog needs a big leash."

The women walked further back into the hills when suddenly Thomas began barking wildly. There in the grass ahead was a rattlesnake. Mae screamed and Sally shrieked. Sally grabbed the leash and yanked Thomas backwards; starting to run in the direction they had come from. Mae scrambled after her, checking behind to see if the snake was after them. She didn't see it, but they kept running anyway, all the way to the big cross where they stopped, gasping to catch their breath. There was no snake around them, but they were both shaken up, and suddenly Thomas's leash broke.

"Oh Mae, that was so close!" Sally cried out in tears. The leash had lasted just long enough to save Thomas from the rattlesnake. It saved both of their lives as well. What a viper. Sally had seen on TV how much venom came out of their mouths when they were "milked" to make anti-venom.

The two women sat down on a bench, Sally holding Thomas's collar as they rested. Thomas sat, breathing heavily and looking around wildly. "I guess I have to hold onto his collar all the way home. I need to get Thomas neutered, and now I need a new lead for him. Oh Mae, I'm so tired," she sulked. God's got me in the eye of a hurricane. Everything is flying around me; things are happening so oddly, and now this. How will I ever recover?"

She didn't feel like talking about Oscar and Simon. She wanted to put them out of her head and live peaceably. So instead she remained quiet with her friend, and then remembering, she asked how James was doing.

Mae admitted that things were going quite well and there were no if very few problems going on. Also they had finally set a date when to get married.

Sally rejoiced with her friend and asked about the date.

"The second Saturday of February. Three o'clock. Mae blushed with pleasure. This had been a long time in coming. "You'll be there won't you?" she asked worriedly.

"Of course, Mae, I wouldn't miss it for all of the moon. You're my best friend, Mae, I rejoice with you."

Carefully the two friends picked their way down into the city outskirts, and down Manger road to Sally's house on the right side. Holding onto Thomas's collar she lead him to his enclosure and turned him loose in there. Sally told Mae to get comfortable in a lawn chair; she would bring out a pitcher of lemonade for them to relax with.

Sally reappeared with the lemonade and two glasses. She poured one for Mae, and waited for hers until she had brought out a fresh bowl of water for Thomas who was very appreciative. Finally she poured her own lemonade and relaxed in a lawn chair next to her friend.

"I baked a batch of chocolate chip cookies yesterday," said Mae.

"Are they soft? I love soft chocolate chip cookies."

"Well, these are so soft they're almost gooey," continued Mae.

The afternoon was warm and balmy, sea moisture in the air.

Thomas had stopped turning in circles and lay down next to his Igloo doghouse.

"I don't think you're crazy, Sally," Mae said. "I've noticed something odd about your two hooligans in Church – but if you don't want to talk about it, I'd understand."

"Good, because I don't want to talk about it. I want the whole problem to disappear. I can't help but feel something creepy up my back when I think of that part of my life.

A little breeze blew through the yard, and Sally got up to refill their glasses with lemonade. "I wish we had some of your cookies right about now," she thought wistfully.

"I'll drop some by later or tomorrow if you want. I made more than James and I can eat by ourselves."

"That would be nice," Sally smiled, suddenly feeling better. Then feeling generous she got up and opened the latch of Thomas's gate, and swung open the door so that the dog could run out. And he did. He tore around the yard, running from front to back to front and all around the little turquoise house they called home.

He was tireless and just needed to run. "Mae, will you come with me to get Thomas neutered? I could get a new lead rope for him at the same time. I'd just feel more secure if someone went with me."

"Of course I'll go with you."

"Great! Let me go make an appointment. My phone is in the house."

Sally got up and went to the back door and in the house, thinking of Mae's chocolate chip cookies. She looked on line to find the phone number at the vet they used. Finding it she called to schedule an appointment for Thomas's neutering.

There was an opening on Wednesday at two o'clock. It just might work, if Farley let her have the car that day. He could easily take the bus home, and it would only be for a day or two. Maybe they would want to keep him over night. Sally made the appointment and started planning ahead.

Mae had already agreed to go with her. So that would be in two days from now.

Sally came back out of the house to Mae who was snoozing in her lounge, her glass held comfortably in both hands across her belly. The glass was empty.

Sally poured herself the last of the lemonade and sat down next to Mae, reclining in the chaise lounge.

There was Thomas, chasing a squirrel up the cedar tree and barking after it.

The rest of the afternoon was relaxing for all three of them. Thomas got to run around the yard, and Sally and Mae found much needed "down time". It was time for Sally's afternoon pills. So she went into the house again and administered the proper doses to herself. Which reminded her, she needed to see Kirk again soon, her case manager, and Farley had to see Nate. Also, her once-a-month visit with her psychiatrist was coming up. Sally and Farley saw the same psychiatrist, Dr. Nett, at the Mental Health and Wellness Center where she worked.

It was starting to get dark, the sun had gone down, and now Sally needed to wake up Mae. She gently shook her shoulders and took the glass out of her hands. Mae came awake slowly and sighed with a big smile. "Oh Sally," she murmured, "I so much needed a nap like this. How long was I sleeping?"

"About three hours. I didn't want to disturb you; you looked so at peace.

"I made an appointment for Thomas at the vet on Wednesday at two o'clock. Does that work for you?"

"Yes. Do you want me to pick you up from work and drive to the vet after we get Thomas? I know that Farley needs the car on work days."

"That would be perfect. Then he wouldn't need to take the bus."

"Good."

"Thank you."

They stretched their limbs and Mae got up slowly. "Thanks for the lemonade and the walk. That rattlesnake might give me nightmares for a long time. What an adventure we had!"

"I'm just blessed that Thomas didn't break his leash until we were well away from danger. Well I'm glad that's over."

"Me too. I hate snakes. They always scare me."

"Well, you go home to your James, and tell him "Hi" from me. We'll have to get together for a Bible study one of these weeks. But for now, - Farley should be here by now. I bet he went to the Red Tornado again. Anyway, -"

"Sally, I'm pregnant. I needed to tell you because you're the only one who would understand. James and I haven't been abstaining like everyone thinks, and now I'm caught." She started to cry and Sally went to her and wrapped her arms around her. "Don't you worry, Mae, God loves all His children and he knows that none of us are perfect."

"Will the Church condemn me?"

"If it does, it's a severely backwards Church. I don't think so. There's no condemnation in Christ, and every child is a gift. I never told you this, it was before I met you, but I have a daughter, Mae, and I had to give her up for adoption, because with my mental illness, I wasn't able to care for her responsibly. I had too much worry of my own. She's twelve years old now, and I've never met her, except when she was born at the hospital. She was the most beautiful thing I've ever seen.

"But I don't believe she was a sin. She was a beautiful baby girl, and I've received some pictures from her family. Someday I will meet her, and be proud that I did the right thing and didn't abort.

"That would've been too hard. It would have been harder than giving her up for adoption. Either way, I did the right thing. I'm sorry, it's so hard, but you get to keep your baby. I will cherish it with you. I will stand up for you. I think the Pastor will welcome the baby to the

Church. Sure, people might wonder, but that's all talk and no chewing gum. Nobody in our Church is perfect. How far along are you?"

"A month and a half."

"So, this is October, you conceived in August?"

"Yes. Late August."

"And you're marrying in February?"

"So the baby will be due in late May."

"Yes."

"Don't you worry, Mae. Does James know?"

"I told him last week. He's not angry. He's actually happy about it. I'm so blessed with him."

"That is a blessing. He would have no right to be angry with you anyway. He's just as responsible as you are.

"Do you want me to tell Farley or not?"

"You can tell Farley. I hope he doesn't judge me."

"He would never do that. Things happen. This happened to you. Take it and run with it. Enjoy your pregnancy and be proud of the little one inside of you. That baby's going to need all the love you can give it. Whatever you do, don't condemn yourself. It was meant to be, and there is no shame on you."

"Oh thank you for understanding, Sally," spoke Mae. "I should probably get going now. James is home and wondering where I am. Where's Farley? I thought he got off work around three."

"Yes, well *he* is probably at the Red Tornado Casino having fun with our money. He keeps saying he wants to stop, but so far he hasn't. I can't get mad at him, but I do let him know that I disapprove.

"Maybe I should go there one day," said Mae thoughtfully. "James and I gambled and we got a baby. Maybe I could win some money."

"Mae, that's no way to look at it. Don't get apathetic now. Really, God has blessed you."

"But I'm cursed, I sinned."

"And God forgives."

"Will he bless me with a healthy baby?"

"As far as I know he will. Don't worry about that. Just be pleased you can have a baby. It'll be your own bundle of joy. Farley and I can't have kids. We're mentally ill, the both of us, and wouldn't make responsible parents. You should be overjoyed!"

"Yeah, I see your point. You know, I really am happy, I'm just afraid that the Church will throw garbage at us."

"Mae, your baby is no abomination. Celebrate life and what it gives you. We have Thomas, but a baby is so much more! Feel good! Don't cry, Mae, God has gifted you with a new life. Look forward to that little bundle of joy. And you and James will get married; the responsible thing to do, and you'll have a Church wedding with everyone invited. People understand, Mae, this isn't the first time such a thing has happened. And remember, there is no condemnation in Christ."

"That's true."

Mae was solemn. "Thanks for the lemonade and the walk with Thomas. Can we do that regularly? I need the exercise and could use your support through this thing."

"I'm here for you."

"Thanks." Mae got up and put her little arms around her friend. Together they carried in the glasses and lemonade pitcher. Thomas followed and was happy to go inside.

"So on Wednesday meet me at work at one-thirty. –To take Thomas to the vet. That works, right?"

"Yeah, that's fine. Will you be ready?"

"I'll be there waiting. And bring some of those cookies with you!"

"I'll bring you some." Mae was morose. She wanted something but knew not what. She knew she had to accept responsibility and stop complaining to herself. She needed to be strong now, and Sally was helping her see that.

Just then they heard the rattle of the engine of the Cadwell car pulling into the driveway. Farley was home.

Mae panicked.

"Don't worry, soothed Sally. Farley is the most understanding creature on the planet. It might help you to talk to him and start to take responsibility for this whole thing."

Farley came through the front door and into the kitchen where Mae and Sally were leaning against the counter munching on their words.

"How's it going?" Farley said as he gave his wife a hug and then hugged Mae, too.

"Fine. How are you? How was the Red Tornado?"

"I lost ten dollars. I'm sorry. At least I knew when to stop," Farley admitted, feeling sorry for himself. He knew Sally disapproved.

"At least I'm being honest about it," he defended himself.

"I understand, you big hunk," said Sally, forgiving him quite easily. It made no sense to argue over money.

"Mae has some news for you. She's already told me. Tell him Mae. It's the beginning of owning your own."

"You're moving," implied Farley.

"No, nothing like that," she said. "I'm pregnant."

Farley's mouth hung open for a few seconds. "You're pregnant. Why that's the most exciting news I've heard for a long time! You lucky little girl!"

"Thanks," she said relieved and encouraged. Farley was a good friend to her.

"Baby is due in May. Wedding is planned for February. James is pleased. I'm just a little worried about how the Church will react. I've fallen in sin," she said sadly.

"Mmm, no." Said Farley. "You're not perfect, and this baby was meant to be. Be happy. Don't get down on yourself. Remember in the book of John in the Bible where Jesus says for the one without sin to throw the first stone? And then everybody ended up walking away, leaving the woman caught in sin to be free with Christ, who says that He neither would condemn her.

"There is not a single person in our Church who could throw that first stone. Take peace and uplifting. Christ understands."

"Thanks Farley. I was just leaving. I'll be back on Wednesday to take Thomas to the vet for his neutering. Sally and I ran into a rattlesnake on our walk today back in the hills. Spooky."

Mae dug into her pocket for her keys and said goodbye to Farley. Sally walked her out to her car. "See you Wednesday!" Mae said; feeling slightly uplifted.

"See you Wednesday around one-thirty."

"Maybe I'll call you tomorrow. Bye!"

"Bye!" Yelled Sally as Mae drove away in her little Toyota. It was plenty big enough to fit Thomas in the back. Sally said a heart felt prayer for her friend, and then walked back into the house.

"So you lost ten dollars," accused Sally who was more than a little bit perturbed.

"Yes, and I won't lie about it. I'm sorry. I'll make up for it next time."

"Next time! Why does there always have to be a next time?"

"Because I like to do it. I'm not doing any harm, am I?"

"I don't want to talk about it anymore. Come here, Sweetheart, and give me a welcome home hug." The two embraced and kissed and said "I love you", Sally, forgiving Farley.

"How was work?" They both said at the same time.

They laughed and hugged and laughed. "My day was fine," said Sally, "and then I went for a walk with Mae and Thomas. We almost got killed out there."

"Rattlesnake?"

"Big, beautiful rattlesnake. And Thomas lunged at it; I caught him just barely, and we ran and ran and ran, and then Thomas's leash broke- you know, the leather one. I'm going to buy a new nylon lead for him on Wednesday. Thomas will probably gentle out a bit after the neutering. I feel sorry for him, but it's the only way if we want to be safe. We don't want him escaping again and mating with all the female dogs in Turnip Bay."

"And that's exactly what he'd do if he got the chance," said Farley.

The next day Farley went to work, but Sally had the day off. She couldn't wait for Wednesday when her dog would be neutered, and safe to bring to the dog park where he could run around and get the exercise he needed. He needed to be free, to run wild, let go, given liberty to use his doggy self in every doggy way except for the reproductive way.

Sally didn't have plans for the day. She baked a cake, a German chocolate cake. Farley would like that. Then she set about cleaning up the house. She vacuumed, swept, dusted, and aired out the house with all the doors and windows open. She prayed that Oscar wouldn't come by with a knife or something. For extra safety, she kept Thomas out of his enclosure and gave him the whole run of the yard.

She took her Bible and went outside to read from the book of Romans in a chaise lounge with a travel mug full of coffee. Eventually, Thomas sought company and came to lie down beside her. The sun was out and the weather was reasonably warm. Sally had on her shorts and a sweatshirt.

She read slowly, and smiled at the parts she knew well. Yet with each reading she was taught something new. The familiarity was a comforting feeling, and even though she often didn't remember the books of the Bible, she had general ideas and feasted on the Word hungrily every time anew.

She took her time with Romans because it was an important book of the Bible that spoke about the receiving of God's Spirit within oneself to have the life of Christ within you. She remembered reading in Corinthians that where the Spirit of God is there is liberty. She felt this was pertinent to her life; that she deserved to make her own choices in purity of Spirit and law. Not to be bound by the sins of the flesh, which lead to death in Christ. She wanted to live to Christ with the Holy Spirit.

Sally sipped on her coffee and stopped reading to massage Thomas at the back of his neck. The big dog was content. He even rolled over on his back so she could scratch his belly. She loved him.

She finished her coffee, lay back, and fell asleep. She was awakened by Thomas's rampant barking and looked to see what he was barking at. It was just the mailman. She got up to go and get the mail to bring inside. The house was airing out nicely. She sorted through the mail and threw everything away except for an invitation from Gilmore to his wedding. Wedding! Sally blushed with pleasure and couldn't wait to break this news to Farley.

First Mae and James, and now Gilmore and – who could it be? Sally realized her Bible was still outside, and her coffee tumbler. Out she went to pick up the objects and bring them inside. Next she went around and closed all the doors and windows of the house. She took a broom to the porch light and wiped away old spider webs.

She put Thomas back in his enclosure and went inside to sit in her chair. She was tired, and didn't know what to do with her day. She decided to call Tina to see if she would want to go to coffee in town. She called.

"Hello?" It was Tina.

"Hi Tina, it's Sally. How are you? Are you busy?"

"Actually I was about to call you," she exclaimed. "For the very same reason."

"Do you want to meet at the Turnip Bay Coffee Shop? Or even better, do you want to have coffee here and have some German chocolate cake that I made – fresh today?"

"Sounds delicious, Sally," said her friend. "When should I come by?"

"Anytime is fine with me. I could just use some company other than my dog."

"Fine. I'll be there in twenty minutes. Is that OK?"

"Perfect. Hurry! I'm hungry."

"OK. Bye."

"Bye – See you soon." Sally hung up. At least the house was clean and fresh, ready for company. Sally took out her espresso maker and decided to fix a double latte for Tina and herself. She hadn't used the machine for quite awhile. She scrubbed the counter top around the sink and put the broom back in the closet. Then she went outside again. The air was stagnant. No wind. A couple of crows were being noisy up in the cherry tree. The grass needed to be mowed. She would get on Farley about that. Her vegetable garden was waning. The potatoes were still probably good.

She heard the front gate and went around the house to see. It was Tina. "Hi!" She said.

"Hi! I got here as fast as I could. That German chocolate cake sounds so good. It's just what I'm craving. Something sweet."

"I thought I would fix us espresso drinks and use my espresso maker. Do you take nonfat or two percent milk?"

"Two percent is fine," Tina said.

"I'm trying to lose weight, so I'll go for nonfat, myself. Here, you can cut the cake, and the plates are in the cupboard over the toaster. Forks are in the drawer under the coffee maker."

Sally went to work making the espresso drinks for each, forgetting to ask how many shots Tina wanted and automatically making two. She made two for her own coffee as well. Next she steamed the milk, each separately, and spooned the foam into the coffee cups above the espresso and steamed milk.

"There," said Sally, and turned to hand Tina her drink, who, in the meantime had cut them two rather large slices of the cake. Tina handed one plate with fork and napkin to Sally, who sat down at the small kitchen table. Tina sat as well, and together they prayed and gave thanks for their snack.

Simultaneously they took forks to their chocolate cake, complete with the frosting and ate their first bites. Both women said ooh and aah, sipping gently on their lattes and concentrating heavily on the cake.

"You're not going to lose much weight eating this," chided Tina.

"I know, but isn't it so worth it?"

"This is really good. I love the coconut in the frosting. I think I'll take some home with me," Tina said, praising the cake.

"You can if you want. Just save a slice for Farley. Guess what? Farley's brother Gilmore is getting married in three weeks. I don't even know who the lucky bride is!"

"That's exciting."

Sally refrained from telling Tina about Mae and James's plans to marry in February. She wasn't a gossiper. "Have you met Gilmore?"

"I met him once at your Thanksgiving Bash a couple of years ago. Seems like a really nice guy."

"Oh, he is. Farley's only sibling, and he's always been there for Farley, when Farley got ill with his schizophrenia. Those early years were nearly impossible for Farley. Then I met him, me with schizoaffective disorder and depression, and we fell in love. We got married about two years ago."

"I wonder if I'll ever marry Leroy," said Tina wistfully.

"How's that going?" Sally inquired.

"Super. But it's hard to abstain. I'm not really sure I can. He just makes me so excited and I get all these flowery feelings. Sometimes I can't help but reach out and touch him."

"It's up to you, Tina. Just be careful, and do what you really believe is right. If Leroy really, really loves you, he should know well enough to save sex for after marriage. If you haven't, you can always repent and start over, clean. There's so much more to loving a person than just having sex. Some people don't know this and they never find out."

"Maybe he'll pop the question." Tina was troubled.

"What's the matter?" Asked Sally.

"Simon is a rapist."

"What?"

"He's a rapist. He didn't know that I was home with Leroy in his room, and I heard him taking vicious advantage of some lady. She sounded so scared, and she was crying for help and saying 'Don't!' and 'Stop!' Then I could hear them wrestling because his bed was bumping around and finally there was a dead silence. I got up and told Leroy that I had to go, we had just been doing Bible study together and I asked him if he knew what was going on. He said that Simon often drugged girls and raped them after they passed out and woke up with all their clothes on thinking they had just taken a nap. It's evil and I said that to Leroy and told him I had to go. As I sat in my car, I saw Simon walking out of their house with *Sandra Naden* on his arm, and he kissed her goodbye.

She looked so bewildered and I saw her go stand by the bus stop. That's all I could take. I went home and prayed for her."

"Oh, Tina! Not Sandra Naden! What an innocent little bird. She's still in her twenties, isn't she?

"Yes, and cute as can be. I wonder if we should talk to her about Simon and how she feels about him; like if she feels fear about him or anything odd at all. What a shame. Poor Sandra. So Leroy knows about this and doesn't do anything?"

"His brother told him he would shoot him if he were to blab what he knows. He calls it harmless fun."

"We need to do something, Tina."

"But Leroy is nothing like him, and…"

"And what? Are you sure you know what you're doing?"

"Of course I know what's happening," Tina said angrily. "I'm falling in love with a wonderful person, and…"

"And what? You think his brother is a suspected rapist and you're going to be fine by that?"

"No. It's ugly and sardonic. It's super human crap. A secret that will only bleed and bleed and bleed until finally it pops open. It's an ugly zit. Leaving a naughty scar and a lifelong fear of intimacy.

"Self-doubt, low self-esteem, uncomfortable social problems, eventually suicide if help isn't found first."

"Believe if you can, that there is something you can do. You can report it to the police. You can break the news in the middle of a Church service. There are a lot of good people who could protect you and apprehend him."

"I could do it, if Leroy helps me. But he lives in fear of his brother - which shouldn't be the case. I know a lot of people who would be highly disturbed by this information. You could bleed to death and never tell the truth of a wart on a finger that doesn't belong there. Let justice be done. You have liberty to tell. Simon does not have liberty to do the things he's doing. He's breaking the law. He's breaking natural law, Federal Law, and the law of sin and truth."

"I'll help you. You need to talk to Leroy and ask him how long this sort of thing has been going on. He should comply, if he knows he doesn't stand alone against his brother. You did the right thing to tell me about it. We have to help Sandra, find out who else he's had, and reveal him to the Church. It's poison in the congregation. We need to bind him, send him to jail. Or let God deal with him on His own terms. I could make a pop speech after telling the Pastor about it. We could have guards at the door so he can't escape.

"What do I say to Leroy?"

"Tell him what we talked about today, and that the secret is out."

"It is out, isn't it?"

"Fresh air."

"Secrets spread."

"That's true."

"I can tell the Pastor what I know, confidentially, and then maybe he can take the steps of getting Simon arrested for multiple counts of rape. Maybe we can have a woman's conference for every girl who has ever been had by Simon and just doesn't know exactly what happened."

"Perfect. These women need help. But we must protect Leroy, who's scared of his brother. . ."

"What about Oscar. Aren't they good friends?"

"Yes, but I wouldn't incriminate him quite yet. We have no proof or any reason to suspect him of rape. Besides, I think he works a different way. I think Oscar is a psychopathic murderer. He's just moved here recently, and I think he's sitting on his ducks, letting some time go by before he strikes again."

"It's scary, but for now keep him out of the picture. We don't want to create any suspicion for him. Just let him be good old Oscar in the front row."

"He follows me around."

"Say something."

"I'm scared. At least I have Thomas to keep me safe, unless he knifed Thomas or something of the sort. We keep him inside at night and outside during the day."

"That's good that you have him to keep you safe on walks and stuff, or like in the yard when you're outside."

"Where are you going after this?"

"I told Leroy that I'd meet him at his place around six o'clock. So I'd better be going."

"Be careful, Tina," admonished Sally to her good friend. "Thanks for confiding in me. We'll get this taken care of. Trust God. Go with God."

They walked out to Tina's car, a Jetta, and said goodbye out there. "I'll pray for you Tina. Stay safe and don't do anything that would get you in trouble, promise?"

"I promise. I'll call you tomorrow, is that OK?"

"Of course. I want to hear from you. I mean it, be careful. We're talking life and death here. I'll call Sandra Naden and have a chat with her. You know, like, what's new? Or, I could ask if anyone special is in her life? I'll just tell her that God put it on my heart to call her. If she cries, I'll know that she knows, otherwise she should be a little mixed up and confused. Don't forget to call me tomorrow. I'll be out in the afternoon, but you can call me morning or evening, or else just leave a message. OK now?

"OK. I love you, Sally, stay safe."

"Bye."

"Bye, Sally."

The little green car sped away.

WHISPERS OF FAITH

Shhhh. Quiet. It's quiet in here. This is the place of healing and mild breezes to ripple the water in glorious diamonds of shards of healing. One more time. Rape had taken place one more time. Sandra and Simon. She was probably crying and didn't know why.

Sally was true to her word and looked at the Church roster to find Sandra's phone number. Taking a deep breath and saying a short prayer for the truth and healing to begin, Sally called.

"Hello?" A small voice came onto the phone.

"Sandra?"

"Yes, speaking."

"Hi Sandra, it's Sally Cadwell from Church. God put it on my heart to call you, so here I am. Anything new going on?"

"Not much. Not much to say. I have a new boyfriend. He's so nice to me. And he cares. I had a fainting spell at his house yesterday, and he stayed with me till I woke again and walked me to the bus stop."

"Did he hurt you?"

"What do you mean?"

"Tina Makron is dating Simon's brother and was at their place yesterday at the same time you were."

"How did you know it was Simon?"

"Listen, Sandra, something must not feel right. Is there anything?"

"Well he did say he would call me today and he never has called since I left and we said goodbye. I got lost on my way home and ended up in a dead end ally and a really mean dog kept leaping at its fence with big teeth, real angry like. I was so lost. I took the wrong bus. I bussed back to Simon's place but he wasn't there.

"So I got lost again on my way home and I stopped on the side of the road to call him to tell him I love him on my cell phone, but Leroy answered and said Simon had gone out drinking.

"That was my first sign that something was wrong. I didn't know that Simon was a drinking man. I thought I loved him but, Sally, I don't know what's wrong but I hate him now and I don't even have a clear reason to. Am I being judgmental? God says not to judge one another. I must be a bad person." Sandra stopped, confused by her monologue and the rich, diseased feelings inside of herself.

"Oh Lord Jesus!" She cried. "His baby, I'm going to have his baby. I remember now. He drugged me. He raped me. I know it because my pants were buttoned up wrong when I woke up at his house yesterday. I feel so silly, like it's all going to go away and I'm left stuck with the baby. It's my ovulation day yesterday and today. I'm so sick. Oh I just want to kill him!"

"Sandra? How did you get home?"

"I ended up on the 48 downtown and transferred to the 72 which brought me home. I hate being lost."

"Listen to me. I know all about it, about what happened to you yesterday. Tina Makron was there with Leroy, the new guy in *her* life and Simon's brother, you know. They were doing a Bible study in his room and she heard all your noises as you were crying out to him to stop. She left Leroy and saw you come out to the bus stop from her car.

"Leroy had explained to her that his brother often did that to girls. He's a rapist and you are his latest victim. Only this time he got caught. I knew I had to call you before it got to be too late. Promise me this one thing, that you won't commit suicide. God wants to save you. He'll heal you, and make mash of Simon.

"Suicide is something that shouldn't even be on your list of options. I'll help you through this thing. Me, Tina, Mae, and there are others who care, as well as others who are in your position. Raped.

"It's an ugly disease of the mind and heart. It's a ruination of something beautiful into a crazy mess of unlearned hurt. Hatred is only natural, and healthy, too. And there should be no shame, although that goes hand in hand with the disease of rape history. It's ugly, shambles, sin. Are you alone?"

Sandra sniffled. "Yes, I'm alone, I live alone."

"Would you like me to come by for awhile?"

"Yes. That would be nice."

"How does chocolate cake sound? I made a cake today and there's plenty left. I could bring some of it over."

"Yum, that sounds good."

"Do you still live on Arrow Road?"

"Yes."

"I'll come over as soon as my husband comes home with the car. What will you do till then?"

"Read my Bible and take a bath. I need a bath. I need to be with my body."

"Perfect. Don't go drowning in the tub now."

"I won't." Tears began to well up within Sandra. "Will I be OK?"

"You'll be fine. Stay focused on the Lord and remember not only that He loves you, but also that vengeance is His, and He is roiling and boiling with anger for you and the trouble you are in. His anger will protect you. Think of Him as "Daddy God", and you can trust Him and in Him. I'll be over soon, OK?"

"OK. I'll just be in the tub for half an hour. Then I'll look for you. Knock four times, OK? It's apartment number 32. Thanks Sally. I love you."

"I love you too."

Sally hung up feeling sick to her stomach. Sandra was like a child robot, not feeling anything but confused thoughts and emotions, upset, denial, but most of all she had hope and was taking care of herself.

Farley drove up outside, and she let him in the front door before he could get his keys. "I have to go, Farley," she said abruptly. "It's Simon. He's a rapist, and his newest victim is Sandra Naden. I have to go see her at her place and visit and pray with her. She needs help and I don't know what else to do. Please give me the car keys; I have to go. Now."

Farley was confused and miffed, but surrendered the keys to Sally and kissed her goodbye.

Sally drove with all alacrity to her Church sister's home and parked quickly in visitor's parking. Hurriedly she mounted the stairs and reached number 32. With a quick prayer to God, she knocked four times. Slowly the door was opened a crack. "Sally?"

"It's me, Sandra, can I come in?"

Sandra opened wide the door and let her in. Everything was neat and organized to a tee. She offered Sally some tea.

Sally acquiesced and asked for orange spice.

Sandra turned on the stove to heat water.

She was very quiet and didn't make eye contact with Sally, who kept her distance.

"Did you bathe?" Inquired Sally, quietly.

"Yes, yes I did, and I almost dropped the hair dryer in the tub after I got out. God saved me."

"He did, and He'll save you again now, with this, this horror you're going through. Nobody should have to put up with that. We'll have to tell the Pastor about it, and find out how many other women he has violated like he did to you."

"I'll turn the other cheek and make him afraid to come near me, as if I'm a teapot waiting to blow the whistle. That will make him fear me, so I don't need to fear him. Poor Leroy needs to be set free from that monster on his shoulder. And Tina was there all the while. She must have been shocked."

"I'll be frank and tell the Pastor about Oscar, too. He's been haunting me for too long, hoping to find a way to make out with me. It sucks and takes so long to process all that outside of myself. I can't let him get at my goat. Or, I can't let him get his harpy talons in me. He follows me around and pretends not to.

"You must be feeling pretty weak after all this. When did it happen, yesterday?"

"Yes, yesterday afternoon."

"So you've been alone with this for a whole day or more. You are a brave lady, Sandra. Take faith that God will deliver you from this sin against you. He cares and loves you, and right now He is incensed about what has happened to you. At the same time, remember that the vengeance is His. Simon has his punishment coming. He'll get it good. Just try to belittle him in your mind. Don't let him be a great big monster. That's what he wants. Rather he's a toad croaking on a mossy log adrift in a sea. He has nowhere to go, no help to come. He's really going to get it."

"You really think so? He's not going to hurt me again?"

"He can't. He'll see that you know, and become very afraid. Maybe he'll get in a car wreck. Agitated, you know, facing a dark tunnel with no other way out but through it.

"Do you think he might call you?"

"I just remembered that he doesn't have my number, and he doesn't know that I live here."

"Perfect. Keep your head low for now and we can go to Church together next Sunday. Do you want to go to the Wednesday night service?"

"Yes, I don't want to be alone in all this. Can you pick me up and take me? Then I could talk to Pastor without waiting until Sunday."

"Of course we can take you. I hope you don't mind if I tell Farley about all of this. I'll need his support, he's my other half."

"That's fine. I trust Farley. He's such a noble guy. He always shakes my hand so warmly. Also, he's a man, and that's another strike against the devil, despite the fact that God will avenge. He can stand up to Simon. Intimidate him. Can we go a little early so we can hide out until Simon comes in, and then act like nothing's wrong. He always tries so hard to attract attention to himself."

"It's settled. We'll pick you up at six-thirty tomorrow night and you can come with us to Church. Dress casual. That might throw him off."

"But we'll talk to Pastor first, right?"

"Yes, of course."

"Thank you for coming over here tonight. Simon will be expecting me to come over tomorrow to go out to dinner before Church. I'll be a no show. Then I'll see him in Church, and he'll be confused. He won't know why I didn't show up, so he'll be pansy nice and try to get me to sit with him, but I'll say something came up and I'll be sitting with you guys, instead."

"What about Tina and Leroy?"

"What about them? They've done nothing wrong. The only wrong is that Simon had Leroy sworn to secrecy upon his life."

"Wow. All this weird stuff is happening. I might as well confide in you, that Mae is pregnant with James' baby. They're planning to marry in February, and the baby is due in May."

"So there's good news among the weepy news. God has blessed them with a child, only they had testified to abstinence until marriage. So there's a little quirk in there somewhere. They're going to have to face reality."

"What about me? I can't have an abortion, but I don't want to raise a rape baby!"

"You can give the baby up for a closed adoption. I had to give up my child for adoption because of my mental illness. I left it as an open adoption, so I get pictures and letters, and someday she'll look me up. What a blessing."

"But was your daughter a rape baby?"

"No, not really. She was just not a planned baby or a baby within wedlock. There's hope for you, Sandra. One step at a time, OK?"

"Yes."

"So take good care of yourself tonight and tomorrow, and we'll pick you up at six-thirty. Be brave and courageous, now, and treat yourself well, OK? No self-punishment allowed. Look forward to being justified. God will work out the judgment."

"OK. I'll be good. Thanks for giving me hope and understanding. I'll pray a lot today and tomorrow."

"Prayer always helps."

"Well, I'll look forward to seeing you tomorrow night. And thanks again for being here for me."

"Anytime. Be strong now, OK?"

"OK."

"I'll be going now."

"Bye."

"Bye." Sandra opened the door for Sally and gave her a big hug as she left.

Sally drove home sadly, feeling sorry and hurt for Sandra. She also felt angry and thought only of Thomas and Farley and their precious little home. She thought of Carla, the spider and her demise. She pulled into the driveway and shut the car off. The house lights were all on. When she went in she saw Farley in the living room asleep on the couch. He must have been up worried.

Gently she planted a kiss on his cheek and smiled as he moaned and rolled over. It was getting late, past nine o'clock and it was dark out. Farley hadn't let Thomas in yet for the night, so she went out into the backyard and opened up his enclosure. Thomas was quiet and raced back and forth until she let him out. Then he dashed to the back door and waited to be let in. Sally opened the back door and Thomas ran into the kitchen. He stopped and went into the living room, licking Farley's face as he woke up to the big dog.

"Hi Sweetheart!" Farley exclaimed. "How did it go with Sandra?"

"Oh the poor darling. She thinks she's pregnant with Simon's rape baby. She's so hurt and stunned. I told her we'd pick her up for Church tomorrow at six-thirty."

"Is she OK?"

"She's shaken, but I think she'll make it until tomorrow night when we can confide in the Pastor and figure out what to do. She's so lost; she's so young! What a tortuous violation."

"Poor thing. What can we do?"

"Stand up for her. Be there. Convict Simon and find out how many victims are in the Church. My guess is that he'll run, but to hell is the only place he can go. God won't let him get away."

"Now as for you and me, my lady, who made that astounding cake today?"

"Oh my goodness, I forgot to bring some of it to Sandra's. Tina and I shared it today. Tomorrow Thomas gets neutered, which is all for the better. He should be fine."

"Is Mae going to take you?"

"She said she would, after work tomorrow at one-thirty."

"We'd better be getting some sleep now. Are you ready for bed?" Farley yawned.

"I'm ready."

Both Cadwell's brushed teeth, took medicine, and changed into bedclothes. Exhausted they crawled into bed and lay there spooning as they passed into sleep.

Morning came with a whiney Thomas putting his big head on Farley's pillow. Farley rolled over and woke abruptly with the dog head in his face. "Oh Thomas," he groaned. "It's only five-thirty," he said looking at the clock. "Couldn't you give us a little more time?"

But Thomas was insistent, so Farley got up and let the big dog out into the backyard where he ran to do his business along the fence.

Farley put him in the enclosure and shut the gate. Then he went inside to get some more shut-eye. Sally slept gently on her side of the bed, unaware of Farley letting out the dog. Farley got back into the bed and buried his head in the pillow to sleep for the next two hours when the alarm clock would go off at seven-thirty.

The two hours zoomed by and this time both Farley and Sally awoke to the alarm clock. They yawned, stretched, and got out of bed before falling back to sleep. Farley went out to the kitchen to make breakfast and Sally hopped into the shower.

She screamed as she saw a big spider on the shower matt. Taking a washrag she squished the little bug and dumped it into the toilet and flushed. Then she turned the shower on once more and stepped into the warm flowing waters.

Shampoo and conditioner provided aromatherapy as well as the gentle Dove soap. She realized that her toenails needed cutting. Stepping out as she turned off the water, Sally wrapped herself in her cobalt blue towel. She dried herself and put on work clothes. She brushed her teeth and fixed her hair, brushing through the dark tangles and fluffing up the long strands.

Farley had breakfast cooking in the kitchen. The smell of bacon piqued her appetite and she looked forward to eggs and toast and grapefruit. Farley would have made the coffee by now, and prepared Sally's morning cup of tea.

"Hi Sweetie," she said as she came into the kitchen. Farley gave her a big squeeze. "Oh Honey," she said, "I forgot to tell you that your brother is getting married in three weeks. Here, here's the letter he sent to us. Who could she be? I didn't know that Gil' was dating." Sally gave the letter to Farley and beamed with exuberance at the good news.

"Well I'll be. . . . My little brother is coming out of the bushes. He's so shy I didn't think he'd ever get married. This must be quite a special lady. I wonder who it could be."

Breakfast was ready and they both sat down to eat. "Thank you, Farley," said Sally considerately. She ate in silence and sipped on her tea. When her tea was gone, she got up to pour coffee. The cake was gone, Farley must have gotten his share. Sally got up and cleared her dish. Then, as Farley continued eating, she filled Thomas' water and food bowls, blue and red respectively, and opened the backdoor setting them on the stairs outside.

She walked through the dewy grass and weeds to Thomas' enclosure, opening the gate and letting the hungry dog out. "Today is your big day, Thomas," she said to him.

He walked next to her to the kitchen door and found his food there all ready so he started to eat, calmly, not quite hurriedly. He looked up at Sally and then at Farley, suspecting something. Finding nothing he finished eating and came into the house where Farley was just rinsing his dish in the kitchen sink.

Now it was his turn to shower, while Sally sat and enjoyed coffee with her companion sniffing all around the small square table. Sally didn't bother wearing make up and did very little in terms of hair styling. She was a natural beauty with dark curly hair, freckled face, and blue eyes. She wore jeans to work, but always wore a skirt to Church. Right now she was contemplating Thomas' next few hours. They were his last few hours before the big operation. She heard Farley whistling in the shower as he turned the water off.

Farley wore heavy work boots, tough jeans and a flannel shirt. He brought his hard hat just in case he might need it. Today they were excavating an old building and tearing it down. It was old and condemned. Farley remembered to take his workmen's gloves, dusty and torn slightly.

He came out of the bedroom ready to go. Sally got up and took her purse. She led Thomas out to his enclosure and locked him inside, for his own safety. She walked through the lawn to the car having said goodbye to her doggie friend. Thomas whined and howled at their leaving. He always did this. Now no one could steal him, and he couldn't get out to hurt someone, if he got the notion in his head to tackle the mailman.

Farley drove Sally to the mental health center where she worked and she kissed him as she got out of the car. They waved at each other as Farley drove away. Sally took a big breath and walked into the office where she assisted.

Both were good, strong workers with great work ethic and enthusiasm on the job. The hours went steadily by, and soon one-thirty came around when Sally left and waited for Mae outside of the building. There she was, in her old Toyota. It was little, but spacious.

Sally waved and wiped a tear from her face. It was good to hear her friend's voice as Mae got out and went to her. Obviously something was wrong. Sally cried on Mae's shoulder, and her friend gently calmed her down and offered to help in any way.

"I love you Sally," Mae said softly. "What's wrong? It isn't Thomas, is it?"

Sally laughed. "No," she cried, "It's Tina, Leroy, Simon and Sandra Naden. Simon raped Sandra a couple of days ago. He drugged her but didn't cover his tracks well and she remembered because of the wetness in her panties, and her pants weren't buttoned up right. Then she remembered. He had tried to be so friendly and cordial, looking ahead to Church when they would see each other again. Only he doesn't know that she knows. It's all messed up.

"Leroy is silenced upon his own life and can't talk about Simon. They're brothers, you know, and Tina Makron is dating Leroy and they want to get married. Oh what do we do? I need help Mae, in approaching the Pastor secretly. We need to do it for Sandra, and any other victims of his in the Church. Let's go, I don't want to keep Thomas waiting for his appointment. I'm sorry. This all happened so fast, and now you, you with your wonderful but stigmatic news being pregnant and having a wedding date. Oh Mae, I just need support right now. I can't handle all this by myself."

"Well, let's go get Thomas and focus on something different right now. You just vented and should be feeling better soon." Sally and Mae got into the small car and she started the engine.

"All that including Oscar, too, and his ludicrous eyes spying me out in Church and showing up all over the city watching me wherever I go. I can't handle this, and my mental illness is really acting up. I'm hearing all kinds of voices telling me to kill myself and be rid of trouble. Telling me I should fear Thomas and that he's evil. Oh bewitchment, if only I could cope better right now."

"You're doing fine, Sally, let's rebuke the devil and his nasty voices so that you may have a sound head. Together Mae and Sally prayed against evil intrusion of any sort, and Sally started to feel better.

She was relieved when Mae pulled into their driveway and they both got out to get Thomas. He was laying on the cool cement in the shade. "Hi Thomas!" She said happily. She remembered that she needed to buy a new lead for Thomas, for his leather leash had broken the other day when Mae was there.

Sally entered the enclosure and took Thomas by the collar to the gate and out into the yard. Mae walked along as Sally led Thomas toward the car. Suddenly he started to growl and pull at the collar. He barked and lunged with Sally losing grasp. Thomas ran head on into the front yard fence, standing up and growling fiercely. Mae looked at Sally questioningly, and saw her friend go pale as she looked too and saw Oscar across the street at the bus stop with his head shaved and his villainous look with white pants and a black jacket. Both girls not knowing what to do, opened the gate and let the dog out. It spooked them. Thomas charged at Oscar who fled and climbed a tree in the yard across the street.

"You'd better get control of your pet or I'll call animal control and report him as a menace. Look, he has me treed! I didn't do anything!"

"You deserve it Oscar," barked Sally, "following me around like that. You deserve to get a bite in the buttocks. But to have mercy, we'll take him and leave. Let this be a reminder not to come around here anymore!" Sally was ferocious, psychotic, and angry all at once, canceling out all fear. "Come, Thomas," she called, and felt for her pepper spray in her pocket. Just in case she needed it against the stalker.

The dog came obediently, looking furiously over his shoulder at his treed prize. Oscar was quiet and climbed higher. "You'd better be gone when we come back, or next time I'll call the cops on you and not be so merciful with Thomas. Not knowing if Oscar was armed, Sally played her cards as though he wasn't. Shy, neurotic, psychotic, two faced. He always worshipped wildly in Church.

Mae and Sally rode away in the little car to the nearby veterinary hospital. It was just five minutes past their appointment, at two o'clock. The operation took only half an hour and after forty-five minutes Thomas came out with a white cone around his head. He was to wear it for a week to prevent him from licking the stitches out prematurely. He was a little bit groggy and the girls were shocked at his demeanor. He was subdued and panting, wild-eyed. While they were there, Sally decided to have Thomas micro-chipped which was a small procedure and relatively painless.

Sally remembered to buy a new lead with a pronged collar, which the vet attached to the lead and put carefully around the dog's neck. She chose red woven with blue. They made an appointment to come back in a week to have the head cone and his stitches removed. Satisfied, they left the veterinary hospital and put Thomas in the back of Mae's car. They still hadn't talked about Oscar, and all the things that Sally had spewed out when Mae picked her up at work.

Dealing with Thomas had lessened the voices in her head, and her memory was scattered, trying to put itself in order.

Thomas needed to get home, so they didn't go out for coffee but straight back to Farley and Sally's place.

Sally tried out the new lead, and let him inside the yard. Opting to keep Thomas calm, she put him back inside his enclosure instead of letting him loose in the yard. Thomas lay down quietly.

Sally and Mae laid down in the chaise lounges, and Mae kept quiet while Sally's mind worked itself into corners and ambivalent recesses. What if Oscar had showed up again. He seemed like a wimp, but at least he'd had the sense to climb a tree out of Thomas' reach.

Thomas hated him. He hated him probably worse than the mailman. Sally would keep him penned up until his next appointment, except for letting him in at night and for morning and nightly feeding.

Farley came home, a little earlier than usual and said that he had to take a shower; he was covered in dust.

The girls remained quiet and a peace came over the neighborhood as the sun made its final descent down behind the hills. It was a great day, all in all, and Sally had survived the onslaught of her mental illness again. Mae had to go and get home to James; they would meet up at Church again. She prayed with Sally before leaving about her safety and peace of mind. She declared healing upon Sally who had broken under the load today.

Mae drove away, and Sally remained in her chair, gently sleeping in dreams of flowering fields and small streams of clear water.

She awakened as Farley came up quietly and planted a kiss on her lips. She moaned and opened her eyes slowly. Farley sat down next to her, where Mae had been. He was quiet and could tell that his wife had been through a lot today. The sun had set and mosquitoes came out so he helped her up and led her to the house where she went in. Next he went out to get Thomas and led him into the house as well. Thomas got his dinner and lay down on the floor by the couch, his eyes droopy. "Ah, Buddy, I feel bad for you," Farley said to the grumpy dog.

Sally was still quiet and sat slumped in an armchair. "This has been a big day, Farley," she said with a deep sigh. "Farley, could you make dinner? I'm much too tired."

"Hamburgers or hot dogs?"

"Hamburgers, if you don't mind."

"I don't know. Do we have tomatoes?"

"What kind of a question is that?"

"Please?"

"Please."

"Very well. Hamburgers it is. Why don't you just take a nap while I whip something up for us. Are we all out of ground beef?"

"I don't know," Sally sighed.

"I'll have mercy on you. How about no more questions?"

"Peace, please. I'm tired and mixed-up. Can we talk later?"

"Of course. You go to sleep now. I'll wake you when dinner's ready."

"Blasted precautions. I don't need to sleep, I need to love you."

"Me?"

"None other."

He walked over to her armchair and squarely put a luscious kiss on her mouth.

"Let's go to the bedroom," she said.

"Of course, my dear. Shall I carry you?"

"I can't be lifted."

"Follow me, then."

Sally got up and followed her husband to the bedroom where the shades were drawn and the bed was made neatly.

"I could do acrobats with you."

"I might break."

"How about if I hold you like this and this and this?" Farley wormed his way around his woman.

"Softly, please."

"Thank you – here, take that off."

Sally sucked in her breath and let herself go. It was over before it started, and both were satiated desperately. Pawing gently, they hugged and kissed and squeezed and came back down to earth.

"How about dinner now?"

"At your service. Hamburgers?"

"Hamburgers. Come get me when you're done – *please*," she emphasized humorously. Farley left her in the room but turned on the overhead light.

He went out to the kitchen where Thomas was snoring on the floor next to the couch.

Sally wiggled around on the bed and stretched and said "ooh" and "ahhh." She giggled when she thought of Farley and his ongoing need. She was his princess, and treated her as if it were so.

The meat was sizzling in the pan and Sally could smell the savory aroma. It brought her out of the room into the living room where she could watch Farley who looked at her and winked. She blushed with pleasure and sent back a sweet smile. Finally, she lay down on the couch above Thomas and drifted off to sleep. Farley knew how to take care of her, especially during and after bouts of psychosis. They had a big cowbell in the kitchen for times like these.

Farley rang the cowbell when dinner was prepared. Sally came rapidly out of her snoozing and sat up. Dinner was on the table. "Is it all ready?" she asked.

"All ready. We even have ice cream for dessert."

"Let's eat!"

Sally made it to the table and pulled up a chair. Quietly the two began munching on their burgers. Farley had baked some tater tots as a side dish, and made a salad for the side as well. Humbly they ate, thankful for the food on their table.

"We have to leave in ten minutes for Church."

"I forgot. We need to pick up Sandra at six-thirty and take her with us. Can we be ready in time?"

"Of course! Hurry – *eat*." Both Cadwell's downed their hamburgers, tater tots and salad. "We have a little time. Maybe you should call Sandra and tell her we're running late. Are you OK?"

"I'm fine. I ran into Oscar at the bus stop across the street today with Mae and Thomas. I let him go and he treed the sleazy sleaze. I had to call Thomas away from him. And Thomas listened, you should be proud to know. He came right to me. That really set off my day. I don't like feeling stalked."

"Get ready, let's go. I'll do the dishes later. Call Sandra first so she doesn't worry about us not coming."

Sally picked up the phone and called Sandra. "Sandra? Hi. It's me, Sally. Listen we're running a few minutes late, so not to worry, OK? Are you all right? Are you ready? OK, see you in a few. Bye." Quickly Sally changed into a skirt and blouse with her nylons and dress shoes. She found her jacket in the front closet and met Farley at the front door ready to go. Out they went and got into the little Fiat.

Sally guided Farley down to Arrow Road and they pulled into Sandra's apartment complex. She remembered it was number 32. "Wait here, Farley, she said to him with a kiss. I'll go get Sandra." She got out of the car and walked up the stairs to Sandra's door. She knocked four times. The door opened a crack, and there was Sandra with gobs of make up and a pretty red dress.

"I'm ready," she said shyly. "I was very self-conscious getting ready. I hope I look all right, she said, and burst out crying. Her make-up smeared everywhere, and she wept.

Sally pushed her inside and closed the door behind her. "Here, Sandra, come, let's wash your face and get you into some jeans and a sweatshirt. You need to feel comfortable, not showy. I love you sweet heart. Here's the facial soap. Wash.

"And get out of that dress. It's – not proper. Get into some jeans. Good. Now put this over, Sally said and handed her a navy blue Boston sweatshirt. Better. OK, let's go. Cry all you want, it helps. I know. I was raped once too. Do you have a seashell or a rock to put into your pocket? It helps to have something to finger when you're nervous."

"I have a little agate," Sandra spoke for the very first time.

"Put it in your pocket." She did. "Better?"

"Ready. Thank you. I hope you're not ashamed of me."

"I hope you're not ashamed of yourself! I'm not ashamed of you. Look at me as your rock. And don't forget the true rock, Jesus Christ. He's here for you. He'll make you well. You will recover. I did. It changes you and you'll never be the same again, but at least you can live with it without blaming yourself. Come now, let's go. We're running late."

Sally led the way out of the small apartment and Sandra followed, locking the door behind her. She forgot her purse and had to unlock the door again to go in and get it. Back at the door she locked it behind her once more, and then followed Sally down to the Fiat where Farley sat idling and concerned.

Sally opened the door and helped Sandra slide in behind the front seat. Next Sally got in to the front seat, and made sure that everyone had their seat belt on. Sandra obediently buckled up.

The little car rolled out onto the road and headed towards Hillside Apostolic Church.

"We're just a few minutes late, and that means we're on time because we always get there early anyway." Farley comforted the odd silence in the car.

In just a few minutes they pulled into the Church parking lot. It was a popular moment for most members arrived at this time. Farley turned the car off and they all got out. Sally took Sandra's arm and led her to the door, Farley following behind. They entered the Church and looked around. There was Oscar, sitting in his front row seat with his i-pad. Oscar looked up and tried to make eye contact, but Sally immediately looked away. There he was, a permanent bother. Sally and Sandra looked around for Simon but he was not there. They took their seats and kept their eyes on the door.

Church worship began and still no Simon. His absence left a black hole in the sanctuary, his evil spirit sitting in for him. Sandra breathed a sigh of relief and disappointment. She had wanted to convict him in his sins.

Farley stood up and started singing and clapping for the Lord. Sally stood and swayed back and forth with her arms raised, singing. Sandra cowered in her seat, half expecting the Church to crumble and fall down on them. She sniffled, and cried. She held her head in her hands and mourned softly for her lost innocence.

Sally saw Mae and James a couple of rows in front of them, and waved when Mae turned around to look for them. There was no sign of Tina or Leroy.

Sally sat down and put an arm around Sandra as the young woman bawled into her shoulder. She was wracked with pain and wanted to break free, but couldn't. She had been caught and violated. A permanent condition, which would settle into a feeling of loss and healing if treated right. Sandra would need counseling to work through her feelings and emotions. It would take time, but facing the enemy was the first step, and by going to Church and not meeting Simon for dinner she had declared her innocence in the situation.

She was buggered out and hunkered down. The praise and worship music was comforting to her, and eventually she lifted up her voice as tears streamed down her face.

She praised her Lord and asked for redemption, cleansing, and renewal. Eventually she would need to forgive Simon, and thus pour coals of fire over his head. He had no escape, for likely he would not turn to God for forgiveness, in self-righteous contempt. He despised Sandra and hated her for figuring him out. By not meeting him for dinner he suspected that something was up.

A miracle happened in a way, as Sandra cried out in a loud voice and went up to the altar for prayer. The Pastor put his hands on this weeping woman and spoke healing prayers over her. She managed to say that she needed to talk to him later. He nodded and moved to the next person to pray over.

Sandra felt somewhat edified and taken care of as she turned to Jesus and prayed to Him, asking for healing, justification, and understanding from others as well.

Mae came forward and put her arms around Sandra and prayed quietly to her; a voice of concern and acceptance. Sandra fell to the floor and began shrieking in utterance of her inner spirit. Immediately a crowd of women stood around her, praying, praising, and lending confidence and healing.

Her tears began to dry up as the worst was over. Now the road was long and tedious, but she could get by, remembering her talk with Pastor, and Sally would be there for that to support her.

By now more than one person had noticed the absence of Simon but no one thought anything odd of that. Oscar shuffled up and down the aisles, dancing and jumping up and down with glee as he praised his Lord. He passed by Sally and the two ignored each other. "The hooligan," thought Sally to her benevolent self.

Praise and worship singing came to a halt as the Pastor took the pulpit and began to lead worship and praising with prayer and hand clapping. Where was Tina? Leroy? Sally made a mental note to call her friend who rarely missed Wednesday services. Perhaps they were all three together, Simon, Leroy, and Tina. Where were they? A dark shadow passed over the service; only a few saw it.

As the worship and praise ended, the assistant Pastor, Duncan Freebes, gave a call for tithes and offerings to be brought forward. Sally and Farley would give on Sunday. A rather large handful of people came forward to give of their finances to God.

Finally, the Pastor led the congregation into his sermon and talked of giving. God gave; people could give back by thanksgiving, praise, and worship; and also prayer and stewardship, including tithes.

As the service ended, the praise and worship team came up to the front and began singing, leading the congregation through words that were highlighted in the front and back of the sanctuary. The Pastor's wife played the piano and sang like a bird. The drummer kept time, and the prayer leader played the bass. It was a musical fiesta. Loved by all, experienced by all.

As Church closed there was one final altar call and people went forward to receive the Holy Ghost, prayer, and healing for all kinds of circumstances.

Sandra was nervous as a clam in a bucket and somewhat dreaded her conversation with the Pastor. She needed the elders to pray over her. Sally waited with her as the people filed out, talking and greeting new members. Where was Simon? Tina? Leroy?

Mae made her way to the Cadwell's and Sandra, full of sympathy and silent compassion, giving her support and being there to encourage the traumatized young woman.

When most of the Church body had exited, Pastor Williams approached the small group of people surrounding Sandra. James was there, Mae, Farley and Sally, all for Sandra.

"What are we dealing with here?" Inquired the Pastor.

"We have a sorry situation and some shocking news to discuss with you, Pastor Williams," Farley was the first to vocalize. He looked around to find the carriage of his remark. Immediately Sally spoke up, and bluntly.

"Pastor, did you noticed that Simon was missing today, and Tina Makron and Leroy, Simon's brother?

"Well, Sandra, here, bears witness that she was raped by Simon in his home not more than four days ago. She had agreed to meet him for dinner tonight at The Old Barnyard before Church, and she didn't go. We think Simon suspects something so he didn't come to Church today. That makes sense, but why Tina and Leroy didn't come is still a mystery. She usually calls if she's not going to make it."

"I was raped, Pastor," Sandra mumbled as tears streaked her face.

"Speak, Sandra," Sally encouraged her.

"I've never been raped before and I feel so dirty and lame. I think Simon knows that I know – I was drugged, you see – and he's afraid. And we think there are others in the Church who have been victimized as well."

"Good, Sandra. It's important to own up to your feelings and your thoughts about things. How do you feel about Simon?"

"I feel like he's a dirty warlock who suckered me into his folds, drugged me, and then raped me while I was in a stupor. Sally told me that Tina overheard the whole thing while she was in Leroy's room and they were doing a Bible study. She heard me yelling 'Stop!' and 'Don't!', and 'help!' Tina told Sally this and then Leroy confided in Tina that his brother often brought girls in from the street to drug and rape. It hurts so bad, I can hardly understand it. No, I can't understand it. A man like that needs to be locked up. And now he's scared so we need to be on the outlook for him at Church.

"I could testify in front of the Church if you think that's wise, Pastor."

"This is all quite shocking and disturbing to me. Would you allow me to anoint you with oil and pray with the elders over you, Sandra? Right now you need extra protection, not only from yourself but from Simon, should he show his face in Church. We don't want to spook him, but he might agree to a meeting with me. What do you think?"

Sandra agreed readily to the oil anointing and prayer from the elders. "Can we do it now?" whimpered the hurting girl.

The Pastor gathered together the Church elders and they all went to work together at once. They anointed Sandra with oil on her forehead and prayed in tongues over the helpless girl who felt so dirty.

"Thank you," she said through tears as the clergy closed their prayers.

"Is there anyone you could stay with for the next week or so while the newness of all this wears off?"

"She could stay with me and James," Mae volunteered readily.

"Would that work for you, Sandra?" The Pastor was both caring and protective. "Everyone around you right now cares for and loves you, Sandra. Try to pray as much as you can, especially if you feel depression moving in.

"I will put a personal call into him, because I am concerned that he didn't come to Wednesday Church like he always does. I will ask him what is wrong and go from there." Pastor Williams stood up and they did a group hug around Sandra who let herself be coddled.

"I'll ride home with you and James, Mae. Is that all right? Just to keep myself safe from myself right now, I don't trust myself to choose life if suicide presented itself. I just feel so dirty."

"Then that's settled. I will put a call into Simon and ask him what kept him from Church today. You guys all be careful. He might suspect that Sally knows where Sandra is, since Tina has confided in her about what she heard and witnessed. It's justification and truth that needs to come out."

No one else had anything to say, other than Mae and James' place was probably the safest place for Sandra to stay right now. Mae took her arm and led her to the door and everyone said their goodbye's.

"We'll see you again on Sunday. God go with you," said the Pastor.

He went into his office and wept over the poor girl and began to prepare for his phone call to Simon.

THE LONE COLD

Brrrrr. It's cold in here. I shiver in the grace of charming fools who sell flamboyant rivers of hope that lead nowhere but to a runny nose and congested chest, and vomiting. Simon was in no way comfortable. He felt evil, he felt ugly and hateful. Why hadn't Sandra met him for dinner last night before Church? He had been too afraid to show his face. What if she knew?

"What do you know?" He demanded of Tina who sat tied up on the floor at Leroy's feet. Leroy's hands and feet were also bound. He was helpless to help her. Simon had gagged him as well.

He sat silently, fuming, angry, ferociously helpless.

Simon nudged Tina with his boot. "Talk!"

She remained silent but couldn't much longer. Just then the phone rang. It was Thursday afternoon. Simon answered his cell phone and it was Pastor Williams. His heart did flip-flops. Should he confess his sins and be made clean? That was possible wasn't it?

"Hello, Pastor," grumbled Simon. "What did I do wrong now?"

"You tell me," Pastor Williams said in a mild voice. "We missed you in Church last night. You never miss Wednesday services. What happened now? You know you have a powerful presence in the Church. I would hate to lose you."

"I was waiting for a date to bring to Church. She never showed up, but I waited just the same."

"That's too bad. Will you be here on Sunday?"

"Of course! I would hate to miss a Church service. I –uh- hated missing service last night. I don't like to lose out, you know.

"Every now and then something happens though and I just can't make it. Was she there last night? Sandra Naden?"

"As a matter of fact she was. She came with the Cadwell's and professed to not feeling good. She reported a cold or flu coming on."

"Is that so? I just thought she stood me up. There must have been a reason. So she's sick? I'm sorry. I guess I won't see her till Sunday, if all goes well. I don't have her phone number. Do you have it?"

"Let me check. No, she's not on the roster. She must have fallen through the cracks early on. Well, we look forward to seeing you Sunday then, Simon. By the way, where was your brother Leroy yesterday, and Tina Makron? I heard gossip that the two of them were merging. Do you know where they are? Or why they didn't make it to Church either?" The Pastor was pushy so as to sound genuinely interested.

"I really have no idea where Tina and my brother are. I left early to go meet Sandra last night and they were gone when I got back. I haven't seen them since." Simon coughed and said he needed to go, because he was getting sick too.

"Now that's not good. I'll pray about you," said Pastor Williams. Hopefully we'll find you in service on Sunday. "If you see Tina, would you have her give me a call? I need to know what kept her from service last night. It looks like I'm starting to lose my flock. - Can't let that happen."

The Pastor waited in what seemed a strange silence. He waited quietly. Perhaps Simon would add some information.

"I really have no idea where they are or why they missed Church too. I'll call you tomorrow after I see Leroy or Tina."

"Can you just tell Leroy to call me? I'd like to speak to him."

"I can't do that, I mean, what if I don't see him before Church on Sunday?"

"Well, if you do see him, have him call me, OK?"

"Sure Pastor, sure. Bye now."

"Bye, and God bless you Simon.

Simon was seething when he hung up. Was the Pastor suspicious of something? He seemed innocent enough, just checking up on his lost sheep. Well there was only one thing he could do to assure his safety.

In his cold, cold heart he realized that Tina needed to be silenced, and he couldn't trust her to keep quiet. She knew something, or was hiding that she knew something. He still couldn't get her to talk. Now she feared for her life and spoke up, swearing that she didn't know anything that she shouldn't know. She simply wanted to date Leroy, and why was Simon interfering?

"Simon, are you jealous of Leroy? Do you covet me?" Tina tried to give him the slip.

"Of course not. I've just started dating Stacy – I mean Sandra. I'm not jealous. I don't need my own brother's girlfriends." He growled and hissed and whistled and swore.

I'm losing this battle, he said to himself. Tina needed to be expunged from the picture. She was not to be trusted. But he needed to be sure that she knew something before he would humanely euthanize her.

Am I homicidal? He questioned himself. Do I enjoy killing people? He had never killed before, but before the Church he must paint himself clean so that no one would ever know what he did to Sandra and Stacy and Becky and Jane. So far, he had never been caught. He made a first date, raped his victim, and set up a follow up date where he would break off the relationship saying there was someone else, and he was sorry. All of his dates were sedated before the rape and it made him wild with pleasure to fornicate in silence, listening to his own noises and the helpless, drugged screams of his victims. It was a type of silence in that he closed off his awareness as he raped, feeling only the sex of the experience. Then he would dress his victims and when they came to, he merely asked if they were all right, telling them they had been dizzy and light headed and passed out. Next he would escort his victim to the bus stop outside, and say goodbye, with plans to meet in a day or two.

Never before had he been stood up. He was in a frenzy, and felt the Pastor's prayers about him, for condemnation and conviction. He felt the onslaught of God's vengeance. "Can't I be forgiven?" he whined.

Back to Tina and Leroy. Both were afraid to move, as Simon hovered over Tina, screaming at her to voice up about what she knew. Poor Leroy was unable to thread a story with her, being gagged and unable to support his girlfriend. His brother flashed a knife.

Just then, the phone rang again, and it was Oscar. Now Oscar was innocent. He knew nothing of Simon's exploits. He was a deceived friend of Simon, who loved the young man's companionship and his warped way of looking at the world.

"Help!" Cried Tina as loudly as she could.

Simon quickly hung up on his "friend" and thrust his knife at Tina's throat. This will be messy, he thought as he saw the bloody knife and the subsequent bloody life spurting out of his victim. He couldn't call 911, he couldn't just let her bleed to death, he feverishly tried to wrap a towel tightly around her neck to stop the bleeding, but blood was already flowing out of her nostrils. Her voice gurgled and gasped, choking and sputtering as Simon only made out "you'll pay for this. . . ." accompanied with silent screams.

Then she was silent, and Simon kicked her hard to stimulate life. But it was too late. The innocent woman was dead. Leroy vomited through his gag and began to choke on his own wretched mess. Simon was silent now, and took off Leroy's gag. With a knife at his throat, he warned Leroy, that should he ever even hint of this event to someone, he would kill him too. I can run, Simon said to himself, shaking in a strange form of glee.

Something told him to go to Church on Sunday with Leroy and he made a plan. Tina had left for Mexico to visit her mother and aunt in Puerto Vallarta. No one would know how long she planned to stay away. Leroy must stand up for his brother, or his life would be next.

Fearing for his life and aghast at what he had just witnessed, Leroy promised to back up his brother if anything of this incident was ever discovered. Leroy went along with his brother, waiting for an opening to overcome him. He had long been intimidated by Simon. But this pushed the cards too far. Simon carefully, coldly explained that if he didn't cover for his brother, well, then the Cadwell's would be easy meat to kill in pay back for any disloyalty. After all, they probably knew too, about Sandra.

Viciously he commanded Leroy to get rid of this messy Tina, and make her gone. He carefully unbound his brother's hands and feet. What to do with the body? For now just leave it in the bath tub until night came and they could wrap it up and carry it down to the dumpster, covering it with boxes and paper. Simon paced back and forth in severe delirium. He found it hard to breathe, and gently wiped the blood from his knife.

Leroy spoke nothing. He was numb. This girl he had begun to love. Now? Murdered. The silence was sickening and Leroy vomited again, grasping himself as he bent over and made gruesome noises, "Aaaagh Gack!"

Obediently Leroy picked up the carcass of Tina and walked her into the bathroom placing her carefully into the tub. She was still bleeding, and Simon turned on the water to wash the blood away. He couldn't stand to look at it, couldn't believe it was done by his own hand. What had he done? Oscar! Oscar had heard her cry for help. He was hemmed in now by Oscar, Leroy, the Pastor, Sandra, and the Cadwell's. He must create for himself a little egg of innocence. He must go out walking with Leroy, to a café and the beach, and Church on Sunday. Hiding out would only make him suspect. His plan must work. Knowing he could flee any moment if things went wrong, he counted on Leroy to be his defender, based on his own life and the lives of the Cadwell's. Simon had killed once. Now swallowing, he realized he could do it again, and decided to pack his revolver and carry his hunting knife.

Darkness came and Simon sent Leroy downstairs to scout out foot traffic around or near the dumpster. Leroy yelled "OK!" before realizing he might be attracting attention to himself. Simon beside himself, didn't know what to do. He needed Leroy to carry the body. He couldn't touch it. It was gruesome. Her black hair was sticky and covered in blood.

Leroy came back up and gave the all clear, apologizing for yelling first. Carefully he picked up the carcass of Tina and placed her on towels that Simon had laid out. Simon wrapped her up in towels and cardboard, only her feet showing. Leroy's heart busted within himself and he agonizingly refused to carry the body downstairs. He would go ahead and signal Simon with a whistle when no one was there.

Simon was lone cold inside, by himself in a world of hate and tremors. He carried the body shakily downstairs, dragging her feet as he swiftly threw her into the dumpster, Leroy holding up the top. He closed the top and the two terrified men raced back upstairs to their apartment, the floor of which was coated with blood. Simon stomached the acrid mess, but Leroy could only wretch again, having nothing left to vomit.

Simon took a bottle of Clorox and poured it liberally all over the floors. The rug was clean, by some mercy, and Simon scrubbed and scrubbed and scrubbed, throwing aside bloody towels as he used them. The job was only partially done. It was the mess that would not go away. The more Simon wiped the more the mess spread. He took to using newspapers to soak up all moisture. There was left a large egg-shaped stain. It reeked of death.

"Tell me what to do, Leroy," whimpered Simon.

"Turn yourself in."

"You're in this too." Simon blurted ignorantly. It was his doing, he was using Leroy to sucker himself out of all this.

"I hate you Simon," cried Leroy, and wept over the loss of his girl, the death, the evil killing.

"It was her fault! She shouldn't have yelled like that. Now Oscar knows about it."

"Oscar doesn't know anything," discouraged Leroy. In defense of Oscar. "You're not going to kill him too, are you?"

"Leroy, you're my only true friend. My brother. Now get rid of this mess!" Screeched Simon. Simon pulled out his knife and waved it at his brother. Then before Leroy could move, he slashed his brother's left leg. It was just a scratch, but enough to bring blood. Leroy squealed in terror as Simon cut his pinky and rubbed his brother's blood with his own.

"Now we're blood brothers all over again," triumphantly spoke Simon.

Leroy looked at Simon with contempt. "You loser. I'm ashamed to be your brother-"

"You will do as I say, and everything will be fine. You're not afraid are you? I could never kill you; but I could kill your friends if you disobey and go against me. Now go to the store and buy two big bottles of Clorox and a bunch of towels. We're all out of towels. You wasted all my towels, you clout."

Leroy went to his room and changed into clean clothes before washing his hands and face in order to go to the store. There was a drugstore just down the street. Out the door he went and wobbled to the drugstore in his shock and pain and hatred, fuming like a cigarette smashed into the ground.

In a haze, he walked into the store and found the Clorox, after asking an employee where to locate it. Next he found a bunch of cheap beach towels and grabbed ten of them. Like a robot, he marched to the check out stand and laid out his merchandise. The cashier said "Good evening," and Leroy mumbled a reply. For the sake of his friends he would do this. He paid for the towels and the bleach, and walked out of the store again, toward the apartment he shared with his brother.

The street was dark and cold and rain came down making the air devilishly cold and lonesome. Leroy stepped in mud puddles and nearly tripped over the curb onto the sidewalk as he crossed the street. He had an impulse to drop everything and run, but he knew Simon would suspect something and run. He couldn't be caught. He would hide out and systematically kill Leroy's friends.

It was evil in a bottle, poured out all over his head. He sucked it up and forced himself to become numb. He treaded nimbly and light footed to his home where he lived with his brother who had just murdered his very innocent, beautiful woman.

He needed to smoke and couldn't wait to get home for his box of cigarettes. He needed to smoke and relax and smoke more and more. He had never been able to quit and had tried many times. Now he needed it. Alcohol sounded abhorrent. He could drink coffee. Coffee and smoke, and let Simon do the rest of the cleaning. He would not touch the mess again. He would have to clean the bathtub, though. Simon would force him to do that. Leroy cried as he entered the staircase to his apartment and cried loudly as he entered the door to his home where Simon was in the kitchen fixing coffee and washing his hands again and again.

"You'll never get rid of all this blood, Simon," he taunted. "You're going to go straight to hell, and I don't want to hear about it. So leave me out of the picture, and clean up that mess by yourself, you loser, you loser, you *loser*. Of course I will clean the bathtub, but the rest is up to you, you big loser. Loser." He could think of nothing to say but attacked the bathtub viciously with Clorox and a towel. Bright lights on, he saw all the stains and got them all expertly. Good luck, Simon, he thought to himself. You'll never get it clean out there. He knelt and cried, getting up to find his last box of cigarettes. He lit one up and went out on the balcony to sit down and smoke. The familiar sensations were comforting.

In the kitchen Simon was whining about a cut on his finger that was burning and throbbing.

After his first smoke, Leroy came in and poured a large mug of coffee. Too bad if his brother had made it, he needed it to clear his head. He took the mug out on the balcony, sat down, and lit up another cigarette. He smoked and drank the coffee, and smoked, alternating between the two rapidly. Then he lit his shirt on fire, not knowing why or what for, maybe to burn away reality. The flames stung fiercely and he tore the shirt off of himself to put in a pile on the balcony floor where it burned slowly to ashes. Nothing else caught aflame. Leroy pressed his cigarette into his chest, burning the skin, needing to punish and coddle himself at the same time.

He whined in vigorous hysterics and carefully put his hand over the burn. He smudged out the cigarette with his boot on the balcony deck. He wanted to lean over the railing and vomit again, but sat back and sucked on his coffee instead.

After a while of interim peace, Leroy went inside and stared at his brother. The monster who had just destroyed his life. Although he had no blood on his hands, he had failed to save the life of his friend.

"I hate you, you bastard," Leroy seethed to his brother, hot tears stinging his face.

"Now don't do that, Leroy, you're my partner, you're on my team. We'll get out of this together. After a year, you won't even remember this except as a big bump in the road of life."

"You don't deserve to live, you begging, behemoth monster." Leroy quaked inside and burned in agitation. He went to the bathroom to look at his cigarette burn in the mirror. I look like a suicidal psychopath. But I'm not one. I'm free. I have liberties. I don't have to die this way. I can save my friends. I just need to go along with Simon until I get a chance to can him. I'll make it through. I have liberties.

This changed his way of thinking and made him think like a robber, waiting patiently to steal away the life of his brother in a most painful and just manner.

"I can't get it all!" Screeched Simon. He was wiping the floors with towel after towel and newspaper to soak up the Clorox when all the towels were wet. "Go throw these in the dumpster, you lout! All the towels are wet with bleach and blood. Get me a hairdryer. Come here you insignificant worm! Go throw these towels in the dumpster."

"You do it, you lazy mushroom! I don't want to see her again. You creep. You murderer. You fat liar. God will judge you. Don't forget about that. You're doomed forever to hell you vampire. You do it!"

Leroy was shaking uncontrollably. He didn't care if his brother killed him. That was his defense, for he was unafraid. He knew his liberties and would use them to rectify the situation.

Leroy watched as his brother gathered together the sloppy mess of towels with Clorox and bloodstains. Miffed, he carried them down to the dumpster himself and deposited them there, within the large container. The mess was stinky.

He slammed the cover shut and raced back upstairs. No one must know, he thought.

Oscar knocked on the door, concerned about his buddy. Simon walked outside and told him that everything was fine.

"Someone needed help? Who was that yelling? Are you OK?"

"Oh that was nothing. Tina and Leroy were wrestling and he had her pinned. It was all in fun. How are you?"

"Oh, just curious. Remember how I told you I was interested in you as a philosophical partner in the truth? I wondered if you'd like to get together with me and study the book of Revelation? I thought we could be prayer partners."

"Yeah, that would be cool," Simon articulated. "When do you want to get together?"

"How about on Saturday? We could meet at the Turnip Bay Coffee Shop."

Simon agreed and sent Oscar on his way.

That was a failure, you wit. Simon began to shake and tremble. What a close call.

There was nothing else he could do now. No way to cover his tracks. Leroy must not go to Church. It would incriminate him. His brother would speak up and tell the truth. If the truth be known. He considered it but would not kill him.

Sleep and exhaustion were overcoming him, and Simon went to his room to lie down on his bed. Darkness overcame him quickly and he found himself in darkness with bats flying at him and merciless clouds of mosquitoes sucking his blood leaving welts all over his naked body. He wanted to cut off his penis.

He found himself in the kitchen with a butcher's knife about to perform the act. He sliced through the skin and screamed, dropping the knife and running to his bed again to curl up tight in a ball, his penis bleeding slowly.

In the meanwhile, Leroy was making plans. He needed to go to Church on Sunday. He thought about lying and sticking to his brother's story about Tina going to Mexico to visit her mother and aunt. But a warm breath blew over him, comforting as he sat on the balcony, smoking calmly. It was 1:00am and traffic below was intermittent and sparse. All these people were driving right past them. Past the dumpster, past his bloody partner, and this bloody apartment which was drying now with minor stains on the wallboards. Simon had used almost three bottles of Clorox to wipe up stains. The rest, Leroy had used in the bathtub.

He grew sleepy and tired and decided it was his liberty to go to sleep as well. Calling the police now would be lethal to his own life. Or jeopardize Simon's life. Which would work and maybe would be a smart thing to do. Turn in his own brother for a murder he was too helpless to prevent. He needed courage now.

Growing sleepy, he lay down and drifted off into dreams of riding an orca through rushing waters and being saved and rescued by this animal.

Morning came and Simon stood at the door of his brother's room watching him sleep so softly, so gently. Leroy groaned and rolled over. Simon backed off and went to the kitchen to make coffee and have some toast. Inside he felt jealous of himself, if that were possible. He knew how to get into this situation, but not how to get out of it. Outside he heard the garbage truck and went out on the landing to observe the dumping process. The dumpster was hoisted up and over the truck and all of its contents fell into the truck to get mashed. It was over soon and the dump truck drove on to its next stop. There were no suspicions. As his head cleared, he went back inside only to feel a psychological hammer hit is head. It was a psychological hammer, but it hurt. He whimpered. He began to feel scared as his glee turned to hate and guilt.

He went into the kitchen and ate his toast and poured his coffee. He drank and poured more coffee. His head felt swollen. He was stuck. He waited and waited for Leroy to get up. Maybe it would be like normal and everything would be fine.

His wishes partially realized, Simon sat down at the table as Leroy shuffled into the kitchen heading directly to the coffee pot. He said not a word and pledged himself with the liberty to remain silent. He went out on the balcony with his coffee and sat down quietly, reaching for the package of cigarettes that was still out there. Automatically he lit one up and puffed gently, thinking of the Cadwell's and what good people they were. Both had a mental illness. They were the nicest, sweetest couple he knew. Funny I should think of them, thought Leroy. Their sweet innocence seemed so far off. Leroy must not let anyone know of this. Simon could be a spider and walk all over them, wrapping them in his web.

He felt a rash break out on his face. Stress and pressure, he alluded it to. The dirty cigarette burned his fingers and he tossed it to the ground next to his chair, letting it sizzle out on its own.

"What are you doing?" Came Simon at the door, looking very troubled and beside himself.

"Drinking coffee, you piece of shit." Leroy cast his gaze out over the bay and appreciated the sun on the water.

Simon was taken aback. What was troubling Leroy?

"I thought we were friends," he croaked, choking on his own saliva.

"Your only friend is the devil."

"Oscar is my friend. We're going to meet for Bible study on Saturday. He wants to be my prayer partner. We didn't do anything wrong, did we?"

"We didn't, but you sure did. It all started with your raping schemes, and then you thought Sandra was wise to you. You porcupine, lit up piece of shit. F-cking bastard. Why did you have to kill her? You know what you are? A God damned sociopath. You'll never get out of this one. Your friend the devil is waiting at the door for you to go home to him. Pick off. You're just going to pick everyone off and stay innocent, are you? What are you going to do when they come for you? Not me. I'm abstaining of all this crap. And I will tell, it's just a matter of whom and when. You dirty piece of crap. Misery will follow you all your days." Leroy was utterly disgusted.

Simon looked around helplessly and stayed in the doorway to the balcony, watching Leroy and weighing his life in his hands. What am I worth? Thought Simon. He was afraid to go to Church on Sunday. He needed to meet with Oscar tomorrow. They hadn't set a time, but Oscar would probably call him, since Simon didn't have Oscar's phone number.

Simon sat down at the computer to check his e-mails. They were all for Leroy and from people he didn't know. Well I have at least one friend, he surmised. So what if Leroy was more popular. He didn't have the devil on his shoulder like Simon felt he had. He would stay home today, planning on who to kill if Leroy were to blab. He could pick off Leroy's friends one at a time if it meant hiding out somewhere and sneakily picking off people one at a time. That's all I have to do. But I'll warn Leroy first, he thought to himself.

"Leroy," Simon said to his brother going back out on the balcony, "you have tons of e-mail messages that you need to check. And just so you know, if you squeal one tiny little bit to anybody, I'll start picking off your friends, starting with the Cadwell's. You don't want to lose them, do you? I'm a rapist, but at least I've come clean. I don't need to be responsible for anything I've done. It's all your fault for stopping me before I was finished. You made me kill Tina. You made me put her in a dumpster and clean up all that bloody mess."

"You rat, I'm going to tie you up and burn you with cigarettes." Suddenly Leroy stood beside himself and leapt up socking Simon in his jaw and hitting up on his nose. Next he hacked at Simon's neck and kneed him in the crotch. The begging behemoth monster fell and slid to the floor. Leroy acted fast, and finding some rope in the closet, he hog-tied his brother and dragged him into the hall where Tina had bled to death.

Shaking violently, Leroy put a piece of duct tape across Simon's eyes so that he would be in darkness. Next he called Pastor Williams.

"Pastor?" He questioned when the beloved Church leader came on the line. "I have some news for you, I need to confide in you before I do anything else like kill my brother. You have to stop me. I'm so filled with hatred. Pastor, Simon killed Tina Makron and got rid of her in the outside dumpster. All because Tina knew about Simon's rapist tendencies, which I confessed to her. Lord Jesus, I've been living in fear for so long, unable to bring up the truth to anyone. Now I've got him tied up and blindfolded. Should I call the police? Can you come over here and help me? I was going to marry her! Now she's dead. Oscar is the only witness. He heard her yell 'Help!' when Simon was on the phone with him. Tina and I were bound and I was gagged. Then Oscar came by to check on things and Simon sent him away, telling him to meet with him on Saturday to do a Bible study. He's a psychopath, sociopath, and a vicious killer."

"Call 911 immediately, Leroy," came back the Pastor. "I'll be at your place in just a few minutes. Remind me where you live."

"Point Six near the harbor."

"Listen to me. Don't run or hide or do anything. You're totally innocent, are you not?"

"I am. I've got him hog-tied and blindfolded. I think I must have knocked him out, as he hasn't made any noises."

"Call 911, and I'll be there in just a few, OK?"

"Gotcha. See you soon."

Leroy hung up and breathed deep. His fear of Simon disappeared as he saw the glutton tied and helpless. He must restrain from killing him. Before he could change his mind, he called 911. He spoke with the dispatcher and explained the situation as best as he could. Simon was starting to moan, and hadn't yet realized that he was tied up.

The police were on their way, and Leroy paced back and forth from the front door to the balcony and back. He heard the sirens as police cars drew near.

It wasn't ten minutes before they came knocking on the door. Leroy froze and burst into tears. He tried his best to explain what had happened and everything he had been through with Simon, unable to turn him in. This was the last straw and Simon was condemned.

The investigators asked him a flurry of questions. "Who was Tina? Where was she now? Did anyone know about this?"

Leroy talked about Sandra, the fourth Church victim of Simon who somehow got wise to the situation, and stood him up. Simon had a string of eight other girls outside of Church whom he had raped in the same fashion. Just then, Pastor Williams knocked on the door and Leroy let him in. The Pastor introduced himself and began to tell what he knew about the situation. The Cadwell's had brought Sandra to Church on Wednesday, and she had confided her sexual violation by Simon.

The Cadwell's knew about Sandra's rape, and so did Mae and James.

Leroy jumped in to explain about Oscar's phone call and then his visit. Oscar was the last to hear from Tina, when she had cried for help.

Simon tried to move and kicked his feet and hands, trying to get the tape off of his eyes. He was convicted, caught.

Pastor agreed to meet with Oscar the next day in lieu of Simon. He had to get to the bottom of this.

The police denied this move on his part claiming the necessity to question him first.

So Tina was in the dumpster. But the garbage man had already come. It was a vicious situation. Belligerent and by far maddening in sexual assault and violent rape abuse. Pastor Williams took Leroy out on the balcony and together they prayed for restitution. He thought it best for the police to question Simon who was becoming coherent.

IDENTITY

Who am I? I speak belittlement, that's for sure. My necessity in life is to do my part and carry my share. Sally penned the words in her journal. It was the journal of her life. What was she to do about Tina Makron's death? Both Sally and Farley were to see their case managers on Friday, Kirk for Sally and Nate for Farley. Sally definitely needed support as did Farley for his own wellbeing, having been informed of the story behind Tina Makron's murder. They drove to the center together, each having a one o'clock appointment.

Sally went in first with Kirk and discussed the situation surrounding Sandra who had discovered her violation and incriminated Simon, a man from Church who had raped three other women from the Church in the way that Sally described to him. She talked of the pregnancy and the murder.

Kirk was very concerned and talked to Sally about her coping skills, and how not to get into a superhero mode, but to take care of herself first. "One thing at a time, Sally," he had said to her. The half hour flew by, and Sally left feeling a little more armed for the circumstances she was in, including the threat there had been to her own life.

When Farley saw Nate, he spoke of Simon as the devil and blamed him for the death of Tina, a wonderful lady who had loved Simon's brother. Farley couldn't come to grips with it and Nate reminded him that he needed to take care of himself first. "Don't forget your medications, and do things to distract yourself," he said to the sullen Farley sitting across from him.

Farley believed that the situation would rectify itself, for God's vengeance could not be denied, nor his loving kindness and mercy. Farley said his first concern outside of himself would be Sally, whom he loved more than life itself. Their half hour went by swiftly as well, and the couple, feeling more centered, drove home in the Fiat to their lives as normal again.

They went to bed early that night, being extra careful to stick to coping plans when their symptoms were aggravated. Both were experiencing devilish voices and warped thoughts of stabbing each other. Something was definitely wrong, and they slept together innocently, rebuking the devil and his evil voices to get out in the name of Jesus Christ.

Night passed swiftly and both had bloody and murderous dreams. They cried together and hugged each other, declaring their love for each other and reminding themselves not to get overly involved with the ugly part of the circumstances.

Being Saturday, neither of them had to work and they stayed home reading books in the sunny back yard. They remembered to pray frequently, and did small things for each other, like fetching lemonade or making sandwiches to eat.

Sally remembered to have Thomas's cone removed, and he was ecstatic about that.

Pastor Williams had called Sally and Farley and explained everything that had happened with Leroy, Tina, and Simon. He didn't mention anything about Oscar, whom he had seen today with the police at the Turnip Bay Coffee Shop. Oscar had nearly jumped his skin when he heard what happened.

Pastor would leave Oscar to explain himself to whomever he chose. He had been "friends" with Simon, and hadn't known about the string of rapes. From the Church, there was Sandra, Stacy, Becky and Jane. According to Leroy there were eight others outside of Church. Simon was arrested for murder and for rape on twelve accounts. He would get life imprisonment. He had begun squealing out what happened as though to clear his conscience. The investigators had the story and apologized to Leroy for what he had had to go through. Leroy needed a place to stay until he found his own place again, without the traces of his ugly pig brother's happenings. Sally offered to let him stay with them until he could find a place of his own.

Sandra was devastated, having tested positive for pregnancy with Simon's baby. What was she to do? She knew she couldn't have an abortion, everything in her told her that was wrong. She could raise the child herself, and have a constant reminder of Simon, or she could give up the child to a closed adoption. Perhaps someday the child would seek her out. She didn't hate the unborn baby, but neither could she love it. Ever. Adoption, then, was her chosen way to deal with the situation.

Sandra, Stacy, Becky, and Jane sought each other out and Sandra told them how she had become wise to Simon's sexual assault. The three other girls remembered passing out and how Simon had eventually broken off their relationships, saying he had found someone else. None of them wanted to believe what had happened, but it was true.

Leroy was heart broken and took up the Cadwell's offer to house him until he found suitable housing.

It wasn't until then that Sally grew curious of Oscar and his involvement in the affair. As far as Leroy knew, Oscar was an innocent young man, if just a little bit introverted.

Sally described the way Oscar had been following her around, and actually had shown up across the street from the Turnip Bay Coffee Shop when she was walking Thomas one day.

Tomorrow was Church again, and everybody looked forward to this time of worship and praise for Jesus.

Leroy couldn't justify the reasons for Oscar to appear at the Cadwell house bus stop on more than one occasion. Sally expressed her dog's guardian behavior to have treed him across the street, and chased him away on another occasion. They agreed to bring this issue up to the Pastor.

Leroy told Sally that Oscar was devastated when he had learned the truth about Tina and her horrendous killing.

Oscar volunteered to help Leroy move his things into Sally and Farley's house. As long as Thomas stayed penned, for Oscar feared the large animal.

Sally was a little bit nervous letting Oscar into their home, but he was polite enough, and quiet. He merely carried belongings of Leroy from the car to the house. Leroy could have the guest bedroom and he didn't have too many things.

Saturday evening, Farley, Sally, Oscar, Leroy, and Pastor Williams ate out at The Old Barnyard. Apparently, Oscar's many advances were efforts to befriend the Cadwell's in his shy and awkward way. He admired their relationship and lifestyle and just wanted to be friends.

Sally scolded him for acting and behaving like such a perpetrator. A stalker. Pastor Williams herded him away from any such behavior in the future.

Everyone ate their fill and went home looking ahead to Church the next morning.

Exhausted, Leroy went straight to bed that night as Sally and Farley talked extensively about Simon and how he had been friends with Oscar. Now Simon was in prison, never to hurt harmless people again.

Thomas rather liked Leroy, but they kept him out of his room. Tired, they also went to bed and made love quietly as Thomas made his bed on the living room couch.

Morning came softly, and Thomas whined in Farley's face, needing to go out and do his business.

Farley got up and let the beast out into the yard where he ran along the fence and peed by the apple tree. He dashed across the yard and came back to the door, knowing it was time for his feeding. Farley filled the dog's food and water bowls and put them on the back steps. He ate politely.

Leroy wandered out into the living room and said good morning to Farley. Farley responded with a big "Hello!" and invited him to sit down while the coffee brewed and he heated water for Sally's morning tea. Leroy was not afraid of Thomas and rather liked the big dog's attention after he had eaten his morning food and drunk some fresh water.

"Can I go out and play with him in the yard?" He asked Farley.

Farley said "why not" and showed Leroy where some of Thomas's toys were. Leroy tossed a tennis ball for Thomas who went berserk with the attention and pounded across the yard to retrieve the ball and bring it back. Leroy was hitched and kept playing with the big dog for the next half hour.

Laughing, he settled down on the steps and put his arms around Thomas, patting his big doggie side as he panted happily, his big pink tongue hanging out of his mouth. Reluctantly, Leroy went inside, finally, having had his fun with the dog.

"He's quite a friend, you have here, isn't he?" Leroy commented on the beautiful Rottweiler. Farley put the dog outside and closed the screen door, so that Thomas would be encouraged to run around the yard and play with squirrels and rabbits and mole holes to dig up.

Sally came out all ready for her tea, which Farley had just made for her. She yawned and greeted Leroy, welcoming him again to their home. Farley fried eggs and made pancakes for everyone. There was only enough hot water for two showers, so Leroy would have to take a cold one, for which Sally and Farley apologized and decided that starting tomorrow they would have to alternate who got the cold shower.

Sally had Tina on her mind and tenderly spoke of her to Leroy, telling him of Tina's fond interest in him as she had spoken to her just the other day. It helped a little, not to ignore the subject completely. She wondered if Oscar would be in Church this morning.

Sally took Thomas's leash and put it on the dog, taking him for a quick neighborhood walk while Leroy took his cold shower. She felt bad but laughed it off. Tomorrow would be her turn. Thomas peed and pooped on the walk and Sally cleaned up after him with a plastic bag turned inside out.

Farley was already in his Church clothes, wondering if Sandra would be in Church today. Her horrible situation was nearly impossible. Did rape babies turn out to be evil? It was a question that continued to bother him. Surely if the baby had a good home and was brought up with lots of love, surely the child would be good in every way. It was a new spice to the population.

Sally returned from her walk and put Thomas in his enclosure, making sure he had plenty of water. The bowl was a little dirty, so she took it out and hosed it off before refilling it with fresh, clean water for her beloved dog.

Leroy got out of the cold shower, fully awake and in good humor. He went through his things and found adequate Church clothes to put on. He fixed his hair and brushed his teeth, hoping for another cup of coffee. He was rather nervous about going to Church. Would Sandra hate him for being Simon's brother?

All three Churchgoers put the finishing touches on their getting ready, including one more cup of coffee for Leroy, who was shaking and near tears. How could he express himself? He hated Simon. He had loved Tina, had wanted to marry her. He prayed for healing.

Finally everyone was ready and they piled into the little old Fiat. Leroy had his Bible, but Sally and Farley went without theirs.

The ride to Church was quick and quiet. They all got out of the car when they reached the Church and Sally and Farley held hands as

Leroy walked in behind them. He looked around and spied Sandra, somewhat relieved. God will take care of this situation, he thought. Everyone must be edified for the Church pulse to keep going. Leroy spotted Pastor Williams and went over to shake his hand. "Welcome and Praise the Lord," said the Pastor.

"Thank you and bless you," spoke Leroy meekly.

Mae and James had spotted the Cadwell's and were making their way over to their friends to sit with them. "Sit with us, Leroy," Farley said to the rather lost looking young man.

Then Leroy saw Oscar and decided to sit with him instead. He thanked Farley and moved over to Oscar on the other side of the Church. He was the closest to the victim, having heard her cry for help. Oscar said he felt dumb for being so gullible by Simon, agreeing to Bible study with him, and not even letting him in the house.

Oscar was crying when Leroy found him. Leroy put his arm over Oscar's shoulders and hugged him briefly. Oscar stopped his crying and smiled at Leroy, a possible friend. Sandra had opted out of going to Church today. Oscar noticed and wondered.

Oscar wept again, thinking of Sandra now pregnant with Simon's child. He had loved Simon and been deceived the whole time. He wanted only to befriend the Cadwell's and not to feel left out in Church. He decided he would go out of his way to greet them and told Leroy to save him a seat while he went to accomplish that task.

Grieving, he walked over to the Cadwell's and saw Mae and James sitting with them. He greeted Sally who responded suspiciously, and Farley who shook his hand gruffly and asked how he was doing.

Oscar complained about a headache and felt like the Church was watching him and judging his every move. Why couldn't he be normal like everyone else?

Suddenly Sally melted and asked Oscar if he had ever been diagnosed with a mental illness.

Oscar suspected it in himself, but had never sought treatment. Was this why he felt so drawn to the Cadwell's? He invited himself over after Church with Leroy, saying it plainly, he said, instead of following them and hanging out at their bus stop, dying to be a part of their lives but totally afraid of Thomas who had treed him once now and charged at him from inside the yard as well.

Sally looked at Farley and together they agreed to invite Oscar over for coffee and cookies after Church. It seemed the only thing they could do, since he had admitted following them in lieu of being open with them.

Oscar smiled gigantically, and thanked them. Then he walked back over to Leroy who had saved him a seat. He sat down, just as the praise and worship team began to sing.

The whole Church stood up and sang along, hands in the air, crying out and clapping loudly.

That day, two people received the Holy Ghost with evidence of speaking in tongues, and four people were baptized. Pastor Williams had spoken about friendship, and what a friend they had in Jesus.

To Oscar, the message seemed aimed at him, in his feeble attempts to make friends, true friends in the Church, having been deceived by Simon and too afraid to approach the Cadwell's, whom he knew to have mental illnesses, of which he suspected in himself. He hadn't sought treatment, believing that none could credit him his story of gradually sinking down into introverted psychotic episodes.

After Church that day, he went home with Leroy to the Cadwell's, and they reluctantly allowed him into their house, not sure if they could trust him. Thomas seemed friendly enough, seeing Oscar with his masters on friendly terms.

They thought it best to sit outside, and Sally and Leroy took the two chaise lounges while Oscar sat in the grass and Farley went inside to fix coffee and open a box of cookies.

"Everyone come and get your coffee!" He yelled after the pot was done brewing. He had put the cookies on a platter in the middle of the table and set out cups for everyone, Sally and Farley having their favorite mugs.

The three outside got up to go and receive their cups of coffee and cookies, too. Back outside they went, at Farley's urging and sat down in the grass, all of them next to Thomas's secured enclosure. Oscar stuck his finger through the fence and Thomas licked it happily. Oscar was tickled and couldn't stop laughing.

Leroy was quiet in the presence of his friends. He was unaware of Oscar's previous "stalking" of Sally. Sally prodded Oscar gently about his mental health, and if he'd ever gone to see a psychiatrist about his painful condition.

Oscar burst into tears and reported that he was too afraid to go to the Mental Health and Wellness Center where Sally both worked and received services.

Sally asked him a few questions and determined that Oscar definitely had a mental illness. He was introverted, confused, afraid of others, and had voices in his head. Voices that denounced God and him. Discussing matters further, Sally volunteered to go to the Center with Oscar and register him to see a psychiatrist. She promised it wouldn't hurt and could only make him feel better.

Oscar was fallen and felt helpless because he had been deceived by Simon on many accounts. The last time was especially awful, since he might have been able to do something – but what? It was in his best interest that Simon had not been truthful with Oscar, because what if he found out? Simon might have killed him, too.

Oscar nodded, responsively, and squeezed out a few more tears. "I feel like I'm being helped for the very first time," babbled Oscar. "God's promise is coming true for me. You understand me," he whimpered. "No one has understood me in my whole life, and I don't have any friends, but God told me that you and Farley would be my friends who could help me and understand. That's why I've been trying to meet you. I'm sorry if I acted suspicious. I don't know how to make friends," Oscar sorrowfully admitted.

"You could go to the Mental Health and Wellness Center with me tomorrow when I go to work. Or you could meet me there after I work, so you won't be all alone in a new place," volunteered Sally.

"Do I need an appointment?"

"No. You can set one up there, after you fill out the millions of papers for your application for services."

"I'm good at paper work," said Oscar, "I've written four books, but I haven't published them because I think they'd be revealing of me." He cleared his throat. "So I have to apply for services?"

"Yes, just make sure you are honest about all aspects of the application process and they should roll you in for help right away. Once you start receiving services, God will begin the healing process in you. You've been hiding all your life, right?"

"Yes."

"You did good to turn to God and begin attending Hillside Apostolic Church where the truth is. Sorry you got mixed up in some shady activities, maybe God wants you to come clean now and recognize good from bad. It's called discernment, my friend. It's an attribute you can learn to better follow your life path, which God has put before you. He brought you to us, because He knew we could help you. You're a strong man, Oscar," said Farley compassionately, remembering his own time for seeking help for a misunderstood mental illness. Which reminded him of Gilmore.

"Sally!" He said aloud, tracing his finger in the dirt, "Gilmore is going to get married?"

"Yes!" She replied excitedly. "You need to call him and find out the details – where, when, who!"

"I'll call him today."

"Who's Gilmore?" Questioned Leroy, who had remained quiet all this time.

"Gilmore is Farley's super cool brother. He understands Farley's mental illness and has been our friend for a long time."

Sally sat back and mulled over all this exciting news.

"Oh, Farley! We're scheduled to see Dr. Nett on Wednesday at one and two o'clock," she said brightly to Farley, who had probably forgotten. Both Farley and Sally saw the same psychiatrist at back to back hours in the same day. Farley always went first.

"That's good," said Farley. "It's about time. I need to discuss my gambling habit with him. I need help to stop it. Maybe he has some ideas for me. I don't think God likes me doing it very much.

"Sally, do you think I am obsessive compulsive?"

"Not at all. You don't obsess on anything. Not even gambling. That's just a nasty habit."

Leroy spoke up. "I love to play slot machines, even though I know God doesn't approve. Is that a catch 22?"

"In a way it is," agreed Sally. "You're doing the very thing that God doesn't want you to do, and you're doing it despite that. You need to turn around and quit, which would kill the habit because you hate loving to do what is wrong in God's eyes."

"Do you really think it's wrong?" Questioned Leroy, coming to life.

"I wouldn't say it's *wrong*, but it can get out of hand, and that's when you have a problem," said Sally mercifully. "You need self-discipline to engage in those activities and not to let the devil lead you on because he can, even if you don't want him to. Just keep things under control.

Farley had a rule to never use more than two twenties in a single day, and he doesn't go everyday, do you Farley?" She probed at him.

"I don't go more than three times a week, and like Sally said, I never use more than two twenties. If I lose, I lose. I don't keep trying with more and more money. I just get hurt. Which keeps me coming back, because I love that winning sensation."

"I'm with you, there," Leroy told them, "but I just go once or twice a month. I hate losing. It brings me down and I have a bad day. But then I try again, and sometimes I get lucky. I don't think it's a sin, as long as you're not out of control. Just like having wine in the evenings is OK, as long as you limit yourself to one or two glasses. Self-discipline is very important in many aspects of life. Even when it comes to eating, people can get out of control."

Oscar nodded agreeably, looking forward to his trip to the Mental Health and Wellness center. He felt good and accepted at the mercy of these so-called friends. He hardly knew them, but detected care and wellbeing in them. Not sure how to be a friend, he remembered Jesus, the greatest friend of all. Jesus had led him to these people who might very well become his friends. All he could do was be himself, and hope that he was accepted.

Coffee was gone and it was getting near time to do something else. Sally wanted to go fishing with Farley at their favorite pier. She stood up and stretched, and seeing no alternative, she invited everybody to come along. Leroy needed them right now; he might kill himself if left alone. Oscar wouldn't be a nuisance; he was filled with intrigue, and both Sally and Farley looked forward to getting to know this stranger.

Farley arose and announced that fishing would be a great idea. He left the group to go and retrieve their two poles, net, tackle box and a bucket. Oscar lit up like a new flower in the sun, and admitted that his Dad used to go fishing with him in their dinghy. The sight of the poles made his stomach swim with butterflies.

Leroy declined and said he would rather take a nap. However, Farley coaxed him into coming along, his company would be appreciated.

Leroy allowed himself to be coddled into going along. He was listless and had thoughts of drowning himself, being unable to swim. He would go along, he said.

Sally asked both Oscar and Leroy if they could swim. Leroy said no, and Oscar said yes. Sally insisted that Leroy wear a life jacket in case he fell off of the pier.

Leroy's secret hope of dying mortified him, and he reluctantly reached out for the safety net of a life jacket to keep himself alive. He felt he would drag along and make sour company.

"Time to go!" Shouted Farley who waited while Sally fetched a life jacket for Leroy.

Then it was time and they all started walking. "Remind me to call Gil' later, Sweetheart," Farley put his arm around his wife and then let go and took her hand.

Leroy and Oscar walked behind them. Neither knew the way so they followed like blind sheep.

The Cadwell's had a strong relationship and Oscar was elated to finally be accepted by them. However, he was having voices in his head that told him to grab Leroy's jacket and push him in the water.

He began kicking pebbles along the walk and apologized profusely when one pebble hit Sally's left leg. "I'm so sorry," he cried out helplessly. "I didn't mean it. I didn't mean it. Oh, I'm so sorry," he sobbed.

Sally stopped and turned around to face Oscar. "It was an accident, right?"

"Yes," he replied like a retarded mutant.

"Then forget it. You didn't hurt anyone."

"OK," said Oscar, apathetically.

They all kept walking, and Oscar wiped at his eyes, growing fatigued with each added step.

"I'm really tired," said Oscar. "I think I'll go home now and lay down. "I don't live far from here. What time should I meet you at your house tomorrow? Are you still going to take me to the mental health center?"

"Of course! Be at our house by nine-thirty. You're sure you don't want to come with us?"

Oscar declined the invitation and thanked them profusely. He shook hands with Leroy, another potential friend and turned left at the next block saying goodbye.

Depressed Leroy mentioned going back to the Cadwell house to take a nap as well, but Farley carefully goaded him into accompanying them to the fishing pier.

The threesome kept walking, and Leroy, feeling silly in his life jacket, removed it from himself and carried it instead of wearing it. Neither Sally nor Farley had noticed and didn't notice until they got to the pier and walked out to the end of it. Farley mentioned to Leroy that he had once seen a dead man float by while he was fishing. It was enough for Leroy to don the jacket once more and zip it up securely.

Sally handed him a fishing pole, and he lit up just a little bit more, loving the feeling of fishing.

Leroy cast out his line and began reeling in. He caught nothing, but kept trying.

Farley had the other pole and cast out his line as well. Then Leroy got a bite and hooked a fish. He reeled in excitedly and Sally netted the fish as it came in close to the pier. It was a nice sized perch and Leroy felt like a success. While the two men fished on, Sally walked down to the water and cleaned and filleted the fish, bring the fresh meat up and putting it in the bucket.

Two hours went by, and Leroy hooked and caught another fish, bigger than the first. He smiled wide and felt giddy jumping up and down and clapping his hands triumphantly. "Thanks for making me come along, this is fun," he said.

Farley nodded and said sarcastically, "Fun for you, Leroy. Why don't I ever get the luck?" They traded poles and Sally took Farley's pole from Leroy. She wanted a turn as well. Farley cast and then Sally cast. Finally, Farley got a bite and hooked a fish. It was a big fish and fought hard. Leroy netted the fish as it came in to the pier. Farley grinned and said proudly, "Mine's the biggest of all three!" Finally.

Sally hooked a fish next and brought it in. It was too small so they threw it back. She gave her pole back to Leroy and went to clean the last two fish and fillet them.

Then, both Farley and Leroy each caught a fish at the same time, these, the biggest two of all. Sally netted them both and took the hooks out of their mouths. As an excited Farley and Leroy fished on, she took these two and cleaned them and filleted them too. They fished for another half an hour before deciding it was time to quit. Five fish! They would eat well tonight.

Farley decided that they should go through town and stop at the bakery to get a loaf of French bread to have with the fish. They each got a donut as long as they were there, and Sally carefully guarded their bucket of fish fillets. Sweet tooth's alive, they each had another pastry before leaving and carrying the loaf of French bread with them. Leroy carried the bread, while Sally carried the bucket of fish and the tackle box and Farley carried the poles and net.

It started to rain as they were two blocks from home. There was nothing they could do but jog-trot as fast as they could, carrying all their gear and the fish and bread.

They came in through the front gate, and Sally half expected to see Oscar at the bus stop. He wasn't there.

They went around to the back door and took their shoes off before going inside. Farley put the poles and net in the storeroom, and took the tackle box from Sally to put there as well. They brought the fish and bread into the kitchen and began to organize a dinner plan.

Sally would fry the fish, while Farley made salad, and Leroy sliced and buttered the bread with garlic salt to put in the oven.

Dinner was done hurriedly, as they were all very hungry. They split the fish evenly among the three of them, and there was plenty of bread and salad for all.

It was over soon and they were all satisfied. Leroy volunteered to wash dishes, and Sally and Farley allowed him to help. They sat in the living room while Leroy worked in the kitchen.

"Do you want to watch a movie?" Farley asked Sally.

"No, not right now. I'm just really so tired," she said. "I think I'll go write in my journal for awhile in the office, and you and Leroy can watch a movie if you want."

"Hey Leroy!" Shouted Farley. Leroy was just finishing up. "Do you want to watch a movie?"

"Yeah, I would, but I think I'll go to my room and read my Bible." He was tired, too.

Farley was left to the living room alone, so he decided to let Thomas in for company. He went out the back door to Thomas's enclosure and opened the gate to let the excited dog out. Thomas jumped up and down and ran a circle around his enclosure coming back to Farley and sitting obediently at his feet.

"Let's go inside, Thomas," he said. Together they walked to the house and Farley realized that they hadn't fed the dog his dinner yet. Obligingly, he filled Thomas's blue bowl with fresh water and the red bowl with food. Poor Thomas was so patient and trusting that he hadn't even howled for his food.

The dog ate happily and quickly, excited to come inside and hang out with his masters.

"It's just you and me, buddy," Farley said to Thomas. Thomas was just happy to be in the living room with Farley, who now turned on the TV to find a movie. Aha! *Trading Places* was showing at nine o'clock – that would be in fifteen minutes. Farley liked that movie. He relaxed as *Little House on the Prairie* finished up.

Farley patted Thomas' side as the dog panted heavily and nuzzled his nose into Farley's welcoming chest. "Good Boy!" He said. The movie came on and Farley lay down on the couch watching the movie with his head propped up on pillows. He thought of Oscar tomorrow and of him going to the Center with Sally. Oscar obviously needed help, and it looked as if God has been trying to hook Oscar up with the Cadwell's as people who could help him and understand his situation. Oscar didn't seem like such a bad guy. He was just really shy and awkward. He needed to find himself; to identify who he was. It was his liberty to seek help. There was no reason why he should stay stuck in a rut for his life. Not when there were many, many people with mental illnesses who have been treated and helped for their illnesses. It was nothing to be ashamed of. Rather celebrated in a way; as the challenge was to learn to live productively with the illness. Farley was curious as to how Oscar would be identified, his diagnosis.

The movie played on and Farley's eyes grew heavy. Soon he was asleep and snoring quietly. Sally came out of the office where she had been writing, and sat down next to Farley on the couch. "Sweetheart," she said gently. "It's bedtime, Sweetheart."

Farley's eyes came open and focused lovingly on his wife. They had had such a good day at the pier. Even wallowing Leroy seemed to enjoy himself. "Tomorrow's a big day, Farley," Sally said quietly. "I'm bringing Oscar to the center with me." The name caused suspicion in Farley, and he reminded her to be extra careful with her charge. - Also to find out where he lived.

Farley sat up, turning off the TV movie, which had lasted two hours. Together they went to their bedroom, when Sally remembered to let Thomas out one more time before bed.

She waited in the doorway as Thomas snuffled around the yard and found places to poop and pee. After that he came gratefully to the house and back inside. Straight to the living room couch he went as Sally turned out the lights.

In their bedroom, Sally and Farley fell fast asleep, curled up together. Morning came, it seemed, right after Sally had closed her eyes and Thomas put his big head in her face and licked her cheek. "Oh, Thomas," she complained, but dutifully got up to let the dog out again. She fed and watered him and then went around the yard picking up his poops and putting them in a plastic bag. The dew on the grass made her feet wet in her house slippers.

Done with that chore, Sally turned to making coffee, and her morning tea. Farley would be up soon, to get ready for work. Also, Leroy was in the house and nobody knew what his plans were.

So Sally sat and drank her tea, eating a bowl of cereal and having a banana on the side. When she was done with her tea she poured a cup of coffee. She was trying to be quiet, not wanting Leroy to wake up. She felt nervous about him in their house and her mental illness was suffering from the stress. Quietly she went to Farley and woke him up for work. Also he had to drop her and Oscar off at the Center.

She hurried her husband, not wanting to be late for work. Oscar should be arriving soon. Back in the kitchen her hands twitched as she held the spoon in the cereal and her head jolted a little, as if little electrocutions were zapping her mind. Then she remembered to take her morning pills and thanked God for that. She needed to be at her best when working, and it annoyed her to be stressed out.

It was then she remembered to tend to Thomas. He needed to get in his enclosure for the day. She put on the blue yard shoes and went outside, calling Thomas; there he was and went obediently into his enclosure where Sally saw he had very little water. Quickly she brought his water bowl to the hose, and turning the spigot she filled his bowl full of fresh water. She put the bowl carefully back in the enclosure.

Inside, having eaten and taken care of the dog, Sally went to the bedroom and pulled out the clothes she would wear. Farley was up and getting ready, having already showered. Next she went to the bathroom and showered off, fixing her hair carefully and applying a small line of eye liner under her eyes. In the steamy bathroom she brushed her teeth and put on all her clothes, getting ready to go.

Farley got ready and Oscar was expected in fifteen minutes.

He needed to fill out application papers. He might need help, she realized and decided to offer assistance if necessary.

Leroy came into the kitchen and poured coffee. "Hello brother Leroy," said Farley. Leroy nodded quietly and raised his cup of coffee to his friend. "Thank you for making coffee before leaving."

"Are you hungry?" Asked Farley.

"A little," Leroy told him.

"Help yourself to cereal and fruit, and there should be enough coffee for three cups."

Leroy sat in the living room and quietly sipped his coffee as Farley got his keys and wallet together and made ready to go. It was already ten o'clock. Oscar was late and now Sally would be late for work.

"What are your plans for today, Leroy?" He asked.

"Well, if it's all right with you, I'd kind of like to hang around here for the day and rest up and reconstitute myself. I could take Thomas for a walk, if you let me, and I could even mow your yard. Do you have a lawn mower?"

"Sure! It's in the storeroom behind the house. There should be plenty of gas in it. Are you sure you want to do all that?"

"Well, at least I'd be helping out and not free loading. Besides I need the exercise to help deal with my psychosocial problems. I'm beginning to think I should see a counselor or therapist to talk about all I've been through and help me sort out my feelings of guilt and paranoia. I've heard of panic attacks, and I really don't want to get one, so mowing the lawn would be good for me."

"Would you be interested in going to the mental health center with Sally and Oscar and me today, the place where she works and we get services? Oscar is coming along with us to fill out application papers."

"You know, Farley, you could be right. Where better to get a therapist, I assume. But I don't think today. I need to be with myself today and God. I need to get down on my knees and pray. And praise."

"Thank you again so much for allowing me to live here for an interim before I find a new place to live, far away from the place where I lived shackled by Simon. I don't want to visit him, but something tells me I should. I don't know. I could someday. I want vengeance. But I guess that's God's, right?"

"You're right."

"Will you pray for me? I'm so mixed up and confused."

"Of course! Right now?"

"Yeah, if you don't mind. . . ?"

"All right. Here take my hand and join with me. Father God, Holy Ghost, Jesus Christ and the Spirit within me, I ask that you take my brother Leroy and heal all his wounds. Keep his mind sound and his paths straight. Lend him a hand in need, and forgive his sins as he also asks you to forgive-"

"Yes, Lord Jesus, please forgive my sins and cleanse my wounds."

"Help him to find the perfect place to live, and keep in his heart the people from Hillside Apostolic Church, who love him and only want the best for this man who has fallen. In Jesus' Name, Amen."

"Amen. Thank you Farley, I feel better already."

"Well, here's Oscar coming in. Thomas's leash is on the hook in the kitchen, and keys to the lawn mower are in the drawer under the sink. Help yourself to the coffee if you want.

"I'll walk Thomas now, if that's OK. Do you have a spare house key?"

"There's one in the drawer under the sink as well. I'll see you later, then. Put Thomas back into his enclosure when you get back and be sure you latch the gate. Bye now."

"See you later."

Just then Oscar knocked on the door and Sally let him in, complaining of his lateness.

Swiftly they all got in the car and Farley drove rapidly to the Center. He let Oscar and Sally out and drove on to his job site.

Oscar turned a full circle taking in all the surroundings. The building was modern and well kept. He was nervous about going inside and leaned on Sally.

"Will you help me at the front desk?" asked Oscar.

"Yes, I'll help you with the forms you need to fill out to get started." Sally introduced him at the front desk as a prospective client and asked for application papers.

"Thank you, Sally," said Oscar, loving the feel of her name on his tongue. She was so friendly. "I can take it from here. I'm really good at filling out forms and I'd rather remain private with my information."

Leroy went out to a very excited Thomas who saw his leash and anticipated a walk. Leroy let himself into the enclosure and leashed up the dog. Together they went out and through the yard to the front of the house. Leroy secured his hold on Thomas and out the front gate they went. Thomas was sniffing everything and peed at every stop in front of interesting bushes and the fire hydrants.

Leroy was enjoying himself and decided to head up into the hills where he soon came across the big wooden cross next to the huge pile of stones. Taking his liberties he folded his hands and prayed for his reconstitution and a new start in life. He prayed that God would avenge him and wipe away any traces of guilt and shame. He wanted to be renewed and thought about getting baptized again. After his prayer he put a rock on the big pile and walked on.

Luckily, Thomas had already done his business because Leroy realized he didn't have any plastic bags on him. Thomas was having a thrilling time and spooked a rabbit, which nearly tore Leroy's arm from the socket. Growing more excited, the dog began running circles around Leroy who pivoted on the spot. Having a better idea, Leroy decided to go down to the dog park and let Thomas run free. He was obviously pent up.

They walked together past the Cadwell house again and Leroy looked at it amiably. It was his temporary home. Sally and Farley were such nice people.

It was already twelve-thirty. The sun was getting warm and the back of Leroy's neck was starting to tingle in its heated rays.

Leroy hummed to himself as they walked happily along to the dog park. Once there, Leroy wondered how he would get the dog to come back. He went out on faith and unleashed Thomas, commanding him to "go play!"

Thomas tore off to the center of the field where dogs were meeting and greeting. Leroy sat down on a log and watched the beautiful Rottweiler running and playing with the other dogs. Thomas paused and came dutifully back to Leroy who patted him rewardingly and sent him off again. Thomas was fast, young, and gorgeous. There were two other Rottweiler's but neither one so sleek and fine lined as Thomas. Two hours went by as Leroy utterly shined and breathed deep. It was getting time to go so he called Thomas who came immediately. Leroy hooked the leash onto the exhausted animal and walked him out of the gates of the park onto the road leading back to the Cadwell's house.

All the fresh air was doing Leroy a world of good and his face was slightly sun burned. They trudged along slowly and Thomas walked right next to Leroy. He ignored a cat that crossed the street ahead of them. He was worn out.

They arrived at the house and Leroy obediently put Thomas into his enclosure, taking his water bowl to the hose and filled it up with fresh water. He turned off the hose and carried the full bowl of water to the enclosure and put it inside for the dog, who lapped at it furiously, stopping once to look up to say thank you.

Leroy surveyed the yard and decided to mow the lawn after he had eaten something and had a soda for himself.

At the Mental Health and Wellness Center, Oscar was busy still filling out forms and reading contracts. Sally was in the front office filing and answering the phones. She wondered if he would set up an intake appointment. She saw him go into an office with an agent and prayed for good results.

Out stepped Oscar who blushed when he saw Sally. Oscar went to her and said that he had filled out a mountain of paper work, which he was good at doing, and through his persuasive demeanor had managed to schedule an appointment immediately. He had tears in his eyes as he told her his diagnosis.

"Dr. Nett saw me, and we talked, and he said I'm an untreated schizophrenic with obsessive compulsive tendencies. He wants to be my Doctor, and prescribed me some medicines to start taking immediately."

"Dr. Nett is our Doctor, too," she said, her heart going out to this quivering individual. Oscar needed to fill his prescriptions and then see Dr. Nett at the same time next week. He also wanted Oscar to sign on with a case manager, and that he would be contacted as soon as that got organized.

"He told me to take it easy and not do anything stressful, and to really monitor what the medications are doing for me. Will you go to the pharmacy with me?" He pleaded. This was a lot to swallow.

Sally went to the pharmacy with Oscar and they waited while his prescriptions were filled.

They sat comfortably in a corner and Oscar looked like he wanted to talk but couldn't think of anything to say. Sally was comfortably quiet.

Oscar had the kind of relieved look on his face that someone in dire need would have just rescued from near death. His shoulders were sloped forward with his elbows on his knees. He was outright crying now, blubbering that he had no one to turn to, he was the only surviving member of his family except for a long lost sister named Cordelia.

"Can you try to contact Cordelia?" Sally asked soothingly.

"She's my little sister who lives in Tennessee. I haven't talked to her for years, ever since I became 'repressed'. I've never talked about my voices to anyone before, and that's why God sent me to you," he said in awe.

"You've been through it all, haven't you?" he said respectfully.

"I have lived with a mental illness for many years. After a long time you learn to live with it instead of running from it or fighting against it. Also medications are important. They give you enough control to organize a quality life for yourself. Farley and I are blessed to have each other. But there was a time when the illnesses had to be recognized and validated. I had to learn to take my pills, and succumb to the mental health system. We wanted to marry for many years before we did, before we were both well enough to work. They take your money away, you know, if you get married."

"I'll probably never meet anyone to marry. Not with my mental illness. There. I said it." Oscar said desolately.

"It's only as bad as you make it, Oscar," said Sally. "You have me and Farley and Leroy now. We're your friends and you don't have to hide from us or follow me around. We could have you over for dinner once a week, or something like that, so you can have us to lean on." Sally was being merciful and tender to this aggravated agate from the sea. Oscar was beautiful and awesome in his own lucid manner.

"I promise not to follow you around anymore," he said shyly, "but maybe you could give me your phone number if I need to call and talk," he suggested.

Sally, her heart going out to Oscar agreed to give him their phone number. She wrote it down on a pharmacy card and gave it to Oscar, who smiled.

"Thank you," he said and wrote down his own number on a card to give her, if they ever wanted to call and talk to him for some reason.

The pharmacist called Oscar's name and he went up to receive his medicines. He came proudly back to Sally and showed her what he was going to be taking. A lot of their medicines were the same, including Effexor for depression and Clozaril for an antipsychotic.

Sally asked Oscar if he was aware of the monthly blood draw for clients using Clozaril. He was. The next time was Wednesday early at eight-thirty in the morning. She volunteered to pick him up on their way to blood draw so the three of them could go together.

Now it was time for Sally to sign out. She would walk home with Oscar, and find out where he lived. Leaving the Center, Oscar directed them to his house, a little grey house with cardinal trim. The small yard was overrun, but the path was clear to the door, up the steps.

Sally said goodbye to Oscar and promised to call him later. Oscar waved goodbye and went up to his house. Their two houses were only about five blocks apart. Sally worried and resolved to call Oscar this afternoon.

Sally found Leroy sleeping in a lawn chair next to the lawn mower. She left him to be.

Already worried about her charge, she called Oscar and asked him if he had taken his pills yet, but he hadn't and was glad she had called because he was too nervous to actually do it. "Now go get your medicines, and set them on your kitchen counter. You don't need to hide them, especially now that you need to acknowledge them." Sally was being supportive and motherly.

"OK, now fill yourself a glass of water, and reading the labels on your medicines, take the appropriate dosage for each one with some of your water." She waited. "Did you do it?"

"I have yet to take my Clozaril," he said determinedly. "OK, here goes...." Oscar swallowed and the rest of his medicines went down.

"Now don't panic. Remember these pills are designed to help you. The best thing to do now is to lie down on a couch and be really receptive to the feelings brought on by your medicines. You should feel a relief as your body accepts the help, and know that the longer you take them the more they will be active in you for your schizophrenia."

"Thank you for calling," said Oscar. "I think I'll take a nice long nap and see how I feel when I wake up."

"Don't forget to eat your dinner, Oscar," said Sally, concerned. "And try to plan out your day if you can, remember one thing at a time. Don't get caught up trying to do a bunch of stuff. You need to be gentle with yourself right now. Right?"

"Right. I'll plan my dinner for tonight," said Oscar. "A frozen pizza. And, I'll get a pot of coffee ready to go. Sound good?" Oscar yawned as he gave into his perpetual tiredness. "Can I call you tomorrow?"

"Of course, Oscar, call us anytime day or night. The Center should be calling you soon to make an appointment with your new case manager. Remember, they're there to help you. Bye Oscar."

"Good Bye, Sally– and thank you."

Oscar hung up the phone and went to get his coffee pot ready to go for later. Then he dutifully lay down on the couch and closed his eyes, hugging a pillow. Soon he was asleep.

In his dreams, Oscar rejoiced with his new identity. There was really a name and a way to treat his condition, the horrid perceptions that badgered him continually were going to be quieted. "I am a mentally ill individual who has schizophrenia. That is who I am."

THE WARMTH OF A STRANGER

In necessity He is there. Always aware, never for sure, the meaning of life so spewed from a stranger. Honor. It is a key issue for life, a remembrance for the figures of your unmade equations. Telling for sure would only phase the remembrance, for you felt His presence at the right time and the right place. Oscar was a believer in the Lord Jesus Christ. He had been baptized in the Holy Spirit and received the Holy Ghost. He was saved. But his life had been horrid, helpless, and frightfully demeaning.

Oscar woke up with the Lord Jesus Christ at his side in his head, quietly affirming his thoughts and feelings of aloneness.

He took his liberties and accepted this stranger whom he had worshiped for so long in his Church. Now Jesus Christ was made real. He felt warm and coddled, cared for and relaxed.

Oscar woke up and made himself a pot of coffee, which he consumed happily, feeling his medicines in their first onslaught of the disease of schizophrenia. Sally had told him that they would work better the longer he got on them. In two months he should be feeling their full effects.

This stranger to him, this visitor named Christ had long been trying to help him, but Oscar hadn't been receptive. He thought back on the many times that the Lord had been there. Now his mind was warm with the energy of the Spiritual being. He was afraid to talk, afraid that this stranger would leave if he didn't talk or worship it properly.

He fell on his face on his hands and knees and sent up prayer after thanksgiving prayer for this help in his head, no longer looming with intruders that chased him around.

He poured himself the last of the coffee and allowed the caffeine to relax his brain. Scared to move, he went to the couch again and laid down on it on his back, hugging a pillow.

Sometime later he woke up again and remembered his dinner plan. He cooked the frozen pizza in his oven and ate the whole thing, giving thanks to God for the precious food. He hadn't thought to stock up and would need to get to the grocery store soon. Maybe Sally could take him. That way he could carry more groceries. Full from the pizza, Oscar went to bed, looking forward to taking his second set of pills tomorrow morning. The warmth of Jesus surrounded him and he slept like a baby.

During this afternoon, Farley and Sally had arrived at home and called Oscar, Sally seeing that he took his pills. Leroy was sleeping in the lawn chair with the lawn half mowed.

Farley awakened him and he sat up looking guilty for not having finished the job. Farley said "no worries" and pushed the lawn mower back into the storage room. Leroy could finish the job tomorrow. He seemed agitated and felt blame on himself for the death of Tina. He needed to befriend Oscar, the only witness to his situation. He felt a connection to Oscar and had no idea of what this stranger was up to. He didn't know about Oscar's diagnosis and ensuing pill regimen.

Leroy felt guilty eating the food that Farley and Sally offered him for dinner. It was a big juicy hamburger. He begged them to let him do the dishes but he needed help putting things away. So he washed the dishes and set them out to dry. He put all the extra food covered into the refrigerator, hoping he was doing a good job. His guilt was consuming him.

The three sat in the living room that evening, watching TV as Leroy heard the news concerning Oscar, and he perked up when Sally told him they had exchanged phone numbers. He asked them if they thought Oscar might like a phone call from him. Sally and Farley both thought it was a great idea. They were two friends in need of friends with a bond to their pasts and futures. Leroy wanted to get baptized again and freed from his sins from the past. Definitely next Sunday he would recommit his life to Christ and allow himself to be baptized. He wondered if Oscar was baptized. He looked forward to calling Oscar tomorrow.

Sally informed him that she would call him as well to make sure he took his morning pills. She wanted to keep track of him to make sure there was no fall through, that he would not miss a dose or more.

Leroy asked Sally if he could talk to Oscar after she was done with him. She replied that this would be a fine idea. Oscar needed to be surrounded by people who cared. Now that his "stalking" behavior had been justified, she felt only concern and sympathy for the young man. She hoped he would call her as well. She wanted to stay on the same page as him.

Farley was surprised at how clean the kitchen was after Leroy had cleaned up. Leroy had also promised to finish mowing the yard tomorrow.

It was time to let Thomas in and feed and water him, so Leroy volunteered to get him, having bonded with the big dog today on their walk and the time at the dog park. He let Thomas out of his enclosure and said "heel", and Thomas walked with him to the house yearning for his food and the friendship of his masters.

Farley provided food for Thomas and filled his water bowl as well. Thomas ate voraciously, wagging his stumped tail excitedly. When he was done he jogged into the living room and occupied a couch. Leroy took the chair, and Farley and Sally took the other couch. They all watched the TV, a scientific documentary on the Brazilian rain forests.

Farley thanked Leroy for all his work in the kitchen, and Leroy ignored the comment, as though he hadn't heard. Then he thought of Oscar, the warmth of a stranger, and accepted the compliment grudgingly. He could do no wrong in Jesus' eyes, yet the guilt he carried caused him to be overly protective of himself and of strangers. Farley and Sally were practically strangers to him, and he couldn't stop thinking about Tina and his wasted brother, Simon.

He had been helpless to stop his brother from killing his potential soul mate. His heart was raw and open, bleeding with thoughts of failure and condemnation. Everything about him was wrong. He could do no right in his own eyes, so he tried to do everything perfectly. Mistakenly thinking that Sally and Farley wanted to be alone, he opted to go to bed early and rest up for the next day. He dreamed of bloody hands on a window, trying to get out, wiping the blood back and forth, stressed and victimized.

He pictured himself going down a chimney and slowly roasted to death as his body got stuck three or four feet above the flames. Neither could he get out of the top. Then the chimney exploded and he flew out into the universe where a mermaid rescued him in her water loving arms.

He felt warm and exotic with this strange apparition and puzzled himself about the Universe and life on other planets.

The rest of his night was uneventful, and he woke mercifully in the morning sunrays that flowed through the curtains on his bedroom window. He cried to himself and sobbed about his aloneness. He didn't want Sally and Farley to see him this way, but he knew he needed to keep going with his life, believing it would get better. He arose and put on his bathrobe, going out to the kitchen, where no one had been yet, but the dishes were put away and he felt guilty again.

Leroy prepared the coffee pot and turned it on. He found cereal and milk for breakfast and taking his liberties, he helped himself to an apple and two bananas. The coffee was excellent and enlightened his mind with the surge of caffeine.

Thomas whined, coming into the kitchen, so Leroy let the big dog outside. He wondered about Oscar and was worried for him. What must he be experiencing, starting on new medications for a newly detected mental illness, the horrid reality of schizophrenia?

After eating his breakfast, Leroy went out into the backyard where Thomas was doing his business. Leroy took his liberties and retrieving a plastic bag from the kitchen closet he went out to pick up after Thomas so the lawn would be ready to mow.

Feeling high on energy, Leroy pulled out the lawn mower and went to work on the rest of the yard that he hadn't finished yesterday. Back and forth, he went, filling up the catcher with freshly mowed grass. Leroy not only finished the job, but dumped all the grass into a compost pile and raked the yard to get all the freshly cut grass into the compost pile.

For once he felt satisfied, a job well done. He put the mower away and prided himself on his perfectionist project. He craved more coffee and wanted to walk Thomas again like he had yesterday. The warmth of a stranger he felt in the dog was gradually filling into the warmth of a friend.

Sally yelled "good morning" to him from the back door and told him there was fresh coffee. They had read his mind. Leroy had washed his dishes and left them out to dry. He had put the cereal box away. Only his coffee mug remained unwashed, ready for more.

Leroy called Thomas to the door where Farley had already put his breakfast and fresh water. Leroy gaily skipped through the grass to the door and entered the kitchen. "How did you sleep?" He asked them together. Sally and Farley had both slept well and asked him what time he got up.

"I think I got up around six o'clock," he replied and told them he had helped himself to cereal for breakfast and some fruit. He asked Sally to let him know when she planned to call Oscar.

Sally told him she would call around nine o'clock in about a half hour.

Leroy boastfully told them that he'd finished the lawn and picked up after Thomas.

They all sat around the kitchen table and drank coffee. It was quiet. Farley thanked Leroy for doing such a good job on the lawn.

Leroy orbited with self-praise. He had done well. Farley started cooking eggs and bacon, so Leroy told him he had already eaten cereal. Farley would prepare breakfast for himself and Sally.

"I'll just have more coffee, thanks," he said

"No bacon?"

"Well, I could have a slice or two of bacon," said Leroy, feeling hungry after mowing the yard.

"Well, I could have a couple of eggs, too," he said coyly. They all giggled, and Leroy accepted a helping of hash browns as well.

"You need to eat to keep your strength up, Leroy," Farley said absent-mindedly. He sipped on his coffee as he made breakfast for them all.

"I was wondering if I could walk Thomas again today. You know, it would get me out and about so I don't sit at home and worry myself sick," he pleaded. He considered Thomas a friend.

"I don't mind if you take him for a walk. You just need to be prepared for an occasional lunge, if he sees something interesting."

"I think it's a great idea," said Sally. "Thomas needs his exercise."

"Thomas is such a good dog," mused Leroy.

"He has a grudge against Oscar. Maybe that's just temporary," Farley said in a weird tone. They had been suspicious about Oscar for a long time, and figured that Thomas had sensed their being ill at ease with the presence of him.

"I'm going to call Oscar right now," said a worried Sally.

"No," said Farley, "You're going to eat breakfast first. Remember to put yourself first and you'll stay out of trouble. Besides, I'm almost done here and we need to thank God for this food. Is three eggs OK, Leroy?"

"I suppose I could eat three eggs, two slices of bacon and a serving of hash browns." Leroy admitted.

"That's more like it," said Farley.

He served up the three plates and put them on the table in front of their chairs. Thomas got up and went outside to run around the yard. Sally, Farley, and Leroy ate in silence after thanking the Lord for their food.

Sally was miffed and a little bit worried about Oscar, which made Farley agitated. Oscar was unpredictable. He was a big unknown.

So he had schizophrenia and had just learned about that. They wondered how long he had gone untreated. They prayed that his medicines would kick in and work for him.

Farley and Sally each took Clozaril for their primary antipsychotic. Upon trying it, they had both improved markedly.

Their morning pills were on the kitchen counter, and they remembered to take those with their orange juice. Leroy asked for a second glass of orange juice and they offered it to him.

"It's sure good you guys don't have allergies," said Leroy "Especially since I just mowed your lawn. I remember that Simon had bothersome allergies every spring. He would sneeze and cough horribly with runny eyes and nose. I don't know why I brought him up, I'm sorry," he said apologetically. He needed to cover up his true feelings. He loved his brother but hated him more and this made him feel guilty.

"Let's not talk about Simon," countered Sally. "Unless you need to vent about him, I can understand that, and we're here to listen," she spoke for herself and Farley.

"I just feel so bad for Sandra, being pregnant with his child."

"I can't believe that Tina is gone." Sally choked. "We were just becoming good friends. She loved you, Leroy."

"Poor Oscar being strung along like that by Simon who I imagine was trying to be his friend. He must have had a huge guilt complex, yet a certain uncertainty that provoked him to rape like he did, and then to finally kill. You saw it all, Leroy. I wonder if it weighs heavy on you," Farley spoke gently.

"I still can't believe it's true. Thank you guys so much for letting me stay here till I find a place. I feel rotten. Maybe we should call Oscar now. He's probably up and around. I feel a need to talk to him." Leroy changed the subject.

"I'll call while you guys clean up. Is that all right?" Spoke Sally.

"Yes."

"Yes." Leroy moved to clear the plates from the table and thanked Farley again for making him breakfast. Then he asked Farley if he should make another pot of coffee.

Farley was in agreement with that, and started to dry the dishes as Leroy washed and handed them to him.

Meanwhile, Sally had called Oscar and only gotten his voice mail. She had left a message but was more concerned than before. "Maybe we should go visit him," Sally said to Leroy.

Farley snarled but did not forbid it.

So they agreed, and after calling again in a half hour with no success, they decided to drive to Oscar's house and check on him. Sally and Farley had to go to work, but the sacrifice of being late was worth knowing the wellbeing of Oscar.

Farley agreed it was the right thing to do. He might need the warmth of a stranger right about now.

Sally and Leroy got into the little Fiat and sped off in the direction of Oscar's little house. They pulled up to the front and stopped and got out.

Up the path they went to the door and rang the bell. "Just a minute!" They heard a call.

The locked door clicked as Oscar unlocked it and he opened wide when he saw who was there.

"Hello, Oscar," both Sally and Leroy said together. "Did you get your messages? I tried to call you twice," said Sally.

"I got your messages," Oscar spoke ethereally. I was on a walk around the neighborhood. I couldn't just stay at home and do nothing. Besides I wanted to try out my new medications. I took them this morning and started talking silly to myself so I left the house and came back later.

"You had us scared."

"I called you back but you had already left. Farley said you were on your way over. I couldn't stop you. I thought you might call this morning but I had to get out."

"Do you have afternoon pills?"

"No, just morning and bedtime."

"You took your morning pills?"

"Honey, I wouldn't miss them for the world. Finally someone, some*thing* is helping me." His words were deep and profound.

Sally found she had little to say, so decided to depart. "We'll see you later, Oscar," she said happily. "I'm glad you're doing well. Remember to call anytime. I'm sure Leroy would like to spend some time with you, wouldn't you, Leroy," she said suggestively speaking.

"Yes, Oscar, I would love to spend some time with you. If you can get over your fear of Thomas, I'd like to go walking with him and you together. We could talk and walk."

"He's a happy dog, now that he doesn't have to wear that cone around his head anymore," Sally spoke, having made a trip to the vet four days ago to have it removed.

"Well, maybe," Oscar said shyly. "Would you like to meet for coffee downtown?"

"Yes, well, I need the exercise and so does Thomas, but I guess I could walk him downtown from the Cadwells' place. How about the Turnip Bay Coffee Shop?"

"Sure, I'll try it. Do you want to meet, say, three hours from now?" Oscar was unsteady but willing to step out.

"How about one-thirty?"

"One-thirty is good for me.

"Well, it's all settled then. You two have your thing downtown today with Thomas, and maybe you guys could hit the dog park as well," said Sally. "Be very gentle with yourself, Oscar. If something seems too hard then don't do it. Are you ready to go home, Leroy?" she asked in a friendly voice. He needed some coddling, she could tell. "Farley and I have to go to work, so I'll drop you off and pick him up and he'll drive me to work and then go on from there. Let's go!"

Leroy was reluctant to leave, but looked forward to meeting Oscar with Thomas later that day.

Leroy and Sally climbed into the car and she drove them home. There was Farley, sitting on the front porch. He got up quickly and in passing Leroy, he reminded him to lock the house up good if he went walking with Thomas. Leroy nodded and wished him a good day.

Sally told Farley about Oscar being on a walk while she had called. They were about an hour late for work, each and decided to eat that cake when they got to it.

Farley lovingly dropped his wife off at work and went on to his job site. Sally rather liked her job. It wasn't strenuous, and it kept her mind alive. She had good organizational skills and fit right in. She explained to her boss about Oscar and was immediately excused, counting this time as fieldwork.

Farley didn't need to explain. He just had to get to work and his job was not as forgiving as Sally's.

The day had begun and the morning flew by and soon it was two o'clock, when Sally decided to clock out having caught up on all the work to be done.

She enjoyed the fresh air as she began her walk home, wondering if Leroy and Thomas were still there. She breathed deeply and walked at a fast pace to get more exercise. It took less than half an hour before she got home and walked in the front yard, letting herself in through the front door.

She looked suspiciously all around the house, even into Leroy's bedroom and he was not there. The kitchen was immaculate, and the coffee pot was all set to go.

Sally looked out the back door but Thomas was not in his enclosure. She relaxed and sat down in a chaise lounge by his gate. The sun felt good on her face and her achy back rested gratefully in the chair.

There was nothing she needed to do so she decided to take a nap for a couple of hours before going inside to read her Bible.

Downtown at the Turnip Bay Coffee Shop, Leroy was waiting for Oscar to show up. He had gotten there at one-thirty and ordered a latte', choosing to sit at an outdoor table. Two o'clock passed and instead of growing antsy, Leroy relaxed, believing that Oscar would show up.

At two-fifteen, he spied Oscar walking toward him from down the street to the left. Thomas picked up his scent and lumbered to his feet, relaxed but sniffing the wind. It was Oscar. He began to pant heavily and looking at Leroy he whined.

"Be good, Thomas," said Leroy, "It's only Oscar. You know Oscar don't you? He was at the house with us a couple of days ago." Oscar neared them and froze at sight of the huge dog.

"Hi Thomas. Nice boy," he said as he approached slowly. Leroy got up and went to Oscar and shook his hand as Thomas looked around worriedly. He stayed calm and lay down by the table again as Oscar took the liberty to pet his massive head and pat his heaving side. "Good Thomas," he said as persuasively as he could.

"How are you?" Oscar asked Leroy and pulled up a chair, Thomas no longer an issue.

"I've been waiting forty-five minutes. What took you so long?"

Oscar hung his head deplorably and admitted he had had a panic attack and couldn't leave when he wanted to. It was by sheer determination that he had managed to get himself out of the house at all.

"I'm sorry, Oscar," Leroy spoke compassionately. "I've never had one of those, but I hear they're terrible. How is your new medication working?"

"It's all right, I guess. It's curbing a lot of my voices that tell me to hurt people. I've had that fight for so long, because I really don't want to hurt anyone. I have a soft heart."

"How long did you know my brother, Simon?" Questioned Leroy. He was searching for closure.

"I met Simon last spring in Church. We always sat next to each other and just sort of struck up a friendship. I would say we were friends, but I didn't know about his vicious, violent side. When I step back, I see that he was using me as a way to curb his guilt."

"I hate him. I just hate him so much," said Leroy resolutely.

"I can understand. I'm not a dumb man, but I do feel I was strung along unfairly. My mental illness made it hard for me to judge character, and analytically speaking, I just wanted a friend."

Oscar stood up and went to the cashier to order a latte'. He liked it with hazelnut and no foam. Considering his tiredness from all that worrying at home, he splurged for a triple shot drink. Coffee always calmed him down.

Thomas lay under the table with his head between his front paws. He was patient, quiet, and sympathetic. He was over his grudge with Oscar.

Oscar came back to the table with his coffee and sat down again across from Leroy.

"What did it sound like to you, when you heard Tina scream for help?"

"It sounded like someone was in trouble, not as if in a game like Simon said. "She sounded desperate and helpless. If I think about it that's how it sounded."

"Why did you come to the door?"

"I was worried that something was wrong, but Simon told me otherwise so I left with plans to meet him for Bible study on the weekend."

"Did you believe him? Or were you suspicious?"

"I just took his words at face value. It seemed the right thing to do."

"I was going to marry Tina," Leroy said quietly.

"You have my condolences."

"Have you ever liked a girl, Oscar?" Leroy made conversation.

"Many times, but I'm always too shy to make a move, so here I am, alone with myself. I'm thinking of getting a dog, but I don't think the timing is right."

"I've never loved anyone as much as I loved Tina. And she was such a Godly woman. We studied the Bible together. We never fornicated. We were going to marry. Now I feel like a bullet hit my chest and stole my life away from me. Simon is such a bastard. He had me shackled for such a long time."

"You know, Leroy, speaking of girls, I've had my eye on Sandra Naden for a long time. She's not like the other girls. She's quiet, and steadfast."

"You know about Sandra and Simon, don't you? She's pregnant with his child."

"She'll probably never trust a man again. How can I let her know my intentions; I just want to get to know her a little, and be there for her."

"You're a handsome man, Oscar, with lots of good inside of you. Look at Thomas, he's totally trusting you."

Oscar reached down and patted Thomas' back. The dog lifted his head and put it down again.

"Do you think that Sandra might go over the edge, commit suicide?"

"That's where you come in. You can befriend her, now that you're friends with the Cadwell's, she'll see that you're a good guy. Let it be known that you have a mental illness just like Sally and Farley do. They're good people, and so are you. Have you ever talked to Sandra?"

"I've said 'Hi' to her a couple of times and every now and then she shakes my hand. How do I get her to notice me?"

"I think you need to make a point of greeting her every service, and maybe try sitting next to her, or near her. I'll sit with you, Oscar, so you won't feel all alone."

"What if she hates you because you're Simon's brother?"

"That's a risk to take and overcome. Look at Thomas. He's over come his adversity to you. Dog's are good judges of character."

"Have you heard about Mae and James? I think Sandra is staying with them right now, because she needs all kinds of care. That includes medical, social, religious affirmation in Christ, and emotional support. I was just going to mention that Mae is pregnant, and she and James are getting married in February."

"Oh how scandalous," chided Leroy. His situation was so much more detrimental.

"You're right. It's not such a big deal than when you think of Sandra's rape pregnancy. She needs the Church to love on her for healing; Mae needs loving as well from the Church. She needs support and acceptance. Simon is such a two-faced piece of crap. He worshiped in Church like he really loved the Lord, excitedly. Then outside of Church he raped Church sisters. I can't calculate how someone could do that."

"Does Jesus hate him?"

"He rejects him."

"Let's just say he has a lot of Hell before him."

"It's courageous to talk like this. I trust you, Leroy, and I know you're in trouble with yourself, which worries me. I need you to turn to me when you can. I'll catch your fall, brother, I won't let you die."

"I am a miserable wreck. I need love and support and acceptance now too. I need to talk to the Pastor for some insight into my situation. I don't want to be sucked in to Simon. That loser can't keep me out of Heaven, can he?"

"Only if you take your own life. Be very careful with yourself, and it all starts with forgiveness. Forgive Simon, forgive yourself, forgive God, and pray for mercy and healing. There is no magic wand to make everything better just like that (Oscar snaps his fingers).

"I feel so angry and cheated. I feel like I betrayed myself and everybody else by keeping Simon's secret. Do you think the Pastor is mad at me?"

"Of course not. He understands; he loves you."

"Do you want more coffee?" Oscar asked politely. Oscar was thinking about Sandra and how to get her to notice him. The Cadwell's were the pivoting point, and Mae and James. If he could only somehow arrange for a get together with all of the above, he might have a chance to talk to her.

Leroy declined the offer for coffee, but made no move to get up. Time had flown by and it was already four o'clock. Then he remembered that he was staying with the Cadwell's; no longer did he live with his tyrant brother Simon. A depression had flowed over him and passed. Suddenly he brightened. "How would you like to go to the dog park with me? We could watch Thomas run and play."

Oscar perked up more. He had never been to the dog park and it sounded fun. So the two young men got up and left, Thomas walking between them.

It was not far, and they enjoyed the late afternoon sun and saw it reflect off of the water. The south end of Washington Park was fenced off for dogs to run free. Thomas grew excited and pulled a little as they got close to the park. Once there, Leroy released him from the lead, and they watched as the dog ran away into the middle of the park and played with the other dogs.

Oscar was in awe. He'd never seen so many dogs together. Thomas came back to them as if to ask permission to play, and then ran wildly across the park and around it, running, running, just running. He snorted and sniffed and played with other dogs. He ran himself crazy and stopped to drink from the water faucet.

Oscar and Leroy sat and watched in amazement. They were quiet, both of them in deep thought. Oscar spoke up and said he should be getting home to rest up. It had been a successful day on the new medicines, despite his earlier panic attack.

So Leroy called Thomas, who came right away and allowed him to hook up the leash. "I'll walk with you to your turn off, OK?"

"Sounds good," said Oscar.

They walked together through the streets to the intersection where their paths separated. They shook hands and hugged one another, pledging to see each other in Church the next night. They wished each other well and went their separate ways.

Oscar went home and lay down on the couch in his living room, feeling the blood pump through his head.

Leroy walked onward to his temporary home at the Cadwell's and went in through the front gate, walking to the backyard where he put Thomas in his enclosure and made sure he had enough water. The Fiat was in the driveway, so he surmised that both Farley and Sally were home.

He went and knocked on the back door, which Farley opened and welcomed him into the kitchen where there were steaks on the grill.

"I'm making a steak for you, too, said Farley. "I figured you'd be getting home soon. How was your day?"

"It was a pretty good day," Leroy said, and told how he had met Oscar downtown at the Coffee Shop, and that they'd all gone together to the dog park before coming home again. "Thomas is very well behaved," he said, "and he seems to have gotten over his grudge against Oscar. Which is a miracle because it says a lot about Oscar's character. If Thomas trusts him, I think I can too."

"I got home and fell asleep in the backyard until Farley got home and woke me up about a half hour ago. Just a relaxing day for me!" Sally cheerfully recounted her day. "But I can't be late for work again unless it's an emergency like today. My boss chalked it up to 'field work'."

"I had a physically demanding day, and I don't want to talk about it," said Farley, and they all laughed.

Now the steaks were done and Sally had made a nice green salad with avocadoes and raisins. Out of the oven, Farley brought three steaming baked potatoes and set the table, giving everyone their share. There was shredded cheese and guacamole, sour cream, and chopped tomatoes to put on the potatoes. They all sat down to eat and thanked God for the meal. Leroy felt a tear in his eye with this unconditional love.

He felt accepted here. He felt welcome. Farley and Sally were good people to take him in. But he knew he needed to find his own apartment soon. Maybe he could look on the East side, far away from his old downtown apartment that reeked of blood and Clorox. The smell of blood is so grounding. It poisons the soul. Luckily the blood was not on his hands. He should have been able to save her. He had been so helpless.

Those last gasping, gargling noises from Tina were haunting him. He hated his brother, hated him so much.

He would never go to visit him in prison. He never wanted to set eyes on that fiend again.

Still, he blamed himself. He blamed himself for hiding his brother's secret raping and for putting up a normal façade for them. If only he had lived on his own, away from his brother, he could have had a normal relationship with Tina. They were so in love. It bereaved him to consider her death.

Farley got up and began to clear the table, as they all were done eating. Leroy offered to help, but Farley declined his offer and shooed him off to the living room where he could watch TV and relax. Sally joined him as they watched Animal Planet, a series of "I Shouldn't Be Alive". They marveled at the dire straits of the characters and what it took for them to come out alive. Leroy enjoyed the suspense and depth of the situations they were in.

Sally got up and went to the office where she wrote in her journal. She wanted to give Leroy his space, and he might like it better to hang out with Farley so things weren't so awkward.

With Farley's consent, he went out and got Thomas and brought him inside. Thomas took an entire couch, so Farley took the chair and let Leroy have the other couch.

They watched the news for a short time and ended up watching Rocky IV. The two men were quiet and absorbed the movie to their liking. Sally came out after awhile and joined them for the company, sitting next to Leroy who felt safer with both of them around.

Things were awkward, but growing more comfortable as they let down their expectations and grew in acceptance of each other. They did not judge one another and avoided direct questioning. Unconditional acceptance began to grow as the Lord had brought them together for a reason. Leroy needed to heal, and there was no better place for him to be right now.

Leroy began to make conversation about Church and Oscar and Sandra, and the interest that lay there on Oscar's part. "He really likes her," said Leroy. He's hoping to get to know her, and feels like the best way would be through you two, if you had a gathering and invited just a few people over. Like Mae and James, Sandra, maybe Stacy, too, you're brother Gilmore, and Oscar and me. That would be a casual get together, wouldn't it?"

"That's a great idea, Leroy. We could have a barbeque outside in the back yard, have some music, and cook hamburgers and hot dogs for everyone. Perhaps someone could provide beverages, and you and Mae could make cup cakes or cookies for dessert, Sally. I know you love to bake and you're always successful in whatever you attempt to make. Like your German Chocolate Cake that you made last week."

"That's the last time I saw Tina," Sally wept. "We had espresso here and that chocolate cake. Oh how I miss her."

"I think we all miss her," said Farley. "In getting together, we could all celebrate her life. It could be a ceremony!" cried Farley. "Why not ask Pastor Williams and the first Lady as well?"

"That's a great idea, Farley," said Sally. Sister Williams is just the person we need to reach out for us. She's so compassionate and loving, accepting and benevolent. She's also very wise about relationships and other peoples' feelings."

"Well, let's do it," said Leroy. "How can I help?"

"You can be our go-between for Oscar, so that Sally isn't constantly worrying about taking care of him. You need to nurture your relationship with Oscar so he'll be comfortable here for the get together. You can help him come open about his mental illness, just like Sally and I have." Farley was contemplative. "You need to be his friend, Leroy. Oscar doesn't have anyone else, even though he's starting to get services now for his hidden mental illness. He has a long healing process to go through."

"Oscar is very shy," noted Sally.

Leroy was jumping up and down in his excitement for the barbeque. It would be edifying for everyone involved. And it was a good mixture of people, including Gilmore and his fiancé, who would be marrying in two weeks. Farley was desperately eager to find out who his brother was hiding in his wings.

"Do you guys want popcorn?" Asked Sally.

Both Leroy and Farley answered positively and melted into the cushions that they sat on. Sally went into the kitchen and pulled out the popcorn maker. She took down a jar of kernels and poured them into the apparatus, plugging it in over a big bowl as butter melted in the cap of the maker. It was done fast and pouring the butter on with a little salt, she took the bowl into the living room and passed it around, taking her turn as the bowl went from person to person around the room.

"Thank you, Sally," said Farley, and Leroy concurred.

There was a peace in the living room as each one of them relaxed in thought and paid attention to the movie.

They sat there entertained, and as the bowl now held a few stray corn kernels, Leroy got up to dump them out and washed the bowl, putting it in the strainer.

Sally and Farley had a few words while Leroy was in the kitchen. They both agreed that he was hurting still, and disoriented. He needed compassion, and help finding his own place.

"When did you want to start looking for a place, Leroy?" asked Farley a little later when they were both in the kitchen getting pop out of the refrigerator.

"Oh, soon," rattled Leroy, not expecting the question. "If I could stay here while I looked that would be great. I'm not a nuisance, am I?" pined Leroy.

"Not at all. Look, you've mowed the lawn, done dishes, suggested a party, and exercised our dog in the time you've been here. I would hardly call you a nuisance. No. You're certainly welcome here while you search for your own place. It will come when you're ready. Have you thought about moving in with Oscar? Maybe he would like the company. You two seem to be kindred spirits."

"That's an awesome idea, Farley," said Leroy, astonished. "Maybe I'll ask him tomorrow. We can walk Thomas again, if that's all right with you."

"That's a big help, because that dog really needs regular exercise, and Sally and I work during the week so there's not a lot of time for walking Thomas, except on weekends. What do you think, should we plan the barbeque for this Saturday? Sally could get in touch with Mae and Sandra and Pastor Williams and his wife, Sister Williams. I'll call Gil', and you invite Oscar. Maybe Stacy would like to come as well, as a support for Sandra."

Leroy was nodding with relief. He wasn't a bother. Tomorrow he would call Oscar and see if he wanted to meet up again. He would bring up the idea of possibly moving in together. Maybe Oscar would be all for it. It would be edifying for the both of them, now in need of a friend through this saturation issue of the ugliness performed by Simon and his artificial friendship with Oscar. Oscar needed to learn how to trust, and there was no one better than Leroy now who could teach him to depend on others again.

The movie was over at midnight so they all turned in to bed and got ready for the next day as sleep sifted everything gently down into the reality of gold at the end of the rainbow. God cared greatly about his apostles and the saints. Hillside Apostolic Church had been hit with a grenade. The bomb was Simon and his lecherous, villainous actions, his murdering God-awful behavior. Now it was time to come together and heal.

The night was long and restful for everyone. They all got up in the morning around eight o'clock, and took showers, this time Sally having the cold water being the third one to shower. They laughed about it. Farley's turn would be next!

The kitchen was a theater of coffee, morning tea, eggs, bacon, and hash browns. This time Sally and Farley got ready for work and left on time. Leaving Leroy in the house to call Oscar and make sure he was taking his medications religiously. He was responsible for giving Thomas his breakfast and fresh water, so as the dog patiently waited, Leroy put food in his bowl and scrubbed out his water bowl, filling it with fresh water.

Thomas ate like a good boy, and lapped at his water. Leroy kept the kitchen door open to the back yard and let the dog go run and play in the yard while he got ready to call Oscar. He wanted to bring up the roommate issue.

First he helped himself to the last of the coffee and sat on the back steps watching Thomas as he chased around the yard and relieved himself by the apple tree.

Leroy sighed and reflected on his situation. His skin crawled when he thought of his brother and the unfairness he had lived with. There was one obvious truth. Tina was dead. He wondered if they ever recovered her body. He thought about all the bottles of Clorox and the ten beach towels he had bought at the drug store. He remembered cleaning out the bathtub, and the alienation he had felt from that moment on.

He looked at his chest and found the cigarette burn. He remembered lighting his shirt on fire, only to strip it off when the flames burned him. It had burned out on its own.

He decided to stop smoking. He had quit before, many times, but this time he was adamant. Oscar could help him with that. Oscar. It was time to call Oscar. First he put Thomas in his enclosure and then went into the house, shutting the door behind him. He washed out the coffee pot and made a new pot. He dried all the dishes and put them away. He thought about calling Pastor Williams first, and decided that was a good idea. He had the number memorized and dialed it quickly before changing his mind.

The phone rang and Pastor Williams answered it on his cell phone. Leroy was nervous and wasn't sure why he had called. He related that to the Pastor who told him to calm down and take a deep breath.

"How can I help you, Leroy?" He asked kindly.

"Pastor, I'm all mixed up and staying with the Cadwell's right now. It's working out, but I don't want to put them out, if you know what I mean? I'm thinking of asking Oscar to move in with him as a roommate and I mean to call him but I thought to call you first."

"Are you all right, Leroy? Are you a danger to yourself?" The Pastor was concerned and had great insight.

"I don't think I'm a danger to myself, but my road right now is so rocky I'm afraid I might fall off. I don't want to be in a dungeon, but part of me thinks I need to punish myself for letting Tina die. It's my fault. I know it's my fault. She shouldn't have been there. I shouldn't have allowed her near my brother. It's her fault too, and I'm really mad at her for leaving me. –"

"No, no, no," chided Pastor Williams, "It's no one's fault but the devil. Satan was in him. Just like he was in Judas who betrayed Jesus. He must have found a comfy nest in Simon, who will pay dearly for his transgressions. It's not your fault, Leroy," Pastor Williams said in his heartfelt manner. It's definitely not Tina's fault, so don't let yourself think that." The Pastor counseled truly and helped to ease Leroy's mind.

"Will I be seeing you in Church tonight?" Leroy remembered it was Wednesday and Church would be meeting this evening like it always did.

"Oh yes, Pastor! Thank you for reminding me that was tonight. I knew there was a reason that I called you. Thank you, you have helped to ease my mind." Leroy hung up after a few more words and got up the courage to call his Church brother, Oscar.

He dialed the number that Sally had left by the phone. Oscar answered on his cell phone and was delighted to hear from Leroy, who took a deep breath and relaxed as he realized he was welcome.

"Did you take your pills last night and this morning? Sally made sure that I would ask you that."

Oscar spoke quietly, saying that he had taken pills last night and this morning.

"That's good," said Leroy. There was an awkward silence until Leroy blurted out a suggestion. "Do you want to walk Thomas today again? We could meet at the coffee shop again and then go to the dog park afterwards if you want to."

Oscar was definitely interested and adamantly agreed to the prospect. "Do you want to meet me at my house and go from there together?"

Leroy agreed readily and then reminded Oscar about Church tonight. "Maybe we can all go with Sally and Farley if they drive. Neither you nor I drive, but if worst came to worst, we could always walk to Church together. I need a friend Oscar, and I think you're it."

"Why don't you meet me here in a half hour or so. Then we could walk to town together with Thomas."

"That sounds great."

"OK, I'll see you soon."

"OK, Bye."

Both parties hung up the phone in anticipation, and Leroy went outside to leash up Thomas. He could pick up after Thomas later when they got back. For now, he started walking to Oscar's house. He kicked himself and wished he had brought a Bible, but then thought better of it and decided they could use one of Oscar's if they wanted to.

The air was fresh and warm, and leaves were starting to turn color. Leroy thought of Sandra and Mae and James. He didn't know where they lived, but Sally did, and she could do the outreach for the barbeque on Saturday.

Leroy stepped lightly and Thomas trotted gingerly next to him. The whispering wind was beginning to blow powerfully, and Leroy looked at the trees around him swaying violently, almost magically in a rhythm that spoke of "Onward Christian Soldiers…"

Leroy began marching down the sidewalk and turned a circle so Thomas went around with him. He was panting and looked at Leroy expectantly. All the wind and excitement served to capture Leroy's imagination and kept him from thinking morbid thoughts. He remembered where Oscar lived and took the left turn that would lead to his house.

Leroy was eager to see his friend Oscar, and anticipated a good day. He heard him before he saw him.

"Hi Friend!" Cried Oscar from his front porch.

"Good morning Oscar!" Yelled Leroy and walked to and up the stairs that lead to the front porch.

"You be careful with that dog, Leroy," said Oscar. "I'm not sure he likes me very much."

Leroy kept Thomas on a tight lead, and the dog sat down, looking about his surroundings like a duck on a lily pad. He was very well-behaved and even laid down at Oscar's feet, smelling his shoes and gazing up to this perplexing man.

"Hey, maybe he does like me!" Oscar was excited and reached down to pat Thomas who rolled over onto his back, begging for attention. So Oscar kneeled down and scratched his chest and his belly, and under his "arm pits". He scratched him and rubbed him all over until finally Thomas got up and jumped up on Oscar, who hugged the big dog and then told him to stay down. He kept petting the dog's head and patting his side. Thomas sat and stared at Oscar.

"Well, how are you?" Asked Leroy in the pressing silence.

"I'm doing really well," Oscar said with no pretenses. "I've been adjusting to my medicines and observing how they effect my moods and my thinking. I think I'm noticing a lot of positive changes, but I haven't put them to use yet, not in a public situation. You know we have Church tonight, right? You'd better leave in time to get Thomas home before it's time to go. Or like you said, I could go home with you and we could all go together in Farley and Sally's car. Doesn't that sound nice? And we could sit together, all of us in Church, and maybe Sandra will sit with us and Mae and James. What do you think?"

"Sounds good to me. So you have feelings for Sandra?"

"I have for a long time. I just don't know how to talk to her. What if she doesn't like me?"

"There's only one way to find out. You're sort of the band-aid in this situation. You're the one keeping everyone sane."

"You really think so? You mean there's some good in me after all?"

"I feel like you in a way, Oscar, I feel like I can't find good in myself and killing Tina was all my fault."

Suddenly Leroy gagged and choked, coughing and spitting as he tried to be rid of the ugly feelings within himself.

Oscar remained quiet. "I'm a good person and so are you," he said finally. "We're not responsible for the garbage inside of us. We need to learn to let it go. Own it, and then throw it away. Don't put it on other people. They aren't deserving of that. That's one reason why self-control is so important. Keeping busy helps. Every energetic or creative thing you do burns away negative energy, and you're filled with a lightness of being."

Leroy nodded and shook his head violently, gasping and coughing hoarsely. He wanted to vomit, but couldn't.

"Let's go in the house, Leroy," said Oscar. Too many bugs out here." They went inside with Thomas and only then did Leroy remember his idea about moving in with Oscar. He looked around himself. Everything was neat and orderly, stuff put away, and TV off in the front room corner.

"How many bedrooms do you have?" asked Leroy.

"I've got two bedrooms and two bathrooms, a kitchen, living room, laundry room, office and crawl space. All neat and decent, why?

"I was going to ask if you would mind me moving in with you, for awhile, until circumstances change and I'm no longer a threat to myself, or anyone else for that matter."

"Hmmm. I think that's a really good idea. I could use some sympathy and support myself. I'm easy to live with and get along well with the people I know, and there aren't too many of those."

"I'm easygoing as well," said Leroy, "and I know we're both in Christ. Maybe this was meant to be." Leroy spoke sadly at his loss but he was beginning to heal. Slowly up that long mountain of wellness he must go. Perhaps he could find counseling at the mental health center where Oscar had started to find help. Leroy didn't think he had a mental illness. Maybe he was suffering from Post Traumatic Stress Disorder.

All he knew was that he was very lost and mixed up inside. Killing Tina over and over in his mind, as though it was all his fault. Over and over again he heard her gaggling and coughing to her death. He saw the flash of the knife, the quick, cruel stroke, and he only came out of it when he saw the knife in his brother's hand, not his own.

"Do you think it would be OK?" Leroy asked Oscar.

"Not just OK, but a lot of fun and freedom for us both. Let us take our liberties and move in together and laugh and have fun and cry and be there for each other. You're nothing like your sibling, Simon; he was deceitful and perverted. I like you because you aren't a control freak or pushy in any way."

"That reminds me, Oscar," said Leroy, "there's a barbeque going to be on Saturday at Farley and Sally's house. You're invited and you could be my guest of honor, since I'm still living there. Sandra might be there too, and I could help to introduce you to her.

"That sounds like a good idea. You can count me in. Now that this dog knows me, he might let me be in the yard!"

Oscar offered Leroy a cup of coffee, and it worked, they got along well. Leroy washed his own mug, and knew it was time to go soon, but he wanted to sit down in the living room first and then see the bedroom that would be his. All the furnishings were clean, dusted, and picked up.

They both liked the idea more and more, and began to talk about rent. "I would have to ask you for $200.00 per month."

Leroy agreed to it, knowing he still had money to dip into from his Uncle Charlie's death.

Leroy mentioned that he needed to get a job, and for Oscar to keep his eyes out for any interesting prospect.

"Can I start moving my stuff here on Sunday? I don't have a lot of things, just some clothes and books and personal stuff. I don't require much space. Hey, do you have a backyard?"

Oscar showed Leroy the back deck above a big lawn that sprawled out forward into blackberry brambles. The lawn was well mowed and there was a beautiful star magnolia in the center of the yard.

Thomas started panting in excitement, so Leroy asked if he could free the dog to run around the yard. It was fenced in. "Of course," Oscar said, and Leroy unhooked the leash and told Thomas to go play.

Thomas ran down the steps to the yard and ran swiftly around and around and around till he circled in to the magnolia and lifting his leg, he peed on it.

Then he ran around, nose to the ground smelling all the grass and found a place to poop.

Leroy apologized, but Oscar said "No big deal," and went inside to get a plastic bag to pick up Thomas's poop.

"Thanks," said Leroy.

"My pleasure," assured Oscar.

"I need to get going back to the Cadwell's so we can get ready for Church. Did you want to come with me?"

"Oh I would like nothing more," agreed Oscar "I'll bring my Church clothes with me in a bag so they don't get messed up on the way to Farley and Sally's house. Lock the back door when you come inside," said Oscar, who went to his bedroom closet to carefully take out his black slacks and shirt, and black shoes. These he put into a bag and came back out to the kitchen where Leroy was unplugging the coffee pot and about to empty the grounds and rinse the carafe.

"I think this might work out for us," said Oscar appreciatively. "Are you and Thomas ready to go?" he said happily.

"We're ready," spoke Leroy.

"OK, let's go!" Oscar followed Leroy and Thomas out the front door and locked it behind them. He had with him his change of clothing.

They walked down the porch stairs to the cement path that led to more stairs down to the street level.

"You sure get your exercise coming up and down these stairs," said Leroy.

Oscar assented and put his mind on the destination before them. It was only a Wednesday, but Oscar felt like it was Saturday. They walked onward to the Cadwell's.

Leroy grew depressed, not wanting to go to Church. He made this known to Oscar.

Oscar declared that it was the devil making him think that way and to focus on Church as a wonderful, beautiful experience.

Leroy smiled and thanked him, letting Thomas stop and pee every now and then.

The walk was not long and there was only a hint of evening in the air. Now Oscar was nervous. Was he intruding on Farley and Sally? Was he something the dog had dragged in? Before he could voice this fear to Leroy they had arrived at the Cadwell's front gate. Thomas whined and tugged at the leash, so Leroy let him go and he dashed around the back to the kitchen door where Farley would feed and water him.

Leroy remembered needing to pick up after Thomas this morning. He went to get a plastic bag but Farley stopped him and told him he'd already done it.

"Thanks, Farley. We had a good walk today and spent some time at Oscar's house. Thomas loved it there. He ran and ran and rolled over so Oscar could scratch his belly. It was sure windy this morning, but I didn't see any broken branches. It must have just been merciful enough to leave us unharmed. See, I think that angels are the winds in the trees, and you can see them by the branches waving, dust devils, and leaves blowing down the street. Tornadoes are very angry angels that do damage at God's will, to prove his existence."

"That's a lot of good thinking," Farley said to Leroy. "I'm glad you had a good day."

"I invited Oscar to the barbeque – is that all right?"

"Yes, we would love to see Oscar here. And you are invited, Oscar, so no snooping around the front gate, OK?"

"Yeah, right."

"Oscar is letting me move in with him! He has a spare bedroom I could have and I think we're compatible in the kitchen and neither one of us is a space hog. There's lots of room to put stuff and decorate. . . ."

"We'll see about the decorating, maybe we could work on that together."

"Yes, and there's plenty of room for hanging out, with a TV in the living room. Kind of like this house, but more bachelor oriented."

"So what time do we leave for Church? – can we all go together?"

"That's fine, Leroy, we have room in the car for the four of us. We should leave in an hour or so –"

"Can Oscar use my room to change into his Church clothes? He brought them so he needn't wear them and soil them walking from there to here."

"That's fine, Leroy," said Farley. At long last Sally walked into the room, freshly showered and wearing a pretty dress. Her flat black shoes were nice. Most women wore high-heeled shoes, but Sally was concerned about her ankles. She didn't want to break an ankle.

Leroy showed Oscar his room and shut the door behind him. Oscar would come out when he was ready. He was thinking about Sandra with a torn heart that she had suffered so much at the hands of Leroy's brother.

"I just have to be myself," said Oscar to himself. "I have a part to play in this drama, and look at me now! Inside Farley and Sally's house and welcome in their house."

He hurriedly changed his clothing and soon came out of Leroy's room wearing a black shirt and slacks, and his good black shoes.

"You look good, Oscar," noted Farley.

"Thanks. These are my Church clothes. I have three sets of Church clothes." Oscar was nervous but forced himself to remain calm.

"I've been taking my pills morning and night. I think I feel something different. Like an easing of the load on my back," he said nervously.

"Just give it time, we'll help you. Why, Sally and I have both been mentally ill for more than ten years."

"Yes, and you two are so successful! That's why I've been admiring you, trying to get close to you and not knowing how. Something about life is a God send, even in the midst of trauma and tragedy."

"Bringing Oscar to life. That could be a part of a missionary field for the mentally ill. We could start a group in the Church for mentally ill and unstable people who could sympathize with each other."

Farley excused himself and went to change into his Church clothes. When Oscar was out of Leroy's room, Leroy went in to change into *his* Church clothes. He hurried, not wanting to hold up the party.

Finally Leroy came out, shook Sally's hand and hugged Farley's shoulder. Oscar was not so touch-friendly. Timidly he remained in the back of things and followed along. At 6:45pm it was time to go and they all left the house, Thomas having been fed during the interim of Oscar and Leroy's arrival and everyone changing their clothes. Now he was safe in his enclosure with water and an Igloo house to curl up in.

They all hopped into Farley's car and sped away to Church, parking in the half full lot. They were a bit early; the way Farley liked it. He parked and they all got out. Farley and Sally led the way, and Leroy walked behind them. Oscar walked behind Leroy. He was glancing around, spying to see Sandra. He must not humiliate her, no matter what.

Sally spied around for Mae and James, and saw them there with Sandra next to Mae on the aisle seat. They were all on the right side facing front.

Sally led the way to Mae, James, and Sandra and her three companions followed along taking seats behind the two friends and their charge. People were bustling around and laughing loudly, praising the Lord. Sally's corner was quiet. Oscar terrified that he might offend

Sandra, and Leroy mulling over and over in his head the thoughts of Tina's decease and trying not to blame himself.

Farley and Sally felt responsible for their friends, as right now they were the centrifugal post that they all clung to. Having been mentally ill for so long, they'd seen nearly everything and could sympathize and be strong for their friends.

One thing that Farley and Sally didn't have together was a child, a decision made by them years ago in the belief that their mental illnesses would cause them to fail in being present for the child. They were not stable enough to take on the responsibility.

That's why Sally was so excited about Mae's pregnancy. Late September now, she would be due in May. And their wedding planned for February. It was an honest mistake, not a curse, maybe a slip in routine, who knows?

Sally hugged Mae, shook hands with James and then came around to hug Sandra, who wept on her neck and held her tight. "Remember, you're in the right place at the right time, Sandra," she soothed the crying woman. Sandra wore a sweatshirt and jeans with black leather shoes. She felt fat and ugly.

Oscar couldn't contain himself and quickly introduced himself to Sandra, who was wiping her eyes and cheeks from the tears. She smiled as she looked into Oscar's roomy, brown, soft and inviting eyes. "I've been wanting to meet you," said Oscar.

"Hi Oscar, I'm Sandra, Sandra Naden. I've come here for three years now. Tomorrow's my birthday."

"Really?" Quivered Oscar. "Which one?" He made no pretenses of games. He listened to her as she gained the courage to speak.

"I'm turning thirty-four tomorrow. My mother's going to take me out to lunch. She usually gives me a gift, something sweet, and then we go to Macy's together and find new clothes for me. I love my Mom, we always have a good time. This year might not be the same. I think my Mom is upset about the baby. She wants me to abort the child, but I can't."

"Thank you for telling me. I already know about the baby. Happy Birthday. Are you going to raise the child yourself? Or put it up for adoption?"

"Adoption, I think. Me being so weak, I couldn't support a child. - I don't think I could support a child. Especially one that I might have trouble loving."

"All very interesting," breathed Oscar. "What if you had help, if someone came alongside you and took some of the load?"

"All very interesting," said Sandra with a humorous smirk. "What sort of help?"

"Well, I could help you," said Oscar. "Just something to think about. Church is starting; I'll talk to you later. By the way, you look beautiful."

Oscar retreated to his seat behind Sandra and stood tall to sing praise and worship songs that began the service. "God is an Awesome God" – the words spoke to Oscar who was trembling inside with giddiness at his successful interview.

All seven patrons yelled and worshipped and clapped their hands, singing with arms raised in the air and dancing in place. Even Sandra felt the Holy Ghost and had a feeling of forgiveness and acceptance.

The music came to a close, and Pastor Williams urged on the steady worship until the whole house was practically shouting and giving thanks for the name of Jesus.

Leroy sat back and listened. He didn't feel like much praising and felt confused having noticed the exchange between Sandra and Oscar. Oscar moved fast. He was a "holy roller". Oscar always went wild in Church. After another five minutes of Apostolic worship, the Pastor brought the congregation down into a focus on the pulpit where he preached.

He preached sadly and honestly, lamenting the loss of Tina, overcoming the evil of Simon, whom he let be known was in prison for life. He paused dramatically, to get his own senses together, and continued to talk, turning his focus onto Stacy, Becky, Jane, and Sandra who were violated in this horrible turn of events.

Pastor called for ten minutes of silent prayer for all the individuals involved, and Leroy took this to mean him too.

Background music played quietly on the piano as some people made their way down to the altar and kneeled there to pray.

Silent, bitter tears flowed down many faces, and hearts were rent in agony at this outcome.

Pastor didn't mention Sandra's condition, or Leroy's involvement in the capture of his hideous brother. Leroy screamed and beat his chest, shocking the people around him. "Father, Please! Help me Please!" He wailed.

Soon he was surrounded by as many men as could gather, who prayed over him and the Pastor anointed him with oil as they prayed loudly and lovingly. Leroy sat with his hands on his knees and cried uncontrollably.

He felt the Holy Ghost working within him, cleansing, him of her blood, smiting the God forsaken blood bath she was in, that *he* had helped to clean up.

He felt the dirty aftermath, the sin, the rape fornication, evil and ugly in the sight of the Lord. It was gross death and bloody mess in the bathtub, which he had volunteered to clean up himself.

Dark bats and evil demons lurked about him, poking accusation and misery at his heart and chewing on his soul.

He phased in and out of service and was unaware of the message that day. His chest hurt like a brick was on it, and his headache throbbed with innocence and revelation of the immutability of his guilty urges. He pined and whined into his knees, unaware of the people around him. He pictured himself under a guillotine with only minutes left to live. God would rake him over the coals and pour ashes on his head.

Then he dove into darkness as he realized he would never see Tina again. He found himself in a dark maze of caves and mossy slopes. Falling out, falling into the fires below. There were great cauldrons with boiling oil dotted all around him, and a waterfall slide to a lake below in eternal relaxation. A river of love ran through it and brought him to the other side where he saw eternity, and God's beckoning finger.

"Come," said the Voice. "Come to me the right way. No killing yourself, you must recover on your own with the help of Jesus and your friends. Do not blame yourself for the death of Tina. You were helpless to keep it from happening. Don't put yourself where you don't belong – in Hell – for you do not want to reside there. Choose Me and come," spoke the Lord.

Leroy shivered in his seat and grabbed Farley's hand. He needed someone to hold onto. Farley put his hand on Leroy's shoulder and started to pray for him. Leroy shook violently and he screamed in agony. Farley led him up to the altar where the Pastor could lay hands on him with the associate Pastor, Duncan Freebes. Leroy cried and cried into his hands and someone gave him a Kleenex. Gradually he quieted down and resolved to get justice for himself and Tina. If he canceled in his life, he could no longer be blamed. He would just disappear. Maybe he would go to Heaven, wouldn't God understand if he just gave up? He could end it all if he pulled the trigger of a gun pointing at his head. No one could blame him then. He thought again. Maybe it would be better to slash his throat so he could die like Tina did. Blood everywhere, ransomed for the sin of death. But then he swore to death that he would not die, unless it seemed the right thing to do. Right now he wanted to die. It was as simple as that.

Farley had his arm around Leroy's shoulders and prayed with him in tongues. Leroy crumpled to the floor. A swarm of brothers surrounded him and lifted him up as he cried into silence. The Holy Ghost tried to permeate him, but he was already hardened in his negativity. He had no right to live. He wanted to die. He wanted Jesus to save him. He was miserable and confused, unable to think clearly, and still wondering about his brother, Simon, the poison in his own blood after he had mixed their blood through the cut of a knife.

Now he was part of what had done that to Tina, to Sandra, Stacy, Becky and Jane, and all the others. It was in his blood. He was evil.

The music played on and Leroy returned to his seat with his head in his hands. He forgot himself and let go of reality. He was poisoned, evil by nature; a part of Simon was in him. He was the devil's spawn. He miscarried his life and dropped it in a cauldron. He wasn't good enough to get to the lake of ecstasy, God's front door.

Gradually he became numb. He found himself talking to the people around him, talking about this and that, pretending to be OK.

He was numb and put a smile on his face. He wanted to talk to Oscar, but Oscar was busy making eyes at Sandra and engaging in conversation with her. She was giggling with mirth; this Oscar was so cute and dapper. Every time she alluded to the pain, he came back with humor, love, and affection. He invested the knowledge to her that he was mentally ill like Farley and Sally, and he had just been diagnosed with schizophrenia. He said he had his own demons too, but they were diminishing as this new medication combated the misaligned wires in his head. He told her he liked Thomas, the Cadwell's big Rottweiler. Then he invited her to the barbeque on Saturday. She grinned widely, showing crooked teeth, and said she would love to go.

Mae and James stood up and told Sandra they were ready to leave now. So she got up and left with them, with a much happier Sandra walking out the door. Oscar had made the baby sound like an opportunity to make things right. To give it love despite the manner of its origins.

Farley, Sally and Leroy left next with Oscar who was on a cloud. They dropped Oscar off at his house and drove home to an ecstatic Thomas who jumped up and down waiting to be let out of his enclosure and brought into the house for the night.

Farley and Sally went into the front door, and Leroy went around back to release the dog and bring him to the back kitchen door which led to inside. Inside was special to Thomas. He got to have lots of attention from his owners, and now Leroy, too. He sensed something was wrong with Leroy and kept licking his hand. Leroy grew angry at this doggy affection and slapped the big dog on his head. "Get away from me!" He cried. He didn't want to be comforted. Thomas lied down and whined, wiping his face with his paw.

Farley and Sally had not seen the violent interchange. They were in the kitchen starting to get dinner ready.

"I'm not hungry," Leroy lied. "I'll just have some coffee if that's all right."

"Coming right up," said Farley who nonchalantly prepared the coffee pot to go.

Sally pulled a large frozen pizza out of the freezer and set the oven to preheat. It was pepperoni and sausage.

The next half hour found the three humans in the living room with Thomas who looked miserable. Sally turned the TV on to Animal Planet and they watched the cutest cat competition.

When the pizza was done, Farley cut it into thirds, still hoping to offer some to Leroy, who wasn't looking very good. Leroy drank two cups of coffee and realized he was uncomfortably hungry so he accepted the pizza when Farley brought him a sliced third on a plate with napkins.

"Thank you," said Leroy gratefully and slowly began to eat the hot pizza, which burned his mouth. He was very angry, but retained it and just waited a little while to eat so the pizza could cool down.

Sally and Farley also waited for their pizza to cool down. They each had a can of Coke with their pizza.

Thomas slept fitfully, whining and kicking his legs in his sleep. He was upset.

After dinner they decided to all turn in for the night and went to their separate rooms. Farley and Sally were fast asleep. Leroy, on the other hand lay agitated with a burning headache. He envisioned a big knife that sliced his throat. Finally he fell asleep and slept like a baby until nine o'clock in the morning.

Farley and Sally were getting ready to go to work, and breakfast was laid out for Leroy – eggs and ham.

They said goodbye, and Leroy reported that he might walk Thomas again today.

Farley assented to this and said to be careful, careful of traffic.

After they left, Leroy ate his breakfast and poured coffee. He brought his coffee outside and enjoyed it on the back steps. He was mixed up in his head and kept seeing visions of red.

"I'll call Oscar," he said to himself, and went inside to pick up the phone. He dialed Oscar's number and let it ring twice before Oscar picked up on the other end.

"Hello Oscar, it's Leroy."

"Well, hello," Oscar replied.

"Do you have plans for the day?"

"I need to take my morning pills. Just a minute, I'll be right back."

Leroy waited while Oscar went to take his medicines. He was back soon.

"No plans, Leroy," he said simply. "No, that's a lie. I'm meeting Sandra today for lunch at the Turnip Bay Coffee Shop. We exchanged phone numbers and she called me today. I love her, Leroy. I'm going to help her raise the baby, after we get married. She's agreed to marry me. I'm so happy."

Leroy was struck with shock and terror. Now he couldn't move in with Oscar since Sandra would be coming to live there.

He felt squeezed out of the picture. "It's the poison I'm carrying," he said to himself.

Leroy found himself grasping at straws. "What do I do? I need to find a place to live. Will you help me find a place?"

"Check the paper, Leroy. There are lots of places to rent. Do you get the paper there?"

"Yes," Leroy said quietly. "I'll check the paper. Good bye."

"Good bye, Leroy."

Leroy went outside and leashed up Thomas. He would go to the dog park and watch the dogs running and playing.

Thomas was excited to get out and pulled at the lead, knowing the way to the dog park and anticipating ever more as they drew near. They entered the park gates and closed them from the inside. Leroy let Thomas off his leash and the big dog ran to go play.

Leroy sat on a log and watched the crowd of dogs interacting and playing and running around within the park barriers.

He felt through his jeans the scar where Simon had cut him and mixed his blood with him. It was a nightmare. But out here in the fresh air the world offered hope. He could be forgiven. He needed to forgive himself. He asked God for forgiveness. He asked for healing and renewal of his spirit and heart. Leroy had been baptized once. Any ensuing sins could be forgiven.

A glimmer of hope spread through him as he watched the dogs play. Where was Thomas? He spotted the Rottweiler in the far right corner of the field. He closed his eyes and mumbled a prayer. "Please save me God, I don't want to die."

Yet his hands itched and he envisioned a knife in his hand, slicing through his throat.

He stifled a roar. "Am I condemned?" He needed to talk to Pastor Williams and decided to call him when he got home. *Home.* He had no home. He needed to find a home and rebuild himself. Find another girl and put this hateful scenario behind him. He resolved to check the paper when he got back to Farley's.

Two hours went by when he called Thomas who came running, totally exhausted. Leroy leashed him up and they left to walk home. He thought of Oscar and hoped his meeting with Sandra was going well.

He closed his eyes and prayed in darkness. "Lord help me recover and put Simon and Tina behind me. I need a nice apartment with lots of light and at least a second story unit so I can have a view. Please help. In Jesus' name I pray, Amen."

His depression ate away at him and clogged his throat. He dry heaved and coughed desperately, but could not come clean.

Walking along he began to see stars. He let the dog lead him, for Thomas knew where home was and he was tired out from his exercise.

A couple of blocks away, Leroy focused on "home" where he was now and decided to do weeding in the yard and pick up after Thomas.

He let them into the front yard gate and brought Thomas to his enclosure. Next he filled Thomas's water bowl with fresh water and the dog lapped at it savagely.

Leroy went back to the front door and found the newspaper on the porch. He took it inside with him and sat down to read through apartments for rent. Thomas was a good boy and he leaned on that. The warmth of a stranger came to him through the Rottweiler that he little knew, but trusted.

CLIMAX

In visions of your inferiority, there is a climax that comes with the envisioning of peace and prosperity. Living alone can make you desperate, and unfounded. Reaching the peak of the highest mountain in your life gives you the sight of everything around you. Don't worry about notions, its just you giving yourself support.

Leroy was terrified at his predicament and remembered to call Pastor Williams. First he had a cup of coffee to calm his nerves. He was alone, so alone.

Finally he picked up the phone and called his Pastor. Pastor Williams answered his phone. "Hello?"

"Hello Pastor Williams, it's Leroy."

"Hi Leroy! I thought I might be hearing from you. How are you doing, my friend?"

"Oh just miserable. I'm afraid I'm going to kill myself, but I don't want to go to Hell. But I feel like I'm already condemned to Hell."

"There is no condemnation in Christ," replied Pastor Williams. "Especially when you are innocent, as *you* are," he said forcefully. "We've been through this several times and you must not blame yourself. I won't lose you Leroy, come to Christ with me." And together they prayed.

Afterwards Leroy felt dense and squashed. He still had Simon's blood in him. He told this to the Pastor who told him he was cleansed by the blood of Christ.

"You're under the blood of Christ Jesus and nothing can soil that."

Leroy whimpered that he kept seeing a knife slicing his throat.

The Pastor told him he needed to overcome that thought with something positive.

"Like finding myself an apartment?"

"Yes! Focus on that for now and make it an endeavor to cleanse yourself by testing your true strength to go forward with your life and to continually walk toward God. He's waiting for you with open arms, if you will accept Him and His promise to forgive whatever is not right in your life."

"Thank you for your advice and hearing me out," Leroy said with a bit of strength recovered from the conversation.

"Call me any time. You are in my prayers, Leroy. What are you going to do with the rest of your day?"

"I'm going to check the paper for a place to live. Please pray that I find a good spot – God ordained. Thank you. God Bless you."

"And God bless you too."

"Good bye, Pastor."

"Take care."

Leroy hung up and a small smile played at his face. He picked up the newspaper and looked through the apartments for rent. Two of them looked promising. They were in his price range and were upper level apartments with washer and dryer. In fact they were both in the same building on the second floor. They were not far from the Cadwell's and Church and downtown. They were in walking distance to the bay and the beaches down there. He imagined himself living in one of those and his thoughts were positive. He had people he could reach out to. He had healing to do, but this would come with God in His own time.

Leroy called the "Sea Breeze" apartment leasing office and expressed interest in the two apartments advertised.

The apartment manager said they would go fast, and asked if Leroy wanted to set up a showing today?

Leroy agreed to meet the manager, John, at four-thirty. He hung up and realized the time was three fifteen. He decided to get there early. He wanted to take Thomas along, but realized that was not a possibility. So he left the house, with Thomas in the enclosure, and walked the short distance to the apartments in question.

"Hi, I'm Leroy," he introduced himself to the manager who professed to be John.

"I'm here to see the apartments you have for rent."

"Of course. The apartments are identical other than differing décor. Both have a balcony facing the water, washer, dryer, full kitchen, one bath, living room, two bedrooms and storage space." John opened the first one, number 7, and Leroy was overwhelmed with what he saw. Thank God he could afford it. He didn't need to see the other one but asked to see it for kicks. When John opened up the next apartment, number 6, he wasn't nearly as impressed. He liked the design of number 7 better. So he applied.

John and Leroy filled out papers and Leroy paid the first and last months rent. Thank God he had money from his deceased Uncle Charlie. Leroy knew he should get a job, but it wasn't necessary at this point. He had plenty of money stored away.

He left the "Sea Breeze" apartments and walked back the short distance to Farley and Sally's place. No one was home so he went to his stranger friend Thomas and exuded happiness all over the dog as he hugged it and petted it roughly. "Good boy, Thomas," he said, "Good boy." He decided next to read his Bible for the day and brought it outside by the dog enclosure, sitting in a lawn chair and browsed through the Old Testament.

Maybe Farley could help him move later today. He should have time after work. Didn't he get home by three?

Thinking back on an earlier thought, he decided to begin weeding the yard with a trowel and a screwdriver. He found these in the storage room by Farley's toolbox.

It was hard work and his back got sore, but he kept at it, doing the northwest corner first and gradually shifting to the northeast corner. With that half done, he called it quits and put down his tools. He longed for a hammock, but decided to lie down in the lawn chair and picked up his Bible again. He would gather the dug up weeds later, and he hadn't run into any of Thomas's business.

As he sat and read, Sally came in the yard, having had a long day at work. They greeted each other and Leroy told her the good news of having secured his own apartment. Sally was gleeful and so happy for him. She had begun to worry about Leroy's welfare, and how long would he need to stay here?

Leroy asked Sally if Farley could help him move later.

"I'm afraid it will be a bit later. When Farley isn't home by now it usually means he's gone down to the Red Tornado Casino to play the slot machines. But no worries, he'll be back later."

Leroy's heart sank. He'd wanted to move in today. He needed the change, but he was patient. Then he realized that he would need a job, or something to engage in that would keep him from being morose alone with time on his hands. Where could he get a job? For now he could keep walking Thomas and cultivating his friendship with Oscar. Which made him think that he should call Oscar to see how his lunch with Sandra had gone. He went inside.

He realized that he was hungry; hadn't eaten since breakfast. Sally sensed this and took out two frozen burritos, one for each of them. She put them in the microwave and whipped up a salad for the side. They still had avocados, which Sally loved and she sliced one up in the salad. She offered Leroy a ginger ale, which he accepted readily. All that weeding had made him thirsty. He asked Sally about her day.

"Oh, you know, it was busy and I got tired. My mental illness kicked in and I couldn't focus after awhile. Just voices and creepy little thought invasions. It was just symptoms of my illness acting up due to stress. My hormones are bothering me too, you know, the woman's curse. It's that time of the month." Sally was not shy about her bodily functions.

"I'm sorry," said Leroy, realizing that his own problems had been taking over as he imagined everyone else's lives were perfect. He asked Sally for a second burrito and more ginger ale.

Sally quickly prepared the burrito and dug a ginger ale out of the fridge.

"Do you want ice?" She asked him.

"Oh that's all right," replied Leroy, not wanting to be a bother.

Just then Farley came in the front door. "Where's the paper?" he asked, aggravated.

"I have it here," said Leroy in a mousey voice. "I was just looking up apartments for rent today. Here you go," he said handing the paper to Farley who accepted it gratefully.

He had already eaten at the casino. "I won thirty four dollars today, honey," he said to his wife proudly.

"That's nice, Sweetheart," she said. "Leroy has some good news for us today. Tell him, Leroy," she told him.

"I've rented an apartment today where I'm going to move in as soon as someone can help me. It's just northwest of here in the "Sea Breeze" apartment complex. I just need help moving my stuff. It's really not a lot, and it would get me out of your hair." He pouted.

"Well that's great news, Leroy. I'm glad you're furthering your life. And don't go thinking you're a bother here. Sally and I enjoy your company."

"Thanks. I weeded the upper half of the yard today. I just have to gathered the weeds that I pulled out, they're lying everywhere."

"Good grief! Leroy – you have gone up and above keeping your weight pulled in this place. Did you walk Thomas too?"

"I did. We went to the dog park for a couple of hours and then when we got back I called Pastor Williams for advice."

"Great for you, reaching out, my friend. And you probably need me to help you move?"

"I was hoping –"

"Consider it done."

"Th-thanks, Farley," said Leroy gratefully. "When?"

"How about tomorrow after I get home from work. I'll come straight home tomorrow so there will be plenty of time."

"Can I keep walking Thomas in the mornings? It would give me something to do. He's sort of becoming a friend of mine. I think he likes to go for walks."

"Splendid. You keep doing that, just be careful, the traffic is so unpredictable around here."

"Gee, thanks Farley. Now I've got to call Oscar. He had lunch with Sandra today and I want to see how he fared."

"That sounds interesting," said Farley. "I'm going to get out of these work clothes and take a shower. See you guys."

"Can I use the phone, Sally?"

"Of course. Remember to ask Oscar about his medications."

"I will." Leroy picked up the phone and dialed Oscar's number.

He answered quickly and sounded out of breath.

"Hi Leroy," Oscar said happily. "I was just doing aerobics, Sandra gave me a DVD to use for an exercise plan. How are you?" He paused and turned off the DVD. "Leroy?"

"Oh yes, I'm doing well. I found a place to live today. Farley is going to help me move in tomorrow. Isn't that great?"

"Wow! You got that arranged fast. Sorry it didn't work out here, but when Sandra and I get married, she'll be moving in. We're abstaining, you know, until after we get married."

"That's exciting! How was your lunch today?"

"Good. Great. I couldn't believe how many things we had to talk about. Then we went for a walk together by the bay. We went to a fishing pier where we just sat at the end of the pier and talked and laughed and talked and cried. It's going to be all right. We're going to raise the baby."

"Wow. I'm floored. You sure move fast, Oscar. I'm-I'm happy for you." It was hard to get the words out.

"What are you doing tomorrow?"

"I have my first meeting with my case manager, Laura, tomorrow at one o'clock. I'm looking forward to checking in with someone who's familiar with what I've got."

"Oh, Oscar, I forgot. Sally wanted me to ask if you've been taking your pills – medicines."

"I take them religiously. I believe God made these through people who can help me. I have so much more control over my thoughts than I used to. Oh Leroy, I've been so miserable for so long.

"Schizophrenia is hell on earth when it's untreated. I'm so lucky that God led me to Sally and Farley who have mental illnesses, too."

"I'm still considering getting some therapy or counseling at the Wellness Center where you go. I'm so mixed up and confused. It's hard to stop blaming myself for Tina's death. I feel hatred for Sandra's baby, which makes me evil, because Sandra is a good person who got caught in a bad way. I could have stopped it. I could have stopped the whole darn thing."

"No sense in blaming yourself, Leroy. You didn't do anything wrong. You just got caught in the wrong place at the wrong time."

"If only I hadn't lived with Simon and known all about his raping schemes and not told anyone. I should have exposed him before it was too late. It just got too late…" Leroy wept into the receiver and let his heart ache with pity for himself.

Oscar was sensitive to his friend and stayed silent on the line. "Are you OK?" He asked after awhile.

"Yes, I'll be OK. You have to come and see my new place. I'm moving in tomorrow. Farley said he would help me move. I really don't have much stuff. A lot of it is at the old apartment, and I don't want those things anyway."

"Sure, I'll come visit you. Do you like it? Is it a nice place?"

"Oh I love it. It captured me from the first glance. It's already furnished, so I'm lucky there."

"What did you do today? – Besides getting an apartment."

"Well, I walked Thomas to the dog park and sat there for a couple of hours. Then I called Pastor Williams and had a talk with him. Let's see, I read my Bible, and weeded half of Farley's yard. Sally got home late – she had a bad day - and we ate burritos and salad. That's about all."

"Cool. It's important to stay occupied and to reach out like you did in calling me and Pastor Williams today."

"I'm just excited about moving into my new place. Farley said I could still walk Thomas everyday. It's not that far."

"Good. Well I have to get back to my aerobics. I promised Sandra that I would try to do the whole program tonight. Then I'm going to call her. Talk to you later, Leroy, and don't hate the baby, it's not yours to hate."

"Sorry. Talk to you later Oscar, Bye."

"Bye."

Leroy wandered into the living room and sat down to watch Animal Planet – it was airing a show on River Monsters. Farley walked in with wet hair suited in sweat pants and a T-shirt. He was bare-footed and carried a Coke.

"Oscar is doing well. He's going to marry Sandra," Leroy blurted out this information.

"Well I'll be. . . that was sure fast. I'm happy for them. Do they have a date set?"

"Not that I know of. I forgot to ask."

"Leroy, I know you haven't been feeling very well for quite some time now. Can I help you in any way?"

"Just help me move. That's all. So I'll have my own place and my own keys, and my own cat. I'm going to get a cat for sure."

"I mean, do you want to seek counseling at the Wellness Center? There's no shame in that. No more shame than sitting back and doing nothing."

Leroy was surprised at Farley's insight. He was a genuine, caring man. "Yes," he sighed. "I admit that I need help. Help so I don't kill myself. I don't want to go to Hell, but I feel like I'm living on wisps of straw, ready to crackle and burn."

"You feel like you're a sinner."

"Of the worst kind."

"God is a loving, forgiving God."

"God doesn't like me very much."

"God loves you."

"I love God, Jesus. I need His help."

"He is helping you."

"I wish I was somewhere else in my life."

"Keep moving forward, toward God."

"He wants me?"

"Right."

"Then why all this pain and confusion?"

"Growth. You'll be able to help other people."

"I give up. God can do with me what he wants. Just remember this if you remember nothing else about me – I love Jesus Christ."

"Perfect."

"Well, I think I'll go to bed now. Good night Farley."

"Good night Leroy."

The lights went off in Leroy's room and Farley got up and turned off the TV and kitchen lights, to go to his bedroom where Sally was sleeping comfortably.

The morning came fast. It was Friday. The barbeque was scheduled for tomorrow. Everyone had their invitations, including Gilmore and his fiancé. Stacy, Becky and Jane were all invited via Sandra who had called them all. Everyone was excited about the Cadwell's; they were such good people.

Oscar was scheduled to see Laura his case manager today for the first time.

Leroy got up, ate breakfast, and went to take Thomas for a walk to the dog park. A car slammed on its brakes as Leroy stepped out into the street at an uncontrolled intersection. It shook him up and he found himself thanking God for the near miss.

Sally and Farley got up, got ready, and went to work.

At Mae and James' place, Sandra was getting up and organizing her things like she did every morning now, just to make sure nothing was missing.

Mae was a comfort to her and Mae's love for James and vice versa was calming for her, peaceful and healing. She knew this was a safe place, and she was no longer depressed. Mae stayed home and worked on her sewing; she was making a quilt for their baby. She slept in the same room as James did now, believing it was not a sin since she was already impregnated and the baby needed love from Mom and Dad, and the benefit of love between Mom and Dad.

Mae had found out that the baby was a girl, and she was excited about that. She was already looking forward to her wedding in February and wanted Sandra to be one of her bride's maids.

James had gone to work that morning. He worked for the newspaper. Sandra and Mae drank coffee and laughed quietly, as Sandra played with their pet bird. Living there with them was therapeutic to Sandra, as peace abounded throughout the house.

Mae and James also had a tame, indoor black cat with white feet. It padded around the house and stayed curled up on the couch beneath the huge Hawaiian Umbrella Plant. Sandra drank cup after cup of coffee until she needed to eat something. So she cut up a papaya and ate half of that.

As lunch came around, she prepared a tuna fish sandwich with a big red Braeburn apple. Then she went to her room to take a nap. She saw the clock and it read 12:53pm. Oscar would be meeting his case manager, Laura at one o'clock and she was nervous for him. She didn't know why. She closed her eyes and prayed for Oscar to get out all his issues while he had this opportunity.

Later Sandra awakened at 3:00pm, and wandered through the house to the kitchen where Mae was beginning to make cup cakes for the barbeque. Sandra pitched in to help, and started making chocolate chip cookies as well, her aunt's spectacular recipe. The two girls laughed and had fun, as flour flew everywhere and covered everything. The first of the cup cakes came out perfectly, as the cookies baked on. Then, as mutual consent, they started to make a raspberry chocolate torte. After four hours working in the kitchen they had prepared more than enough sweets for the party.

Sandra called Oscar to inquire about his appointment.

"Hello, Oscar?" She mouthed as he picked up his phone. "Ahem, Oscar?"

"Hi Sandra, how are you doing?" He asked.

"Really good. How are you? How was your meeting?"

"Oh the meeting went great. Laura is a perfect match for me. She's kind, sensitive, knowledgeable, and a great counselor. We talked about everything. Like how long had I known there was something wrong, when did it start, how did it start, how I've been coping, if I ever wanted to hurt myself or someone else."

"Wow, that's a lot."

"Yes, my little merry-go-round, I came out of that meeting with all kinds of new ideas, advice, and homework. You're part of my homework, to cultivate a meaningful relationship with someone in my life. I chose you.

"How are you?"

"I'm fine, relaxed. Mae and I have been baking all day for the party tomorrow. I invited Stacy, Becky, and Jane. I don't know if they'll all show up though.

"I think Farley or Sally were going to invite the Pastor and Sister Williams. Then Leroy will be there, Mae, James, and Farley's brother Gilmore and his fiancé.

"I'm really excited about it. That's a good handful of people. I told the girls to bring drinks – pop – no alcohol."

"I hope they all show up."

"Yeah, it should be a pretty good time, it's just that I'm so shy, sometimes I don't enjoy social events."

"You just stick by me if you start to feel awkward or out of place. I'm a warm companion and pretty darn shy myself. We could hang out with each other and eat sweets and barbeque and have pop in the Cadwell's back yard. I think they have plenty of chairs and I think they'll have music too."

"We could dance!"

"Not a chance. I have three left feet."

"Are you a beast?"

"Not at all, like I said I'm very shy."

"Good – it was just a test, I wanted to see what you would say."

"Don't trick me!" cried Oscar.

"I'm sorry, I hope you didn't take it the wrong way."

"I'm fine. I need hope. I keep slipping into depression. But when I think of you I get all warm and happy inside. I love you, Sandra."

"Why thank you, Oscar, you make me happy too. And I think I love you. . . I look forward to seeing you at the party. I hope it's going to be a sunny day, warm and blue skied. And Thomas will be there. I hear from Sally that Leroy has taken quite a fancy to Thomas. I know you're sort of unsure about him, but really I think he's a really nice dog."

"Thomas hated me when I was first trying to meet Farley and Sally. Now he likes me, since I'm accepted. I walked Thomas with Leroy the other day. He is a good dog."

"Well I better go and help clean up the kitchen. I love you!"

"Bye Sandra, I love you as well."

"Bye Oscar."

The two lovebirds were dealing with the odds of life together. Oscar accepting that he has a mental illness, and Sandra bearing the child of Simon who raped her. They accepted and loved each other.

Leroy was getting nervous about the barbeque, although he knew he was invited. Today Farley was going to help him move to his new apartment. He had clothes and a few bags of stuff, but luckily the apartment was already fully furnished.

He waited in the back yard next to Thomas in his enclosure. His lawn chair was comfortable and he relaxed as he leaned back and pondered his life. "It's not my fault," Leroy said to himself. His chains were heavy and he bound himself in their accusatory links. He couldn't do what he wanted. "If I take my liberties," he said aloud, I can just lie here and wait for Farley to come home without stressing out about the move, the party, or my life. I can give myself liberties. I can go get a cup of coffee if I want, or a lemonade."

Leroy got up and went inside for a lemonade pop and brought it back outside. He took his liberties and again laid down in the chair while he waited peacefully for Farley. He finished the lemonade and decided to get up and let Thomas out so they could play fetch. It was his liberty to do so, and the dog was enthralled.

Leroy threw the tennis ball and Thomas dove after it in slobbery ecstasy. He retrieved the ball and brought it back to Leroy. This went on maybe ten more times until both dog and man were tired of it. Leroy put Thomas back in his enclosure. He was sure growing fond of the big animal.

Sally came home and met Leroy in the yard as he lay there relaxing in the chaise lounge. She noticed the lemonade can and made a mental note of positive thought for Leroy to have helped himself to the drink. She wanted him to feel comfortable here, and to eat and drink whatever he liked.

"I've been here all day after walking Thomas this morning. He sure is a good companion," Leroy testified. He had a soft spot for the animal who was helping him deal with his pain.

"Farley should be here soon," Sally said, reassuring Leroy.

"I have all my stuff packed and ready to go. We can probably do it in two trips. I just have to get my stuff there and then take my time and liberties organizing everything so that I like it. I really like this place, and it's walking distance to you guys and it's on your way to Church so maybe you could pick me up regularly."

Sally nodded positively, agreeing to picking up Leroy for Church services.

Just then Farley drove up in the old Fiat and parked in the driveway. He came in the yard and saw Sally and Leroy talking together. This made him happy, to see Leroy coming out of his shell.

"Hello!" He called as he came into the backyard. Thomas jumped up and down excitedly. Here was his master.

"Are you about ready, Leroy?" Farley cast his line.

"As ready as I'll ever be," said Leroy, "let's go carry out my stuff to the car. I think we can do it in two loads. Is that all right?"

"Sure. No problem."

Leroy and Farley filled the car with Leroy's things and sped off to his new apartment. Farley was impressed with the lay out and the view of the bay. They unloaded everything and went back to get the rest of his things. They packed everything into the car and once more made the trip to "Leroy's place." After unloading everything there was an awkward moment as Leroy thanked Farley and prepared to begin organizing.

Instead, Farley asked Leroy out to dinner with his wife to The Old Barnyard.

Leroy agreed readily and taking his liberties, he changed into a different shirt and locked the apartment behind them, putting his new keys into his pocket.

He walked a step behind Farley down to the car and together they drove home to Farley's. They got out and went into the house, where

Farley told Sally that he had invited Leroy to dinner with them at The Old Barnyard.

Sally smiled and said it was a wonderful idea. To celebrate Leroy's home coming.

Sally took her liberties and went to wash her face and change into comfortable shoes. It was time to go, so they all got into the car and drove to the restaurant.

Farley requested the attic room and they sat down together in the booth overlooking the old farming equipment. They all ordered and waited silently for dinner to come. Sally looked at Farley who looked back at her and then said, "Congratulations, Leroy, on finding your own place. Do you want to spend one more night with us, or should we drop you off at the Sea Breeze so you can sleep your first night there?"

"I guess it would be best to drop me off at my new place. But can I come walk Thomas in the morning?"

"Yeah, sure. He likes you and he needs the exercise that you give him. You're so patient with him. I trust you with him, just that I want to warn you to be careful of traffic."

"Thanks. I'll be careful."

Their food came and they ate quietly, Sally and Farley being sensitive with Leroy whom they knew was suffering right now.

"How's Oscar? Have you talked to him?" Farley prodded.

"No, we haven't talked for awhile. Last I heard he's going to marry Sandra and raise the baby with her. Also that he's being careful to take his medication. I think he's doing really well, and I know he loves you guys."

"So what about the party tomorrow," asked Sally. "Are we ready for it? I haven't had time to prepare anything. I need to call Mae, she was going to do some baking for the barbeque. We can stop and buy hamburger at the store, and buns, and –"

"I'll pay for the veggie tray for the burgers –" volunteered Leroy.

"That would be nice, Leroy, thank you. And the three Church sisters, Stacy, Becky, and Jane are going to provide drinks, as far as I've heard, I hope they show up."

Farley looked at his beloved gold watch and asked Sally if she'd invited Gilmore and his fiancé.

"I'll call him tonight, and Pastor Williams and Sister Williams. I really do hope they'll come. Are you nervous, Leroy? I know you're going through a lot right now, but I really hope you show up as well."

"I'm nervous, but I'll be there. I need to be around people, you know. You guys are my friends. Thanks for being there for me and offering up your home."

"Is everyone done?" Asked Farley who also asked for the bill when the waitress walked by.

"I'm done," said Leroy, and Sally said she was done as well.

"Well let's go to the store on the way home. We need to buy hamburger patties and cheese, and Leroy, you were going to pay for veggies. Let's buy a couple of two liter Cokes just in case the girls don't show up. We can always make a store run tomorrow if we have to."

"I'll call Mae when we get home. Hopefully she did some baking."

Up they arose from the table and Farley paid for the bill on their way out. The food had been good as it usually was.

They got into the car and drove to the grocery store near their home. After twenty minutes they had found all they needed, including onions, lettuce, and tomatoes for the veggie tray with pickles as well. They paid and left the store with their groceries. Farley was getting tired now. His mental illness was starting to pull him in different directions. "Honey, can you drive, Sweetheart? I'm not feeling so good. All this running around is making me psychotic."

"Of course, Darling," Sally said with concern in her voice. "Tell me how to get to your Sea Breeze apartment, Leroy. She was all business. Farley needed to get home and relax.

Leroy guided her to his new home and she stopped the car as he got out. "I have my keys, I might come by to walk Thomas tomorrow. I guess this is good night."

"Good night Leroy. Enjoy getting settled in. Bye-bye now." Sally made a u-turn and drove through the streets to their house. Farley stumbled out of the car and went straight for the front door to let himself in, where he curled up on the couch and hugged himself.

"I'll feed Thomas," Sally said and went outside to let him out of his enclosure so he could come inside. She half expected to see Oscar outside the fence.

She filled his food bowl and gave him fresh water to drink. Thomas was a polite eater and came inside when he was all done. Sensing his master's confusion, he went over to Farley on the couch and stuck his big head in Farley's face who nuzzled his nose affectionately.

Thomas lay down next to Farley on the floor by the couch. He put his head between his paws and laid his head down docilely.

Sally called Mae although it was getting late. She was delighted to hear that Mae and Sandra had spent the whole day baking together and had more than enough sweets for the party. She thanked them, and then went into the living room to sit in a chair across from her husband.

"Are you OK, Sweetheart?" She asked him gently.

Farley groaned and said he would be all right. "Just let me sleep," he said.

So Sally got up and put in a call to Pastor and Sister Williams.

"Hello?" It was the Pastor.

"Hi Pastor Williams, it's Sally Cadwell."

"Well Hi there Sally, is there anything I can do for you?"

"Well, yes, as a matter of sorts. I would like to invite you and your wife to our house for a barbeque tomorrow around one o'clock. There are a handful of us from the Church getting together to celebrate and support each other through this trial that we've come to face with Simon and Tina and Sandra, Stacy, Becky, and Jane. Together with Oscar, who has just found out he's mentally ill, Mae, James, and Farley's brother Gilmore and his fiancé."

"Sounds like a blast," cried the Pastor; thankful to be included on the guest list.

"Oh and yes, Leroy is coming too. He just moved into his own apartment tonight."

"Well I'll be . . . we were just talking about that yesterday. Prayer really does work. I'll be blessed. You can count us in. Anything we should bring to contribute?"

"Could your wife make potato salad? A big batch."

"I'm sure she could, or I could, well, yes WE can come up with something like that. How about deviled eggs?"

"Yes, and chips as well. I just remembered chips and dip – oh but I don't want to load you down –"

"Consider it done. It's our pleasure"

"Oh great! I'm so glad you can make it! Thank you, thank you, thank you." Sally babbled in her excitement.

"God bless you, Sally. We'll see you tomorrow at one. Thanks for the invitation."

"Thank you again. See you tomorrow."

"Bye."

"Bye."

Sally was all shook up but keeping it together. She needed to go to sleep and dream hard to balance herself out. Carefully she pulled at Farley and tugged him out of his sleep on the couch. "Farley, Farley," she whispered gently. "It's time for bed. Come on, we need to get some good sleep before the barbeque tomorrow. Do we have enough propane?"

"Yes." Farley sat up on the couch and gave his wife a tender hug. "Let's go to bed now. I'm very tired. I stretched myself too hard today. Work was hard, and then Leroy. I'm glad that's over." Together they turned off lights and took a peek into Leroy's room, which was empty with the bed made neatly. Then they walked to their own room and changed into bedclothes. Together they lay down and went to sleep.

Morning would come fast with a whiney Thomas needing to go out. Sally got up and let him out so he could do his business. Maybe Leroy could volunteer to pick up after Thomas later. She put the thought aside and putting on yard shoes she took a trowel and a bag and started scouring the yard for droppings. She found poop in three places and put the bag in the dumpster at the side of the house.

Better to get it done, she thought.

She looked at the clock when she came inside and fed Thomas. It was just past nine. She made breakfast for herself and Farley, having her morning tea and then putting the coffee on. Farley liked bacon and eggs and hash browns with his coffee and chopped up fruit. She decided to wake Farley so they could eat together.

He woke up with bright eyes, fully rested and looking forward to the barbeque today. He remembered that he didn't have Leroy's new phone number, and he was worried about Leroy for some reason. He couldn't put his finger on it. He said a little prayer that all was well with Leroy.

Farley and Sally ate breakfast together and sat in the living room with their coffee. They prayed together about the day and that it would be a success. Farley had to bring out a couple of folding tables from the storeroom, as well as their eight folding chairs.

Excited about the party, Farley set up the table and chairs in a circle. Next he pulled the barbeque out from the shed where the tools were, and made double sure that there was plenty of propane. That done, he found their battery operated radio in the storeroom and put it on an end of one table where the food would go. He found an easy Classics station. Feel good music from the eighties.

There was nothing to do but wait, so Farley had more coffee and read his Bible. This helped to center him and keep his mind on Christ. He decided to call Gilmore and make sure that his brother knew of his invitation to the barbeque.

He called the number but no one answered, so Farley left a detailed message about the party and his invitation. He stressed that they would love for him to come with his fiancé so he could meet her. The wedding was in one week at a Lutheran Church across town.

He was excited for them, especially for his sensitive brother. He fingered the gold watch and thanked God for its recovery from the depths by the fishing pier.

It wasn't long when Leroy came around to the back door and greeted them. He asked if he could help. When there was nothing to do, he volunteered to walk the dog down to the dog park to get Thomas and himself some exercise.

Farley consented and the young man and dog left through the front gate. He had promised to be back by noon when guests might start arriving. Leroy took deep breaths and walked slowly with Thomas who was obedient and stayed at his heel.

At the dog park, Leroy let his charge run free. For two hours. Then it was time to head back. He called Thomas who came quickly.

Back at Farley's house, the first guest had arrived. It was Stacy, and she had brought a cooler full of ice and energy drinks. She laughed and giggled a lot, and Farley became irritated that Leroy wasn't back yet. Thomas was such a good conversation piece. There they were, coming in from the front yard. It was five minutes after twelve so he was nearly on time.

"Hi sister Stacy," greeted Leroy cordially. He put Thomas in his enclosure and went to get a drink that she offered.

They sat together in the circle of chairs and commented on the nice day. As they made conversation, Mae, James, and Sandra came around the corner carrying stacks of trays filled with cookies, cup cakes, and a raspberry chocolate torte. Close behind them came the William's carrying a big bowl of potato salad, deviled eggs and chips with dip.

Sally came running out and welcomed her guests, helping them spread the food on the table. She went inside and brought out paper plates and plastic forks.

Oscar came around the corner, shyly, as Sally helped to arrange the potato salad, deviled eggs and chips, for which she brought out a big plastic bowl to dump them in.

She spread out the cookies, cup cakes and the raspberry chocolate torte on a picnic table with the other food. Oscar came empty handed but felt invited nonetheless. He spied Sandra from a ways off and zoned in on her immediately.

As he approached, Mae, James and Sandra were taking seats in the circle with Pastor and Sister Williams and Leroy. Stacy was helping herself to cupcakes before she sat down as well. Everybody had a drink and started to get comfortable in the ring of chairs. Thomas ran back and forth in his enclosure, nervous about all the guests.

Finally Farley came out and began to prepare the barbeque. Sally laid out the hamburger buns and veggie tray.

As Farley put the first burgers on, Becky and Jane came around the corner carrying a cooler full of pop and ice between them. They were giggling together and made their introduction quickly, shyly, as they deposited the cooler next to Stacy's cooler and lost no time to take their seats in the circle.

Pastor Williams got up and blessed the food and company, and everyone got up to help themselves to food. Becky and Jane greeted Stacy, and Sandra joined them with a group hug. "I'm really glad to see you here," said Stacy to Becky and Jane and Sandra. "We're glad to see you too, all of you," they said to each other. All four sat down next to each other, Sandra on one end who found a handsome Oscar next to her ready to engage in conversation, but waiting for her to begin.

Just as everything was getting underway, there was a big cheer as Gilmore with his fiancé, introduced as "Fay" joined the party and introduced themselves to everyone there, many who had heard about him as Farley's kind brother. There were chairs enough for everyone, including the lawn chairs that were always outside. The pressure was mounting as people couldn't help but think about Tina who should have been here with Leroy. There was a sadness in the air but an uplifting presence as well, as Gilmore and Fay chatted mildly with Pastor Williams, who invited them to be married at Hillside Apostolic Church; he would love to perform the ceremony.

Gilmore and Fay took his offer to heart and agreed to the prospect. The following Saturday was the chosen day, and they sealed the deal with a shake of hands.

Stacy was being much too loud as if she needed to be heard. Leroy was quietly suffering in his guilt and trauma. Becky and Jane kept to themselves and engaged in their own conversation as people got up to help themselves to food and drink.

Farley announced the first burgers to be done, and Pastor and Sister Williams were the first to claim theirs. People lined up at the barbeque, Leroy next in his nervousness that there might not be enough, and Stacy who was laughing loudly at something that Oscar had just said. That Oscar is so charming, she thought to herself, but recognized his paramount interest in Sandra. This was Sandra who was carrying Simon's child, Simon who had raped her, Sandra, Becky, and Jane.

Oscar stood up to make an announcement. "Sandra and I want to announce to the people here that we have become engaged to be married."

There was a cheer and many congratulations. Oscar sat down again and stuffed a cupcake into Sandra's mouth, who was happy and laughing uncontrollably. She was in love with Oscar, and now everyone knew it. They all knew about the baby too, and Oscar's decision to help raise the child.

Leroy was wishing that there was alcohol at the party. He wanted to drink himself drunk and pass out in blissful ignorance. His heart tore at him as he thought now about Tina and how perfect she had been for him.

Mae and James politely stood last in line to get their hamburgers and took paper plates with cupcakes, cookies, potato salad, deviled eggs, chips, and a piece of the raspberry torte, which Mae cut into pieces for all.

"I heard him with you and you and you and you," Leroy spoke rudely to the four girls who had been victims of his brother.

"Leroy, would you run inside and get the coffee pot?" Sally clamped down on him and changed the subject. "Now, is everyone OK? Does everyone have a burger?" She turned up the music a little bit and conversation slipped into itself as Leroy returned with the coffee, miffed and ashamed of himself. He quieted down after that and sat and listened listlessly to the talk going on all around him.

Stacy stood up and started dancing shamelessly, and grabbed Gilmore and Fay out of their seats to join her. Farley joined in, to help his brother's embarrassment and Sally turned up the music. "Let's all dance!" cried Sally. And soon even the William's were dancing. Everyone was dancing inside the little circle of chairs and they committed themselves to God as He moved through the party with the Holy Ghost coming on everyone. The dancing lasted ten minutes and even Pastor Williams cried out with pleasure as they all sat down again, laughing and out of breath.

"Thank you Stacy," spoke Oscar, who had appreciated her wild gutsiness. "You sure got us out of our seats."

The party was more relaxed after that, and Becky and Jane decided they had to go, for more pressing issues at home. They thanked the Cadwell's for the good afternoon and took their cooler with them. Everyone said goodbye to the two girls, who had become fast friends in knowledge of Simon who had raped them both, only to be discovered later in questioning of who in the Church had been with Simon, and the stories were all the same. Even Leroy had had to come forward with his knowledge of his brother's activities. The proof was there, now Simon was locked up and no one had to fear him anymore. Except for Leroy, who was tortured with his knowledge and the mixing of their blood.

Pastor Williams took Leroy's hand and asked him how he was doing. Leroy talked about his new apartment, and immediately felt better as he focused on the positives in his life.

"I'm going to look for a job as well," said Leroy. "And I have the Church to keep me centered and my friends Sally, Farley, and Oscar to confide in." He felt better after flipping the penny and looking at the shiny side.

Stacy avoided conversation with Leroy, whom she associated with Simon and who had let the vicious behavior continue until checked by the death and revelation of Tina.

If only Tina hadn't known. If he hadn't let her into their home the day that Sandra was there. It was hopeless, and then there was the God d-mned baby to think of. Leroy was vicious, the baby didn't have the right to live, he thought.

Cupcakes were getting eaten and cookies as well. Mae and Sandra took compliments on the fantastic baking. The torte was divine.

The radio was humming along and Sandra conversed brightly with Oscar, whose shy charm won her over magnetically. Sally kept Leroy's cup filled with coffee, to deter him from any other angry outbursts. If Oscar was being completely charming, Leroy was being utterly rude, and told Gilmore to divorce Fay, when they weren't even married yet. He pulled the plug of the party and knocked over the barbeque on his way in to the house to the bathroom. Everyone screamed and Leroy ran to the house in fear. He was being hunted. At least Becky and Jane were gone. He remembered clearly their days of violent violation. He reached the bathroom and sat weeping on the toilet. Maybe he should walk Thomas now. He finished peeing and went back outside, where the barbeque had been lifted up again and the party was holding itself together at the seams.

Sandra relaxed and invited Gilmore and Fay into her conversation with Oscar, noting that there were three engaged couples there today.

Mae and James, who were not phased by Leroy's outward belligerence quietly celebrated about their upcoming wedding as well. Pastor Williams would be the presiding minister over all three ceremonies.

Leroy went into Thomas's enclosure and sat down next to the big dog, leaning against the fence. "You understand me, don't you Thomas?" who allowed himself to be scratched affectionately. Farley noticed but didn't say anything. If Leroy wanted to sit with the dog, there was no reason why he shouldn't.

Stacy requested a second burger, and Farley put one on for her. She was relaxing after her awkward initiation of dancing at the party. In fact she was getting quiet and gently social with Sally, as Sally explained her job and admitted that both she and Farley had a mental illness. Stacy was quiet and understanding, relating that she had a brother with schizophrenia as well. He wasn't doing as well as Sally and Farley, though, she said.

Sally told her that it would take time to heal and learn to live with the illness.

Oscar overheard the conversation and told Stacy that he had recently been diagnosed with schizophrenia as well.

Now Gilmore wanted another burger, and he felt concerned for Leroy who was alone with the dog, so he asked him if he would like anything else, perhaps another burger?

Leroy looked up gratefully and assented to another burger. Then giving Thomas a big pat he got up and came out of the enclosure to take a chair next to Stacy. He was apologetic and said he was sorry for his outbursts. He didn't mean to be rude. He was just grieving Tina's death severely and felt very unstable. "I need friends right now," he said.

"We're all your friends," spoke Pastor Williams for the group who agreed readily and acknowledged their proffer of friendship to the suffering young man.

Leroy looked around gratefully and accepted a burger from Gilmore, who pointed to the veggie tray with tomatoes, onions, lettuce, and pickles. Leroy loaded up his burger and became quiet, not wanting to be the center of attention.

Mae asked Fay how long she had been engaged to Gilmore. "Three months tomorrow," said Fay proudly. She was quiet and looked searchingly at Gilmore who smiled affectionately.

"Where did you two meet?" asked Mae.

"Actually, we met at the Laundromat. After three Saturdays of concurrent meetings at the Laundromat, Gilmore asked me out to coffee, and it just sort of went from there."

"James and I met at the Library," said Mae shyly. He always took the computer next to mine, and finally we got to talking about each other's work, and found we each liked writing. James works for the newspaper. I don't have a job yet, but I'm writing a novel."

Fay professed to be a freelance writer and Gilmore was a car sales man. He was a shy man, but not on the job. He could be very outgoing, assertive, even a little aggressive at his line of work.

Sally was talking with Oscar and Sandra, when suddenly she realized that she'd missed her appointment with her psychiatrist, Dr. Nett on Wednesday. "Farley! Farley!" She called. "We forgot to see Dr. Nett this last Wednesday. Remind me to reschedule on Monday. This is the second meeting we've missed now. At least we're caught up with Kirk and Nate. We also need to go in for blood draw."

"My case manager's name is Laura," said Oscar proudly, who also needed to have his blood drawn. He was getting tired from socializing at the party. Sally looked at her watch and it was already five-fifteen.

"Maybe we should help you clean up," volunteered Pastor Williams who was keeping an attentive ear and eye on Leroy.

"That would be nice," said Farley. "Leroy, feel free to pack up some food to take home with you."

"Thanks, Farley. Do you think you could drive me home?" Now Farley was also getting tired with the stresses of the party and hesitated.

Pastor Williams jumped in and volunteered to drive Leroy home. That way he could see the new place.

Leroy was thankful and tried to help clean up.

Sandra was still, waiting for Mae and James to go. She was in no hurry. She could sit here for a couple more hours with Oscar and Gilmore and Fay. Stacy was holding her own, and hadn't decided to leave yet either. So Farley boxed up a couple of burgers, cupcakes, cookies and chips for Leroy and sent him on his way with the William's to the Sea Breeze apartments. The car ride was pleasant, and Leroy looked forward to showing off his place. The ride was less than ten minutes. "So I can go walk Thomas whenever I want because it's so close," Leroy boasted.

"Come on in and see," he urged Pastor Williams and his wife. They climbed the stairs to the second floor and walked down to the second door on the right. Leroy let them in and proudly displayed his new home.

"Very nice," said Pastor Williams. "Excellent view."

"Would you like to stay for coffee?" Asked Leroy.

"Of course we would," said the Pastor.

"Could you put a blessing on my new home?" Asked Leroy as he rinsed the coffee pot and got it ready to brew.

"Jesus put your blessing on this home, may the Holy Ghost reside here and prepare a place for Leroy to learn to live again and to heal. We pray in Jesus' name, Amen. That should do," said the Pastor. He looked around at the nice furniture and took a seat. "This place is really, really nice," he said.

Sister Williams agreed and took a seat as well. Nobody knew what to talk about, so they remained silent for a while, as Leroy nervously waited for his coffee to brew. "Would you like a cupcake with your coffee?" He asked. "I brought some from the party. Wasn't it a nice party? I even spent some of it with Thomas."

"The party was spectacular," Pastor Williams agreed. "And yes, I would like a cupcake with my coffee. How about you, dear?" He asked Sister Williams.

"I would also like a cupcake," she said and grew quiet, not knowing what to say. Finally she focused again on the party. "That was a good mix of people at the Cadwell's today. Gilmore and Fay decided to let our wonderful Pastor marry them in the Apostolic Church. That was a great thing. The girls were happy to celebrate together, and you, Leroy, handled yourself very well, considering what you've been through." Sister Williams was very sensitive and understanding. She believed in the Holy Ghost, and prayed also that the Holy Ghost would bless this abode with prosperity and life.

The coffee was done, and Leroy poured two mugs for the William's and one more for himself. He dug in the bag and produced three chocolate cupcakes, giving one to each of his guests.

"I like the view here, it's relaxing," said Leroy.

"Oh, I agree," said Sister Williams, "the water is always so calm to look at, even when it's stormy out. It's exciting to watch it then, when God calls a mild tempest. Those are thrilling times. You have the perfect view – and the hills, too, to the South."

"I wish I had my girl back," Leroy voiced his sorrow.

"God will help you carry on," said the Pastor "Don't turn your back on God. Now is when you need Him most to recover. It helps to think He's a good God and wants the best for you, despite your circumstances."

"My life has been upside down for a long time. I think when Sandra found out what he had done to her, it spooked him crazy-like, and learning that Tina knew about it, he struck out to save himself. But it didn't work. I pray he never gets out of prison. I might kill him if he did."

"Those are valid thoughts," said the Pastor. "But for now you should concentrate on peace, and peace in your life. Make peace with your situation, understanding that you can't turn back events. Tina was a wonderful woman and you were blessed to have time with her. God gives and God takes away. But look where you are now! You have your own place; you have peace knowing that Tina is ecstatic and looking down on you with love and appreciation. She's in Heaven, Leroy, if that's any consolation to you."

Leroy sipped on his coffee mug and took a small bite of cupcake. He was grateful to have his two visitors. It gave him life, hope, and happiness. He wasn't some kind of an evil leper; he was loved, and he hated his brother, as Cain hated Abel.

Only, Leroy hadn't done anything wrong. So it mixed up the nuances.

"I found myself, out there, when I was suffering under Simon. I would have killed him when I had the chance, but God stayed my hand. Instead I gave vengeance to Him, so I hope my brother has to pay for what he did."

"God will deal with him accordingly, and his outlook doesn't look very bright."

"Do you think he'll go to Hell?"

"I think he is in Hell," Pastor Williams said quietly.

They had all finished their coffee and cupcakes and the William's made ready to go. "Are you going to be all right here?" the Pastor asked Leroy.

"I really believe so. I think God wants to heal me, it will just take some time."

"Be sure you keep coming to Church, all right? We need you there, your place is very important. Besides, both you and Oscar need a friend, and I think you are there for each other." Pastor Williams got up and so did his wife.

"Thanks for coming by and praying for my place. I think I'll like it here, it has positive vibes, and there's no blood on the floor – I'm sorry, I shouldn't have said that . . . ."

"Oh you're all right. It's normal for you to be a little mixed up right now. Just keep thinking positive, and give Oscar a call if you need to talk."

"Thanks, I will."

Leroy opened the door for them and they said their goodbyes. He closed the door behind them and picked up their mugs to wash in his new kitchen. He felt alone and hurting. It was climbing on him, this wishy-washy negligence, keeping him upright but hurting his ego. He needed to let go. Let go and forgive. He needed to forgive his brother, and turned his attention to that, rather than blaming himself.

At the party, Oscar had left and gone home to rest himself. Mae, James and Sandra helped put chairs back and folded up the picnic tables. Stacy was lingering and hovering around Sandra as she talked shyly and they compared notes on boy friends. "Oscar is my boyfriend," Sandra said boastfully. "I'm going to heal and marry Oscar and have my baby."

"What do you think of that baby?" Stacy questioned her.

"I really think the baby deserves its life. It's not the baby's fault that it was conceived recklessly. Simon wasn't a *bad* person; just the devil had a hold on his life. I feel sorry for him, and want to make things right by saving this baby's life. Oscar and I have talked a lot about it, and we want to forgive Simon for all he did wrong. It wasn't his fault, it was the devil in him, who had somehow gotten control of his destitute life. I wonder how he felt, desperate?"

"I hadn't thought about it like that," said Stacy, an intelligent woman. "I feel sorry for him as well. Not just that we got hurt, you and I, but he even killed a person when he killed Tina, not knowing what he was doing, I believe he was helpless and lost in a world of evil spirits."

"You mean, you think he was a victim as well?" Sandra was surprised.

"You might say that. The devil's pawn, not his spawn."

"I see what you mean. So we should forgive him."

"I think that's what God wants, as hard as that is to do. I like Him, Jesus, who can forgive and bring new life. Not that Simon shouldn't suffer like he does now, but that he deserves to serve his sentence here on earth, maybe never getting out of prison, but given the God given chance to redeem himself through his daily conduct. He also could choose not to do well, but God won't forgive that. Simon is faced with a choice. I pray he makes the right one."

"Stacy, you make everything so clear. You don't carry the burden that I do, but in your heart you can share it with me. I envy that. I'm a little listless myself, having been violated, it hurts to think about and I need healing. I think healing comes with forgiveness. It's not a lost situation; even Tina is in Heaven now. I feel horrible for Leroy, he must carry such a huge burden right now. If anyone falters now, I think it will be him. We have to stick together. We all belong to this experience, and Oscar does too, having witnessed the evil in person, and without knowing it."

"I'm glad Becky and Jane were here today. We should make a point of getting together, the four of us, for coffee now and then. What do you think?"

"That's a great idea! We all have Simon in common and we need to spiritually cleanse ourselves from his raping, to put it rudely."

"Rude is what it is, no doubt about that. It's something ugly we have to face. Together we can heal ourselves, instead of breaking off and being consumed by the pain."

"I have Becky's and Jane's phone numbers. Should I call and have us arrange something together? Oscar and I like to go to the Turnip Bay Coffee Shop. It's open and spacious. I like it there. Should I try to organize something?" asked Sandra.

"Yes, let me in on it so we can all meet together. Maybe we could make a pilgrimage to Leroy at his new place. He needs forgiveness too, for himself he needs to forgive his brother. We can help him. That brings me to my favorite NIV Bible verse: Ephesians 4:3 'Make every effort to keep the unity of spirit through the bond of peace.' It speaks to my heart, especially now."

"That's really beautiful, Stacy. Maybe Oscar could come visit him with us. They're friends with each other. Leroy really needs Oscar right now. I hope we can work something out."

"I'll call you tonight or tomorrow after I talk to Becky and Jane. I want to arrange something as soon as possible so we can facilitate healing and growth among us. Like you said, we need the bond of peace."

"Well, I'd better get going. It looks like everyone liked the drinks I brought. This cooler was full when it got here. Do you want to take some drinks home with you? There are a few left."

"No, maybe you should offer some to Sally and Farley in thanks for their party."

"It was nice meeting you," Fay said as she got up from her seat. I know your situation and I really admire your fortitude. Gilmore and I don't normally go to Church, but I think we want to look into going to your Church. There are good people there. You are all really good people." Fay was a natural at filling in the blanks and managed to stay quiet as Sandra and Stacy exchanged words. Gilmore was inside talking to Farley, about possibly going camping with each other and their wives after he got married. He wanted to spend more quality time with his brother.

Mae and James were ready to take their leave, and collected Sandra as they moved to go home. Sandra hugged Stacy and promised to keep in touch. She thanked her for her bravery, and her willingness to face the truth with forgiveness and healing. "I love you, Stacy," she said.

"I love you too, my friend," Stacy replied. "Good night to you all."

"Good night," said James and Mae together.

The threesome left and Stacy sat down by Fay. "Would you care to take some of these energy drinks home with you?" She asked her.

"Oh thank you," She replied, "but maybe you should offer them to Sally and Farley."

"I'll just leave the cooler here and pick it up another day. Thanks."

"Thanks for what?"

"Well, for being so understanding. You seem like such a peaceful person.'"

"You'll come to our wedding?" Asked Fay.

"Of course I will. Thank you again!"

Stacy walked to the house and poked her head inside. "Goodbye, all, and thank you for the wonderful party," she said. "I'm leaving you the cooler with drinks in it for you. I'll pick it up another day, OK?"

"OK! Thank you for coming Stacy."

"It was nice meeting you Stacy," said Gilmore.

"Likewise. Goodbye now!"

"See you in Church," said Sally.

"See you in Church tomorrow. Bye."

GARDENS OF HELL

Burning in the freezing winds, you are too cold to be a fire, so you die. That's where you will see paradise. In the ignorance of Hell there is fruitfulness of behavior, turning the wrong to the right and chasing winds to their sources.

Gilmore and Fay stayed until everything was cleaned up and put away. They agreed to meet Sally and Farley in Church tomorrow, who were overjoyed with the prospect.

They left with a few energy drinks, and left the rest in Stacy's cooler. Stacy had really stepped out, having come alone to have accomplished so much peace making at the party. There was little to forgive from her. She had made herself a star, along with the William's.

Sally and Farley realized that Thomas needed his dinner. It was close to dark outside and Farley went to get the big dog out of his enclosure so that he could come in for the night. It was hard to tell which he liked better, to come in at night, or to go back out in the morning. Possibly he liked both equally well.

Farley also brought the garbage out to the front of the fence for the truck to pick up tomorrow. He had just about had it and was nearing psychosis in his exhaustion. When Leroy had knocked over the barbeque he had fretted violently, not wanting the lawn to go up in flames. He took his liberty and didn't blame the young man for his recklessness. He understood. That was part of his mental illness – an uncanny understanding of others.

At his apartment, Leroy took his liberties and dove into the Bible, re-reading the book of John. He grew tired, and taking his liberties, he used the new bathroom to brush his teeth, turned off the light and allowed himself to crawl into bed comfortably.

Morning came and Farley was awakened by Thomas's whining. He needed to go out. He ran out the door when Farley opened it and ran to the fence where he peed gleefully. He trotted around the yard in search of something – Leroy? – his new pal? He found a spot and took a dump. Then he came racing back to the house where Farley had just filled his food bowl and water dish. Delighted in breakfast, he ate like an avid hormone, consecrating his energy in dapper excellence. He growled at his food and barked at the dish, looking around himself and preparing for an intrusion. This was his moment. His breakfast. But where was Leroy, his new friend who walked him every day to the dog park? Farley watched the dog's strange behavior and credited it to the excitement of yesterday's get together.

Then came a whistling, and around the corner there appeared Leroy who was coming to walk the dog. Thomas jumped up on his friend in dapper elegance, dancing with him as the young man held his front paws.

"Hello, Farley," said Leroy.

"Hi Leroy," said Farley. "Did you forget about Church this morning? There's no time to walk Thomas right now – did you want to go to Church with us?"

"Yes, if that's all right. I don't have any wheels right now and the bus system scares me."

"You're welcome to ride along. We'll be leaving in about an hour. Does Oscar need a ride too?"

"I'll call him if I can use your phone. He's probably too shy to call and ask for a ride. I think he usually takes the bus."

"You can call him and see what he prefers."

"Thanks. Where's your phone?"

"Over there on the shelf in the kitchen."

"Thanks." Leroy dialed his friend's number.

"Hello?" Oscar picked up.

"Hello Oscar, it's Leroy. I'm here with Farley and Sally, they're going to drive me to Church. Do you want a ride too?"

"Thanks, but I'd rather just take the bus like I usually do. Besides, I don't want to get in the way."

"OK. I just thought I would ask. See you in Church."

"Right. See you in Church."

Leroy hung up the phone and reported the news to Farley. Sally was just coming into the kitchen, itching for her morning tea. She sat down at the table and sipped on her cup. "How are you today, Leroy?" She said. "How was your second night alone in the new apartment? Do you like it there?"

"Oh I slept like a new born puppy in my new surroundings. I woke up feeling peaceful. It was great to eat my breakfast overlooking the bay. I think I found the right place to live. But I thought I might get a ride with you to Church, if that's all right?"

"Well of course. You rock my world in all your endeavors, Leroy. I'm very proud of you, reaching out for help. I know it must not be easy, what you're going through."

"I forgot about Church this morning. Good thing I came to walk Thomas; Farley woke me up to Church and it's perfect if I can ride along with you."

"We wouldn't have it any other way," said the sensitive Sally.

"OK guys. Time to go in half an hour. Let's not be late today." Farley was ornery about getting to Church on time. "So Oscar is taking the bus?"

"He said he always does and wants to keep it that way. He also doesn't want to be a bother."

"How thoughtful."

"Can I have a cup of coffee to pass the time?" Leroy didn't realize he was being a bother. He was innocent and nonchalant.

"Sure have a cup of coffee."

"That man makes me nervous," Farley said to himself. "He's too needy." But he went along with the ebb and flow of the morning. "Perhaps I'm just being a stickler," thought Farley. "I need to give him a chance; he's been through a lot. But it's not my problem. I have my problems, I don't need more."

Leroy sat blissfully at the table, drinking his coffee slowly as Sally switched from tea to coffee and began drinking that as well. She and Farley had had oatmeal this morning, and needed nothing else.

"Are we ready?" Farley was peaceable.

"All set," said Sally.

"I'll put Thomas in his enclosure," Leroy volunteered hastily. "He's my dog too. I really feel like I have a connection with him."

"Well," drawled Farley, "he actually belongs to us, but I don't mind you befriending him."

"Thanks Farley, I need all the friends I can get this time, I'm not wasting away on my brother, I'm learning to live for myself and God."

Farley was humbled and patted Leroy on the back. "You can consider us your friends," he murmured.

Leroy looked up and met Farley's eye. There was genuine concern. He understood. Farley understood. But Leroy must be very careful with his friends and not use them to his own purpose.

They all got in the car, after Leroy locked up Thomas and Farley drove the twenty minutes to Church. The parking lot was full and Farley found a small space between two SUV's. They got up and went in, and Leroy was shaking like a leaf in his nervousness. Was he to be blamed like his brother?

Sally and Farley walked to their usual spot and Leroy spied Oscar across the room on the other side. "If you don't mind, I'm going to go and sit by Oscar," he said.

"That's fine," said Sally, "Give him greetings for us. Where is Sandra? – oh yes, she'll be coming with Mae and James. We'll save three seats here, and, yes, two other seats for Gilmore and Fay. They said they were coming this morning."

"Great. I'll catch you after Church." Leroy made his way over to Oscar who looked a little nervous as well.

"Hi Oscar! How are you doing this morning?"

Oscar mumbled something unintelligible.

"What was that, Oscar?"

"Hi, how are you doing?"

"I'm fine, I came with the Cadwell's. I guess Sandra and Mae and James aren't here yet. Are you nervous? You look a little bit ticked this morning."

"I had a panic attack this morning after I got up. I was so scared, I felt like my house was haunted. I felt like ghosts were chasing me, trying to get to my soul. I almost missed my bus ride to Church here today. I was so afraid, I'm just now coming out of it."

"I'm sorry, Oscar, I'm glad you could talk to me about it. I'm your friend, remember? I hope we can be there for one another. I guess I'm a little nervous today myself. I feel tainted and I can't shake the feeling. Like I'm a poison to the world. I feel so dirty."

"That's enough, Leroy," stormed Oscar, "I'm tired of you blaming yourself for something you didn't do. I'm sorry, I have a short fuse today. Please forgive my outburst, I'm not being very understanding."

"I understand I can be tiresome. But that's where I am in life. I'm needy and people don't like that. It's over, my life is over."

"Would you stop talking like that?! There's nothing wrong with you and you didn't do anything wrong. Why can't you accept the grace of Christ and move ahead with your life?"

"Well, I have my own place now; that's a start. I walk Thomas every day, so that's something to do. But I know I can't depend on everyone else for support. I have to lean on me and God, right?"

"Yeah, I guess so." Oscar was not particularly friendly right now. He was worried about seeing Sandra and falling to pieces in front of her. The panic attack had really shaken him.

Leroy kept quiet and soon Oscar was pouring out his soul to him.

"My only family is my sister Cordelia. There's no one else to care for me. But it's not my fault being mentally ill. What if Sandra changes her mind and doesn't want to marry me? I'm a stranger to myself, I'm not a rich man, and I sometimes get psychotic. I would have died if she saw me this morning in that wretched state. I believe I was consuming the devil and spitting him out bite for bite. I was crazy with exhaustion. I don't know why, I had such a good time with her at the party last night. We were all dancing there for awhile and everyone was in a good mood except for you, Leroy, but that got covered over thanks to the Pastor and his wife. Let go. Don't blame yourself; just be my friend. I need a friend like you, and I'm friends with Farley and Sally too; they both have a mental illness like me. They understand what I'm going through, and believe it or not, they understand you too. So be my friend, Leroy, you don't need to cry in front of me, but you can if you want to."

Both men were wiping at there eyes, when suddenly Leroy spied Sandra across the room sitting with Mae and James and the Cadwell's. As he watched, Gilmore and Fay walked in and sat down in the seats saved for them. They were all chatting together, and Sandra looked beautiful in her mercy, as she prayed in her seat and swallowed her fear; fear of being exposed in an unnatural way. She didn't want the Church to blame her for her decision to keep the baby and marry Oscar. As she looked up, she saw him from across the room and excused herself from Mae and James to go sit with him.

"Here she comes," Leroy said to Oscar. "Look good now, and remember to meet her eye." Oscar looked thankfully at his friend who was here for him at this nervous moment.

"Hello Oscar, Leroy! Do you mind if I sit with you?" She scrambled into the seat next to Oscar on his right side and took his hand. "I missed you last night after you left. I've been looking forward to seeing you all morning."

"Thanks, Sandra, I've been anticipating seeing you again as well. Yesterday was sure a fun party, wasn't it, Leroy?"

"Oh yes, I had a great time."

"You shouldn't have knocked over the barbeque, Leroy."

"I was nervous, I didn't mean to."

"Boys, boys, stop fighting. What happened, happened and what happens today is meant to be. Remember, we're all friends here."

Sally was watching Sandra from across the room, and admired her guts to be outspoken with her relationship with Oscar. Bless the baby, she thought.

Mae was kneeling before her chair and praying. Sally put a hand on her shoulder and prayed over her as well. Farley was entertaining Gilmore, who wasn't sure what to expect at this service. Fay wasn't a Christian (yet) but came along out of pure interest. She favored one of her legs, having been in a car accident long ago. She was of sound mind and body other than that, and a very stable individual. Farley liked and approved of her; approved of her coming to Church today.

As the whole Church socialized, the praise team came out and they were in full vigor today, singing songs of love to the Lord as the congregation sang along.

The Holy Ghost was present in full force as healing was taking place all over.

Farley felt encouraged, after his near breakdown last night when the party ended. He had used all his courage to deal with the upset barbeque and needed Gilmore to help him. Otherwise the party went well for him, and he praised the Lord, singing and lifting up his hands.

Pure eloquence went through him as he imbibed on the Holy Ghost and felt the rush of the presence of God.

Becky and Jane were sitting together in the middle of the Church. Both were crying big, lopsided tears, figuring their innards with the price of victimization and healing from torture. For torture it was, although not noticeably acknowledged until the truth of Simon came out. They were purged of their fears, and stood tall with hands raised praising and singing along as their tears came down in forgiveness of sin.

Praise went on for half an hour before the assistant Pastor came up and called the Church to order. He made an announcement of a Church picnic the following Saturday at Washington Park. Next he called for tithes and offerings as he did every Sunday. Sally brought up hers and Farley's and put them in the basket. They believed in giving to God. They gave one tenth of their earnings and intermittent offerings each month. Leroy, Oscar, and Sandra each brought up their gifts and took their seats again.

Now Pastor Williams took the pulpit and told the Church to pray for sunshine next Saturday. There was laughter and interest. He spoke about the right to forgive and the healing of the Lord through time and positive experiences, and people too.

He mentioned the small get together yesterday, and made the Church aware of the intentions of Christ in healing and forgiveness. Overcoming rudeness and obstinate behavior with peace and love. Stubbornness in the Lord was a perversion of the truth. It took faith to pry open the vats of love in God's forgiveness. He turned truth to incident and caused action to fix brokenness and immediate danger to the self.

The devil liked to seep into cracks in personalities and take his liberties there. The dwelling of the Lord does not allow that, and when one comes near to the Lord there is a cleansing of evil and sin from the soul, and a renewing of the spirit and heart, which in many people are called broken.

Rearranging the symbols of Heaven to reach down and deliver peace, The Father, Son, and Holy Spirit are gifts to God's creation. Embitterment and sloth are rebuking evil for good, and though they don't taste good, God gives the gift of milk and honey for healing and significance of perpetual lucid and acrid behavior.

Lunatics today would be counted as people having demons in themselves, which Christ cast out of many people. Today, people with mental illness are not cured but made better with the gift of medications. Therapy, treatment, care and understanding can bring about a whole change in a person. Christ still casts out demons, but it figures with medication and tolerance of avid behavior. Nectar sweet as lemons can cleanse the soul today. Facing responsibility, overcoming intolerance, and expecting positive outcomes are new and relational. Thank God for medicine.

The Pastor talked on and there were several healings in the Church that day. Including Leroy's acceptance of himself.

Three people, including Gilmore and Fay, received the Holy Ghost with evidence of speaking in tongues, and both Gilmore and Fay were baptized in the name of Jesus Christ. They each came out of the water rejoicing and immediately got hooked up with brother Clarence and sister Audrey to have Bible study sessions. They were both eager to go out and buy themselves Bibles. It was a true conversion.

Farley rejoiced for his brother, now coming into marriage and being healed by the Holy Ghost as well.

It could have gone another way, but even Oscar felt relieved as Sandra paraded in his presence, flaunting her feminism in his spirit of masculinity.

Sally prayed for Mae's healthy pregnancy and for a strong healthy baby. James quietly suggested that he and Mae have Bible studies with Farley and Sally like they used to, just the four of them. Both Sally and Farley agreed to the idea. They had been doing a lot of outreach since the big Simon fiasco, and deserved some peace and enjoyment in their lives.

The ride home for Farley and Sally was a little bit stressful with Leroy in the car. He kept blabbing about what a good friend Oscar was turning out to be. Then he put himself forward and nearly demanded to walk Thomas to the park again today.

Farley grumbled about wanting to walk Thomas with Sally, since the dog was Sally's animal and they hadn't walked him for a long time.

Leroy nearly begged to go with them, or to the fishing pier to go fishing like they did last time. He said he had good memories of the place and wanted to go again with his good friends, Farley and Sally.

Farley put his foot down and told Leroy that he would drop him off at home, for Farley and Sally needed the time alone together this day. So much had happened including the conversion of Gilmore and Fay at Church today. He suggested that Leroy call Oscar if he needed someone; that they wanted to enjoy the company of their dog, their little family unit, with peace.

Farley got to Sea Breeze apartments and Leroy nearly begged them to come in for coffee, but Farley flat out said "no". Reluctantly, the wistful Leroy got out and walked and waved and walked and waved till he got to the downstairs door. Finally, he closed it behind him and walked up the stairs to his apartment, which was welcoming and inviting when he opened the door. He realized that he would be OK. This was not Simon's place, it was his own apartment where he would live and heal and prosper.

Leroy made himself coffee and took out his Bible to read. After about forty minutes of reading, he finished the coffee and lay down to nap on his cushy couch. He tried to weep but couldn't. He thought of calling Oscar, but decided to save that for later when he really needed somebody. He could always call Pastor Williams for prayer, direction, and guidance.

He needed to do something, but didn't know what to do, thereby not turning on the TV lest he get lost in it, or fall asleep with a bad show. He got out his pocketknife and a stick of wood he had been working on and began to whittle as he leaned back in a chair and put his feet up. He was designing an intricate walking stick for someone to use, he hadn't found the right person to give it to yet. Encouraged he turned on the radio to a good old Classics station and prepared more coffee. He wondered jealously how Farley and Sally were spending their day. He grumbled against them and their high-mindedness. Obviously they didn't like him very much. He wondered why. "What's wrong with me?" He thought.

He had a hamburger for lunch with a few cookies left over from the barbeque. He was jealous of Oscar too. Now that Oscar had Sandra, there was no more room for Leroy in his life. So he thought. The food lifted his spirits as he remembered the party with fondness. Things had gone all right, except for knocking over the barbeque and then the hiding in Thomas's enclosure with him for a spell. Hadn't Gilmore encouraged him to come out? Maybe Gilmore would be his friend.

Jesus is my friend, he said finally to himself. I'm not a bad guy, I'm just going through Hell. When I get to the other side, I'll be able to help people by having healed from my experiences. I need exercise, he thought. Sea Breeze apartment complex sported an athletic room with treadmills, weights, and a rowing machine. He took his liberties and went downstairs to let himself in. He looked around with glee and turned to run back upstairs to change his clothes into something fit for working out. In running shorts and tank top with tennis shoes he practically ran downstairs to the athletic room and mounted a treadmill. He turned it on and looked at his watch. He would time himself for one hour. And he went for it, huffing and puffing, sweating and getting out all his hatred and negativity.

Forty minutes went by when he started really laboring. But he must keep on, he told himself. He screamed out to God as he pushed for the last twenty minutes. Beads of sweat ran down his face and his tank top was soaked. This is really good for me, he thought, and felt positive about his life at that moment.

Finally an hour had gone by and he stopped, bent over and wheezed. He was the only one in the room and walked over to a stretch pad where he sat down and touched his toes, feeling the stretch. He twisted from side to side and spread his legs leaning forward from the waist. Next he stood beside the wall and lifted his right shoe behind him, grabbing it with his hand. It pulled on his hamstrings, and he switched sides stretching his other thigh. Next he sat down with his legs crossed and leaned forward to pray quietly. He gave thanks for this opportunity, this outlet for his fears and agitation.

He realized he hadn't brought a bottle of water with him, and with a wave of contentment left the athletics room and walked back up to his apartment. The coffee was done. He poured himself a tall glass of water and proudly drank it down. I'm working on myself, he thought. He stepped out of all his sweaty attire and took a long, hot shower, soaping everything and washing his sweaty head of hair. His body felt wonderful, pulsing with endorphins.

Out of the shower he climbed into sweats and a clean, cotton T-shirt. He stepped into his house slippers and sat down on his couch, feeling the good effects from his exercise. Now he turned his attention to the view ahead of him and watched the sun as it set over the bay. Night would come soon, a good time to call Oscar.

He faced himself here in these gardens of Hell, realizing he needed to work for salvation. Jesus saved him, but now he must save himself.

He must not commit suicide. He begged for mercy and poured himself more coffee. Then he ate the other hamburger and the last of the cookies and chips. He had an apple on the counter and consumed that too. Now he was tired. The view was spectacular and he thanked God for this place to live.

Finally he let go and called Oscar, having memorized the phone number. As he called, Oscar picked up on the other end.

"Hello?"

"Hi Oscar, it's Leroy. How are you?"

"Hi Leroy! I'm all right, just having some coffee with my Bible. What are you up to?"

"I exercised today. We have a workout room downstairs in my apartment building and I did the treadmill for an hour. I whittled earlier on my walking stick, and I read my Bible earlier too. I also took a short nap . . . which I may do again soon."

"Gosh. You're busy."

"I got dumped off by Farley and Sally after Church today. Then I didn't have anybody, so I sort of just made my day, you know?"

"Yeah. Sometimes you have to push it to get through the hard times. Nobody knows how hard it's been for me, I'm good at faking socially. What a nuisance I can be."

"That's exactly how I feel. Like I'm a big nuisance to everybody. Nobody wants to pay any attention to me. I must be an ugly mess." Tears were coming now and he apologized to Oscar for crying on the phone.

"Oh, you don't have to apologize. I cry all the time. It's getting easier now that I'm treating my illness with medication and therapy. Sally used to think I was a stalker because I kept following her around. For some reason, God told me I needed to speak to them, her and Farley, about my condition. God didn't tell me how to meet them. It was a miracle the day I became an acknowledgement to them.

"They're good friends but Sally and Farley have their own lives too, and can't be baby sitters."

"I wouldn't want a baby sitter. I'd be too nervous. I can't get close to people right now. It's really hard to be around people because I always make such demands on them. Do you think we could get together, you and I and spend some time doing healing stuff, like working out together, or doing Bible studies? I remember you were going to have Bible studies with Simon. That's what he said. He used you for an excuse to get out. I need you as a friend. Do you understand?"

"I understand. I like you, too, Leroy, and don't worry, I don't mix you up with your brother, although it is weird, we used to do stuff together, he and I. We were naughty chasing girls, but I never knew to what extent he was chasing them; you know, the raping."

"My brother is evil. He deserves to be in the Penitentiary. He deserves to live there and to die there. But I have to forgive him, and I'm working on that."

"Me too. I need to forgive him too for using me like he did. We never did anything, but he made it known to me that he had homosexual tendencies."

"Yikes. Even I didn't know that," said Leroy. "I just have to remember that he was and is the devil's pawn not his spawn. There's no hope for him in his gardens of Hell. He deserves what's coming to him. So do I. I deserve to have good things happen to me. I'm a good person."

"Yeah well, I'd better go, Sandra's coming over to watch a movie with me. Do you want to do something tomorrow? Like take a walk in the hills or something? I need to get out and do something. If you want, I'll call you tomorrow and we can plan to meet somewhere. Bring your Bible in case we want to do a study. OK?" Oscar was itching to leave the conversation.

"Sure. Call me tomorrow morning. I don't think that Farley and Sally want me to walk their dog any more. Maybe I should get my own dog. What do you think of that? I don't travel, I love walking dogs, my apartment is plenty big for a small dog, maybe a Pug. I don't know. It's just a thought."

"Good thought. I have to go, I'm getting nervous."

"OK. I'll pray for you. Call me tomorrow, all right?"

"Yeah. Bye now."

"Bye."

Leroy hung up his phone. He turned on his music station and sat still, listening to the soothing music as he let his thoughts go. He wondered what Farley and Sally had done today. Maybe he could call them in the morning. He wanted to be on good terms, in order to have a ride to Church twice a week. I'm desperate, he thought. Nobody likes a desperate person, but I think Oscar understands me. "Lord thank You for my friend Oscar. Please bless his time with Sandra tonight, in Jesus' name, Amen."

He had kept his word and prayed for Oscar. Finally he turned on the TV and watched a show about Chimpanzee rescues on Animal Planet.

When ten o'clock rolled around he got ready and went to bed, murmuring Jesus' name into the pillow as he drifted off to sleep.

Oscar answered his door and let Sandra in at eight o'clock. She had brought the movie with her. She had all three DVD's of *The Lord of the Rings*. "We can make a long night of it and watch all three, she said gaily.

Oscar recoiled in terror. He needed his sleep in order to function the next day. Neither did he trust himself to spend a whole night with his fiancé. He wanted to preserve their purity until after marriage.

"Honey that was splendid of you to bring all three. Maybe, though, instead of watching them all in one night we could watch one every night for the next three days. I don't know how to break it to you, but I need my rest for the next day, I don't want to fall to pieces. I could make you a toasted cheese sandwich, if you want. Have you eaten yet?"

"Not yet," she said, a little bit miffed. "Sandwiches sound good to me, and fruit, too, do you have any fruit or fruit juice?"

"I have bananas that are still fresh."

"Can I have one of those, and maybe a Coke, if you have one?"

"Is Pepsi all right? Diet or regular?"

"Diet Pepsi sounds great. Do you need help in the kitchen?"

"No, I just need company."

"Great. Here I am."

Oscar got out sandwich makings and turned on the stove. The cheese sandwiches were done in minutes, and he gave a banana to Sandra who accepted it graciously.

Next he got out a diet Pepsi for Sandra and a regular one for himself. He put the cheese sandwiches on plates for them and suggested that they start the movie before it got too late.

Sandra succumbed to his probing, and produced the DVD's. "So just one tonight?" She wasn't fussy, and got along easily. She was grateful for Oscar who cared so much about her.

They sat at opposite ends of the couch as the movie began and they ate their sandwiches. The movie was entertaining for them. Oscar had never seen it before and he liked science fiction/fantasy. Both were intrigued in this well-made movie and enjoyed themselves carefully, making comments now and then.

Oscar thought of Leroy and remembered to call him in the morning. He hoped his friend was getting along OK.

It was a long movie, and ended around eleven o'clock. Oscar got up and sat next to his fiancé. He kissed her and carefully put his arms around her neck. He breathed into her ear and told her he loved her. Then suddenly he released her and got up to bring the plates to the kitchen. This is hot and steamy, he thought carefully. I must not go wrong here.

Sandra followed him to the kitchen and said 'Thank you."

"Thank you?"

"For not taking advantage of me. That's important to me. You're not a loser and I'm not a slut."

They hugged each other and Oscar walked her to the door. "Do you want to watch the next movie tomorrow?" He asked carefully.

"Yes, let's do that. I'm sure you'll like it."

"I'm sure I will."

"Good night."

"Good night," she said and Oscar closed the door behind her. Then he opened it again and said loudly, "Call me when you get home so I know you're safe. Are you going to stay with Mae and James?"

"Yes, for a few more nights before I feel ready to stay on my own. I'll call you soon! Bye."

"Bye, Dear," Oscar closed the conversation and shut the door. She said she would call when she got home. He went in and straightened up the couch, putting pillows in place. He thought of calling Leroy but it was probably too late by now, so he refrained. Poor Leroy, he thought, he must have it really hard right now. Well, God is with him.

The phone rang and he jumped. Who would be calling him now? He picked up the phone and it was the Times, advertising for free Sunday papers. "No thanks," he said and hung up. Leroy had mentioned wanting to get a cat. Maybe that would be good for me, too, he wondered, cat or dog? Probably cat, he thought to himself. Maybe two cats. He could pick one out with Sandra and she could pick the other one. Just an idea, he thought.

Finally as he sat down and started drifting off, Sandra called to say good night.

"Good night, Dear," he said. "I love you."

"I love you too," said Sandra.

They hung up and Oscar went to take his nighttime medications before turning in for the night. He pulled the covers up around him and went to sleep peacefully, dreaming of pigs and cockroaches attacking Simon in droves.

Farley woke up early in the morning to a whiney Thomas whose head was next to his face. He got out of bed dutifully and walked the big animal to the door outside. Thomas ran around the yard and peed and pooped and ran into and out of his enclosure, coming back to the door where Farley had prepared his food and water bowls. Farley turned the coffee on and prepared Sally's morning tea, which he brought to her in the bedroom. "Can I climb in here?" He asked setting the cup on a windowsill.

"Sure honey," said Sally slightly aroused. Farley's heavy breathing made her excited to have him near her and she wrapped her arms around his back as he lay on top of her, gliding in and out of her, rising to a peak and then exploding on top of her. She came too and squealed as the natural shudders danced through her body.

"Is it time to get up already, honey?"

"Yes, dear, here is your morning tea," and he handed her the cup from the windowsill. He kissed her passionately and begged for more, so once more she allowed him inside of her and the passion broke all over them, together, powerfully.

"Thank you, Sweetheart," he said softly, holding her as he lay astride her body. Then he got up and went to take his morning shower, first setting out his clothes for the day.

Sally propped herself up on the pillows and slowly sipped her tea, reeling in the ecstatic feelings of her body. Body language was important, and she and Farley communicated perfectly.

She finished her tea and slid out of the bed, heading straight for the kitchen where Thomas sat wagging his tail, happy to see his master. "Go play, Thomas," she directed him and he obediently went out into the yard. So Sally started cooking eggs and frying bacon and hash browns. It would be done by the time Farley was ready. She prepared two plates and drank coffee as she waited for him to appear.

There he was, fully clothed and relaxed this morning. He thankfully took his plate and they ate breakfast together. Sally had a second cup of coffee before going to take her own shower and getting dressed.

It was a Monday, and she prayed to have a good day. After she showered and came out dressed and ready to go, she reminded Farley of their missed psychiatrist appointments, and told him she would reschedule for a new time today. "Are Wednesdays good?"

"Yeah, probably. It doesn't really matter. Whatever works for you will work for me." Farley was easy going.

Sally went outside and scoured the yard for Thomas's droppings. She found them by the fence and with a trowel put them in a plastic bag, which she put into the garbage bin up front. She threw a ball for Thomas and he chased after it, bringing it back to her proudly. She threw it again and then three more times as he chased after it and brought it back to her. Finally, she let him keep it and went back inside.

Farley was getting organized to leave and had the keys to the car in his hands. "Ready?" He asked her.

Patiently he waited as she put the dishes in the sink and ran water over them, leaving them for later. Then she grabbed her coat and her purse and her house keys, and told Farley she was ready. So they went outside, and Sally put Thomas into his enclosure where he had plenty of water and shade.

They went to the car and got in, and just as they were pulling out, Leroy came running down the hill around the corner and stopped in front of the car. "Is it OK if I walk Thomas today?" He asked imploringly.

Sally sighed and looked at Farley. The leash was outside by the steps and hung on a peg above the dog's bowls. "Of course you may walk Thomas, Leroy," said Sally, patiently, and told Leroy where to find the leash. Farley leaned over Sally and said out her window, "You be careful, Leroy. Traffic around here is treacherous. Be careful and look both ways when you cross the streets. Are you going to go to the dog park?"

"I might walk to Oscar's house and go into town from there. I just need a companion, and Thomas likes me."

Farley nodded and they both wished each other a good day. Farley put the car in gear and drove Sally to the Wellness Center where she worked at her clerical job.

"Goodbye, Sweetheart," Sally said as she got out.

"Have a good one, my love," Farley rejoined.

Sally walked toward the building as Farley drove away to his work site. He worked hard, Sally knew, and the heavy labor was good for him, not driving him insane. It was straightforward work and he managed OK on the job.

Sally entered the building and immediately went to the front desk, where she mentioned her need to see Dr. Nett for herself and for Farley, and when did he have any openings?

The receptionist knew Sally well and pulled up Dr. Nett's schedule. "We have a Friday at three, or a Wednesday at one. Tuesday's and Thursday's are booked.

"Can we have Wednesday at one and at two?"

"That would be just fine," said Joyce, the receptionist and put both Sally and Farley on the Doctor's schedule.

"Thank you, Joyce," Sally said and walked around to the back of the office where there was some filing all ready to do, and the phones to answer. Sally rather liked her job and innocently treated it with affection.

Leroy was walking with Thomas now, and making his way to Oscar's house. He would surprise him. He had gotten up early and didn't want to wait for Oscar's call, so he had taken advantage of his liberties and gone to Farley and Sally's house, in a panic to do something, go somewhere.

He climbed the stairs to Oscar's front door and knocked on the door. There was no answer so he rang the bell.

Oscar came shuffling to the door in his slippers, t-shirt, and shorts and opened the door, surprised to see Leroy and Thomas.

"Hi," said Leroy.

"Hi! How are you? Come on in, both of you. I was just going to take my morning pills, so excuse me for a moment. Leroy waited with Thomas in the living room as the dog took *his* liberties and began to sniff all over everything. Oscar was in the kitchen taking his pills.

Leroy wondered about his mental illness and decided to ask him about it later. "Do you want a cup of coffee?" Came Oscar's distant voice. "Yes, please," Leroy came back. "Is it all right to have Thomas in the house?" He asked Oscar.

"Oh, that's fine. He's a good boy, now that he likes me."

"Have you showered yet? – or had breakfast?"

"I've showered but I haven't eaten anything yet." Oscar appeared lost when confronted with this surprise visit.

"I thought I could take you out to eat at the Coffee Shop down town this morning, if you haven't had breakfast yet. It would be on me, since I'm making this intrusion. I should have waited for you to call, but I was just getting too jumpy."

"That would be nice. Could you get me a bagel with cream cheese?"

"Anything you want. We don't need to bring our Bibles, we have Thomas to keep us entertained. Are you ready to go?"

"Let me just change my clothes. I'll be right out."

Leroy sat down on the couch where Oscar and Sandra had sat the night before. He noticed the *Lord of the Rings* DVD's.

Oscar came out all ready to go in his jeans and T-shirt and running shoes.

Leroy questioned him about his night with Sandra yesterday and pointed to the DVD's. "Have you seen these?" He asked.

"Sandra and I watched the first one last night. We had a good little visit. You know, taking our time with each other and no forcefulness. She's a wonderful woman, you know? I really like her."

"You're a lucky man," Oscar, "Count your liberties."

"Well, number one, I have faith in Jesus Christ. Number two, I have Sandra, number three, I'm going to get a cat, number four, I'm finally being treated for my mental illness, and the list goes on, including you as my friend, Leroy," he said.

"You're very lucky," announced Leroy, who was glad to be counted among Oscar's list of liberties.

"Well, let's get going."

"OK. Let's go."

Oscar opened the door and locked it behind them. "Are you still going to get a cat?"

"I'm thinking about a cat or a dog. I like walking Thomas so much it makes me want to get a dog of my own. It would have to be a small dog, but those are cute, too."

They walked along, side by side with the dog between them. "Can I try?" Oscar wanted to hold Thomas. He was deeply pleased at the opportunity to walk this dog that had at one point treed him outside of Farley's house. They were friends now, and Thomas didn't pull. They were crossing the next street when a car came around the corner faster than they thought and slammed right into Leroy. As Oscar jumped out of the way with Thomas, Leroy went down under the green Volkswagen

Bus. He crunched and died upon impact. Shock and trauma filled the air, as Oscar floated above the whole accident holding onto Thomas and desperately trying to keep himself together on earth. He sat back on his haunches and howled at this apparition. Grief filled his face and his hands shook as he placed one hand on Thomas' head, and the other on his own forehead.

A witness must have called, for an ambulance came swiftly and medics examined Leroy's body, which was destroyed upon impact, and they pulled him out from under the vehicle. Where was the fault? The driver of the bus was frantic and in shock, unable to digest this turn of events. Oscar wasn't believing his eyes. As he looked upward, horrified, he saw Leroy's soul disappearing away. It vanished at peace.

Because of Oscar's illness, he had heightened senses, which allowed him to see that especially in the gravity of this tragic situation. Leroy waved goodbye to him, and rose out of sight, into the coming clouds of Heaven.

Oscar talked to the police and the driver, as more ambulances arrived and the driver, whose air bag had released on his steering wheel and cushioned his head leaving him with a neck injury and a dislocated shoulder, and smashed knees. Oscar gave them as much information as he knew. Crying, he admitted to being a friend of Leroy's and that Leroy had no family other than a brother in prison. Choking, he had no idea what to do with the body. It was his friend who had just been walking with him. It was over, just like that. Oscar went into pilot drive and said he must return the dog to its owner. He could walk there. But now what about Leroy? Oscar began to bawl, heaving as his shoulders drew inward and down. He sat down on the sidewalk and cried for fifteen minutes. He was shaking and the medics examined him for damage, but there was nothing done except a state of shock.

Would Oscar be all right?

He would. He must take this dog back to its owners. The second ambulance left with the driver whose car was moved to the side of the street. If only he hadn't been speeding. If only he had reacted sooner. Leroy was pronounced dead. The other ambulance took his body away. That was the last that Oscar saw of Leroy, who was consequently buried in a small graveyard with a massive ceremony. Leroy never knew he had so many friends. The entire Church showed up for his funeral as Pastor

Williams presided. The driver that hit Leroy paid for his funeral. It was the last thing he could do.

"And we all knew him as a kind, loving young man with struggles more than most people face. Right now our friend Leroy is in Heaven with Tina, and with Jesus. So we should rejoice for him as his spirit is liberated and he is free to be who and what he has always wanted to be."

The day of the accident, Oscar had blindly walked Thomas home to the Cadwell's, and put him in his enclosure. He sobbed as he turned to leave the dog, and left the leash on the back steps. He walked home and made lunch, a tuna fish sandwich with a banana and pop.

He called and left a message with Farley and Sally on their voice mail. They came home to the message that day and immediately Sally called Oscar for details and wanted to know about Leroy. What had happened? Whose fault was it? Where was Leroy now? Was Oscar safe with himself?

Oscar called and relayed everything that had happened so suddenly with Leroy and the dog, and the Bus that came screeching around the corner and hit him; Leroy was buried partially under the car.

Oscar and Thomas were untouched, having jumped out of the way before Leroy did, although he had tried.

The funeral took place on Monday a week later, where Pastor Williams gave the epitaph. A wave surged through the Church as everyone remembered Leroy and the hero that he was.

Farley and Sally saw Dr. Nett the Wednesday after the accident, and they were both blinded by their ignorance of having judged Leroy too harshly. He was a good man, plagued by problems too big for him to handle alone. The Lord had called him home.

Sally was the first to see the Doctor and she sat down in his office. She cried about Leroy as she sat there with Dr. Nett who was sympathetic and understanding. Sally's medications were working well for her, she was holding steady at her job, and she needed to walk Thomas. Everyday she needed to walk Thomas, for Leroy, in place of Leroy whom the dog had befriended.

Sally's relationship with Farley was steady and loving. They were there for each other always.

Sally still attended Church twice a week and had a healthy relationship with God.

She had no plans or thoughts of hurting herself. She weighed in at exactly the same weight as last time, one hundred and eighty two pounds. She agreed she was overweight, but that this was a side effect of her medicines. She and Farley were managing well financially, they still liked to go fishing. Fishing made her think of Leroy again and she sobbed.

Dr. Nett conceded that she appeared fine, and if there weren't any other hidden issues, she was all done.

There were no hidden issues, but this blatant one with Leroy that she would need to work to process and cycle through herself.

Seeing her trouble, the Doctor prescribed her an added two milligrams of Lorazepam to adjust to her anxieties.

Sally agreed that would be helpful and sniffled as she finally got up and exited the room. It was two o'clock, Farley's turn with Doctor Nett.

"Hello."

"Hello," said a quivering Farley as he sat down with the only other person than Sally who knew his weak side, his vulnerabilities and fragility. "I'm a strong man, but this catastrophe with Leroy has really shaken me up."

"How so?"

"I see visions, visions of collisions happening all around me. I'm afraid to walk in front of our own car when it's parked. I'm afraid of the cars across the street parked there. I'm afraid for my wife now that she's pledged to walk our dog everyday. I'm afraid one of us might suddenly die, and then how could the other one of us cope? I'm afraid of getting cancer or having kidney failure. I don't want to die yet, but I feel like I might die at any time unexpectedly."

"Nobody knows when their time will come, but you can't go through life expecting it to happen in the next breath or else you won't be able to live. You have no greater chance of dying today than you did before the accident."

"I was so rude and impatient with Leroy. I let him bother me when I should have given him the attention he needed. I wasn't a very good friend to Leroy and I feel bad about that."

"You did what you could, Farley. You took him under your wing and gave him a place to live while he recovered from the trauma caused by his brother, Simon. He had no other place to go, and you were very gracious to take him in."

"I allowed him to walk Thomas everyday, thinking it was good for both of them. But then I started feeling protective about the dog, not wanting him to love Leroy more than me. Thomas is our dog, but he was Leroy's friend."

Farley wiped two small tears from his eyes and the Doctor offered him tissue to wipe his face.

"I'm a small person in the big world of things. My life is insignificant to many, many people. I work everyday, I love my wife, and she works everyday, too. Together we live peaceably, and have joy in our lives. But I don't know what I would do in Leroy's shoes. He was friendless, plagued, traumatized and then made to feel a bother. I'm so sorry, Dr. Nett, couldn't I have been kinder towards him?"

"You did what anyone would do in your shoes. You have your own life to live, and you can't go around going out of your way for everybody. They need to live their own lives, and it looks like your friend Leroy was starting to do exactly that. No one knows why he was called home, as you say, but together we can know that he's much better off where he is now than when you had him at home with you and Sally."

"He's free. He's liberated. No more chains to tie him down, or to the wall."

"Now you have to make allowance for yourself to grieve and not accept responsibility. You can overcome this, day by day as you live your normal life and do the things that make you happy. You still like to go fishing, don't you? You can do it alone if you need think time, otherwise what better way to spend time alone with Sally? What else can you do together?"

"We can have over our friends Mae and James for a Bible study. Or invite my brother Gilmore and his soon–to-be-wife, Fay over for dinner or lunch or coffee sometime."

"Do you still intend to go to Church together twice a week?"

"Yes, and the other thing we can do is to walk Thomas together, so I won't be so worried about Sally going by herself. I'm possessed. I think every passing car will be the car that runs me over. I'm afraid of the streets."

"Maybe you could walk up in the hills rather than through the city streets. And if you feel up to it, why not go to the dog park and let your Thomas run and play with other dogs. Isn't that what Leroy did on his walks?"

"Yes, it would commemorate our time with him to do as he did and walk Thomas to the dog park. Then we could walk through the park. Washington Park is very beautiful and boasts many woodsy trails where we could go and enjoy nature."

"That's sounding better already!"

"Yes, I think we will recover from this misfortune. We just need to keep living our lives together, and go to Church, and walk the dog, go fishing, and relax at home when we're not working. Work is essential for both of us, otherwise we couldn't live on the disability income we get as a married couple. Luckily we got help finding jobs that match our abilities. I bless my lucky stars for that."

"How is your diet?"

"Fine. I'd like to lose a few pounds here and there, but I can't complain. I have enough to eat, unlike some people, and I can even go out to eat every now and then. That's always a luxury."

"House payments?"

"We're holding steady there. Plus tithes, phone and internet, and light and heating bill. Those always go out first, and with our jobs we can afford to eat until the end of every month."

"Sounds good. Your meds.? How are they working?"

"Fine I just might need a little extra of something to get through this tragic event."

"That's fine. I'll do what I did with Sally and prescribe you an extra, optional two milligrams of Lorazepam to have under your belt if you need it. I'll give you a two weeks supply. By then things should have settled back down to normal for you. So great! You're doing astounding under all the circumstances. Keep holding it together and realize that all things pass and everything balances out."

"Thank you, Dr. Nett. Are we good for the next month?"

"If anything comes up, let me know, otherwise I'll see you in one month. Here's your prescription and your date time on my business card."

Both men stood up and shook hands. Farley felt very small. But he knew what he needed to do. It might even include a couple of visits to the Red Tornado Casino, as long as he set limits and could bear loss without going over his budget. He knew when to stop; at two twenties on the slot machines. What harm could it do? He wasn't hooked. He didn't go often. Just for enjoyment now and then. But he knew that Sally didn't approve; she took it with a couple of grains of salt.

Dr. Nett guided Farley out of the office to the lobby, where Sally was waiting for her husband. "See you in a month, both of you!" Said Dr. Nett and called in his next patient.

Sally and Farley drove home slowly in silence. Sally needed to talk to Mae about Sandra, and how much longer would she be living with her and James. Guilty as she felt, she was glad that Leroy was out of their home. It was taxing having another individual who was so desperately needy. They had done their best, and even kept tabs on Oscar with his new diagnosis and pill regimen.

Oscar had been friends with Simon and then Leroy. He didn't blame himself for any of the outcomes. He was liberated now and could be with Sandra without Leroy's critical eye and hell damning issues about the baby. To be truthful, he didn't really miss Leroy who was so needy. At the same time the two had begun to be buddies and close friends. However he hadn't been able to offer his home to Leroy, not with Sandra moving in, in the near future. He thought that Leroy was beginning to do well for himself. He had found a nice place to live, and even tried to fill his days with activity. He was scared to be alone, but had Oscar's phone number to call at any time, and he hadn't taken advantage of that privilege. Hope to hope, Leroy was in Heaven. Oscar had seen his soul rising. In a way, now, he stood in awe of the situation. People would miss Leroy. More than he would've ever known.

Farley and Sally reached home and got out of the car. There was a profound emptiness. They both mourned for Leroy and counted their blessings to have each other as one of them. They both agreed it would be the right thing to walk Thomas now.

It would have to be a short walk, as it was Wednesday, a Church night and they didn't want to miss the service. They headed left into the hills and came to the big cross with the pile of stones nearby. Each Farley and Sally said a prayer and then added their stones to the pile, giving thanks to Jesus Christ their Lord and Savior.

It was enough. Farley walked the dog on the way back and put him in his enclosure for the evening. Together they hung the leash by the back door, and then turned and kissed one another. No words needed to be spoken.

Farley looked forward to seeing Gil' and Fay this Wednesday before their wedding on Saturday. Farley wanted to go and worship the Lord. Sally wanted to pray at the altar and sing praises with songs to the Lord. It was a safe place, and it needed to remain that way.

Getting ready, Farley and Sally kissed as they passed each other in the house, each tending to personal needs. Sally put on a nice blue skirt with a pink top and nice black flats with black nylons. Farley wore a button down shirt with black slacks and black shoes. They both dressed up casually.

They decided to skip dinner and go out for a bite to eat later. They didn't want to be late for Church, and being ready early, they left a little early to pray for the service and their friends and each other and their selves.

Once at Church, Farley parked their little car and they got out and went in. The choir was practicing and being early, they went in and sat down in their usual seats, saving room for Mae, James, and Sandra, and Gilmore and Fay. Oscar always sat across the room, and more than likely, Sandra would go and sit by him.

As they were praying, Gilmore and Fay walked in and sat down next to Farley and Sally. They were respectful and quietly sat. The choir was done and the Church began to fill up. Everyone missed Leroy. There was a hunger in the air and a chill that went with it. The Holy Ghost settled upon the congregation in full power as everyone gave thanks for the goodness in their lives, and acknowledged that accidents do happen, and that nobody knew when their time on earth was through.

It was a short service, in utter gloom, and even the praise songs came out slow and sloppy. The Church was rickety and threatened to up heave itself, blowing smoke into the reaches of nowhere. Leroy's funeral was announced for next Monday. The entire Church was welcome to show up. On that day and occasion there was no shortage of comrades. Many women, too, attended the service, with bleeding hearts at the loss of one of their Church members.

Leroy would be buried in a small graveyard, funded by the driver in the accident. It was programmed together to work that way. Leroy was given free release. Sorrow blew through the congregation that Wednesday night, and many people turned around to forgive grudges that had been held for a long time.

Finally Oscar showed up and sat across the sanctuary by himself, hoping that Sandra would come and sit by him. She did. As Mae and James arrived with her, she excused herself to go and sit by Oscar. He was elated and poked her tummy, which wasn't really showing yet.

They sang together, listened together and prayed together. At altar call, they both went up and kneeled before the altar. Oscar was crying; still in shock from the sudden loss of his friend and his own near escape. But he focused on the Lord and gave thanks for his life and the many blessings he had.

Darkness fell, and after service, when Pastor Williams had preached that day, the congregation moved out to their designated vehicles. Sandra went with Mae and James in their car, while Oscar took the bus back to his house and Farley and Sally drove home, alone.

Gilmore and Fay were especially pleased with the service and couldn't stop talking about Saturday, when their wedding would take place.

They drove in Gilmore's car and he dropped Fay off at home.

When he got home, Gilmore walked around his place thanking God for his Fay, and praying against such accidents as had befallen Leroy. Life was that little bit more appreciated. He loved his brother, Farley, and Sally, his sister in law. They were such a strong couple and both dealt with their mental illnesses. He was glad to be there for them, and pleased that Farley had found his golden watch with the diamond on the minute hand.

He had been devastated long ago when his brother took ill. There was nothing he could do to help his suffering. Farley was so angry and had needed to be hospitalized for two months. Gilmore had gone to visit his brother nearly every day that he could, and Farley had come to live with Gilmore after being discharged from the hospital and was no longer a threat to himself. For a time he was suicidal, but that had passed.

Farley started taking groups at the Mental Health and Wellness Center, and slowly accepting his medications he had recovered from his "break". When Sally came into the picture, Gilmore was relieved. His brother still had it in him to live a normal life.

But Leroy was pronounced dead, and he couldn't decipher whom that benefited if not Leroy himself.

The accident had come out of the blue, totally unexpected. Leroy hadn't had a caring brother like Gilmore, but neither did he have a mental illness like Oscar, Farley and Sally. If enough time went by, the story would wash over as a bad clip of news.

Gilmore picked up the phone and called his brother.

"Hello?" Spoke Farley.

"Just checking up on my favorite brother. Are you doing all right?"

"Hey, thanks for calling, Gil'. I'm doing all right, holding it together. I hope this all washes over soon, because I must admit I'm a little bit psychotic under all the stressors that are pulling me different directions. I hope peace settles back upon our house, and life can go on normally without this gigantic zit popping in our faces. It should all heal up. Leroy will be remembered fondly in the hearts of everyone. Especially me. He really turned to me for help, and I was glad I was able to help him. Thomas most of all appreciated Leroy. No one knows just how tormented he was. We want him here with us still, but could we have helped him in the way he needed to be helped?"

"Forgive yourself and let go. You did help him as much as you could. Now forgive him for all his trespasses. Leroy wasn't perfect like many would like to believe. He clung and he needed and he had false hopes without a future. We miss him now, but it's time to let go and let Leroy take his liberties with him, to miss this place, but be now in paradise."

"You put that very well, dear brother. How are you doing?"

"Jumping up and down about my wedding on Saturday. You'd better be there for the ceremony, brother."

"I wouldn't miss it for all the money in the world."

"Good. Well, I'm going to say goodnight."

"Goodnight, Gilmore."

Farley hung up and sat on the kitchen stool, with shoulders draped forward. Besides Sally, Gilmore was Farley's most important person in the world. He felt stretched out, like his entity was covering a lot of ground at once. Sally came into the kitchen and rubbed his shoulders. He prayed he would never have to leave her. Maybe the Rapture would come and they would both be caught up in Heaven with Jesus.

"It's time for bed, Sweetie," she said. "Just leave everything till tomorrow. We need to get our sleep and go to work tomorrow. Do you follow me?"

"I'm coming. I'm just so thankful for Gilmore. He's been there for me ever since I got sick. I used to live with Gilmore. Then I met you, and, well, you know what happened," he said slightly embarrassed. "We have to let the dog in and feed him." He said suddenly.

Sally ran outside to the enclosure and let Thomas out who bounded out to see her and ran to the house where Farley was just filling up his food bowl and putting down fresh water.

The dog ate voraciously, and wagged his stump of a tail as he pushed his way into the living room onto the couch.

Satisfied, Farley and Sally changed clothes, took their pills and brushed their teeth, and got into bed together. It was a sad, sorrowful night and they lay together, arms around each other as they each drifted off into dreams of hope and future.

As morning arrived, Thomas whined in Sally's face and implored her to get up and let him out to pee and poop.

Very quickly she got out of bed and ran to the kitchen door, opening it to let the dog out to do his business. She poured food in his bowl and washed out his blue water bowl, filling it with fresh water.

Thomas came back and politely ate his breakfast, only to go running around the yard barking at a squirrel and sniffing the smells of the day. He waited for Leroy, but Leroy never came, and never again would come. He lay down in the grass outside the kitchen door, sunning himself.

"The day rises," spoke Farley as he shuffled into the kitchen and turned on the radio. He half expected to hear about Leroy's accident, but he didn't. Instead he appreciated the classic hits that this station played which reminded him of his youth.

Sally was in high spirits as she faithfully made her morning cup of tea. She sat with it on the back steps and sunned herself as well. There were crows dotting the lawn, going after what she did not know. Worms?

Sally drank her tea slowly. She had risen early and had plenty of time before she must leave for work with Farley. Just as she finished her tea, Farley brought her coffee and exchanged cups for the empty one. Now she took sips of her coffee and enjoyed the caffeine rush that she was getting. She smelled food and realized that Farley was cooking their breakfast.

Gardens of Hell, she thought to herself. Had Leroy been plucked like a weed that didn't belong? Was he nourishing himself on borrowed time? Could God water a garden like that, that had no place to grow?

He filled it up with noise and battering rams, guilt and complexes of suicidal envy. Belonging to hatred, growing in sin, caught in determination to pull through, his gardens had been in Hell, while I live here on earth, voiced Sally. It was better to be in Heaven than to live in gardens of Hell among weeds and polluted soil, lucid in the imagination. Freakishly living Holy Hell while everyone around him was on earth and gardening our planet.

Sally sat with her ankles crossed and her knees up, balancing the coffee cup on her left knee. I'm lucky I belong and don't live in gardens of Hell. That's where I would be if either Farley or I would be unfaithful to the other of us. Luckily that won't happen, she pondered, as they were so in love with one another.

"Sally! Sally! Breakfast is ready." Farley called his wife.

"I'll be right there," said Sally. She leaned her head back and appreciated the morning sun with Thomas. Well, at last it was time to go eat breakfast. She got up and went in, seating herself and her coffee cup at the kitchen table. Farley brought her dish with eggs, bacon and hash browns. Together they ate and got up and washed their dishes, putting them in the dish strainer to dry. Sally couldn't help but think of Leroy, realizing he would not be coming to walk Thomas. She confided this in Farley, and together they prayed and had a moment with silence.

"We've just got to let him go. We appreciate who he was, and the many lives he's touched; really there's nothing bad to say about him. He was just a turkey in a tight spot, kind of stuck there fearing for his head to be cut off."

"Maybe if he was mentally ill he could've handled his life better. He has no one to blame for his torture, other than his hellion brother Simon. Leroy told me that Simon had cut them both and mixed their blood together. It was eating him up inside, there was no one who could keep him from harming himself, but he chose to live. He found an apartment, was thinking about getting a job, wanted to walk Thomas everyday, he simply got side swiped. It was an accident, but maybe a blessing in disguise."

"You're right about all of that, Farley, I couldn't agree more. But you know what? We have to be leaving now; can't just sit forever and mull over the loss of our friend."

"You're right. Let's go!" They locked Thomas in his enclosure and walked around the house to the front yard, having locked all the house doors and made ready to leave.

They both got in the little car and Farley drove them to the Wellness Center, where they said goodbye, and waved as Farley drove on.

Sally went in to her nine-to-one job and began organizing the reception area where clients came in to check in for their arrival. She manned the phone and began the morning's filing job. As she was working Oscar called to set up an appointment with Laura, his case manager. He was desperate and needed help right away. Apparently he had spilled all his pills down the toilet in rebellion to the weight he was gaining and for the many voices that plagued him, one of which had told him to throw away his medicines. He needed refills and to talk to somebody.

"Let me see if Laura is available, otherwise you can see the on call nurse."

Oscar held on, sweating and cold footed, shaking with despair and ready to beg for help and new meds.

"Laura is out today, but you can come in and talk to Rebecca, today's on call nurse. She should be able to set you up with a new supply of medicine. Oscar, it's me, Sally. I need you to promise me that you won't do that again. We'll talk later, but for now, get some exercise and walk on down here. You need to get out of the house and move your body."

"Hi Sally. Thanks for your help, and I'll be there pretty soon. Thanks again, Bye."

"See you soon Oscar."

The troubled young man was beginning his life as a medicated, mentally ill individual. Mistakes like these were bound to happen. She remembered her first or second prescription paper, and in spite of her madness, she had ripped it into little pieces and chewed on them, spitting the bitter paper out in a grass field and grinding the paper into the earth with her heel.

She had needed an emergency refill and became terrified of the way she felt having not used her medications for three days. Hopefully Oscar had caught himself before that.

She looked out on the lobby and gazed at the many different types of people who were here for some type of treatment. God sure made a crazy world, she said to herself, and kept working around the office.

It wasn't until two hours later that Oscar came shuffling in, covered with sweat and breathing paranoia. "I'm here to see Rebecca the nurse, he said at the receptionist desk. Sally was taking her last fifteen-minute break and so missed him when he came in. "Where's Sally?" He asked the receptionist.

"She's on break," replied Niel who had just come back from break himself. "You needed to see Rebecca?"

Oscar nodded hysterically, drool running off of his face.

"One moment while I call her."

Oscar waited patiently, knowing that now everything would be OK. A young woman with blonde hair came up to the desk and asked if he was Oscar. He nodded vigorously and shook her hand as she introduced herself. He was so relieved that he almost forgot to let go of her hand. "Oh thank you for being here to help me."

"Let's get an office so we can talk." He followed her down the hall to the right and went inside an open office to which she closed the door.

"What can I do for you, Oscar?" She questioned intently.

"Well, to put it short, I have a friend that just died, he was hit by a car while our dog and I jumped out of the way just in time. I've been a little psychotic since then, and I miss him, and then I started hearing voices telling me to get rid of my medications, that they were doing more harm than good. But after two days I've started to feel a lot worse. My emotions are going haywire, and I'm scared to see my fiancé like this because I might do something abhorrent to her. I'm scared. I need refills on all of my pills."

"I see. Who is your Doctor that prescribes you pills?"

"That would be Dr. Nett."

"Hang on a minute while I give him a call."

Oscar sat nervously in his chair, fighting demons and bats in his head. Rebecca reached Dr. Nett and explained the situation to him. "Yes, yes," she said, and "of course", and "no – Oscar you're not feeling suicidal are you?"

Oscar shook his head, no, adamantly and Rebecca went on. "That's right. He flushed all his pills down the toilet."

She waited and listened. "Very well. So you don't need to see him?"

"Not at this point," said Dr. Nett. "He seems to have found the folly of his ways."

"Yes, I'll send him to the pharmacy right away. Two milligrams? I'll tell him. Thank you Dr. Nett."

Rebecca turned to Oscar and told him that all his pills were being called into the pharmacy, including an added two milligrams of Lorazepam to pull him out of this funk.

Oscar thanked Rebecca and went across the way to the pharmacy where he checked in and waited for his medicines. He would treat these medicines kindly. They were there to help him.

Finally his name was called and he went up to receive his full prescribed medications. He paid the small co-pay amount and took his pills, searching through the bag to see that everything was there like before. There was the new Lorazepam. Everything else he recognized.

Walking back out to the lobby, Oscar spied Sally behind the receptionist window and he went up to the window to wave hello.

Sally saw him and waved hello back. She came up to the front and greeted Oscar, who told her he had been able to get refills on all his pills – plus a new one, and he promised never to throw away his pills again.

"That's good Oscar. If you ever want to be stable again, you've got to take your pills like they're prescribed to you. I'll leave a note here for Laura that you came in to see her. She'll call you and you can reschedule."

"Thank you *SO* much," said Oscar and wished her a good day. After that he left and started back on his way home. When he finally got there, he took his Lorazepam, prescribed for afternoons, and put his other meds., for night time and morning next to the kitchen sink.

Before calling Sandra, he would wait to feel better.

Gilmore and Fay were becoming nervous little clowns, jumping up and down about their wedding the day after tomorrow. Mae and James had actually contacted them to suggest the idea of a dual wedding. They didn't want to wait until February to get married. Something didn't feel right in their relationship, and they decided to stop sleeping together until after they were married. It was time for Sandra to move out on her own again, and they spent all of Thursday moving her things back into her old apartment. They asked if she was OK, and she agreed it was the right thing to do. She had enjoyed living there before the rape trauma, and she would enjoy living there again. Now she had healed a lot emotionally, had accepted the baby with love, and was quite ready to marry Oscar, when he was ready to take care of them. She had quit her old job, selling shoes, and could easily find another one.

Sandra and Mae and James packed up the old Toyota, making two trips to bring all of Sandra's things to her apartment. They said goodbye emotionally, and Mae made sure that she had plenty of groceries. "Call us anytime, Sweetheart," said Mae as they prepared to leave Sandra to organize her things.

Sandra hugged each of them and thanked them profusely for taking her in like they had. She promised to be at the wedding ceremony with Gilmore and Fay together on Saturday.

As Mae and James drove home, they felt in the pits of their stomachs that she was going to be all right. They sighed and looked at each other. It was the Christian thing to do, what they had done, and Mae had enjoyed Sandra's company.

Mae and James soon to have the combined last name of Wilburton drove into their driveway and got out of the car. James made a quick scan of the back seat and trunk to make sure Sandra had all her things. He found nothing so they went inside ready for dinner. They had fried hamburger patties and salad.

That night they slept in separate rooms and prayed for forgiveness for their situation, being caught in pregnancy out of wedlock.

Gilmore was making his house as inviting as he could for his precious Fay who would be becoming Fay Cadwell. He loved her intensely, and couldn't wait to start their married life together.

Sally and Farley each had Friday off, something they did every now and then to have more quality time together. Doing what they liked best, they took their gear to Farley's fishing pier and set out to spend the day fishing. They brought a picnic basket including sandwiches with Brie Cheese. Neither one caught anything for the first two hours, when suddenly Farley had one on. It was a lovely perch of nice size and they put it in the bucket after clobbering its head so it remained motionless. Then, instead of fishing on, Sally took the fish and scaled it and cleaned it, putting the fillet in the bucket after chopping off its head.

They neither one had any more luck and walked back grudgingly as they remembered morosely having been there with Leroy last time. They both felt depression and walked on quietly.

Farley didn't know how to handle his feelings, and tried to ignore them by whistling Amazing Grace. Sally joined in and they whistled all the way home as their emotions rearranged themselves and processed through, carefully falling into place. It was a healthy feeling of acceptance without expectation.

At home, Sally fried the fish and they shared it. Still hungry, they pulled out a frozen pizza and stuck it in the oven on bake.

Sally wanted to make cookies. She got out flour, sugar, butter, raisins, eggs, oats, chocolate chips, vanilla, salt, and baking soda. As Farley sat down to read the daily paper, she prepared the batter, mixing all the ingredients together. Next she pulled out a cookie sheet and started making balls of dough and setting them in rows of four by five. The oven had room for two cookie sheets, and when they were all finished she put them in for twelve minutes.

She found herself weeping about Oscar, and how innocently desperate he had seemed yesterday at the Wellness Center. She understood how he felt, having done a nearly similar sort of thing in her own life. So Oscar was hearing voices again.

She needed to be there for Oscar. It was God ordained that they had been brought together. She could mentor him these early years of diagnosis until he had finally accepted it within himself. Now he had Sandra, and apparently they were in a great relationship.

Both couples; Gilmore and Fay, and Mae and James wanted a small wedding with a few chosen friends on both sides. Mae wanted Sandra, Sally, and Stacy to stand up with her, and James chose Farley, Oscar, and that was all. Fay had two friends, and then Sally, while Gilmore also wanted Farley, and two of his close friends.

Preparations were made and the weddings promised to be small and intimate. Sally was nervous for Gilmore, knowing what a kind, shy person he was. Finally he was taking the step towards marriage. And James and Mae Wilburton the newly weds would be, having waited too long to marry and having been caught out of wedlock. The time was theirs to shine.

The cookies were done in twelve minutes and Sally took them out of the oven. They were soft and chewy. She set the two cookie sheets on top of the oven to cool down a little bit. Irresistibly, she lifted one up with a spatula, and brought a fresh, hot cookie to Farley as he sat reading the paper.

"Thank you, my Queen bee," he said appreciatively.

"Careful, it's hot," said Sally, proud of herself.

As she watched Farley consume the cookie, she couldn't help but go get one for herself. She ate it in the kitchen, leaning on the counter, and decided to have a cup of tea.

She heated the water and poured it over a bag of Chamomile Tea. She played with the tea bag, dunking it up and down and swirling it around in the cup. After it had steeped and cooled a little, she took another cookie and sat down at the kitchen table where she mulled over her day and tried to make sense of all that had been going on around them. She realized that she needed to call Oscar and check on him. So she did. She dialed his number and he picked up on the other end.

"Hello?" Oscar's voice sounded cool and together.

"Hi Oscar, it's me, Sally."

"Hi Sally, thanks so much for helping me yesterday. How are you doing?"

"I'm doing pretty well, considering our circumstances. Farley is pretty stable, and I'm still processing my feelings about Leroy and Tina. She was a friend of mine. I miss her."

Sally hadn't called to vent, but realizing that Oscar was a good outlet, she began to pour out her feelings, first of all checking with Oscar about his medications.

"I'm taking my new Lorazepam," said Oscar, "and I'm getting ready to take my nighttime pills really soon. I can't wait to get them in me."

"That's great, Oscar. How are you doing emotionally?"

"Oh, I'm a little bit shaky myself. Starting with Simon, I hope he goes to hell and wanders in hell's gardens for the rest of his days. Blistery pools of hot oil, thirsty, burning, flaming gardens of Hell. Those days will never end for him, either. That's how I feel about that. He was like an automated killing machine, and nearly killed Sandra's spirit when she learned her condition and what happened to her. I feel so sad for Tina. Now she's in Heaven with Leroy, though, and I guess that joy is meant to be regardless, forever."

"Oh Oscar I feel the same way. A young man struck down in his youth, terrorized in life and innocent in death. I can't really follow his history, as I only knew him from Church and that was on brief terms. Wasn't he fresh out of college?"

"Virginia State. He left there to come out here and live with his brother. He had no idea what an ugly creation Simon had become. Simon was someone full of Satan, ready to do evil at any turn. Maybe he needed help. Who cares now?"

"I certainly don't," muttered Sally. She didn't know if it was proper, but she hoped that Simon would burn in hell's gardens forever, forever burning, continuously, non-stop eternal flaming consumption. "Let him walk through pools of burning oil, and dry his feet on burning stubbles of hay, thrown everywhere, sneezing, trees bearing grenades, never to end, unable to die, but be tortured forever. Flaming flowers, bare footed, pathless, messes of eternity, and every mistake ever made come falling down upon his shoulders. Total, eternal destruction, every disease visited with nothing good to hang onto. At the devil's beck and call, tortured by demons who play with fools in the grace of evil orgy."

"Pitiful, pitiless we know that only now, everything good will happen to Leroy. He will be surrounded by love forever, and the good will of God in Jesus Christ will bring him every good thing that he could possibly imagine. And then some."

"Yes," said Sally, "he is in eternal paradise which is beyond what we can imagine. I'm happy for him. Maybe his death was a blessing. We earthlings just have a hard time of letting go."

"That says it right and true. Now God has given me the gift of Sandra, baby and all, and we will marry soon, as soon as I'm ready. I want to have a job, like you and Farley have jobs, so we can live a good life."

"Oh Oscar, what do you want to do?"

"Maybe work as a gas station attendant. I don't know. I like cars and I like helping people. But I think I need help from the Wellness Center's vocational program to help the process work with my disability. It hurts to say disability, but that's what I have with my mental illness. I always thought I was crazy and weird, but now with my diagnosis, it all makes sense. It's a sad story with a happy ending."

"You couldn't have put it better. Well Oscar, I'm glad you're all right and being a good warrior for the cause of mental health recovery. Will I see you tomorrow at the dual wedding ceremony?"

"Yes, I'll be there. Thank you."

"You're welcome to call any time for any reason OK?"
"OK. Have a good evening."
"You too. Goodbye."
"Bye Bye."

Stacy was pleased to be part of the wedding and arrived first, early at the Church on Saturday. The small ceremony was scheduled for one o'clock. She waited outside because the doors were locked. As she waited, Sandra arrived, and the two girls hugged each other with joyful mercy. Each knew about the other's tragedy. Next came Pastor and Sister Williams and they unlocked the door and opened the Church made ready for entrance. Sandra and Stacy went quickly inside and to the sanctuary where they sat down and waited expectantly.

Oscar walked in and gave Sandra a big, warm hug and a peck on the cheek. Here was his soul mate, the woman of his dreams. She perked up when she saw him and now sat smiling next to an embarrassed Stacy. Oscar shook her hand and greeted her with a "Praise the Lord." She responded likewise and smiled, sitting on her hands.

There by the door was Fay, in a beautiful shell colored gown trailing three feet behind her. Gilmore followed her in and went to talk to Pastor Williams. "Would it be OK to have a ceremony without rings?"

The Pastor affirmed that it would be fine and happened quite often. It was a casual setting, and soon Gilmore's two friends entered and went to sit by their Buddy. Fay sat with Sandra and Stacy, having met them at the barbeque last Saturday. Fay's two girl friends walked in and waved excitedly and ran to give her a big hug, telling her how beautiful she looked and they were in awe.

Farley and Sally entered the sanctuary and smiled and waved at everyone, closely followed by James and Mae. Here was everybody and the ceremony was ready to start. Everybody took their places and the Pastor contended to each couple, one at a time, asking questions to be answered, "I do." It was a quick ceremony and almost as though it had just started, it was over and the two couples were married. Everybody welcomed Fay and Gilmore Cadwell, and Mae and James Wilburton.

Stacy had run out to her car and came back bearing a large wedding cake beautifully frosted with two couples standing in the middle of it. She placed it on a table and ran out to her car again, this time returning with napkins, paper plates, and plastic forks, plus knife and spatula for cutting and serving the cake.

Everybody thanked her and she demurely accepted the appreciation. The cake was good with raspberry filling and everybody ate.

After this small ceremony Fay and Gilmore were off to a two-week stay in Hawaii, and they left first, after Fay changed her clothes and Gilmore also changed. The whole party wished them well, as Mae and James changed clothes, they were already prepared to take the next flight out to Sydney, Australia. They wanted to experience the ocean beaches at a resort, where they would also tour the outback and see Ayers Rock. They were both avid surfers, having grown up by the California beaches. They, too, planned a two-week vacation with side trips to New Zealand and Malaysia.

Sally hardly had time to see the two couples off. She cried on Mae's shoulder and told her how happy she was for her. It had been a long time coming for them. And now the baby was due in May, while Sandra's baby would be coming in June. Sally hugged Fay affectionately and gave Gilmore a gigantic hug. "I'm so happy for you, Gil'," she said with tears in her eyes.

The whole party saw the four newly weds out the door and to their waiting cabs. There was a sense of loss as they drove away and each person was wondering how to spend the rest of the day. It had all happened so fast. And it was such a beautiful ceremony. Mae and James were made right in the eyes of God, and they had a healthy baby on the way.

Oscar stood next to Sandra and asked her if she wanted to see the other two DVD's from *The Lord of the Rings* that day. She agreed readily and hopped on Oscar's bus with him. Stacy volunteered to stay behind and clean up after the cake. She would go home and go for a good, long run.

Pastor Williams and Sister Williams helped Stacy with the cake, and she offered it to them to take home. They accepted readily so after the mess was picked up she went on home alone.

Sally and Farley left that day in high spirits, glowing with the matrimony and harvest of souls that day. There were two unions, beautiful as could be, and now it was time to rest. The excitement was in the air, however and they needed to do something productive. "Let's walk," said Sally. "Let's go down to the Viking High School track and do some laps. What do you say?"

"Not in these clothes," said Farley who would rather lie down and rest. But he succumbed, and after swinging by the house to change clothes, Farley realized that Thomas could come with them, and they took him in the back seat of the car to the track where they got out and started walking.

After four laps, Farley was feeling warmed up and experiencing his endorphins. They kept at it until the threesome had walked twelve laps, or three miles.

"Let's go to the beach," said Sally after their walking was done.

"Sure, why not. Then we can get something to eat on the way home." Farley was feeling energetic.

The beach they chose was Turnip Bay Cove, a little inlet within the bay. There was a small stream feeding it that came from the Western Mountains. The surf was beautiful, calm and rippled with sun reflecting off of it. Dogs were allowed on leash and they were astonished to see two seals sunning on the beach. The clamshells scattered about were entwined with lengths of seaweed and there was a purple starfish on a rock partly submerged in the water. Here and there were tide pools with tiny fish and crabs, and barnacles laced the rocks along the shore.

As they walked, their feet left imprints in the sand among the rocks, which appeared randomly scattered about. The beach opened up into flocks of driftwood lying strewn upon the high shore. As they walked on, they passed over mounds of small rocks mixed with flat sandy fissures.

"We should go fishing," said Sally, who loved the beach and the oysters still under water. "No, we ought to go swimming!" she grew excited about the idea, and soon enough, with no one around, they stripped down to their underclothes, and taking Thomas, they waded out into the cool water, still warm from summer months. Thomas loved the water and Farley kept him leashed as together all three began to swim in the outgoing current. They were careful to avoid oyster shells and floated on their backs. Farley made a lot of noise kicking his feet and began to swim back to shore. Sally kept swimming further out. She was in no danger, being a strong swimmer. She stopped and floated on her back with her arms crossed behind her head. Finally, she, too, headed back to shore.

The wet threesome walked around to dry off, as Thomas shook his coat repeatedly. Hiding in the driftwood and rocks, Sally and Farley stripped out of their underclothes and put their dry clothes back on, carrying their wet makeshift swimwear.

They went back to the car exhilarated, hungry, and in good moods. They drove back through town and stopped at the bakery where they bought French bread, and to the meat store where they bought pepper jack cheese and salami to make sandwiches at home. Their waiting car outside brought them home with a wet dog, hands carrying wet underwear, and bags of bread, salami, and cheese. Farley knew they had onions and tomatoes, which would complement the sandwiches perfectly.

Farley let Thomas off the leash once in the yard and he raced around and around until he came to his water bowl on the other side of the fence of his enclosure. Sally had compassion and immediately let Thomas into his enclosure where he lapped furiously from his water bowl. Sally brought the hose over and filled the bowl with fresh water and Thomas drank and drank and drank.

Sally closed the enclosure with Thomas inside and went into the house. Farley had already broken the loaf of bread and was cutting up cheese and slices of salami, on which he strew onions and tomatoes. He crammed the sandwich into his mouth, stuffing it full to sate his hunger after playing in the salty waters.

Sally thought about Oscar and wondered how he was doing. She fixed her sandwich a little less hurriedly than Farley had and took smaller bites.

Then Sally called Oscar to find out how he was doing and lending an ear if he needed to talk. Oscar picked up on the other end.

"Hello?" His voice was suave and alluring.

"Hello, Oscar, this is Sally calling to check up on you."

"Hi Sally," he said a little more brightly, having obviously had someone else on his mind and the switch over was lost in communication.

"How are you doing? Are you taking your afternoon Lorazepam?"

"I am, and it's making life a little easier for me. Doctor doesn't want me addicted to it so I only have a two-week supply. Otherwise, I'm doing really well. I've cycled out of my psychosis, and Sandra doesn't think I'm acting weird. I don't know, I'll just see how it goes, you know?"

"I know. That's the way life is. You never know what's going to happen before it does. And if you do know, you make pretty good predictions."

"So you're taking all your medicines again and starting to feel better?"

"Yes. Thank you for checking in on me. It's nice to know that people care."

"Yes, that is always very nice. OK. Well, if that's all, I'll let you get back to whatever you were doing."

"Sandra and I are watching movies together."

"How nice. Tell her hello from me!"

"I will. Bye now."

"Bye."

Oscar hung up the phone and put his arm back around Sandra, telling her "Hi" from Sally.

"You should have let me talk to her," said Sandra, her feathers ruffled.

"I'm sorry. I didn't think about it. She was just checking up on me to see if I was being faithful with my medicines. I got really rattled when I stopped taking my pills last week. I was afraid to see you, I didn't want anyone to see me like I was."

The movies were ending and it was eight o'clock. Both Oscar and Sandra were sleepy from watching two movies in a row. Oscar made coffee and they both had a cup. Then Oscar said, "I want to write in my journal. I want to remember my experiences this week. Do you journal?"

"I do. In fact I have my journal with me in my bag. Why don't we journal together, and then share our writing with each other?"

"That's a great idea, Sandra! Do you need a pen?"

"I have one. Can I sit at the kitchen table?"

"Sure. I'll sit right across from you. Here, help yourself to coffee, I find it stimulates my mind. I just don't like having too much."

Oscar and Sandra began busily scribbling in their journals. They wrote about Leroy's accidental death, about the weddings, about the baby, and about each other. Oscar mentioned his mood swings and psychosis having dumped his medicines down the toilet and missing them for three days. He described his feelings of paranoia and helplessness, of curling up on his bed in a little ball, and having been rescued by Sally and the nurse, Rebecca, at the Wellness Center.

He wrote about his recovery and his adamant love for Sandra. She was more choosey about what to write, realizing they had agreed to share. She wrote about her pregnancy, about the scandalous Simon who was infected with Satan, and about the death of Leroy and Tina, that it was destiny for them to be together in Heaven. Then she wrote about wanting to marry Oscar and to move in with him, and she wondered when that could be. Also she was determined to save herself until after their wedding.

After half an hour of busy writing, they both came to a conclusion and closed their journals, putting pens down.

"Did you still want to share?" Asked Oscar.

"Sure. I'll go for that." They each opened their journals up to today's writing and gave them to each other. Sandra was curious to see Oscar's scribbled handwriting, which she was able to make out. He liked her big, flowery letters, smooth and artistic.

Quietly each one read the others journal. They stopped at the same time and looked up, eyes glowing. "You wrote *this*?" They both seemed to say breathlessly. "I had no idea you were such an artist, Sandra," said Oscar. "And you are so talented in your craft," gaped Sandra. "I feel like I know you better."

"I feel the same way," reiterated Oscar. "Wow, this is heavy, personal stuff. Thank you for sharing," he said in awe.

"Thank You," cried Sandra. "I had no idea that psychosis could be so frightening."

"And I wasn't sure if you wanted to marry me." Oscar was sullen. What had he to offer her?

"Sandra Naden, I don't have a ring for you, but I'm asking, will you be my wife?"

"Oh Oscar Thadeus, I couldn't be prouder to marry another man."

"Let's do it!"

"Should we talk to Pastor Williams?"

"I think so. We need jobs."

"I can be a nanny. I'm good with kids."

"Really? I could be a courtesy clerk at Sanford's Grocery."

"Do you really think so?"

"I could try!"

"Let's talk to Pastor Williams tomorrow."

"Why not."

"I'm worried about finances," Sandra said cautiously.

"What do you mean?"

"Well, neither one of us works. I lost my job selling shoes since the pregnancy. I'm not worried about finding another job, but I'm worried about you working with your mental illness."

"What do you mean? I can work."

"You have a disability. It flares up sometimes, like how you wrote in you journal. You couldn't be a courtesy clerk and then have psychotic episodes."

"Well what could I do? I must be able to do something for pay!"

"Let's think about it."

"I could walk dogs for a kennel company. I love dogs and they love me—"

"Thomas used to hate you."

"Well that's when I was sneaking around following Sally and Farley. Of course he was suspicious. But he loves me now. Which reminds me of the last time I walked him. We were with Leroy. Leroy got hit and me and Thomas got away unscathed."

"That reminds me of Tina, and how she heard me being raped by Simon that night at their apartment. Tina heard it and lived to tell."

"And Simon is roasting in Hell, where the ivy chokes and the poison oak blooms and thrives. Where thorns and nettles strangle and dig into the skin, and then with serpents in the oil cauldrons, and where there is no water."

"That puts it well, Oscar, but what about us getting married? Do you think we can really do it?"

"Not until I have a job. I'd be the man of the house and want to be the provider. I need income, we can't just depend on you."

"Well how do you get by now? Where's your income?"

Oscar grudgingly said, "I have income from my Dad after he passed away. I'll be getting SSI soon, but it's not going to be enough for the both of us. I need work. I feel responsible."

"Yes, I understand. But what could you do? Could you do landscaping with Farley? He has a mental illness and gets by just fine at that job. Or maybe there's a job moving boxes or something at the Wellness Center. I think that physical work would be best for you. It's affirming for your body and relaxes your mind."

"Moving boxes? I don't think so. Maybe I could be a ticket taker at the local theater. Or check receipts and membership cards for people coming and going at Costco. Maybe even be a food demonstrator. What do you think?"

"Those sound like good jobs that are low stress. What else? I like the dog walking idea the best. You could walk dogs and I could teach kindergarten. That way when we get married, we can have a dog – any kind you want – and I'll have lots of practice dealing with kids. We'd be a shining example to the community of what true love is all about. And being blessed, the Lord counts us for something, that's why we're both so hardy."

"Yeah, we deal well with adversity. We're over comers. We're friends and soul mates. We care for each other and want the best for each other."

"It's true, Oscar, I love you madly."

"And I love you too, madly, Sandra."

"Well, let's get started finding you a job. I know of three dog kennels around here. Surely one would hire you. Just be open about your disability and reiterate the fact your disability wouldn't affect your job in a bad way, rather, it makes you more sensitive to animals and would be an attribute to your job."

"You think so?"

"Of course! It's getting late now, but how about if we go around to the dog kennels tomorrow after Church? By the way, can I sleep on your couch; it's getting too late to catch the bus back to town where I transfer to my bus line home."

"Actually, you can sleep in the spare bedroom where I was going to have Leroy stay with me. When I found out about you, I told Leroy he couldn't live here because of you. It's too late to matter now, but just think of it as your room, and your bathroom, the one through the door on the right as you go into your bedroom. It's only accessible from your room so you'd have complete privacy. Feel welcome here, and remember I'm not like Simon. I wouldn't dare lay a hand on you without your permission."

"That's generous of you, Oscar. Do you have a big T-shirt and boxers I could sleep in?"

"Yes, of course," said Oscar nervously. He got up and went into his bedroom and took out an X-large white T-shirt from his closet and flannel shorts from his dresser. These he brought out to Sandra for her to inspect.

"Thanks," she said and accepted the clothing. "Did you want to go to bed now? Or stay up talking?"

"Actually I'm pretty darned tired. I think it's about time for bed. It's just after eleven."

"Do you have a spare tooth brush, some floss, soap and shampoo/conditioner? Also I need a brush for these tangles in the morning."

"I have all those things and more. We could throw your clothing now into the wash and get up early enough to put it all into the dryer. Then you'd be dressed for Church again tomorrow. I wonder how the newlyweds are doing? That's going to be us pretty soon."

"I'll go change out of these clothes so we can put them in the wash tonight. I'll go to 'my' room and change," she said with a flirt.

She came out a few minutes later and had on Oscar's T-shirt and shorts. Oscar had never seen a more beautiful sight. "OK," he said. "The washing machine is over here," and he led her to a room behind the kitchen. Together they put her skirt and top and personals in the washing machine and as Oscar added detergent, they turned on the clunky appliance.

"Now, for your bathroom supplies, follow me," he said. He opened a drawer in his bathroom and produced a brush, soap, toothbrush, floss, toothpaste and an unopened bottle of shampoo/conditioner in one. "There are clean towels and wash rags in your bathroom. Now I have to take my pills, and then get into bed, myself."

"I don't know how to thank you, Oscar," whispered Sandra. "I'll go to bed now. Wake me up at eight-fifteen tomorrow. That should give me enough time to get ready for Church. What time do you usually leave on Sunday's?"

"Well, Church starts at ten-thirty, I usually catch the nine-thirty bus and it gets me there about twenty minutes early. I'll wake you at eight-fifteen. Good night."

"Good night," said Sandra and crept like a bug into "her" bedroom where she pulled back the covers and crawled into the bed with its firm mattress. Then realizing she hadn't brushed and flossed, she got up again and went to inspect her bathroom. It was neat, clean, and tidy. She flossed her teeth and brushed them, spitting into the sink and rinsing with her hand, then wiping her face and hands on a blue towel.

She crept back out to the bedroom and crawled into bed once more. She wasn't sinning. Oscar was making sure of that.

She heard Oscar in the kitchen taking his pills, and then under her door, she saw all the lights go out. So she turned out her bed lamp and snuggled into her pillows.

Morning came without event and Oscar knocked on Sandra's door. Then he opened it slightly and peered in. There was his Sandra curled up in fetal position, breathing slowly. "Sandra!" He said loudly, not wanting to go into the room. "Sandra!" He called again and heard a moan as she rolled over and stretched. "Sandra! Get up!" He called once more.

"I'm coming, Mom," she said and jerked herself awake as she took in her strange surroundings. Then she remembered. It was Oscar. "Oscar?" She questioned suspiciously. It was him. "Hi Sandra. It's eight-fifteen. You have to get up for Church. You have to shower and get ready and we need to put your Church clothes in the dryer."

"I heard you. Thank you for waking me, Oscar," she said gratefully. Oscar closed the door as she pulled back her covers. He took his liberties and went to put Sandra's clothes in the dryer. Next he went about making breakfast, which consisted of a bread roll, butter and raspberry jam. He cut up some fruit on the side and made the coffee.

Oscar had already showered and was dressed for Church. Today they would approach Pastor Williams about getting married soon.

In the meanwhile, Sandra showered, soaped, and shampooed, brushing out her tangled hair with its dark, natural curls. She brushed her teeth and washed her face. Then she put on the T-shirt and shorts that Oscar had let her borrow and padded barefoot out to the kitchen. She smiled sleepily at Oscar who looked a little sleepy himself. "How did you sleep?" She asked him.

"I slept great. Not so peaceful for a long time. I just liked to have the thought that you were in the next room. It relaxed me and I dreamt about waterfalls."

"I dreamed about butterflies and dandelions, and a little spring flowing through a meadow."

"I'm going to try to contact my sister, Cordelia. I want her to meet you. She's the only family that I have. Last I heard she lives in Arkansas. She doesn't know about my mental illness diagnosis. She's been used and abused, too, like you, Sandra. I think you would really like her. But look, now, eat. Your clothes are in the dryer – I put it on gentle cycle."

Sandra buttered a roll and put jam on it. Then she bit voraciously into it, hungry from the lack of food last night. She had two more and then a bowl of fruit. The eclipse came when she sipped on her coffee, her morning companion.

"Thank you, Lord, this was good," she said, satisfied completely. "How are my clothes coming?"

"Ten more minutes in the dryer." Oscar couldn't help running his eyes up and down Sandra's body, her hair wet and styled. Sandra asked for more coffee. He brought it to her and poured it into her mug. Both were nervous and uncomfortable, not sure how to act and react. So they both responded to the situation and went together for an embrace.

"I love you Sandra Naden," whispered Oscar in her ear. "And I love you, Oscar Thadeus", she whispered back, trembling in his embrace. "Look up, Sandra," he said, "you don't have to hide from me or be afraid of me. I'm not going to do anything. You can trust me."

She broke down and cried, cried over the rape, the violation by Simon, and confused about the baby within her. She had the urge to talk to Sally.

"The dryer is done," called Oscar from the laundry room, seething in his anger at Simon who had betrayed him as well.

Sandra swallowed her tears and went to the laundry room where Oscar stood, trembling, holding her clothes, which he handed to her. She received the bundle of clothes and went back to her bedroom where she changed into her clean Sunday garb. She put on her nylons and slipped her feet into her brown spotted high heel shoes.

Sandra found her jacket in the living room and put it on, all ready to go. Oscar put on his jacket as well as his shiny black shoes and together they went to the door, prepared and ready to go get the world.

The bus stop was a block and a half away, and the gorgeous couple walked carefully step-by-step down the to the sidewalk. Oscar had remembered his medications and felt fairly stable. Sandra was full of mixed emotions, and the tenderness between them could be felt from a block away.

As they reached the bus stop they had a few minutes to wait. Oscar commented on the blue sky and how beautiful it was. Sandra pointed at the crows in the trees, and the squirrels running dangerously across the street. Then the bus came.

Oscar and Sandra boarded the bus and took front row seats. This bus would go directly past the Church. It was about a forty-minute ride, arriving at their destination at ten after ten o'clock. They stepped carefully off the bus and stood for a moment as the bus drove away.

"Can I hold your hand?" Oscar asked Sandra. She smiled and said, "Yes."

They walked hand in hand up the path to the Church front door, flanked on either side by cherry trees, now beginning to lose their leaves.

"Let's sit with Sally and Farley," suggested Oscar.

"That's fine with me," Sandra said.

Mae and James wouldn't be there, nor Gilmore and Fay. Sandra looked around for Stacy and hoped she would come to sit with them.

There was Pastor Williams, greeting people in the front of the Church. Sandra and Oscar whispered to each other that they would talk to him after the Church service.

Not seeing their friends, Sandra and Oscar sat down where the Cadwell's usually sat and waited expectantly. Then Sandra saw Stacy coming in alone and called and waved her over. Stacy broke into a big grin and made her way to them. As they sat and chatted, Sally and Farley appeared and greeted them all and sat down behind Sandra and Oscar. It was good to see them. Oscar stayed quiet in his horrible shyness and focused on Pastor Williams who was just now taking his seat on the front platform.

Sally and Farley were sensitive to Oscar's shyness and didn't poke or prod. Soon the music would start. Sandra and Stacy were talking like best of friends, and Oscar was mute in front of Sally and Farley whom he placed on a pedestal.

"If they have jobs, why can't I?" He wondered.

"I don't think I could work hard like Farley. He's so strong," Oscar thought to himself. "Maybe the dog walking job is best. Sandra was going to check out some places around here with me. I like animals and they tend to love me. Maybe it's my instinctive passions. Animals pick up on intuition."

The music started and everyone stood up to sing along. The noise escalated as people broke out in adoration, singing, shouting for the Lord Jesus Christ. It went on for minutes, and then a half hour. Saints were hugging each other and crying, feeling the touch of the Holy Ghost. The Holy Ghost swept through the congregation and finally people walked up to the altar and knelt, praying as others kept singing and the praise level was ultimate.

Oscar liked being surrounded by the Holy Ghost. Sometimes he felt its presence in his life, but almost always he was touched by it in Church.

It carried on for forty minutes, when finally the Pastor broke through and led the congregation to a reverent silence. There was a call for tithes and offerings, and Oscar, having already paid tithes for the month brought up a dollar for offering. He didn't have very much money, but he always got by somehow.

After tithes and offerings the Pastor spoke about tithes and the biblical truth (in Malachi of the Old Testament) that spoke of giving tithes and not "robbing God."

Everyone had returned to their seats and sat at attention.

Today the Pastor would talk about forgiveness versus condemning the devil. Should the devil be forgiven? Was it responsible for everything wrong in peoples' lives?

Because it was an implement of God, an omnipotent God who used it to cause danger, wherewith in the midst of danger, turning forth the efforts of God's love, you would be lazy or nonchalant without the translucent, adequate, responsible affection of God, who loved us first, but realizes the truth that many people don't love Him in return.

Believe the truth; that scandal comes as a reiteration of evil being stirred up in the face of reality. Confusing reality and sanctification belongs to the Lord. He chooses who shall suffer for what and why and for how long. He makes examples of sinners who are brought to humiliation, over the reaction of overwhelming catastrophe in times of peace.

His sympathy is hard up, and given to all who try to live for God. For it is the new foundlings that the devil swipes up so greedily, having not had time to grow in the faith.

A mighty perpetrator, the devil looks for weak spots, and attacks in due order. It claims as many lives as it can get a hold of, meaning that some people choose to walk in its way. It clarifies evil with intent of troubling further in a most seductive manner. Drugs, alcohol, war; these are its friends. It perpetrates nastily whenever given a chance.

Finally, the Pastor spoke about Simon and his great troubling. Could he have been forgiven in time of need? Was he steeped in evil at birth? Or did the devil claim his life early on? Was there any goodness in his life?

The Church believes in the devil. Many people don't believe in it. It is real. If you can, forgive those who have trespassed in your life. The devil is a liar and a cheater and delights in these things. You have power over it in God. Stand up to block out evil, where it tries to make mush of your integrity. You can block it out and fend it away from your life, and when adversity happens, know it is God's truth speaking war on the ignorant.

The devil is evil, and you can't forgive that. It was sent as a tempter, and caused Eve to commit the first sin, that of eating of the fruit from the tree of knowledge of good and evil. In turn, she fed it to her mate, Adam. This was the first infection of evil into the Human Life that God created. This life had been perfect. It was the first act that spurned innocence and revival of truth. Adam carried a sore spot where he opened himself to sin, which carried on for generations and is with us today, although it can be forgiven through Jesus Christ the atoning sacrifice for love in God's way.

We can seek peace, so rebuke the evil in your life. Don't let it carry you. Don't let it control you or cause you to react on random impulses without consideration of events ahead of time. Be careful with your life and the choices you make, to be sure you are always following after God and running towards Him. He can set you free from sin, and heal you where you have been injured. He will heal the broken heart, mind, soul, spirit, and body through the faith. Remember to rebuke evil, and never give it a foothold. Pray to God for mercy when you are out of control. Only the Lord knows where you will land. The devil is a cheap skate with shadows and mirrors to draw the innocent toward him. Unfortunately, sometimes it breaks through and puts its grimy hands on lost souls.

The Pastor finished by asking for a handclap of praise for the Lord, and a reminder not to fear evil, but to recognize it and be glad of its well-deserved future, to burn forever in a lake of fire. Pouring coals over you enemy's head results from forgiveness, but not necessarily love. Don't love evil, and don't forgive it.

As he finished up, the praise team began to sing and saints poured down to the altar to pray and have hands lain upon them. Each person must go home and understand that evil is ugly, bad, and wrong. It can be ignored, conquered and kept at bay. God has the victory.

People cried and sang out in the midst of prayer and worship to God. Jesus touched many sore hearts that day and gave a lesson of hope.

Sandra pondered to herself about her baby and how she should feel about it. She was confused and wanted to talk to Sally. Or maybe she could confide in Oscar. She had already promised him she'd go visit the three dog kennels in the area, where he might get a job.

"Sally, is it all right if I call you later?" She asked her friend. Just then Becky and Jane walked right up to her and Stacy and invited them out for a girl's coffee. She couldn't resist and decided to tell Oscar that her plans had changed as far as investigating dog kennels. She told him of her wishes to go to coffee with her friends after Church. She would call him later, and maybe he could have some reports on having gone around by himself.

Oscar was mildly hurt but didn't let it on. "I'll call you later," he told Sandra. Sandra mentioned that they talk to the Pastor another day. Stacy volunteered to drive the foursome to a Starbucks nearby where they could sit together and relate their current issues, troubles, and successes.

Sandra hugged Oscar, apologized in his ear and whispered that she would look forward to his phone call later. She thanked him for letting her sleep over and suggested that they plan to do swap journaling again. "I love you so much, Oscar. I need this today. I hope you understand, I –" He put his finger over her lips, and whispered, "I'll see you later my true love. I have some dog walking to do, if I get hired. Have fun with your troop of girl friend survivor friends. I'll check out these places on my own. I'll look up addresses on the Internet, and I'm good at getting around on buses, so don't worry about me. I'll see you later, Sweetheart."

Sandra gave him an extra passionate squeeze and then parted, meeting up with Stacy, Becky, and Jane, all Simon's handful of victims.

BARKING UP THE WRONG TREE

Sometimes life casts illusions and we suffer delusions, envisioning hope where there is only death. Following after that is a new life that must be learned how to live.

Stacy drove herself and her three friends to the downtown Starbucks that had a fireplace in it. Stacy guarded the four chairs placed around the fireplace as Sandra and Becky and Jane ordered their drinks and a double tall white mocha for her. "These four seats are taken," she said sternly to a little old lady who would sit there.

"I'm sorry," said the old woman and moved on.

Finally the drinks came and the four ladies sat down around the fireplace holding their cups. Nobody knew what to say, and for once Becky and Jane were quiet. Sandra crossed and uncrossed her legs, shifting in her seat and holding her coffee until it had cooled a little.

Becky came right out and asked, "You carry his baby, how do you feel about that?"

"Becky!" Admonished Jane, "You don't ask questions like that."

"Oh, it's all right," said Sandra. I don't mind talking about the truth, especially after Pastor's talk today. I feel like a target for the devil, but I'm not going to let it get me. I'm going to love this baby for the fact that he or she is human, not a monster. The Creator created him for some fault or defect, I don't know.

"What do you mean, 'for some fault or defect'?" Pushed Becky.

"I mean he or she can't be hated for something he or she didn't do. If he – I keep wanting to say 'he'; if he is born evil, which I don't think is possible, he'll be caught and punished like any bad boy. That's why I have Oscar who wants to take responsibility for the discipline of this boy. There is really no harm or danger. This baby is being derived out of innocence."

Jane asked, "How does your body feel physically?"

Sandra replied softly, "I've never been pregnant before, but I think my hormones are doing the regular things. I feel strong by nature and I'm starting to show. It feels like there's a baby in there. And I'm hungrier."

Sandra was quiet and then began to cry. "Are you guys judging me?" She said defeated. A wrecking ball was swinging back and forth over her head. She needed support, not derision.

Stacy spoke now. "It's cool that you have Oscar. He's a great guy. But I think that before any of us gets judgmental, we should all remember what we have in common with each other - Simon. Sandra could have been any of us. This is a weird question, but what is our order? I mean, who was first and who was last? – We all know who was last, but what about the rest of us?"

"I think I was first," squeaked Becky. "It makes me want to cry a river, being so violated, so helpless, and so unaware."

"Now that you know, do you remember what happened?" Asked Stacy.

"Yes. It all makes sense, how dirty I've felt since that night at Simon's house, when he walked me out to the bus stop and told me to call him.

"And then he broke up with me just like that in a single phone call. He avoided me ever since in Church and told me there was someone else. And I guess there was," she said bitterly.

"Then comes me, I think," said Stacy.

"Yes, I think you're right," agreed Jane. "I'm number three. My turn happened in August, early on."

"Yes, I was in July," Stacy muttered, as all girls started feeling dirty and victimized as the topic continued.

"What about you, Becky? Which month were you?"

I got taken in early July. He got busy that month," she said venomously.

All four girls were seething as they realized their victory. "We won't let him get the best of us," cried Jane.

"What do we do? Forgive him like the Pastor said? Feel sorry for him, but know that his transgressions were perpetrated and infused on us, not by our consent, and certainly not by our approval?" Becky was floundering.

"Are we damaged goods?" Asked Jane.

"We aren't damaged goods. We'll all heal in time, and there might be an ugly scar, but I think we can get past it," replied Stacy.

"I'm good! I'm not walking evil because I carry his child. There's nothing sinister about me. I'm hurt but not weakened. No. I think I'm strengthened and I have a huge responsibility. Love the unloved. That's my gripe. I must teach this child the ways of God from birth. He will be loved and not forgotten, because I don't plan to disappear. I'm not going to hide my pregnancy, and I don't care what other people think, as long as I have you guys and Oscar to support me along this road to destruction – destruction of evil.

"Like the Potter with his clay. He'll throw away the broken pieces of ugliness and create something beautiful."

"That's beautifully said, Sandra," spoke Becky in awe.

They sat in silence for a few minutes, sipping on their coffee drinks, and experiencing the horrible feelings of rape. It's easy to ignore until it rears its ugly head.

"I feel like crap," said Jane.

"Me too," agreed Becky. "Why do guys rape girls?"

"If we only knew the answer," spat Stacy abhorrently.

"Is it the devil?" Ventured Sandra.

"I would guess so," said Becky. "But even Adam never raped Eve."

"And lots and lots of people don't experience rape in their relationships," offered Jane. "But a lot of people have it in their past."

"That's true. But then there are degrees of rape, which I don't want to talk about. It's too ugly what happens out there. Was Simon a serial rapist? Was he a psychopath or a sociopath?" Becky asserted her curiosity.

Sandra whispered, "He's probably all of the above. At least he didn't murder – never mind. He DID murder, and that makes the situation for us even uglier."

"We're free, Sandra, but you got caught!" Becky said astonished at the gravity of the situation.

"I'm here for you Sandra, whatever you need," cried Jane.

"Me too, Sandra, you can count on me," said Becky.

"And of course I'll do my best to be whatever you need," sobbed Stacy.

Their drinks were getting mostly consumed but no one wanted to end this gathering yet.

"Should we get refills?" Becky popped the question.

"I think so," said Stacy, wiping tears from her face.

"Sandra, you stay there, I'll get you another Hazelnut Latte."

"Thanks, Becky," said Sandra as she began to perspire from the topic, the coffee, and her hormones. She thought about Oscar and wondered how he was doing with the dog kennel job search. She cried silently for herself and her three friends. They hadn't even spoken about Tina and Leroy. It was all the more damage. She sat quietly as her friends were refilling on drinks – one for her.

They returned and took their respective seats as Becky gave Sandra her coffee.

"Thank you, Becky," Sandra coughed.

"Does everybody feel crappy now or is it just me?" Prodded Jane.

"I think we all are experiencing some pretty disgusting stuff. – I'm trying not to swear," bit Stacy.

Now Jane was aggravated. So far she had been able to ignore those feelings of victimization. Now she feared for her dreams and felt afraid of going to sleep that night. She voiced her thoughts.

"We all have the danger of crappy dreams, frightening dreams," said Stacy, "but if we pray before we sleep, about overcoming and being victors, not victims, we might have some pretty terribly beautiful dreams with overcoming and rescue. Recovery, resiliency, healing."

"Stacy, how can you be so strong?" Asked Jane, who was weeping.

"My father used to beat me and my brother raped me. So I've been through some tough stuff that I've needed to process. This is just another cherry on the devil's food cake.

She demoted herself to childhood and came out weeping. She had only talked about these issues with her therapist, and that's been for a long time. She began seeking therapy at the early age of twenty-two.

Her therapist had helped her through these ordeals, and was there now to talk about Simon's rape. "I'm really not that strong, I've just processed a lot of my junk and pulled the plug on its electricity in my life."

"Stacy, you're so brave," whimpered Becky. I feel like I've been soiled, damaged some."

"Me too," said Jane. "I have a horrible, yucky feeling. It's gross, so opposite of what the bible teaches about men and women relationships and the love that is meant to be there when you are with Christ. We should all love like He does."

Sandra sipped on her Hazelnut Latte. She felt quiet and protective. She didn't want to be ugly and perpetrated. Simon was a pervert. She put it simply to herself. He had slyly left behind some semen that bonded with her egg, and created a child. Her mothering instincts overcame her rejection of the creature within her. Now she was getting tired, exhausted. All four of them were. It was time to wind things up. They had a group hug and promised each other to meet again, maybe next Sunday.

"Stacy, could you drop me off at my place? —And we should all exchange phone numbers first, don't you think?"

"I agree," said Becky boastfully. She didn't like feeling so yucky. They each had a Bible with them and wrote down respective phone numbers for each other within its pages. Then it was time to go.

Stacy dropped Sandra off at her place and took Becky and Jane back to their cars at the Church. They all waved goodbye after hugs and kisses, and promises to be there for each other as they processed through their experiences with the demon, Simon.

Stacy drove home deep in thought. She was scheduled to see her therapist tomorrow. She thanked God for that.

Sandra let herself into her apartment and right away called Oscar. He was not at home so she left a message. "Hi Oscar, it's Sandra, about two o'clock and I just got home. Please give me a call. I love you, bye." She hung up and would go to her Bible but decided she needed to nap instead. Remembering their talk about dreams today, she prayed for positive, uplifting dreams while she slept. She lay down on her couch and curled up into a fetal position. She slept.

As she slept her body rearranged the emotions within it and put up barriers to all evil. She slept fitfully and cried out with moans and jerks. "I'm not a bad person," said her conscience. It weaved around her many feelings of responsibility and rejection. It was rejection of the baby within her. Something was not right. The baby had to go.

Go where? Go to a bad place. It didn't belong in her. She smothered her thoughts with feelings of responsibility. But she must not go to the bad place with the baby.

In her dreams she was bruised and purple on her face from beating it against a wall. She terrorized herself and saw a pitchfork coming at her. She dodged the pitchfork and fell down at the feet of Christ. He reassured her that all would work out for the wellness of her life.

Becky was going to spend the night at Jane's place. She didn't want to be alone tonight. They both remembered to pray for positive dreams that night. She slept on the couch with Jane's black cat curled up around her feet. Tomorrow they would go to work, and pray for a good day. Becky worked at Goodwill, and Jane was a massage therapist. They both had good jobs and helped people. Jane had gone to school for a long time to be a massage therapist. She was advanced in the field.

Becky worked in sales and inventory, sometimes manning the cashier and accepting donations. She liked her job because there were a variety of tasks and she never got taxed or overburdened by her work.

Stacy worked at the Nordstrom's Rack in customer service. Her loud and boisterous personality was appreciated there.

As Sandra slept she grew depressed. Depressed to have this baby in her. What should she do? She needed to get a new job so she and Oscar could marry. But should she wait until after the baby? She wanted out with it.

Oscar called her around eight-thirty and she woke up and picked up the phone on the fourth ring. Oscar apologized for waking her up, but she told him "no worries" because she had been sleeping all day.

"What better activity to do on the Sabbath," Oscar said with a smile.

"Yeah. Now I have to eat dinner and go right back to bed. Sleep allows me to process my emotions. We girls got into it at Starbucks today," she said slowly.

"Was it a healing experience?"

"I'd say it was a 'revealing' experience. We all feel the same way, dirty, except for me, I feel dirty and imprisoned with this baby on the way. I don't want it to come. Oscar, I don't want this baby." Sandra started to cry.

"Whatever happens, it's the Lord's will. He gave us a free will to do what we want. But he also gave us a set of instructions, including 'You shall not murder.' You can't abort the baby, Sandra, and don't worry about it, because I'm here to shoulder the load with you. Don't do anything rash like killing yourself, that's murder too."

"I hate this baby."

"Farley would know better what to say. He's very sensitive and understanding."

"Funny you should say that, I've been thinking about talking to Sally about it. Aren't they such pillars in our Church? But I can't be jealous of them, because they've had it bad, too, being mentally ill – like you."

"I'll stop thinking about the baby, maybe I can ignore it. But still, it's inside of me, foreign material. I didn't want to cleave to Simon. I want to marry you." Sandra was coming close to self-punishment.

"What are you having for dinner?"

Sandra groaned. "Do I have to think of dinner? Baked potatoes and onions, I guess. I better turn the music on so I don't fall asleep while it's baking."

"How about if I call you in an hour? You need to eat something to keep up your strength."

"Yeah, sure, call me in an hour. Thanks."

"Bye."

"Bye."

Sandra got up and lugged herself to the kitchen where she started peeling and cutting potatoes in small pieces. After five she determined that was enough, and chopped up an onion to sprinkle over the potatoes in a pan covered with olive oil. She set the timer for fifty-five minutes. Then she got up and picked up a novel she had just bought at the store. It was about a woman who had walked across the outback of Australia with a band of Aborigines. She sucked on a rock to stimulate saliva in her thirsty mouth.

Sandra lay on the couch reading and just as she was totally absorbed the timer went off.

She got up and pulled the potatoes and onions out of the oven and put them on the stove. Next she sliced up cheddar cheese and laid the pieces all over the pan. She put it in for five more minutes to melt the cheese and took it out again. All done. She sprinkled it with garlic salt and pepper, and then the phone rang.

"Hello?" She said doggedly.

"Hi my sweet platypus. How was dinner?"

"Oscar I haven't eaten yet. It just came out of the oven and needs to cool down a little bit."

"Then talk to me."

"What do you want me to say?"

"Whatever's on your mind, I love you."

"Oh Oscar I love you too. What are we going to name the baby?"

"Well, we have to know if it's a girl or a boy."

"OK. What if it's a girl?"

"How about, 'Sarah'?"

"Good. What if it's a boy?"

"How about, 'John'?"

"Those are two good, Biblical names. That's a good start for the baby. Surround it in Biblical innuendos."

"I had a dream of dodging a pitchfork that was coming right towards me. Does that mean I won't kill the child? I'll protect it?"

"I don't know what it means, but it sounds positive. At least you didn't get pierced. Maybe it affirms that you won't have an abortion."

"Maybe. Do you think Jesus loves the baby?"

"I don't know. I can't prove that either way. Maybe it's an abomination to Him."

"Maybe. Or maybe He feels sorry for it and wants to take care of it."

"That's probably true. Anyhow, I shouldn't worry about it. God knows all about this baby and He will treat it accordingly. I wish you were here."

"That would be nice."

"I love you."

"I love you too."

"So tell me how the dog kennel search went."

"Oh, I have good news. I applied at all three places and got accepted to two of them. I think I'll take the one closest to me. That's also my favorite one. They have a big green field for the dogs to run and play. You can walk them all around the field and then there's clean up in their kennel runs. They also teach dog obedience there. People come for lessons with their dogs. My job would be exercising the animals and keeping their kennels clean, as well as feeding."

"That's really great! Do you think you can do it?"

"I think so. I want to train to be an instructor. But cleaning kennels is fine work for me. The sad part is getting to know the dogs and then they leave. But I could handle that."

"When can you start?"

"Actually, tomorrow they want me to come in for orientation. Then I'll start on Tuesday."

"What are your hours?"

"I'd be working Monday, Tuesday, and Thursday for four hour shifts. That's twelve hours a week. I think my mental illness and I can handle that. I hope. Maybe I could increase hours as time goes on. But that's a little bit of income," he said feebly.

"Good for you. I have faith in you, Oscar. If you put your mind to it, I know you'll succeed."

"That's what I'm hoping. I see my case manager tomorrow at four o'clock. Maybe she'll help me adjust to having a job."

"Why don't you call me tomorrow after you see Laura and let me know how orientation and your counseling session go. I'm getting hungry and my dinner is ready now."

"OK. I'll call you tomorrow around five-thirty or six."

"Great. Have a great day and just go with God. Remember prayer works. I'll probably have a lazy day tomorrow. I'm almost two months along now, I think, and my gut hurts. I need to rest and relax. I'll look forward to your call. – Wait! Isn't Leroy's funeral tomorrow?"

"Yes, thank you. What time is it?"

"One o'clock down on Holden. Do you want to go?"

"No. Funerals make me depressed. Besides, it will be crowded there and I don't like being around a lot of people."

"Well if you're not going, I won't go. Sound good?"

"Sounds good. Will you pray for me? I'm nervous about tomorrow."

"I will. Love you. Bye-bye."

"Love you too. Bye."

Sandra went to the kitchen and filled a bowl with her potatoes, cheese and onions and brought it to the living room where she sat watching TV and eating. The food was good. She went back for seconds. She braided and unbraided her hair. She picked up her Bible and saw the phone numbers of her friends from earlier today. She felt encouraged. She delighted in herself and taking her liberties, she got down on her knees by the couch. There she prayed quietly for God to be gentle with her and take care of her every need. Then she spent some time thanking God for protecting her this far. She hadn't been killed, like Tina, but she felt perpetrated and questioned God.

"God, why did you let this happen to me?"

She listened and beckoned toward him. The only answer she got is that this situation would turn out to glorify God. Somehow she would be redeemed from this short stay in Hell. She would come back a much stronger person able to help others.

She lay down on the couch, dealing with her pent up emotions. Small tears came down and she hugged herself as she lay there. She relaxed into her feelings and gently rubbed her stomach. She closed her eyes and saw only darkness, and then a beam of sunlight shining into her. It was a beautiful sensation, which God had brought her to. This baby was causing all kinds of problems. Her head swooned and had radical thoughts of ravens flapping in her ears. Their claws clutched at her belly and pierced it.

The ravens carried the baby away and dropped it in the ocean. Little Sarah or John wasn't going to make it. She already felt sick. She got up and ran to the bathroom and puked in the toilet. It was a nasty mess that went up her nose. This is normal, she thought, it's like morning sickness.

She got up and blew and blew her nose to get all the vomit out, and spit into the toilet to cleanse her mouth. Next she got up and brushed her teeth thoroughly. She craved a cup of coffee and walked to the kitchen to turn on the coffee pot. It was ready to go.

Then she sat down in the living room and drew a deep breath as the TV droned on. She turned off the TV and turned on the radio so she could read. She read her book on the Australian Outback journey. She felt like she needed more protein, so she got up and fried two eggs over easy. She sprinkled cheese on top of them and slid them from the pan onto her plate.

It was really hot so she had to wait a few minutes of desperation; wanting to inhale the eggs, she needed them so bad. So she poured herself a cup of milk and drank that. The coffee maker beeped so she poured herself a cup of that, and let it sit for a few minutes to cool down. While waiting for her coffee to cool, she picked at the eggs and blew on them so they were palatable. The eggs went down easy and she got up to wash her plate and let the pan sit and cool down first. Finally, she took her coffee into the living room and decided to call Jane. She picked up her Bible and called the number within.

The phone rang and Jane picked up on her end. "Hello?" She said. "Hello Jane?"

"Yes, is that you, Sandra?"

"Yes it's me. I need to talk to someone,"

"I'm here and so is Becky. Are you all alone?"

"Except for Jesus and this baby I'm all alone. I'm having a crappy time coming to grips with this baby. I feel more and more like rejecting it. But I won't get an abortion. What should I do? Be miserable for the rest of my life?"

"Oh, don't go talking like that. I thought you loved the baby and you and Oscar were going to get married and raise it together."

"That's what I thought, but I don't think I deserve that responsibility. The baby's not my fault." Sandra whimpered.

"Of course, but that's why we're all here, to bear the burden with you."

"I want to be a nanny so both Oscar and I have an income. But I'm unpredictable. I just vomited about twenty minutes ago. I feel sick, ugly, and sinful."

"Sinful? Why that?"

"I guess because my total psyche is turning toward rejection of the baby."

"Have you thought of putting the baby up for adoption?"

"I'm thinking that. But how can I carry it to term when it makes me feel so loathsome. I just want to die."

"Toughen up, chicky, we all have hard times, some harder than others. Remember, God selected you, out of all of us to bear a child from Simon. I understand your hatred and bitterness, but it's a life and as it is a life, you need to wait it out."

"I will. Thank you for validating me."

"Of course. Do you want to talk to Becky? She's spending the night here."

"Sure." Sandra was feeling a little better with the aid of Jane's perspective.

"Hi Sandra," it was Becky.

"Hi Becky, I guess you overheard my conversation with Jane. Are you in agreement with her? It's just something I have to put up with for a time?"

"Certainly, and put it out of your mind so you don't start to dwell on it with misery. It's a burden, and you need to bear it."

"But I want to work so Oscar and I can get married and raise this Hellion, obedient to the Lord's wishes. He doesn't want to punish me, He's just making a point, I guess, that evil is out there and sometimes we get suckered into it. He's going to help me overcome."

"He'll bring you out a victor, and you'll be able to help others in your position or similar. Don't get caught up in all the small stuff. The fact is that there's a baby inside of you, and the normal process goes for nine months and then the baby comes out of you. Remember that. This isn't eternal or forever. God won't hurt you, you just ran into a wall without realizing it."

"What am I supposed to do, climb over the wall?"

"I guess you could try, but that gets all philosophical and I don't understand it. Honestly, I don't know why you had to get pregnant. It doesn't seem fair. Pregnancy should be a beautiful thing, not a horrible terror."

"Maybe if I had had a relationship with Simon, and the baby wasn't an accident… but that can't happen, he's a terrible person and hates everybody. I'd kill him if I could. Maybe that's why I feel so sinful. Because I hate everything about this baby who shouldn't be."

"Are you taking care of yourself physically? You need to eat and walk and stay clean."

"I guess I'm doing all that, sort of. Maybe I need to walk more to keep my strength up. OK. Well, I'd better go. I need another cup of coffee. And I don't care if it hurts the baby. I'm not going to stop my coffee drinking for some implant that I shouldn't even think about."

"That's lousy, but I guess you have to do what you have to do to get by."

"Yeah." Sandra responded shortly.

"Promise me you won't hurt yourself."

"I promise, Becky, thanks for talking to me."

"Let's keep in touch, OK? I'm glad you called and I was here."

"Thanks again. Tell Jane goodbye from me."

"Will do. Love you.

"Love you too. Bye."

"Bye and bless you."

"Wait – are you going to Leroy's funeral tomorrow?"

"We talked about it and both feel it's best if we go. I take it you're not going?"

"No. I'm not feeling well. I'll pray about it. I hope it's a good time for everyone."

"Thanks. I'll let you know how it went."

"Thanks. Bye now."

"Bye-Bye."

Sandra hung up.

She went to the kitchen and poured a cup of coffee for herself and her burden. That's all it is, a burden. I'll just have to bear my burden and take my liberties, like this cup of coffee here.

But I want to work, she thought, and I don't know if my burden and I can handle that. What am I going to do for seven more months? I guess that's not that long considering my life span.

She sipped on her coffee and turned the radio louder, to block out negative thinking. Then she just lay there, thinking about Oscar and wanting to marry him. What does he see in me, she thought. I feel like a big ugly oaf who's fat and blubbery, and a horrible sight to see."

She rocketed into sleep and bore no pain as she floated through the skies on a pink blanket, covering her genitals, and softly soaring around dark skies as stars came and shot by her. It was galactic approval, overcoming the ignorant, the Hell, the "why?", and the worship. She worshiped God and tears poured out to moisten her pain, invisible but ornery to put a dull thud on the rapture of her moist insides, carrying a begotten life. It angered her, and she woke up punching pillows and shrieking.

The loud noise comforted her and she crept around her apartment looking for ants to smash. She had had an ant infestation at one point in this apartment, but it was put to an end.

She crawled out of anger into acceptance and sarcasm. I will but I won't. She couldn't care or even understand the situation.

She couldn't sleep and crawled all over the apartment till she got to her bedroom where she fell asleep on her bed finally, wetting the bed in the middle of the night as her bladder insistently expelled it's contents.

She woke up in a mess, her hair awry, wet on top of her comforter where she had urinated.

Her legs itched from the urine and she was cold and troubled. She immediately got up and ran to the shower, needing to feel clean. She must stay clean.

The warm water and soap soothed her and she basked in the warmth, soaping her legs and between them. She shuddered with release as the soap gently rubbed her there. She turned the water as hot as she could bear it, and gently washed her hair, which felt dirty too.

After she was done showering, she filled up the tub with gentle bath salts and warm water. She sat in the bath and stared at her belly. Then she glared at her belly, feeling sorry for it.

After soaking for a half hour she slowly stood up and stepped out of the tub, wrapping herself in her soft blue towel and drying herself all over. She wrapped the towel around her and walked to her bedroom where she stepped into her bathrobe, soft and luxurious. She padded barefoot to the kitchen and emptied out yesterday's coffee pot. She got it ready and hit the 'brew' button to start the gurgling apparatus. She got funky with her coffee and decided to use her hazelnut syrup to flavor it sweetly. An old friend had given her the syrup as a Christmas present years ago. She didn't use it often, though, because of the calories.

She poured herself a bowl of Grape Nuts and milk, gasping as she saw the old milk poured out lumpy and clumpy into the bowl. "Dang!" She shouted. "Why this? Why now?!" She sat down at the table and cried. She didn't want to go to the store. But she needed milk. She got up and went to her room, and found clothes to put on for the day. I guess God doesn't want me lying lazy around the house.

Back in the kitchen she made two pieces of toast and had a small cup of yogurt. She poured orange juice and the container was full.

"God, You drive a hard bargain," said Sandra out loud.

The sound of her voice shocked her, and she realized she was dealing with the blows. God was making her strong.

Thankfully she poured her coffee and took it to the living room, on second thought going out on her small balcony that sported two basket chairs and a fake potted palm.

She took a seat and relaxed back into the chair. It was raining outside and the sky was grey. Her balcony stayed dry. There were little blessings, shining through the muck. Oscar was probably on his way to orientation. She said a small prayer for him, that he would keep it together and not get psychotic in the new situation.

"What about me?" She thought. "What do I do with my day? I need to take my liberties and go buy a cat or something. I would like to have a cat." She smiled at the thought and looked on her computer for pet stores in the area. Then she changed her mind and called the Humane Society. They had plenty of kittens that needed a home. Sandra got the address and figured out which buses to take to get there. Now she was glad she was dressed for the day. First she would go to the store and buy kitty litter and milk. She needed a litter box and found one which she put on hold because she couldn't carry it all.

When she got home she dropped off her booty and went back out to buy the litter box —and cat food. She brought these home and then sat down in the kitchen again, tired and hungry. She ate the rest of last night's dinner and washed the pan. The potatoes and onions filled her up.

Now for the fun part, she thought. She went out and caught the first bus into town, and then the 93 that went east across town, stopping at the Humane Society. She stepped off the bus her pulse racing. She'd never owned her own cat. Her experience at the Humane Society was both shocking and humbling. So many to choose from, decisions to make. Finally she made up her mind on a little boy kitten, a shorthaired tabby with a striped tail. She paid $100.00 for the kitten which needed neutering in a couple of months. She bought a carrier with the money as well and took her cat outside to the bus stop. She was freaking out. Nothing bad must happen to this kitten. She made sure the carrier was secure and boarded the 93 back into town where she transferred to her home bus and rode home smiling to herself. She was all set up at home for the kitten.

As though meant to be, the kitten started using his litter box almost immediately. Then she realized she hadn't given him a name. Her first thought was "Simon", but she loathed the idea. Instead she called him "Peter", like the disciple of Jesus in the Bible. "Peter." She liked it.

The small kitten was so cute to watch as he explored Sandra's home and ended up in the arm of the couch, curled up sleepily.

Sandra admired Peter from afar, and didn't want to touch the sleeping kitten. She wanted him to have all the liberties she could afford him, and if he wanted a nap, that's just what he would get.

Sandra went to the kitchen and picked up her journal from the shelf and sat down at the table with a pen. She wanted to record this era of her life.

Then Oscar called.

"I got a kitten, Oscar," she bragged. "I went to the Humane Society today and picked out a tabby kitten. His name is Peter and he's asleep on my couch."

"Wow. That's really cool," said Oscar in admiration.

"He even uses the litter box already. He's so cute. I think he'll fit in here perfectly."

"That's great!" Said Oscar with enthusiasm.

"What about you? How did orientation go?"

"I can't lie to you. I flopped. I freaked out, froze up, and threw a tantrum. I really had a fit and found myself yelling at the employer with sarcasm and bitterness. I blamed him for my symptoms. I blew it."

"Oh Oscar, I'm so sorry. That must have been awful!"

"It was. I nearly died of embarrassment when I came back into myself. I felt like such a pathetic fool. I let my guard down and messed up, for lack of better words. We'll never have enough money to get married –"

"Oh Oscar don't say that. One mess up doesn't mean you'll never have a job. Aren't there vocational specialists at the Mental Health and Wellness Center who could help place you in a position where you don't stress out and you can handle the work?"

"I don't know what that job would be."

"Maybe they have ideas for you."

"Maybe." Oscar was morose; he was letting his illness get the better of him.

"Just keep trying, that's all I can say. Don't give up, I'm sure there's a job out there that you can do and enjoy."

"I hope so. What about you? You could get a job anywhere. I bet you'd be a good Starbucks barista.

Sandra laughed. "I love coffee. But not while I'm pregnant, it would be too hard on me. I need to pay the bills, though, so I'm thinking maybe a job at the Library in the kid's section would be good. They'd hire me in a snap; I'm good with kids and children's literature. I think I'll go apply for a position tomorrow. There's probably nothing available at the library anyway. What else could I do? Maybe the Bremerton Shoe Store will take me back. It's only been a month or so since I had to leave that job. But now that things are more under control… I don't know; I don't have any dream jobs. Just something I can do to pay rent, you know?"

"I have the perfect idea for you. Why don't you apply at the Turnip Bay Coffee Shop? It's not so hectic like Starbucks, and you'd be around people, maybe do a little baking, and make coffee for people. Do you want to try?"

"I can ask them if they're hiring. I don't mind sweeping floors and wiping down chairs and tables. That's a good idea, Oscar, thanks."

Oscar was depressed. He hadn't had such an onslaught of symptoms for a long time. He was just so shy and kept to himself a lot.

"I want to see Peter," said Oscar emphatically. He was jealous that Sandra had a cute, fluffy kitten.

"Do you want to come visit me here? It's just two buses away from you. Go downtown, and then catch the 72 North to Heiden Hill. I live on Arrow Road at Sky Hills apartment number 32. Why don't you stop by for the evening and we can hang out and talk."

"I'm on my way! Seriously, can I?"

"Of course. I trust you. Do you trust yourself?"

"I most certainly do," replied Oscar who was itching to be with Sandra momentarily. "OK, I'll be there in a half hour or so."

"Good. I'll be waiting, bye."

"Bye."

Oscar hurriedly changed into casual clothes; he was still dressed up for the orientation. All ready, he locked his door and ran to catch the bus downtown. He caught it on time, and rode into the city. At the bus station he looked for the 72 and saw it approaching. As the bus came to a stop and the doors opened, Oscar leapt into the coach and took a front seat. Patiently he waited till the bus approached Heiden Hill and he told the driver he needed Arrow Road.

The driver obediently stopped at the nearest bus stop, just a block South of Arrow Road.

Oscar thanked the driver and got off. He nearly sprinted up the block to Arrow Road and began scanning for Sky Hills Apartments. There it was, to the left. He crossed the street and slowed down to catch his breath. Then he climbed the stairs in front to the third landing and found Apartment 32 just to the right. He knocked on the door three times and then two more. It was a friendly greeting.

Sandra opened the door holding the adorable kitten in her hands. "Isn't he cute?" She asked.

"Can I hold him?" Asked Oscar.

She carefully handed Peter over to her fiancé, who cradled it in his arms as he leaned forward to give her a kiss. Their lips met mildly and pulled apart in satisfaction.

Here Oscar felt right at home. He surveyed her apartment and saw that it was clean and well decorated. He sat down on her couch and played with the little kitten. It mewled and made little squeaky noises. Then it purred. He held the tiny kitten purring. It didn't get cuter than that.

But before he forgot himself, Oscar put the little kitten down on the couch and stood up to wrap his arms around the woman that he loved. She was soft and tender, and tears trickled down her face.

"Why the sad eyes?" Asked Oscar wiping away a tear.

"I'm just so miserable about this stupid baby," she ejaculated and coughed, catching her breath. "He feels so sinister in me."

"How do you know it's a boy?"

"I just feel that way. I could be wrong. But for now I call him 'he'."

"You don't like the baby."

"I hate this baby. I feel like my body is rejecting It."

"Oh my God, no. I forgot to meet with Laura today at four. It's already six-fifteen now. Oh darn. Something always goes wrong. I'll have to reschedule tomorrow. Darn it!"

"Oscar, don't get all worked up over it. Part of it is you feel like a failure after orientation today, right?"

"Yes, and now this goes wrong too. I could have used her counseling today. I was supposed to call you after that, but I called you earlier, instead. I just had to tell you how awful my day went because I knew you would understand. You always understand me."

"I'm faithful to you, Oscar."

"Thank you, Sandra. I love you. I guess we're both feeling a little abominable, right?"

"Yes, I think so," Sandra sighed. "Today was Leroy's funeral."

"Yeah. I bet there was a large turn out."

"Yes, I pray that it was edifying for everyone."

"Yes, well let's sit down and play with the kitty."

"Yeah, look how green his eyes are. Jewel eyes."

Oscar rolled him over and scratched the kitten's belly.

It wiggled and pawed in every direction.

"Let's see if you need to pee before you do," said Oscar and carried the kitten to his litter box. Sure enough he made a little stream and then pawed all around to cover it up.

"That's a good boy, Peter," said Oscar.

Oscar became aware of Sandra sitting so close to him as they sat on the couch. He felt turned on and wanted to kiss her. But he was angry and didn't. He wouldn't take his aggression out on his beloved Sandra. Instead he leaned back on the couch and asked about the girls' meeting yesterday. "Where did you go?"

"We went to Starbucks with the fireplace and all sat around it and had our coffee drinks. We talked about Simon; we talked about strength and healing. Then we talked about this baby. We all got exhausted and went home after a couple of hours. It was a good experience.

"Then I called Jane, and Becky was going to stay the night at her place too. I needed someone and now I have Peter and you!"

"I hope I make good company tonight."

"Oh don't worry about that. Just relax and kick back and spend some time with me before you have to go home again. You can't sleep here, you know, that wouldn't be right."

"You're right about that, but I must admit I'm tempted to stay."

"That's the devil tempting you."

"Oh my goodness. I'd better behave myself and look up." Oscar made a silent prayer begging the Lord not to let him sin with Sandra.

"Do you want to watch TV for a bit? I like to watch Animal Planet."

"Sure. Turn it on." Oscar was disgruntled. He had imagined sleeping here tonight. Now he couldn't.

Sandra turned on the TV and Oscar picked up the newspaper. His pride was hurt. Angrily he stared blankly at the print and then put the paper down again. He whined. "Sandra, couldn't I sleep on your couch with Peter?"

"No, Oscar, don't even think about it. You can stay for one more hour and then I have to go to bed. I'm exhausted, you know, this baby is killing me. You're barking up the wrong tree, Oscar. Don't take your aggression out on me, just like I can't keep hoping for good to come out of this pregnancy. It's eternal, it's engraved; 'Thou art ugly, Sandra.'"

"Oh how could you say that, my sweet pickle? You are so beautiful to me, unless you think that I'm ugly, too."

"You're not ugly, Oscar. You're gorgeous, and you should know it. Inside and out, I love you."

"You mean you're not mad at me?"

"Mad about what?"

"About me wanting to stay here and complaining when I can't."

"That doesn't make me mad, Oscar, to me it's just an unjustified compliment. I know how you feel, and the way guys and girls get attracted strongly sometimes. That's why I simply say 'NO', and send you away, no less concerned for your wares."

"Thanks Sandra, you just edified me. You're great. I'm stupid."

"Stop putting yourself down, accept who you are. You are Oscar Thadeus and you have a mental illness called schizophrenia. Take it and work with it. Don't fight it. Accept it as who you are, and then you can be."

"I do tend to be hard on myself but I usually try to hide that. Nobody knows some of the things I've called myself before I finally got to call it schizophrenia. Now I have an explanation for who I am and why I get this way sometimes and worse. I've been all through it. Things are supposed to start getting better now."

"That doesn't mean the road won't be bumpy or free of potholes."

Oscar jerked up from his reverie and looked at his watch. Nine-thirty. "I'd better get going Sandra," he said. "Thanks for having me over for a little visit. Next time you come to my place. I'll see you in Church on Wednesday, right?"

"If not before. Thanks for coming over, Oscar. We talked about some pretty important things. I love you Sweetheart."

"I love you too. Bye-bye little Peter," said Oscar as he picked up the kitten once more to hold it and squeeze it.

Then he handed the cat to Sandra and gave her a small kiss. He made his way to the door and saw himself out. "Good night!"

"Good night! See you soon." Oscar closed the door behind him and went down to the bus stop across from where the 72 had let him off. He was cold. The bus came. He sat morosely in the front seat all the way to town where he transferred to the bus that took him home.

Once in the house, Oscar took his pills and lay down on the couch. The phone rang and Oscar picked up.

"Hello?"

"Hi Oscar, Sandra here."

"How's my little butterfly?"

"I'm fine," Sandra giggled. "I'm just calling to remind you to reschedule with Laura tomorrow. I think you did really well managing your disappointment tonight. It must be ghastly when your mental illness takes over like it did at the orientation today. I'm happy for you."

"Thanks, Sandra. I'll get over it." Oscar pouted.

"Remember, tomorrow's a brand new day. Get some sun. I'm going to go to the Turnip Bay Coffee Shop and apply for a job there like you suggested. I'll try to call you when I get home, OK?"

"OK. Should I meet you there? – I mean for coffee. I'm dying to see you and more of you.

"I don't think so. It wouldn't look professional, if I'm applying. I might even get an interview tomorrow. No, just wait until I call you after I get home."

"OK. Good luck."

"Thanks, don't forget about Laura."

"I won't. Give Peter a little petting for me."

"I will."

"Thanks. See yah.'"

"Bye-bye"

THE FULLNESS

Reigning as the King would, here he comes walking across the waters, and Farley, near death in his disfigurement gravitates to his King to worship Him. It is Jesus, the lover and savior of his soul. All is quiet at the Cadwell house. As Farley dreams of his dying day, his soul fills to fullness as he goes to meet his Savior. "I love you Jesus, he mumbles in his sleep.

The phone rings and jerks him out of his sleep. It is Sandra. "Can I please talk to Sally?" She whimpers.

"Sally, Sally wake up! Sandra needs to talk to you." He hands the phone to his sleepy wife.

"Hello?" Sally's scratchy voice goes across the lines and she clears her throat.

"Sally, I have to talk to you. I started having contractions so I called 911 and went to the hospital. Sally, my fetus came stillborn this morning at two-thirteen. It happened so fast and was so painful. It was dead before it was born. I think my body rejected it. Am I a murderer?"

"What?!" Cried Sally aghast. "Are you OK? Stillborn? Are you serious?"

"Yes, and much as it hurts me, I'm relieved. Oscar is here with me. He came right away.

"I don't know what to say. It's all so shocking, so sudden. Did you get to see it?"

"They showed me. It was the ugliest thing I've ever seen. Like some alien from out of space."

"What did you do?"

"Well, for now I'm staying the night in the hospital. They want to watch me in case there are any complications. This is really scary,

I mean, I was carrying a dead thing inside of me for God knows how long. Do you care? Do you know what I'm going through?"

"Of course I care, Sandra," said Sally trying not to be hurt and take this lashing out personally. "Do you need me there, Sandra? Where are you? Which hospital?"

"Four Corners Hospital on Benson. Third floor room 3161. Can you come?"

"Yes, I can stay till nine, and then Farley needs the car to go to work. – I have to go to work too. But I'll be there in a few minutes. I'm praying for you, Sandra."

Sally got up and got dressed, briefly telling Farley what was going on and that she had to go down town to see Sandra at the hospital, that the baby was stillborn and Sandra needed her support.

All dressed, she ran to her car and drove in the night to the Four Corners Hospital. She parked in visitor's parking and quickly went inside to go up on the elevator to the third floor where she remembered Sandra's room number (3161) and found it quite easily. There was Sandra resting easily, a small smile on her face. It was a miracle. She had been delivered.

Sally sat down at the foot of the bed in a small chair. Gently she reached out and squeezed Sandra's left toe. Sandra moaned and rolled over to her side. Her eyes opened and fluttered when she saw her friend at the foot of the bed.

"It's all over, Sally," whispered Sandra. "The devil is no longer inside of me. Please pray over me, that I heal completely without any complications."

The two women prayed together for a total and complete healing and no complications or after effects.

Sandra was smiling, and the guilt she bore was gone. "I'm here, Sally, I'm really here."

"You're really here and so am I. Where's Oscar?"

"He went to get some food. He's hanging in there, not doing so well. His job interview collapsed on him yesterday, and he became psychotic. I think he's kind of glum and feeling like a total failure.

"As long as he keeps taking his medicines, he should pull out of it OK. He's feeling hopeless, like he'll never get hired anywhere. I told him not to worry and used you and Farley as a successful example of mentally ill people holding down steady, stable jobs. He just needs help getting one that works for him."

"Are you in pain?"

"No, they have me on something strong for the pain of the delivery. My stomach and genital area are all red. I hope that's not a bad sign."

"It's in shock, I think you'll come out of this just fine, and you can put an end to Simon in your life."

"Did I tell you I got a kitten? I named him Peter, after Simon Peter in the Bible. He's really cute and the perfect addition to my home. He uses the litter box and everything. I love him, my little kitty-cat friend." Sandra began to doze off, feeling sedation from the relaxing medications they had her on.

Oscar walked into the room with a tall diet Pepsi. He had gone to McDonald's across the street for a burger and brought back this drink for his precious Sandra. He didn't want to show it, but he was doing back flips and cartwheels over the death of the fetus. He felt no remorse, rather he felt revenge on Simon who could not leave an heir to his wicked ways as would have been had the baby come to term and been delivered alive.

Apparently the gender of the stillborn fetus was male, just as Sandra had thought. He wondered where the little baby's spirit had gone and its soul. To the center of the earth where spirits and souls bonded to form angels who worked for glory. It wasn't the baby's fault. It wasn't evil, but its circumstances had been. God would give it a second chance to become an angel in the legions of God's angels.

This is what Oscar believed. He kept his thoughts to himself. Sally and Oscar were awkward in their presence with Sandra sleeping peacefully. Secretly they were both pleased at the turn of events.

Morning came and Sally had to go to work. Farley needed the car to get to his job. She told Oscar, who kept nodding off, to kiss Sandra's cheek for her and let her know that she would be checking up on her friend soon.

Oscar was pleased at this, that Sandra was not alone in her struggles. Sally hugged him and reminded him to take his morning pills.

"I have to see Laura today. Wait, is it Monday or Tuesday?"

"It's Tuesday."

"I have to reschedule with Laura today because I missed our appointment yesterday, after I flubbed out on a very important job interview, and my symptoms acted up and I failed highly, making a fool of myself and falling to pieces. It was my mental illness. It was the trap door that I fall into sometimes. There are rats and snakes down there. It's a spooky, scary place. Slowly, I'm coming out of it and trying not to blame myself."

"Don't worry, Oscar. It took me several tries and failures myself before I landed a good job that I could do. Your job is out there. Get help from the vocational team at the Wellness Center. That's my best advice. I've got to go now. You take it easy and don't abandon your special lady."

"But I have to see Laura."

"Maybe you could reschedule for tomorrow."

"That's a great idea. I don't want to leave Sandra's side."

"Well, I'll see you soon, OK?"

"OK. Bye, Sally, and thanks for the advice - and thank you for being here with Sandra. I know she really wanted to talk to you."

Sally took her leave and walked outside to her car in the cool, morning air. The sky was blue with intermittent fluffy white clouds. She got into her car and drove home to Farley and Thomas. Farley was just waking up and Sally took a quick shower before she got dressed for work and went out to prepare breakfast for her husband. She made her breakfast tea first, and sipped on it as she went about making bacon and eggs and hash browns, not forgetting to turn on the coffee after making it ready.

Farley came shuffling into the kitchen and gratefully poured himself a cup of coffee and sat down to eat with Sally, who was also drinking coffee now. Farley finished quickly and they both looked around to see where Thomas was. Usually he was the first one up. Suddenly worried, Farley got up to look for their dog. There he was, breathing heavily in his fitful sleep on the living room couch.

"Thomas!" Farley called sternly. "Thomas!"

The big dog lifted his head and slowly came down off the couch to his master Farley. "What's the matter, big boy?" He asked slightly concerned.

Thomas wobbled a little and walked to the kitchen back door. There he collapsed and fell to his side.

"Thomas!" Sally screamed. But it was too late. The big dog lay there lifeless. "What? Why? Farley? What's wrong with Thomas?"

"I don't know what or how. Thomas isn't breathing."

"Shake him!"

"Thomas!" Sally bent down and wrapped her arms around the big Rottweiler. "What's wrong, Thomas? I think he's dead!"

"I don't know why or how… let's bring him to the vet. We need to find out what's wrong with him. I'll take the day off work so we can bring him to the vet."

"Me too. Let me go with you, Farley. He's my dog too, you know."

"He was yours in the first place."

Sally wept as tears flowed down her face and her heart squeezed up agonizing her wretchedly.

"Let's go now."

"Yes. Call work first and tell them you can't come in today. I'll do the same thing."

They took turns using the phone and secured their days off of work.

"Let's go *now*." Farley was short and curt.

"I'm coming." Sally put her jacket on and together they lifted the body of the dead dog and brought him out of the back door, securing it, and then carried him to the car. Farley tucked the dog into the back seat and held back a tear.

They drove through the streets until they got to the vet where Thomas had been neutered. They carried their dead dog inside. Immediately the doctor took him in and examined him for causes of the death. He was slow to say but said it appeared to be an aneurism or a blood clot in the heart. He was sorry and asked what they wanted to be done with the body.

"You take him, Doc." said Farley trying to be brave and responsible.

"Yes, we'll leave him here with you," said Sally breaking into sobs and falling onto her husband who put his loving arms around her shoulders. Sally wailed as reality set in, as she realized they wouldn't be taking Thomas back with them. No more Thomas. Thomas gone. No more Thomas who had been a guard dog for Sally and a friend to both Sally and Farley. Thomas had come as a defense against Oscar, before Oscar had gone from stalking stranger to fellow mentally ill friend.

Sally denied being able to accept this. Thomas was part of their routine, their daily lives.

There was an awful quietness when they got home, and Farley went out to dump the water out of Thomas's bowl. He locked the enclosure behind him, and taking a bag from the shed he picked up the last of Thomas's droppings.

Sally whimpered and stared blankly out into the backyard as she sat on the steps watching her husband. There, to her left hung Thomas's lead rope. She was stunned, in shock. It was so peculiar that Thomas died the day that Sandra's fetus had come out dead.

It was an ugly scenario. Death hung over Sally and she knew what they had to do that day. Go fishing. She packed up a lunch for herself and Farley, and got all their gear ready.

They wandered the streets until they got to Farley's fishing pier, and together cast out their lines in grim silence. Neither one of them caught a fish that day, but instead went swimming in their clothes and floated on their backs, relaxing into the buoyant water.

They walked home dripping wet and took a short cut that would get them home without having to walk through town.

Dripping wet they opened the front door of their house and went in through the hall to their bedroom/shower on the left. Farley called out for the first shower, and got out a set of clothes to change into.

Sally removed her wet clothing and wrapped herself in her bathrobe, shivering. Finally Farley was done, and grabbing herself a new set of clothes, she got into the shower and let the hot water woo her pain as she gasped and choked on little wails of torment and destruction. She cried out, finally, and Farley left her to herself. He would see her when she was done with the shower. As Sally shut off the water, all clean and soaped she bowed her head and gritted her teeth, in anger and frustration. "Things can't be this way," she thought. "My Thomas, my Thomas...."

She climbed into her dry, comfortable clothes and walked out to find Farley reclining on their bed. She ran to him and lay in his arms, sobbing hysterically. "My Thomas, my Thomas!" She cried out. Her heart broke and she sobbed recklessly, having wild and passionate sex with her husband. They both lay spent and warmed together on the bed, unable to face the truth. But they must. They gathered their strength and went out to the kitchen, Sally desiring a cup of orange spice tea.

Farley wandered aimlessly around the kitchen, bending over to pick up tufts of dog hair that inhabited the corners of the room and rested under the table. Finally he went to get a broom and tackled the job with broom and dustpan, cleaning up Thomas's fur from the floor. He was intent on doing the job. Sally finished letting her tea steep and slowly began to sip on the spicy concoction to which she added sugar and honey.

They turned on the TV but there was nothing good on to see, so they turned it off again. Sally decided to go do some journaling in the office. Farley picked up his Bible and began to browse through it, searching for some sense, some explanation about the death of their dog. "God gives and He takes away." Farley mused over this thought in his head. Was it true? Or was it hearsay? He couldn't find it in the Bible right then and wondered about the wisdom of it anyway. It made him feel very small.

He looked at the couch and saw Thomas's fur all over it. It needed to be vacuumed. He heard a meow at the door and got up to open it. There in a little basket was a black kitten with a small note attached. It read: "Here is small remorse for tall losses. Keep him safe and warm. His name is Starskie and he is a blessing for your home in lieu of the dog you lost. My name is not important. I love you. Take care of Starskie and let him live inside. Around the corner of the house is a bag of food and a litter box with kitty litter in it to bring inside. Thank you for taking Starskie; he needs a loving home. Signed, Jehovah.

"Sally! Sally!" He called, flabbergasted. "Sally! Come here now!"

Slowly he bent over and picked up the little black kitten, "Starskie". Sally came into the kitchen, and wordlessly, Farley handed her the small bundle of love with the little note, which she read with delight. Farley went around the corner of the house and there was a litter box filled with litter, and a bag of kitten chow. He reached down and picked up both items and brought them to show Sally who had just read the note. "Jehovah?"

"Jehovah. In the name of God this cat is presented to us."

"Oh Farley, he is so cute. Come, bring everything inside."

Farley put the litter box by the kitchen back door and made plans to create a kitty door so he could go in and out as he pleased.

The kitten was making a big noisy fuss, wiggling in Sally's gentle hands. She put him down in the litter box and he peed. When he was done, Farley picked him up and held him to his chest, where the ache was, where Thomas had dwelt.

This cat would have a lot of love, that's for sure. They didn't question who had sent the little cat. Obviously he was Heaven sent. He couldn't be more than six weeks old. He needed neutering, soon. Farley didn't want to let go of the little beast. It licked and nibbled at his finger. He held it in one hand on its back and scratched the little tummy. Starskie squeaked and squirmed so Farley put him down on the kitchen table, and told Sally that he would set out a bowl of food for the little critter. Sally picked up the kitten and hugged it to her as her chin brushed its baby soft fur. She cried at its helplessness, at its total innocence.

Farley put a bowl of food on the floor and Sally set him down near the bowl. Starskie walked firmly to the bowl and began to ingest. He chewed each mouthful thoroughly and looked around as he ate. Finally Sally acknowledged this situation to her husband. "We have a cat!" She said with alacrity and a sudden suddenness as was true to the circumstances. Here was a friend to welcome into their home, to ease the ache of losing Thomas that day. Starskie was too small to climb onto the furniture, so Farley put him on the couch in the living room. The cat rolled around and stretched, purring and making small cute noises.

It was getting late, and Farley and Sally wanted to go to bed, so he put the kitten down on the floor by the litter box, and on second thought, put a pillow from the couch next to the food and litter where Starskie climbed up and curled into a little ball, sleeping. There was too much activity for a little cat all in one day. Lord knows where he came from.

Farley took Sally's hand and together they turned out the lights in the kitchen and living room on their way to the bedroom where they undressed slowly and went to bed.

It was Wednesday and time to get up and go to work. They both rolled over and fell out of bed. Sally got the first shower, so Farley went out to the kitchen to make breakfast and there curled up on his new pillow was Starskie, their new black cat. He was motionless and breathing small, quiet, and shallow breaths.

Farley stepped around him to get to the refrigerator and opened the door. Out came the bacon, eggs, and the hash browns from the freezer. Then remembering himself, he started heating up water to make Sally's morning tea. The water heated and he poured her a cup of Earl Grey tea. Then he got the coffee pot ready and turned it on.

Before he could start on breakfast, Sally came out all dressed up and ready to go to work. "You go shower now. I'll make breakfast for us." Farley walked out of the room and Sally bent down to examine the little black miracle that had appeared on their doorstep last night.

She let it continue to sleep and started making breakfast. She fried four eggs over easy and five strips of bacon. Farley would have three and she would have two. In another pan the hash browns began to thaw and sizzle.

As breakfast neared being done, she found her tea on the counter and began to sip on it slowly. Despite herself she sat down on the floor with Starskie and scratched his little head. Two eyes popped open and a big yawn stretched over his face. The little cat tried to get up, and Sally helped him to the litter box where she let go and watched him squirm over the side into the sea of cat litter where there was a little clump from yesterday. Starskie took his time and pooped and peed and then jumped out of the box, attracted to the smell of his food. He walked on stilted legs to the food bowl and dropped his head in it as he chomped on the kitten chow.

Farley came into the kitchen and found his wife on the floor with Starskie. "Come on, it's time for *us* to eat." Sally stood up and sat down at the table. Together they gave thanks for breakfast and began to eat. Sally finished her tea and went to get a cup of coffee. Farley was already drinking his. Suddenly they both laughed. "Look at us!" said Farley. "Like two proud parents we are."

They finished eating in gleeful silence and realized it was time to go to work. "Starskie will be fine inside while we're away. He already knows his litter box manners and – oh! – I need to put down some water for him. Farley got up and filled a small bowl with water and set it next to the cat's food bowl. Starskie lapped at it furiously. He was thirsty.

"OK. Now he'll be fine," said Farley with assurance. "As for us, we need to get going."

Sally agreed and got up to get her keys, purse, and jacket. Then she remembered her water bottle. She tried to bring it everyday to stay hydrated. She could think better when she included water in her day.

"Bye Starskie!" cried Sally.

"Bye Starskie!" cried Farley. Then they left the house locked and went out to the car and got in. Farley drove Sally to work and dropped her off. From there he drove to his current work site.

Sally was overflowing with emotions and couldn't help telling everybody about the little black kitten who had appeared at their door in a basket with a little note. She sadly explained the death of Thomas and cried a little as she felt her heart ache. Some how, little Starskie helped ease the pain.

At noon, Sally was manning the front desk and Oscar walked in. They made joyous hellos and hugged each other as Sally told everything to Oscar. She couldn't help giggling like a little girl when she told him about Starskie.

"That's funny," said Oscar. "Sandra just got a little tabby kitten and named him Peter. Peter is so cute. Sandra is thrilled with him. I'm sure she'll be happy to see him when she gets home from the hospital."

"She told me about Peter. How is Sandra doing?"

"She's holding her own. So far there have been no complications. I think they'll release her tomorrow afternoon. Are you going to Church tonight?"

"Yes. What are you doing here?" She asked.

"I see Laura at twelve-fifteen. I just need to check in."

"Sign here and put the time of your appointment and whom it's with," said Sally professionally, just doing her job. It had taken her a long time to get comfortable with the front desk. Now she could answer most questions and knew how to refer the ones that she couldn't answer.

"Good luck," Sally said warmly.

Oscar sat down in the lobby and waited, looking at his feet. He looked at the clock on the wall. It said twelve-eleven. He took a deep breath and started to nod off, tired from being up all last night with Sandra.

"There you are, Oscar," came a feminine voice around the corner of the waiting room. He jerked his head up and nodded and got up to follow his case manager to her office. He walked through the door and sat down by the window.

"How are you doing, Oscar?" Questioned Laura.

"I'm OK. I'm sorry we missed our appointment on Monday. I had a really bad day and failed at a job interview."

"Failed? Did you try? What happened?"

"I seized up and started having voices and delusionary thoughts and fell apart in front of them. I never even got to the interview. I never got past shaking hands. I shattered. I convulsed. I blamed them for not hiring me before we even got to talk. I think I was scared, nervous or something."

"Well at least you tried. It must have been a very uncomfortable situation for you. I'm sorry things didn't go well. Are you over it?"

"Yes, I have more important matters to attend to."

"Such as…"

"Such as my fiancé, Sandra, who just gave birth to a stillborn child last night. She's doing well, I was with her all night long."

"Is she the one that got raped and impregnated?"

"Yes, that's Sandra. She's a very strong woman."

"I'll say. She must have strong faith to get her through all this."

"She just got herself a little kitten named Peter, and Peter's going to be a friend for her when she gets home. Peter is *very* cute. I've been taking all my pills like I should, and except for the interview, and now this with Sandra, things have been going quite well. All except that the Cadwell's dog died yesterday. Thomas. Thomas was my friend. Now they have a cat that someone gave them in a basket on their back porch. It's black and its name is Starskie."

"Animals make good friends, don't they?"

"Yes, they really do. I can't decide if I want to get a puppy or a kitten."

"Well don't rush it. You'll know when the time is right."

"I think Sandra might need some counseling after she gets out of the hospital. Can she use a therapist here?"

"Of course she can. She just needs to fill out the necessary papers and signify if she wants a male or a female therapist. I find it's best to let the client make that decision."

"I'll get her to call and make an appointment. She has a lot of stuff to work out. I don't want her to blame herself for anything. Nothing is her fault. She was taken against her will. God killed her baby. She didn't want the baby. I want her to have my baby. I want to marry her. We both need help, you know, me being Schizophrenic and all. We both need jobs. We both need to heal, and I have to still keep on managing somehow."

"You're very clever, Oscar. Your wisdom shines through your disability."

"Thank you. When do I see Dr. Nett again? I lost my appointment card."

"Just ask the front desk. They should be able to tell you. So other than that, do you have any questions?"

"Will you come to our wedding?"

"I would love to. Do you have it planned out yet?"

"No. I need to talk to Sandra so we can work this out together. We have a lot of issues facing us. First of all, I'm mentally ill. Secondly, she can handle that; she has a background in psychology. She wants to go back to school and become a therapist herself. But right now she needs therapy for her own wellness."

"If you want to, we can put her on my load, however it might be more therapeutic for both of you to have separate counselors for confidentiality. Howard Edson is a very gentle therapist. He has a great listening ear and tons of wisdom. Clients give him high ratings. What do you think?"

"I'll bring it up to Sandra, I think she'll like the idea. Does he understand issues like rape and conception?"

"Violation is his specialty. He's very healing and has a touch of God in his therapy. You and Sandra are both Christians, aren't you?"

"Yes, we are. Devout Christians at that."

"Talk to Sandra about Howard Edson. I'm sure he would take her on. It's liberty, you know, being able to choose your own will. Steps to healing are her right."

"That's fantastic. I never thought about it that way."

"Yes, it's your right, and violation is a tragedy of force against your will."

"It kills your liberty?"

"That's right. That's what's wrong with this world. People steal other peoples' liberties and smash us against the pavement. It's like a wave of deceit that decimates your compatibility with justice and misunderstands conception as an ugly deed, a forced happenstance."

"I'm old enough to understand that. It's like being hung. Your liberty gets pulled out from under your feet. Then there's crap. It creeps up on you. The devil tastes like shit, and we shouldn't have to swallow its crap. It's ugly and seditious, a burden to society and an ill to the healthy. It's a piece of crap. It follows around the innocent and smothers them in crazy circumstances."

"I believe it enjoys stealing peoples' liberties. Their rights to choose their own will, until it comes to functioning after the fact, like Sandra has the right to healing therapy, a choice she can make to help herself.

She doesn't need to, but she can. It's her choice how to deal with her crazy circumstances."

"How are you doing now, Oscar?" said Laura searchingly.

"I'm doing OK. I missed my friend's funeral on Monday. I didn't want to go and be around all those people where I felt so squished as to the loss of my companion. Leroy was my friend. He got hit by a car and was killed. Now the Cadwell's dog, Thomas is dead, the dog that Leroy and I were walking when the VW Bus hit him. I hate death when it cheats life. But there is liberty even in death, for the Spirit is present at death and the Lord is the Spirit, and where the Spirit of the Lord is, there is liberty. That's from the Bible- 2 Corinthians 3:17. The liberty of death is that you get to exit this life and face up to your path, where you've sinned and been liberated by forgiveness. It's a big mess. Not everyone is going to Heaven because they chose to do evil in this life."

"What a statement."

"Sandra comes home today. I want to meet up with her so we can both go to Church together – if she's feeling up to it. It's a good thing to focus on amidst the entrails of something more disgusting."

"You really love her."

"I love her completely. I will never leave her."

"Well, things are sounding good. I'm glad you were able to make it to our appointment today. I was worried when we missed out on Monday."

"Monday's the day that Sandra got her kitten, Peter. Also the night she went into convulsions and had to call 911 to take her to the hospital. Luckily she's alive, if not the baby. What do you call it, a miscarriage?"

"Yes, it sounds like she's had a miscarriage. Be very careful with her. Let her feel the fullness of life again before you ask her to do too many things. She needs rest and continuity."

"Well, I'll try to take her to Church today. – If she wants to go."

"Somehow we have to come out of this darkness that surrounds you. Are you sure you're managing your symptoms OK?"

"I'm doing my best. I'm following my pill regime. I've been using the Lorazepam that Dr. Nett gave me after Leroy's death. I'm still sad that I missed his funeral. But I let go anyway. Leroy was a good friend with a big sack of troubles. I think they buried him in a cemetery not far from our Church. The driver responsible took care of the costs. Like I said, it's time to go, I'm starting to repeat myself."

"I'm worried about one thing. First of all you're not repeating yourself, you're emphasizing your points. Secondly I'm scared you might go psychotic over this 'job failure' problem. I can tell it's eating away at you."

"It will, and it will for awhile, until I get my confidence up again. So don't beat down the door. Just wait till I open it, OK?"

"At your liberty, Oscar. You must choose your own will, and no one can do it for you successfully.

"Take care, Oscar and let's plan to meet next week. Which day is good for you?"

"How about Tuesday at one o'clock?"

"Sounds fine to me. I'll see you then."

"Thank you." Oscar stood up. "Wish me well with Sandra and Church tonight."

"Good luck, Oscar."

"OK, Bye."

"Bye."

Oscar walked out of the room and past the front counter to the front doors. Sally was nowhere in sight. He wanted to talk to Sally so he sat down and waited. Most likely she was at lunch.

Oscar flipped through the magazines and tapped his foot. He watched the clock on the wall. It read two-fifteen. It was then that he realized she had probably already gone home. "I was in a long meeting with my counselor," he thought to himself. "Almost two hours."

Oscar got up and started to walk home. When he passed the 16-bus line he urged himself and boarded the bus that would take him to the hospital to see Sandra.

In five minutes he was there and Oscar nearly dove off of the bus toward the hospital. Room 3161. Sandra. She was there resting easily. The Doctor came in; there had been no complications.

"Did she have a miscarriage?" Oscar asked the Doctor.

"She did."

"Is she safe to go home today?"

"She should be fine and doing better everyday, considering the circumstances she was under."

"Can we take Hope Link? I have Medicaid and she is my charge. Neither of us drives."

"Sure. Would you like me to schedule a pick up time?"

"What time is it now?"

"Almost three o'clock."

"Do you think she could be up and ready by four?"

"Most probably."

"Then schedule us for four-ten. Thanks."

"No problem. You can do the scheduling at the nurse's station just outside."

"OK, Doctor, thank you Doctor."

Oscar went out to the nurse's station where he requested a Hope Link pick up at four-ten to go to Heiden Hill, Arrow Road, Sky Hills Apartments.

Oscar went back to Sandra's room and roused her gently. "Don't you want to go home, dear sweet Sandra?"

There was a moan and she turned on her left side. Then she saw Oscar and sat up as well as she could. She wanted to go home.

"I've arranged a ride for us to bring you to your home in about an hour. Do you want to go or stay?"

"I want to go," cried Sandra. "I'm feeling so much better than yesterday. Can you get the nurse to get my discharge papers?"

"Will do."

Oscar made Sandra's wishes known to the nurse at her station and the nurse complied immediately.

Then she came to Sandra's room where Oscar was sitting in the chair and holding her hand.

"I'm prescribing you Percocet for the pain, they should last about a week and a day. By then you should be a lot stronger. Let us know if the pain continues or any problems arise."

"Thank you."

"Are you ready?"

"All ready, just need to get dressed. And I might need help putting on my socks and shoes."

Sandra giggled as Oscar helped her into her clothing. "Let's go down to the pharmacy so I can fill this prescription pronto. I'm in a bit of pain down there. She rubbed her abdomen and tummy area. Let's go. Can you carry my purse?"

Oscar was all over her, helping, soothing, steadying as she took her first steps.

She was walking on her own shortly, and bent over just a little for the pain she was in.

They got to the pharmacy, which filled her prescription immediately. She asked for a drink of water and took one of the pain remedy pills. Then they walked to the front door and out. Sandra felt liberated. She could make her own choices now, with no difficulty, with responsibility for herself and her new freedom.

"I feel like I'm out of bondage," Sandra murmured, not sure if the devil was on the attack."

"There's no devil around here," Oscar said adamantly when she voiced her worry. "Satan we rebuke you and resist you. Be gone! In the name of Jesus Christ, Amen."

"AMEN," said Sandra.

Oscar saw the Hope Link van coming up the hill. "That's for us," he said happily. We're bringing you home! – To your new kitty."

The van stopped in front of them and they identified themselves and got on. The ride was short up to Heiden Hill and the driver knew Arrow Road. He let them off at the Sky Hills apartments where the two love birds disembarked and made sure they had all their belongings. They thanked the driver and said goodbye. Then they walked up to apartment 32 and Sandra let them in. There was Peter in the middle of the living room floor.

"Welcome home."

"Thank you so much, Sweetheart!" Sandra put her arms around Oscar and nested her head in the curve of his neck.

First she sat down and took a deep breath. "It's like a nightmare is over! God has cut my shackles. He has answered my prayers for things to work out in the best possible way.

The pain of delivery was over; the Percocet was doing its job.

Oscar took his chances and asked Sandra if she was up for going to Church that night. He would call the Cadwell's and ask them for a ride for the two of them.

Sandra was delighted by the idea, and took her liberties to ask him if he thought she was well enough.

"You need to decide. That's your liberty."

"Call them. I want to go. I need a touch of the Holy Ghost."

Oscar was relieved, and taking his liberties he called Sally and Farley. Sally picked up on the other end.

"Hello?"

"Hello, Sally?"

"Speaking."

"I'm calling to ask a favor," said Oscar asserting his personality.

"What can I do for you, Oscar?"

"I'm at Sandra's place, we just got here from the hospital, and are wondering if you and Farley can pick us up on your way to Church tonight."

"I don't see any problem with that. Just a minute." Oscar heard her call the request to Farley and heard a muffled reply that sounded like assent.

"What time should we be there?" Asked Sally.

"Well, Church starts at seven-thirty, so how about six-forty five?"

"All right. We'll be there then. How is Sandra doing?"

"Remarkably well. She's having a little bit of pain, but the Percocet is helping her there. She really wants to go to Church. It'll be a cleansing experience for her. A way to let go and let life back into her."

"Perfect. Can I talk to her quickly?"

"Of course. Here honey," he said and handed the phone to Sandra.

"Hello?" She said quietly, subdued.

"Hi Sandra. I'm glad you're feeling up to going to Church with us tonight. Are you sure you're not pushing it?"

"I need to go to Church, to get me on the right track in the middle of this chaos."

"Is that what it feels like?"

"Yes. There's a whirlwind around me calling me crud for killing my baby."

"Sandra, that's the devil, don't you believe that. It was not your doing. You didn't choose to give birth, did you? No one knows what caused your miscarriage, but if God calls the shots, He calls all of them. You got pregnant for a time, then God called the baby home."

"Home?"

"I'm sure if it's a good baby it's in Heaven as an angel, but if the baby was bad, well, then good riddance. No one knows, and it doesn't matter, either way you are liberated from being the address of that baby. No more baby; life open for Sandra. Think of all the possibilities that disappeared when you got raped. Now all you have to do is heal and be good to yourself."

"Thanks, Sally."

"All right, honey, we'll be by at six-forty five. Remember, dress comfortably!"

"OK. See you soon."

"Bye now."

"I think I'll wear what I have on," said Sandra after she hung up the phone. "We have about an hour and a half. I think I'll rest right here for now and play with little Peter," she said, reaching down to pick up the kitten from the floor.

"I don't want to throw everything at you at once, but when I saw Laura today we talked about you maybe needing a therapist right now to get you through this mountain in the road, or at least a way around it. There's a therapist who specializes in violations of the nature of what happened to you who is very good and she recommends him for the time being. His name is Howard Edson. He gets rave reviews from troubled clients."

"That sounds good, like a God thing coming my way in time of need."

"Exactly. You need to talk to people who can really help you navigate the next few steps in your life until you're not so wobbly anymore. Do you want me to have him call you to make an appointment?"

"Yes. Definitely yes."

"Good. I was hoping you'd say 'yes', to give you professional support right now."

"Thank you for caring."

"I couldn't care more. – Do you have anything quick to eat? Sally and Farley will be here soon and you need some sustenance."

"I'll have this orange and a banana. I feel a craving for fruit."

Sandra peeled her orange and ate the juicy pieces. After that she shoved down a banana. Next she poured a glass of milk. "I think I'll be fine now," said Sandra.

They both sat quietly on the couch as Sandra played with her kitten. "My little Peter," she said. "You couldn't have come at a better time."

Oscar hummed Amazing Grace, and watched the girl of his dreams playing with what might be the cutest cat on the planet.

Then there was a knock on the door. Sally? Farley?

Oscar opened the door and let both Cadwell's in. "Hi Sandra," cried Sally and ran to give her a hug. "Are you all right? Are you in pain?"

"A little, but it's a healthy sort of healing pain."

"Good news! Farley she's all right! She's FREE!" Sally couldn't contain herself, she was so overjoyed to see her friend happy and alive."

"It's good to see you well," mumbled Farley self-consciously. "Are we all r-ready to go?"

"All ready," said Oscar who took the kitten from Sandra and helped her up.

"See my new kitten? His name is Peter."

"How cute! We just got a black kitten. His name is Starskie. Oh look, he's so cute. Look at his mottled belly and striped tail. Wow. That's nice, Sandra."

"Let's go!" Said Farley sternly. "We don't want to l-lose our seats in Church!"

"Yes, let's go," said Sandra as though she were on a cloud, soft and wispy.

Oscar closed and locked the door behind everyone and they all made their way to the little Fiat. Sandra got in first with a little discomfort. She had remembered her water bottle and the bottle of Percocet. Just in case.

Soon the little car was speeding towards Church and they arrived in plenty of time. They all got out, excited about the Holy Ghost and the message, excited about coming to worship Jesus.

The four saints found their seats humbly, being the first ones there. Sometimes Wednesdays weren't as packed as Sunday services.

There was Pastor Williams conversing with associate Pastor Duncan Freebes up by the altar. Someone came and put water bottles by their seats and on the pulpit.

Sandra focused on the Pastor and wondered what he would speak about today.

Sally felt important making sure that Sandra was OK. Oscar put his arm around his fiancé.

She appeared a little disheveled, but no one would comment. Everyone was so happy for her being out and healthy. People continued to flow in, and there came Stacy, Becky, and Jane. Sandra cried as they all gave her hugs and kisses and well wishes. Sandra smiled, and that was all she had to do. She felt accepted and loved by her Church family.

The lights were dim and the Church began filling up. Becky and Jane stayed to sit with Sandra, and Stacy sat across the room with her new boyfriend Stanley. Stanley was well liked by all and people approved of this new relationship. Becky and Jane sat in front of Sandra and Oscar. Farley and Sally sat next to Sandra.

"I can't wait till Mae and James and Gilmore and Fay return from their honeymoons. I miss their company," spoke Sally to no one in particular. "They'll be back soon," said Farley to his wife who was riding the Spirit in the Church. She faded in and out, it was her way with dealing in complex situations. She found she was thinking of Thomas and suddenly broke into tears.

"Thomas died yesterday," she said aloud, not caring if anyone heard her. That's why she needed Mae, who always listened as a good friend.

She might as well be speaking to the Lord in conversation with what happened yesterday when he called the dog home.

The lights brightened and music began as the praise team sang in time with the music, singing a song of praise to the Lord. Halfway through the next song Sally and Farley stood up and started singing along. Sandra stayed seated because standing was painful, but she sang loudly and Oscar stood by her side.

Becky and Jane started to clap their hands with the song and continued on into the next song. Soon music and singing, praise and clapping filled the whole Church as the Holy Ghost swept through the sanctuary. Tears were flowing down Sandra's face as she realized she was delivered. No more abominable baby to tie her hands together and force her to squat. No. She was free. The inkling began to grow inside of her that she really was set free, liberated from a curse of hell, without a reminder of the awful circumstances that set off her walk through Hell. She thought about Howard Edson and looked forward to his cleansing understanding and therapy.

Praise was wild tonight as people worshipped with their hands in the air and swayed back and forth. Bright youthful saints took their liberties and ran around the Church, up and down the aisles. Sandra cried quietly as people stood and sang all around her, clapping hands and tapping feet.

Finally the music came to a close as Brother Duncan Freebes stood up at the pulpit and called the Church to attention. There were some announcements about upcoming events to prepare for. There was a Church call for women to lay hands on Sandra and pray for her delivery and recovery. Sandra got up and made her way to the front where women surrounded her and prayed loudly calling on the Lord to send healing and blessing in this situation. They prayed for her future, her recovery, and gave thanks that God had liberated her of the burden of Simon's son.

People were in awe at the situation. Then Pastor Williams took precious oil and anointed her head with it as he spoke in tongues to pray about the delivery of this Christian woman. For her healing and recovery, and praise for the future of this woman.

Slowly it got quiet and Sandra made it back up to her seat next to Oscar who put his arm around her proudly.

Next order of events came with collection of tithes and offerings. More singing, and then Pastor Williams began to speak. He spoke fluidly and easily, almost joyfully like he didn't get to do it everyday, setting someone free.

It was achingly beautiful as he settled into his main topic, "liberty".

"Liberty," he said, "is the right to choose your own will. For you to be able to direct your decisions without forcefulness or other willfulness. It is your autonomy, which keeps you from being persuaded by others to do things you normally wouldn't do. It was the right to skip breakfast if you wanted to. It was your liberty to light a fire in your fireplace on a cold, snowy day.

"It is faithfulness, not tied down, found in the freedom of every day. It is a new rising of callings made by you to enforce your life securely. It often allows you to lead, and it often allows you to follow. You are at liberty to pick your own friends, and avoid those whom you don't want to be around. Blockage of liberty, as in the case of Simon and his sordid violations with innocent young females, stops up like an overflowing sink that won't drain well. Dirty water overflows onto the floor with messy and gruesome effect. Seeing faces in the furniture, or patterns on the wall, we all cry out to be free, to see the desire of small steps, floundering in the liquid with bonds of steel and rope blocking the freedom to move about, losing out on the life of creation to be drowned by the heated freeze of negligence that nobody good gives to freedom where movement is restricted at risk of being covered up and blocked head on.

"Religious nuances, obvious to conspiracy with avid flirtation among the saints and their faith, both blocks walls and tears them down. Refusing the timely thought, and a purposeful disaster is the ache to be free in all of us. We all desire to take our own liberties, broken or damaged. Our bodies are malleable and easily subject to damage. Bodies break and leave a set of new bodily rules in motivation. Like a lemon in the refrigerator, it shrivels if not used in due time. A wasted lemon is like two spoonfuls of sugar that sprinkle on the ground, instead of coming together as blessed lemonade. So take your liberties when the time is right, don't spoil opportunity.

"Dark coffee brings light and awakening to the eye of those free to indulge. You have the liberty to choose coffee or tea, or neither."

The Pastor went on to speak about the virtues of liberty, the meaning of it in our lives, and the foundation of our country in the Constitution of its birth. "Life, liberty, and the pursuit of happiness."

"There is a trail of dust leading to the point where one can say, 'I have the power to choose my own destiny.' Digging and planting in the dirt, brings us the liberty of creating an experiential economy, a government that protects our liberties. People coming forth for denial of an unfair deal or judgment bring the quaking truth, shouting at denial, which puts us forth by the opportunities of the pure necessities of truth. Belonging to necessity allows urgency to make decisions, your liberty based on wisdom, although often covered by foolishness. Dust covers the face of shame, where liberties have been slighted to bring awareness of broken purity, shame on the sodden path of life. It is retroactive to the symphony of truths within your garden of faith. It perplexes the devil and sends it running for cover.

"Astute and orderly, only Jesus can set you free. It's your choice to choose Jesus. It's your enigma to relax into. There is the truth of the situation, setting you free and binding you with the God of Heaven and Earth. Here you are liberated as you follow the fundamentals of religion and rebirth. Can you choose the color of the car you want to drive? Can you decide between apples and oranges at the store? Can you choose both? Does Jesus live?

"In our perspective, He does live.

"You can choose to come to Church and worship God, Jesus Christ, who claims you with a lead rope that never pulls taut. He guides and leads you along the way. He is the Prince of Peace, Mighty Counselor, and a friend to the lost. He is King. We are his children, children of the Father who gives us to Him. If you believe in peace and truth, there is recovery, open arms to run to. Our devil the adversary hunts back and forth for situations to undermine and to twist with evil. It cannot steal us from Jesus, but the liberated can talk back to and rebuke and resist it, causing it to flee as the little overblown nitwit that it is. The devil tries to steal your peace, to overturn the work of your hands. It causes evil to travail and to pity those seeking help.

"God resists and rebukes the devil, causing it to flee as it realizes its time is short, and it grows desperate as it realizes that its destiny is to burn forever in a lake of fire.

"Just as avidly, it tries to overturn the faith of the innocent, and leads them in tempting forages, seeking evil that looks like goodness, for the devil is a schemer and a trickster and trips you up whenever it can get that hidden rope across your path.

"As you fall, you have the liberty to catch yourself in fields of brambles, where thorns chastise your life, and belief in yourself is reiterated with the loss of a good way. Barking up the wrong tree, we plead for recuperation of necessary outlook, narrowing our faults to zero and pinning the blame where it belongs, back on the evil face of Satan.

"What you lose to the devil, God will replace with a plan B. He holds your truths within Him, and desires to put you back on the right path."

The Pastor was sweating and drank water. "The recovery process is beautiful," said Pastor Williams, who had been talking for a while. Now he brought up the deliverance of Sandra from a life of walking the gardens of Hell. "Purified, free, liberated to choose any action in her life that might glow with the love of the Lord. He is a Lord of Love. Love heals and beckons to its own. It calls on the nitty-gritty, and the preponderance of prayer. You have the liberty to talk to God. And He listens.

"Everyone can take their liberties and set themselves free of bondage whether conscious or unaware. You can choose your own destiny; you can choose your own will. God guides and loves along the way, pulling you out of the brambles, which would consume you with fiery thorns. God sends miracles in disguise. We squirm in His presence so awesome and true.

"Bitterness causes you to squirm. You spit it out like a bad raspberry.

"Sin causes a bad taste in the mouth, a feeling of rejection and servitude. Serving the devil sometimes goes along unbeknownst, and it uses people to reject retroactive positivity.

"Like a rainbow on a sunny day, there proves to be rain in the midst of the sunshine. When Sandra became impregnated, -to use you as an example, Sandra,- she lost the liberty of a free and easy being. She bore the rotten fruit within that caused her health to fail. Breaking her fall, God used her as an example to the faithful. Anyone who can believe can be redeemed, remade and whole.

"Everybody has liberties of which they have no idea that they have. People are stuck in ruts, not knowing that they can change, or knowing they can change but not knowing how. You have the right and ability to make a cup of coffee. You have the liberty to drink three cups or more. You have the wisdom to know when enough is enough. That's enough," said the Pastor and motioned for the music to start again. "You see?" he said, "I have the liberty to wind up my message right here, and I believe it will sit well with you without going long-winded."

Sister Williams began to sing as she played the piano. The Pastor spoke saying we have the liberty to go to the altar and pray to God about anything and not to limit our choices about which to pray. We have the liberty to dance in the aisles, and to kneel before our chairs in prayer. We have the liberty of active prayer, communing with the Father, Son, and Holy Ghost who are all One. "God loves us," he said.

"'Therefore if the Son makes you free, you shall be free indeed.' John 8:36. We can laugh in His gardens, and walk hand in hand down His lanes. Proof of laughter is spontaneity, springing forth from our liberties to be happy. Everyone wants to be happy. Prayer furthers us down those roads.

"Laughter instigates mirth, the beauty of Creation, the recklessness of joy. The terrible truth that we are indeed free to choose our own paths exists if and when we walk with Jesus.

"Remember when you go home today, to examine yourself and take your liberties, the beauty of truth and justification. Let yourself in on the secret that you, too, are free if you will arise and claim that freedom for yourself."

Sally and Farley put their heads together in deep conversation and decided it was their liberty as well as their obligation to mentor Oscar and Sandra through these troubling times.

The Pastor dismissed service with a blessing and told his congregation to go their own way, and to experiment with taking their individual liberties.

Becky and Jane were talking busily and decided it was their liberty to go get coffee together.

Oscar decided to take his liberties and go stay at Sandra's for the night while she rested so she wouldn't be alone. First he asked her permission, and she took the liberty to say "yes".

Sandra took her gracious liberties and depended on her friends to get home, for she was very tired and very sore. She took the liberty of using another Percocet. She heaved a huge sigh and let her headrest on Oscar's shoulder. There she waited expectantly for Sally and Farley to mention that it was time to go.

Sally wanted to go down to the altar and receive prayer for her mental health, now that Thomas was gone. She needed help in dealing with the loss.

Gradually, the Church filed out of the building, each going their own way. Farley found himself thinking of little Starskie and decided it was his liberty to claim the cat as his own, for he had found it.

Sally came back up from prayer, and mentioned that it was a good time to leave, if everyone was ready. Becky and Jane bid everyone goodbye and left in Becky's car to go get coffee.

Oscar and Sandra stood up and Oscar helped Sandra walk as they made their way to the Cadwell's car parked outside.

They all got in, as Sandra gingerly maneuvered into her seat.

"I'm in a lot of pain," she took the liberty of saying.

"Well we'll get you home just as soon as we can," said Farley as he pulled out of the parking lot. Carefully he drove through the streets up to Heiden Hill, found Arrow Road and the Sky Hills apartment complex. Oscar would be spending the night on the couch. He didn't think that Sandra should be left alone in her circumstances.

Sally and Farley bid their adieu, and drove home silently to their little house with the little cat to welcome them. It was then Farley spoke up. "I've decided that Starskie is my cat since I'm the one who found him."

Sally spoke, "with all the nerve! How could you claim him for your own when I live here too?"

"I'm not saying you can't have him too, to love and cherish and feed and play with, but he belongs to me, just like Thomas belonged to you."

"All right, I understand, it's sort of like the baby that we can't have. But being an animal, Starskie needs an owner. If he picks you, that's fine, but if he picks me, well then he's all mine."

"What do you mean 'picks'?"

"Well, when we get home, the first person he approaches should be his owner."

"OK. No cheating though, you can't get there before me."

Farley agreed to the plan.

They went in the front door and found Starskie sitting on his little pillow by the food and water and litter box. There were two tiny clumps in the litter where he had peed. There were not yet any poops.

Sally and Farley sat equidistant from the kitten on either side of him. The kitten mewed loudly and waddled over to Farley who triumphantly picked him up and held him to his chest.

"OK," said Sally, "He's yours."

They let it rest at that and Sally suggested making a pot of coffee, even though it was after nine o'clock. Farley assented with a gruff "sure", as he played with the little cat.

"We have to get him neutered. How old does he need to be to get neutered?"

"I don't know, you can call the vet tomorrow and find out. The number is right here by the phone."

Farley realized it was up to him to call.

Sally took her liberties and called Sandra to see if everything was all right.

Sandra answered the phone holding her kitten. She squealed a "hello?" and then handed Peter to Oscar.

"How are you doing, Sandra?" Asked Sally. "Does Oscar have his medicines with him?"

Sandra gave the phone to Oscar.

"Hello?"

"Hi Oscar, it's Sally. You didn't forget your pills, did you?"

"No, thank God. I brought enough for tomorrow morning as a last thought before I left for the hospital yesterday."

"You're not lying are you?"

"No, I swear, I have my medicines with me. I know I need to take care of myself before I can take care of Sandra."

Sally was satisfied with this last answer and said her goodbyes. Next she went over to Farley and demanded the kitten to hold and squeeze and play with. Little Starskie nipped her finger and she screamed, "Ouch!"

"Sorry Sally, I think you're a little too rough with him. He needs a gentle touch, not a crazy, coveting touch.

"I guess you're right. Maybe he has to get to know me slowly. I'm a great greeter, but below the surface takes awhile to arise.

"The coffee is done, Sweetheart," said Farley, throwing the ball back in her court."

"Yes, my loving man. How much do you want?"

"I would like one full cup, please."

"Coming right up my sire."

"Oh Sally, don't be bitter."

"Sorry, I'm just missing Thomas. A lot."

"I miss Thomas too, but Starskie is helping to cushion the loss. For me."

"That's nice, I think I'll go journal for awhile in the office. Your coffee is on the table."

"Sally, don't leave me alone! Come play with the kitty *with* me. We don't have to fight over him."

"OK, Sweetheart. Here's your coffee. Can I hold him?"

"Yes, here, take him. He's yours, I just gave him to you."

"Not mine, *ours,* silly. He needs a Mom and a Dad."

"That's right. We need to share responsibility for the cat. I'm sure we'll develop a system. We did with Thomas. We both took care of feeding and watering him, and letting him in and out of his enclosure. I sure miss that bugger." Farley took the liberty to squeeze out a tear, which trickled down his cheek. He gulped.

Sally carefully held their new cat and sat quietly with her husband. She stretched out its paws and scratched his little belly. The kitten squirmed but then relaxed into Sally's gentle hands. She shed a tear too.

Then sensing a change in the kitten's demeanor, she carried him to his litter box where he squatted as well as he could and pooped two little lumps into the box. "Now he has accepted us," thought Sally. She left him on the pillow by the box and he curled up to sleep.

"That's a good cat," said Sally.

"A gift from God," replied her husband. "Too bad we can't go fishing tomorrow."

"Yes, we have to work, you know that."

"Maybe after work if it's not raining and we're not too tired."

"Maybe."

"I miss Leroy."

"So do I. I'm glad we're still friends with Oscar. What do you think of Oscar and Sandra together?"

"I think it's a great start. They have this common history to call upon, and futures as bright as the stars."

"He really loves her."

"I know. I think she knows it and loves him too."

"That's the fullness right there."

"Yes, that's where the ball starts rolling. Our ball has been rolling for how many years now? At least ten."

"Probably more. I'd have to really think about it. When did we first meet?"

"Was it as the center?"

EPILOGUE

Liberty is an essence, a choice, an activity and a freedom. Sometimes you may feel "stuck" and not sure what to do. It is then that you take your liberties and choose an action, a choice, or a decision.

Painful circumstances come upon everyone in life. It is dealing with pain that is so taxing. It is then that you are able to get a photograph of your life and see where the best paths lead out to victory.

Hating doesn't help, controlling is not freeing, and exuberance lands the right words at the right time.

Throughout this book there is a sprinkling of situations in which a character is seen to "take liberties" and motivate from there, by allowing them a freedom that is inherent to everyone.

Autonomy is a gift created by God. He gave us our own true will, the choice to make a decision in certain circumstances, and the vision to discern right from wrong. Lifting your head you face reality and there are many choices to make on the road of life.

Autonomy is the core of the being, the judge, the saint, and the perpetrator. Liberties are sometimes taken away at will of an imposing force. This is evil and wrong in every way.

We are judges of ourselves and renew each day with the passion for righteousness, to be free of sin, and to live regarding God, Jesus, as Savior and interloper of sinful natures. He regards death as something He has conquered, and those of us who are living free from sin are those who are forgiven and true to the Lord as His chosen followers. It is a choice to follow Christ, it is a liberty to go to Heaven.

Made in the USA
San Bernardino, CA
26 November 2014